COMPLETE.

PAT O'CONNOR'S SCHOOLDAYS

THE BOYS OF THE SHANNON

EDWIN J. BRETT, LIMITED.

RAILWAY HOUSE, 4 WEST HARDING STREET,
LONDON, E.C., AND ALL BOOKSELLERS.

PAT O'CONNOR'S SCHOOLDAYS.

"'SHURE, AND IF IT ISN'T TERENCE O'RAFFERTY'S OWN LITTLE CABIN,' SAID PAT."

No. 1.   *NOTICE.—With this Number is presented a Gift Plate.*

PRICE ONE HALFPENNY.

[Published Every Friday.]

PAT O'CONNOR'S SCHOOLDAYS;

OR,

THE BOYS OF THE SHANNON.

CHAPTER I.

"THE COACH FOR TIME."

"SHURE, and is it yourself that employs bullocks for horses? Maybe, as ye know I'm an honest boy, you'll be afther telling me to help the poor beasts up the hill. A miserable gossoon. God help yer honour; away you go. Divil a bit of the journey ye'll make, though, between this and Ballinara."

Such were the words, given in rapid changes of "alouds" and "asides," that came from the mouth of the ostler at the "Pig and Whistle," a snug little roadside inn nestling at the foot of the "winsome hills o' Clare."

The object of his anger was a man of some forty years, the driver of the coach—the express coach—a vehicle, which, in the neighbourhood, had been nick-named the "Coach for Time."

It had earned its reputation in a dubious way.

Certainly, it had never been reported that it broke down more than three times in a journey of a few miles, and as no one had a chance of choosing between anything else, except this and Connor O'Calloran's jaunting car, which had one sound wheel out of two, the "Coach for Time" was generally patronised.

The company which Mike O'Hara had upon his coach was of a mixed nature.

On the box seat—and it was a box seat, nothing more draughty, tumble-down, and Irish could have been found out of Ireland—were seated two of the most cross-grained, miserable creatures that ever disgraced a civilised country.

The one was a tall, lanky fellow, who looked a cross between an unsuccessful Methodist preacher and the keeper of a lunatic asylum.

The other was a fat, podgy party, whose principal business in life seemed to have consisted in growling at his fellow-creatures, drinking bad port, and nursing his gouty toe.

They were both of different temperaments and different forms, and avoided one another, looking uncomfortably forward on either side of the driver.

Behind them, revelling in all the joys of the glorious sunshine, and the splendid verdure of dear old Ireland, were four boys, lads varying in age from fourteen to sixteen.

They were all returning, after their holidays, to the school on the Shannon, the school kept by Doctor O'Shaughnessy, a worthy son of Erin, and one who, by his kindly heart, had won golden thoughts from all.

Most boys returning to "work" after a time of fun, and jollity, and play, feel a sinking at the heart as they approach the scene of their labour.

But there was nothing of that about "our lads."

O'Shaughnessy had made them a home; they were emphatically "his boys," and there wasn't a man within a mile of Shannon Tower that would have dared, in the presence of the doctor, to have spoken ill of the smallest boy under his care.

Swish! crack! went the driver's whip, and the "bullocks" began lazily to move out of the courtyard of the "Pig and Whistle."

Heaven save the mark!

Courtyard!

An expanse of dry sand, bounded by the rutty high road on one side, and on two others by a range of black board buildings full of cows, horses and pigs.

On the fourth lay the inn itself, with its bulgy windows, and tumble-down porch, and green (it's all green in "ould Ireland") blinds and so forth, and the vine-clad, white-washed walls, that spoke of jolly cheer and comfort.

The driver gave one more touch-up to his horses, and away they went.

The boys gave a cheer.

"Hurrah!"

They weren't all Irish, but still, they all—Irish or English—felt the effects of the bracing air and the bright sun, and never for a moment thought of the black clouds that were rolling softly over the tops of the hills that the "Coach for Time" had to climb on its journey.

Off they go!

Even the ostler, having received some "poteen" from the boys, gives them a cheer, flinging his ragged hat in the air, and never noticing that it had fallen into the horse trough.

"It's themselves that are raal jintlemen,

and no mistake; but the divil a bit do I like that Mike O'Hara. The fair's coming on soon, and the first crack—Lord be praised and the Blessed Virgin!—will be on the head of that same."

Meanwhile, the coach began slowly, by the aid of four wretched horses, to make its way up the hilly lane towards the mountainous country.

The light-hearted boys had taken no notice of the evidences of the coming storm.

But the others were far from being in such a quiet state of mind.

The thin party appeared, as it were, to shrivel up into himself, while the fat man seemed as if his gouty toe was a lightning conductor, and kept pointing in a most agitated manner to the heavy, cold bank of clouds that stared them in the face over the ridge of the mountains.

"It's really dreadful," he said, "coming over these hills in wet weather."

"And it's yer honour as is right," said the driver; "but, ye see, surr, if you'd only stopped at home, it would never have occurred. It's myself that's driven the 'Coach for Time' all these blessed years, and unless a jintleman like yer, as is bred and born, can prevent it, I've had to put up with all the thunder and lightning of Ballinara, and the bad whisky at the 'Mountain Top,' which I'll show a small portion of to your honour's self when we get there."

There was no time for further conversation.

Suddenly the storm broke.

The thunder boomed.

The forked lightning darted from one edge of the horizon to the other, illumining the mountain tops and away yonder the bright waters of the Shannon.

Down upon the coach descended the unmerciful shower.

The driver was all right.

Wrapped up in one of those mysterious coats which seem to have had a lappet added to them at each century, he didn't care much for rain or wind.

The two travellers behind him, however, fared differently.

The lean man who delighted in the habit of wearing low shoes, was sitting in a pool which filled them to the brim.

The fat man, who had bought a pair of cheap high boots, had forgotten to see whether they were a fit, and consequently the water from the seat, which was copious, ran in at the tops, and added to his discomfort immensely.

"This is pretty travelling," growled the fat man.

"Yes," growled the lean man; "but I don't see you've got much to make a fuss about."

"How's that?" exclaimed the other, rather fiercely.

"Why, I noticed when you left the inn that you stole—aye, sir, stole—the only thing which would keep the wet out from anyone on the box seat—a piece of tarpaulin."

"Which has been the means of my sitting in a cold bath ever since the storm began," returned the fat man. "If you've any sense

in your head, keep your tongue between your teeth."

"Bad cess to ye both!" exclaimed the driver, as he whipped his wretched team of horses, "and it's a quarrelsome lot ye are, I'm thinking——"

"That it ud be betther if ye'd all stop talking, and wait till we reach the 'Mountain Dew Girl,' when I'll stand Mike O'Hara a dhrap o' the best poteen, and buy some patent sates (seats) at the sign of 'O'Rafferty's Gridiron.'"

The speaker was a fine, handsome lad, about sixteen, with curling hair, the bright blue eyes of the sons of the Emerald Isle, and a lithe, well-built figure.

"Shure you're right, and that's thrue, Master Patrick, dear," said the driver, winking at the fat man, to his infinite disgust. "There's parties here that are getting wet without that might be civiller and betther-looking, maybe, if they were a little more wet within.

"Did ye ever hear," he added, "now maybe ye might up at Ballinara—did ye ever hear the story of the lean pig and the fat one?"

The boys all burst into a roar of laughter.

"That's too bad, Mike," cried the lad addressed as Master Patrick, laughing, though, with the loudest. "We'll hear that story another time, when it's not such a chance of being personal.

"Now, here ye are, Master O'Hara," he continued. "Turn to the right, then to the left, and—there we are. Now, boys, no more wet seats. Follow me."

As a rule, Mike O'Hara was not supposed to stop at the "Mountain Dew Girl," as the "Coach for Time" was imagined to dash along the road and arrive in Ballinara in a few hours.

But there was not a traveller "on board" who was not glad to have a "warmer," and the tall man and the fat both descended willingly into the courtyard, and entered the bar.

Having here regaled themselves, they returned to their wretched seats on the rickety old coach, and were preparing to make themselves as comfortable as spongy seats and a foot of water would make them, when a yell of delight rose into the air, and glancing round, they saw the four lads prancing wildly about the coach.

They were waving something madly about in their hands.

What could they be—these things which seemed to have inspired the four Irish lads with so much jollity?

Gridirons.

"Bless my soul! yes, they are gridirons," growled the fat man, appealing to his lean neighbour. "What can they be going to do with them!"

The driver was now climbing to his seat.

"Is it the gridirons ye're wondering at, then, jintlemen!" he said. "Ye see yonder there?"

He pointed towards a building next to the inn, a building where the glow of the furnace within and the swarthy forms at work formed a contrast to the clean, blinded windows and the green climbing plants and flowers, that made it pleasant and happy-looking.

"Truly, yes," said the fat man.

"Well, they shoe horses there, and on occasions they make a gridiron or two, and as gridirons don't keep wet in so well as the sate you're a-sitting on now, the bhoys have jist bought some to sit on."

And Mat laughed loudly.

At this moment, just as the "bhoys" were mounting the coach, the ostler got up on the first step and whispered something in the ear of the driver.

A scowl passed over the hitherto laughing face of Mike O'Hara.

"Is it spies they are?" he growled, as he gave a backward glance of hate, which comprehended both men. "Then it's the upper road I'll take."

The ostler nodded, apparently with pleasure, and with a muttered oath, the driver urged his horses on towards the mountain tops.

CHAPTER II.
THE MIST ON THE MOUNTAINS.

WITH many a shout of laughter the lads of the Shannon School arrayed their gridirons on the coach top, which now, as they sat on their strangely improvised seats, discharged its deluge of rain into that where the fat and lean men were huddled up, in the fulness of their misery.

"I think, instead of making such a confounded row, you might think of other people," said the fat man, addressing Pat O'Connor, who sat nearest to him, laughing loudly.

"Shure and it's myself that did that same," said Pat. "I thought of my schoolmates."

"You might as well have had a little consideration for your fellow travellers, too."

"Is it a gridiron ye're wanting?" asked Pat, winking at his schoolfellows.

"Well, absurd as is the idea," said the traveller, "they really do seem to answer the purpose."

"Ye'd like one?" asked Pat.

"It's that same I would," said the fat man.

"Well, then," cried Pat O'Connor, raising above his head a bran new gridiron of the same size and strength of the others, he had bought at the forge, "I've always been taught to keep a reserve."

The fat man extended his hand to receive the coveted prize, but Pat O'Connor flourished the gridiron over his head.

"I've been taught also," he cried, "never to give to strangers, unless they are destitute. There's a price, you must know, for this gridiron."

"Well, what is it?" growled the traveller, impatiently, as he moved himself out of a puddle of water.

"You see, I paid two shillings apiece for these gridirons," cried Pat, with a grin which distended greatly his handsome mouth.

"Very well; be quick. I'll give you half a crown," cried the traveller, again extending his hand. But Pat once more waved him back.

"No, not yet," he said; "ye see, five gridirons at two shillings each comes to ten shillings, and two for profit makes twelve; so if ye'll hand over twelve shillings, the gridiron's yours."

And with a true Irish laugh in his twinkling eye, he extended his hand.

"Why, ye little extortionate imp," began the man.

Then he stopped.

The rain was coming down in a perfect deluge.

Every moment his seat became more sloshy, and the foot boarding more flooded.

"Come on, then," he cried, "here's the money, and much good may it do you."

He had passed the money and received the gridiron before he uttered the last savage words, or Pat O'Connor would certainly never have completed the bargain.

"You're an ongrateful omadhaun," exclaimed Pat; "I'd sooner have kept the gridiron to cook steaks with, or given it away to the witch on the mountains, than you should have had it, if I'd known what gratitude I'd get—but there, the divil fly away wid ye for a thieving Saxon. You know no better.

"Now, then, boys," he cried, as he turned to his grinning schoolmates, "here's three shillings apiece for us, which is a profit of sixpence each to drink the health of ould Ireland, and confusion to all guagers and spies."

The two men on the box seat exchanged glances at these words, but neither spoke, while Mike O'Hara whipped his horses with greater energy, saying—

"It's meself that echoes those words, Master O'Connor, and good luck to yer."

The boys now laughed and joked, and made merry in every way, while the two men on the box seats lapsed into slumber, or, at any rate, seemed to do so.

They were now ascending a rugged mountain road, and the mists above were rapidly thickening.

"It's a puzzle to me, Mike," exclaimed Pat O'Connor, addressing the driver, as they ascended the road, which every moment became more rutty, "it's a puzzle to me why you're going up this road when the lower one's open."

"Shure thin, Master Patrick," returned Mike, "if a ship is going from one harbour to another, why does it put into another port on the way?"

"To deliver goods, maybe."

"It's yourself that's right," exclaimed Mike; "I've got two bales of goods to deliver right up on the mountain top."

"Bales of goods. Shure, it's small ones they are then," cried Pat, "for divil a bit of goods is to be seen in the coach."

"Shure, and goods may be packed away in a very small compass," said Mike; "not that I say that it's the case now. Ye'll see me deliver them in a few moments."

He spoke in a serious voice, and winked back at Pat O'Connor in a way which seemed to tell him to be quiet, and on the *qui vive*.

So Pat turned once more to his companions, and in spite of the rain, they talked of the fun they had had during their holidays, and the fun that would come in the approaching schooltime.

As they went higher and higher towards the peaks of the hills, the mist became denser and denser, until, at length, the "Coach for Time" was so enveloped in the thick atmosphere, that nothing could be seen around it.

Mike O'Hara lost now all his pleasantry.

A stern frown settled on his brow, and when they reached the crest of the hill, the coach was stopped.

Mike raised his hand to his lips, and a shrill whistle echoed over the hills.

The two passengers on the box seats glanced uneasily at one another.

In an instant, some dark forms sprang out of the mist.

"Hould there," cried a rough voice, as the leaders were seized by a couple of strong hands, "who's your passengers?"

"Shure," exclaimed Mike O'Hara, "shure, and it's four boys for the Shannon school I have on the coach top sitting on gridirons."

"The divil fly away wid ye for a joker always," cried the man; "and who are?"

"Who else!" cried Mike, in a thundering voice; "why, two spies, two hateful, sneaking Saxon spies, who've come here to ruin the widow and the fatherless, the hungry and starvin'. Away wid them to the caves."

The two men on the box seat now seemed endowed with a new life.

From the pockets of both were drawn pistols, which were presented at the heads of those who sprang up to seize them.

"Back there on your lives," cried the thin man, rising to his full height, and showing, in spite of his leanness, a tall, military figure; "we're no rabbits in their holes to be taken unawares. We are Englishmen, and know how to fight for our lives."

"Ah, shure and we know that; and it's a little bit o' fighting we can do on this side of the streak o' rough water," returned the man; "we're not wanting to harm ye, only when we find the ' Coach for Time ' coming up the wrong way, we know that something is up."

The Englishmen both knew now that there was a plan in all that had been done.

They were well aware of the state of the country.

It was 1847.

The potato famine—that fearful scourge for poor Ireland—was raging everywhere throughout the dear old country.

Emigration was carrying away into far-off lands the bone and sinew of the country, but yet over the green-clad hills there wandered starving thousands.

In the towns they dropped and died, on the hills they fought and plundered.

An empty stomach does not breed much charity to others, and the Irish looked to England as the cause of their disaster

Who can tell hungry men to reason?

English soldiers held their towns, English people ate and drank; English rifles and good living seemed to go together, and so English tyranny seemed connected in their minds with the gaunt faces of their wives and the constant deaths of their children.

So the two Englishmen, who until this moment had so successfully concealed their mutual friendship, understood with what they had to deal.

"If you will tell us what you want," cried the fat man, "we will reason with you. But

we are not the ones to be attacked by robbers and say nothing about it."

"Shure, and we are not wanting any of this palaver," began the man who had first spoken.

And scarcely had he spoken, when there was a whizz in the still murky air, and a heavy stick struck the lean man full in the face.

In an instant, while insensibility was upon him, he was seized—dragged down from the coach top and hurried away.

The fat man, however, seemed disposed to fight till the last.

With wondrous agility, considering his size and shape, he sprang down the steps of the coach and blazed away right and left with his double-barrelled pistols.

One of the assailants was at once shot dead, while another fell bleeding to the ground.

This sealed the fate of the unfortunate Englishman.

Two blows from a heavy bludgeon from behind hurled him senseless to the earth, and as he fell, prone upon his face, a knife driven through his back sent him into eternity without a groan.

There was a pause now for a moment.

The Irishmen, famished and wolf-like as they might be, had never bargained for such bloodshed.

But their fury was in the ascendant, and they cared for nothing but revenge—revenge on those whom they regarded as their cruel oppressors.

After a moment, however, when one of their number had handed round a bottle of whisky, "the darling stuff that had never seen the exciseman," the head of the party spoke to Mike O'Hara, who had throughout the scene sat stolidly on the box.

"Mike, we want the boys now," he said.

"What for?"

"Shure and they've seen too much," cried the man, "and as sure as my name's Dark Dennis, they'll have to stop in the cave until we shift quarters."

There was a loud laugh from the top of the coach.

The boys had seen something of what was going on, though they knew not the terrible extent of the catastrophe.

At any rate they were resolved not to be taken.

"But what are we to do, Patrick?" asked Tim O'Reilly, a lad somewhat of the same age as O'Connor.

"Fight for it, lads," cried Pat O'Connor, dropping his broad Irish, as he could at any moment. "We've got our gridirons, and a crack from one of them wouldn't be healthy for a man, even if he'd a skull like a nigger. Follow me!"

Preceded by Pat O'Connor, who somehow or other was certainly the leader of the party, they scrambled down at the back of the coach.

The men saw them descending with their gridirons, and naturally enough they imagined they were doing so for the purpose of surrender.

"This way, bhoys," cried the captain of the plunderers; "we'll take every care of ye, and ——"

Crash went a gridiron in his face.

He saw at once a thousand stars.

Murderous curses were upon his tongue, but he could give no vent to them and he fell helpless, stunned, to the earth.

Pat O'Connor had never for a moment dreamed of such an end to the attack.

But as he stepped down from the coach, he saw, despite the mist, in the circle of light cast by a torch held by one of the party, the dead body of their fellow passenger.

Pat O'Connor didn't believe in spies, but neither did he believe in cold and deliberate murder.

So, without a word, he dashed the gridiron in the face of the Irishman, and then shouting—"Follow me, lads," he sped away through the mist.

His companions were close behind him.

Rushing up the hillside after their beloved young leader, they joined him on the crest of the next hill, just where a dim light shone through the grey cloudland.

"We shall never reach the school to-night, lads," cried Pat, as they paused out of breath; "we must, as the redcoats say, camp out to-night."

"Then we'll make for yonder light," exclaimed Tim O'Reilly, "and see what shanty it is."

The lads at once started off, and presently as they came nearer to the spot where the light was shining, they saw standing at the door of a tumble-down-looking hut an old man, clad in his tail coat, his heavy corduroy breeches, ribbed stockings, brogues, and on his head a battered caubeen.

"Shure and if it isn't Terence O'Rafferty's own little cabin," cried Pat, relapsing once more into his brogue; "it's himself that's the proper bhoy. Terence! Terence!"

"Aye, aye; and that's the voice of the young masther, for fifty pounds," exclaimed the old man. "Here, mind yer way up the rocky path there; that's roight. Shure, and it's my eyes are brighter for seeing ye. Ah! Master Patrick, darlin', what did ye come out in the mist on the mountain tops for, this blessed night?"

"I didn't come; I was brought in the 'Coach for Time,'" said Patrick O'Connor. "But we've been attacked on the road by some of the starving peasantry, and a man—a guager—has been killed."

A strange look passed over the face of the old man, a far-off look, a look which seemed searching into the past.

He pressed his hand to his brow.

"A guager!" he murmured. "Bad cess to them all! a bad lot, a bad lot. Come in, bhoys; I've some poteen here, brewing on the hob, and it's yourselves'll be wanting some comfort from the mist that's choking ye."

The lads were nothing loth.

In a few moments, five steaming glasses of poteen were standing upon the table, and they were about to partake of it, when—

Bang—crack!

Dully through the mist-laden air came the crack of a rifle.

The old man started to his feet.

"What on the earth is that now?" he exclaimed, and he rushed to the door.

There all was still.

The mountains were veiled in impenetrable mist. All seemed drear, desolate, lonely.

But then again the echoes of the night were awakened.

The ping, ping, boom! of several rifles was heard.

Then the sound of rushing feet, and as Terence O'Rafferty started back in astonishment, a dark figure loomed up in the darkness—staggered forward, and plunged into the shanty.

A smaller figure was with him, led by the hand.

"Conceal me, for the love of Heaven; if only for a moment, conceal me!" exclaimed the stranger, as he tottered to a chair.

"Shure, and it's yourself will spake better for a drop o' the crater," said the old man as he bolted and barred the door. "Though you're one o' the murthering decaitful Saxons, I'll not see ye murdered in cold blood, while I've a bolt to shut, or an arm to waild my shillelagh!"

He poured out a bumper of strong Irish whisky hot for the stranger, and then passed his great horny hand through the golden locks of the ten-year-old boy, who stood pale, but defiantly by the side of the man, whose face was bloodstained and whose eyes glittered with the glare of a hunted wild beast.

"You've a good-looking gossoon here," said the old man. "What are you doing with him up here in the mountains?"

"Don't ask me," cried the stranger; "this I will say, I'm saving his life. I was taking him up to Shannon Tower, the school by the river, when I was attacked. Oh! if there was anyone here who would let me escape and take him, the blessings of a hunted wretch would fall like grains of mercy on his head."

Pat O'Connor in an instant stood before him.

"Sir," he said in a gently-modulated tone, "we four boys are bound for school at Shannon Tower. Tell me only what to do, and I will do it."

The stranger glanced at him.

He saw in a moment with what class of lad he had to deal. He extended his hand.

"I will trust you," he said, as he grasped firmly the hand of the brave young Irish lad; "take my boy to the Tower with this letter, and——"

Crash! came the blow of a heavy bludgeon on the rickety door, and he started up.

"I leave him to you and Heaven!" he cried, and opening the window at the back, he leaped out into the darkness.

As he did so, the door was burst open, and four masked figures, armed with rifles, rushed in.

At the same moment there was another report from without, followed by a shriek of mortal agony.

"He has met his death," exclaimed Terence O'Rafferty, springing to the door, and gazing out into the darkness.

CHAPTER III.
THE BOYS OF THE SHANNON.

THE school towards which Pat O'Connor and his companions were bound was situated on the banks of the river Shannon.

It was known as Shannon Tower, or Shannon Academy, and was a mark in the landscape for miles around.

It was a grand old building of red brick, with high walls surrounding its grounds, and large, waving trees were in the playgrounds.

On the one side a lawn stretched down to the river's brink, where boats were ready in the pleasant summer time for the use of those boys who understood the art of rowing.

For Mr. Thaddeus O'Shaughnessy was one who believe in kindness and rewards.

Curious stories were rife about O'Shaughnessy's predecessor, who had illtreated the boys right and left.

His son Thaddeus resolved if ever he obtained the school himself, to carry it on on a different principle; and he kept his word.

He taught well, he fed the boys well; he was stern, strict, but just, and while he almost wept when he was compelled to punish, he gloried in distributing rewards.

There were two ushers in the school.

The one, Laurence McMahon, was a man nearly as tall as the schoolmaster himself, and of a military appearance, that had gained him, among the boys, the title of "The Marshal."

He was well liked by the boys.

Then there was Timothy Finnigan, who in consequence of his propensity for a certain dried fruit, had earned the pseudonym of "Figs."

He was a stout, podgy little man, with reddish hair stiffly curling all over his head, a fiery nose, and deep-set, twinkling eyes.

He was somewhat of a butt for the boys, but he readily forgave an affront, and was voted not such a bad fellow after all.

The sun was shining brightly, as the lads were seen coming down the hillside on foot.

Mike O'Hara had not made his appearance with the "Coach for Time" at the shanty of Terence O'Rafferty, and so, *minus* their luggage, the lads made their way from the misty mountains to the Shannon school.

Mat O'Grady, the serving man, was the first to see them, and with a loud "hurroo!" he rushed into the house.

Thaddeus O'Shaughnessy met him in the hall, where the serving man nearly knocked him over in his excitement.

"Bad luck to you for an ignorant, madheaded omadhaun!" exclaimed the master. "What on airth is the matter?"

"Shure and it's Master Pat O'Connor and four more coming down from the hill-tops on foot, and divil a bit of a box, or a bag, or a blessed parcel with them."

"Bless me! what can the meaning be—and Mike O'Hara's coach due last night?" said the master, with some concern. "Be quick, and open the front gate and let them in. Dear me! I hope they've not been in trouble."

Mat O'Grady looked as if he would have liked to have made a remark about this, but his master's manner stopped him, and with another "hurroo!" he darted towards the front gate.

The boys just disappeared, as it were, behind the top of the gate at that moment.

With a wild Irish "hurroo!" he flung open the gate, and embraced the first object standing there. The next moment he received a terrible blow.

With a terrific howl he went spinning back again into the school grounds.

When Mat O'Grady recovered his equanimity, and rose from the place where he had fallen, he found himself surrounded by five grinning boys.

"Well, and be shure, Master Pat," he cried, addressing young O'Connor, and rubbing away at his shock head, "and it wasn't the act of a jintleman to pitch me in here, head foremost, when I came to embrace you."

A roar of laughter greeted these words.

"And it's yerself that embraced Mike Murrigan's donkey that's standing out there with the vegetable cart," cried Pat, hardly able to articulate with merriment; "sure and the donkey —poor beast!—doesn't like liberties, and he tould ye so plainly."

The donkey's head was now partly visible at the gate.

Mat O'Grady saw his blunder, and scratched his head all the harder.

"Shure and I'm sorry," cried he, "that I——"

"Sorry is it," cried Pat O'Connor, "and it's sorry ye ought to be to confess that you mistook Mike Murrigan's donkey for me. Is Mr. O'Shaughnessy in?"

"It's himself that's standing at the door this blessed minit," cried Mat.

The boys at once hurried along the avenue, and in a few moments they had reached the broad stone steps, upon the top of which stood the schoolmaster with beaming countenance.

"Well, bhoys," he cried, as he shook hands all round.

Then he paused as his eyes fell upon the English lad.

"Shure, and whom have we here?" he cried. "What new pupil is this that has come here unintroduced?"

"He comes with a strange introduction, I'm thinking," said Pat O'Connor; "I brought him here myself. Here is a letter to you, Mr. O'Shaughnessy, and when we go in, sir, I'll tell you how we met."

Thaddeus took the note, glanced over it, patted the boy on the head, and said, in a kindly voice—

"Ah, my little man, I've heard of you before; your name, I believe, is Reginald Graham?"

"Yes, sir."

"I hope you'll be happy here, then, my child. It shall not be my fault if you are not, and I am sure your companions will do their best to be kind to one who, for a time at least, will be without any friends but me and them.

"And now," he added, "come in to breakfast, and tell me your adventures, and why you came the day after the fair, and on foot instead of in the coach."

While partaking of the breakfast provided by the master, Pat O'Connor told the story of the previous night's adventures.

Thaddeus O'Shaughnessy listened very gravely to the narrative, especially when he heard of the attack on the suspected spies, and the flight of the mysterious friend of Reginald.

"Who was this gentleman who brought you here, Master Graham?" he said, glancing at the lad.

The boy turned slightly pale.

"'SO YOU ARE GOING TO SHOW FIGHT, ARE YOU?' SAID THE IRISH LAD."

"Am I obliged to tell, sir ?" he asked.

"Why do you ask, my lad ?"

"Because," he said, "I promised never to tell anyone."

"But you know him ?"

"Yes, sir."

"And he is a good friend ?"

"Yes, sir ; a dear friend, the best I have," said the lad.

"Ah, just so," said O'Shaughnessy ; "I am glad you feel obliged to keep a promise ; I respect you all the more for it. But this is very vexatious about your luggage, boys ; as for your gridirons—ha, ha, ha !" he laughed, throwing himself back in his chair, and bursting into a roar of merriment, "you can afford to lose them as you were paid back for them ; but your clothes, pocket-money, books, and so on, are not such nice things to lose sight of."

"Oh, I suppose, sir," responded Pat, "Mike O'Hara'll turn up some day—ah, what is this ?"

He jumped up, and rushed to the window, and there, sure enough, as the schoolmaster and the rest followed him, they saw whirling down the road from the hills, a jaunting car, with all the luggage jolting and bumping about in indescribable confusion.

The driver was Mike O'Hara himself.

"Well, I wonder what the vagabond will have to say for himself," cried the schoolmaster. "Keep back, boys ; don't let him see ye. I'll send O'Grady to ask him to come up here to the hall."

The boys, enjoying the fun, at once crept away from the window, and ensconced themselves behind the half-open door, where they could hear all that was going on.

O'Grady then, having helped O'Hara in with the luggage, told the latter that "the masther" wanted to speak to him at the Hall entrance.

The driver came with many a bow and scrape.

"And it's good luck to ye, yer honour, and long life to ye," said he.

"Good morning, O'Hara," returned the schoolmaster, quietly, "good morning. You've brought the luggage, but where are my young gentlemen ?"

The driver dropped his jaw quite an inch, and stood grasping his whip in comic amazement.

"Shure, and it's myself cannot say, yer honour," he said slowly, feeling his way, as it were, through his words ; "if the bhoys—I beg your honour's pardon, the young gentlemen—haven't reached the school, shure, and it's themselves as is to blame."

"How's that, Mike ; I hope nothing has happened to any one of them ?" said O'Shaughnessy.

"And that's the thing that I can't tell, your honour," said O'Hara, cautiously, "by the token that I don't know. Ye see, we had two jintlemen aboard my coach, raal jintlemen, bred and born, surr, and as they wanted to be dhropped a trifle out o' the way—maybe yer honour's following me ?"

"I am," said Thaddeus, drily.

"I went up a little on the upper road, and then the young jintlemen—Lord save 'em, they're only bhoys, after all, and maybe yer honour'll not punish 'em—they pulled out some gridirons, and began fighting the chaps that were takin' out me horses, and pullin' down the jintlemen's luggage."

"Well ?"

"And then they all went whooping away in the mist, and—Lord save us !—I lost 'em altogether."

This was said with all the bold effrontery imaginable, and evidently under the impression that O'Shaughnessy believed him.

He was unprepared, therefore, for the stern look that came over the brow of the schoolmaster.

"Mike O'Hara," he said, "I have listened to you, and know your whole story is one tissue of lies. The whole of the young gentlemen have arrived here, and I know all—the murder of the spy and so on. Quit my premises, and never let me see you here again."

At first a scowl struggled with the set smile on the face of the driver, then the smile returned as if by magic, and he took his hat from his head, and bowed respectfully.

"And it's your honour's been misinformed, thin," exclaimed he ; "I'm sure I took good care of the young jintlemen, and——"

The schoolmaster waved him away.

"I want no more of it, O'Hara," he said ; "go away, and don't presume to come across my threshold again."

The man turned his back as if with a sudden resolution, and then hurried away to his jaunting car.

"Ah, Misther O'Shaughnessy," he muttered, as he whipped up his lean horse, and rushed away up the mountains, "wait till the red lights are glowing on the hills, and thin see who'll cross your threshold. Sorra for you thin, who turned the O'Hara away from yer doors."

CHAPTER IV.

THE SCHOOL FÊTE.

"THAT is a thorough-paced rascal, and I hope you boys will have nothing to do with him," said the schoolmaster, as he returned to the room where he had left his scholars. "Come now, let us go into the school-house, and you can join in the sports which the rest of the lads are engaged in. You know we always have a holiday on the first day of term, and as this happens to be a fine one, I hope you'll enjoy yourselves in every way."

The jolly old schoolmaster kept speaking thus as he passed from his own dwelling, through the large door which separated it from the school-house proper.

They knew it was Liberty Hall for this day, at any rate, and after giving a cheer for the jolly old man who presided over them, they went whooping away into the playgrounds at the back.

The beautiful playgrounds, with their gymnasiums, and their tennis courts, and their recreations of all kinds, and the beautiful lawn, too, sloping down to the waters of the Shannon.

Their arrival was greeted by the boys with uproarious shouts of welcome, and Reginald, the new boy, came in for more than his share of it.

Indeed, his hand was shaken till the tears

came into his eyes, and Pat O'Connor had to interfere to prevent his being, as he said, "torn all to pieces."

Reginald, of course, felt proud of his welcome, and being of a handsome presence, and a frank, ingenuous nature, he very soon ingratiated himself with his new companions.

But new boys and old companions were soon lost in the general whirl of fun and play, and Pat having told his adventures again and again to admiring audiences, who yelled with laughter as they heard of the gridirons, joined in the rabble rout, and ran, and jumped, and rowed with the rest.

Reginald, to whom the games were new, gladly took advantage of a moment when he was unobserved to escape from the rest, and wander down the green slope towards the river's bank.

The water looked so beautiful as it glided by the broad emerald expanse, and sparkled between the trees that girt it on either side, that he could not resist the temptation.

He forgot his sorrow in the bright summer landscape.

"How lovely," he cried, "is all this scene! This old school and its surroundings, and this sunlit river and——"

"Shure the people too that dwell by it entirely," cried a voice near him.

A thick voice, husky with whisky and tobacco.

Reginald started round, expecting to see a sturdy son of the hills, some ruffian of the same type as those who had attacked the coach on the preceding night.

But he found himself most wonderfully mistaken.

Instead of this he saw before him a lad about eighteen, clad in a variety of coloured rags that gave him somewhat the appearance of a scarecrow.

His caubeen was stuck jauntily on one side of his head, his feet were bare, and in his hand he flourished a goodly shillelagh.

His eyes had a mixture of low humour and cunning in them, and his mouth wore on it a heavy and animal expression.

Unused as young Graham was to Irish manners, he knew at once that this fellow must be an interloper in the schoolgrounds, and he said, somewhat haughtily—

"Pray, who told you to interrupt my conversation?"

The Irish lad half stooped, stuck his shillelagh under his left arm, and clapped a hand on each knee.

"Shure and is it conversashun ye're after calling it?" he cried. "A-praching to yerself; or, maybe, you were a-talking to the river or the fishes or the birds, eh?"

"At any rate, it is no business of yours," remarked Reginald, "so go about your business"

And he turned to go.

"Is it my business ye're talking about?" cried the Irish lad. "Then I'll be after doing that which you tould me. So come on with me, and no squealing, or I'll crack you over your head wid this in the fastening of Father Dominic's shoes."

And as he spoke, he seized Reginald by the arm, and raised the shillelagh threateningly above his head. Reginald was no coward.

He had often, before this, roughed it in various latitudes, and had passed, young as he was, through innumerable perils.

And now, faced by this ruffian of nearly twice his age, he did not yield.

He stooped and picked up a large stone which lay on the river's bank.

"Stand back, you ruffian," he said, "or I'll dash your brains out."

"Ha, ha! my young Saxon cub," exclaimed the Irish lad with a laugh, "so you're going to show fight, are you. Well, fire away! my head's hard enough to stand a blow from the best stone that ever rolled down from the hill of Clare."

"Have it then, since you wish it," exclaimed Reginald, and with good aim he launched his weapon.

Had it caught his enemy on the temple, he would certainly never have reappeared during our story.

As it was, the Irish lad dodged, and the stone, catching him on the side of the head, inflicted a wound which made the blood spurt freely, but did not stun him.

In an instant he sprang forward, with a cry of fury.

"I'll be the death of ye, as sure as my name's Dan Hooligan," he cried.

"Which, shure, can't be your name thin," said a voice.

And before he knew whence the sound proceeded, or what new foe he had to encounter, someone had run between his legs from behind and flung him high in the air.

It was useless to attempt any resistance.

Up he went like a rocket, and being so near the river's brink, he went head foremost into the water. It was Pat O'Connor who had performed the feat. And now his voice resounded loudly across the greensward.

"Bhoys, bhoys, come and see the Irish pig that can't swim," he shouted; and as Dan Hooligan, fierce and yet dripping like a drowned rat, scrambled ashore, the river's margin was crowded with school lads.

"Shure, and the Shannon's rayther deep jist hereaway, Master Hooligan," exclaimed Pat, with a broad grin; "it's hoping I am that ye've not caught cold."

A roar of laughter was the response from the boys, but a scowl of hate darkened the brow of the Irish lad.

"It's yerself has the pull of a poor bhoy now," he said bitterly, "but the day will come when the Hooligans——"

"Will get praties widout paying for them agin, and sorra a bit of gaol for it," exclaimed a tall boy near him.

Dan turned savagely.

"And ye needn't be talking so, Master Barry of Barrymore," he cried; "ye're not so rich yerself that ye can afford to scoff at a poor bhoy."

"I'm not quite so rich in impudence, no doubt, as you are, Dan Hooligan," said The Barry, "but I'm as rich in bone and muscle, and I'm thinking you'll have to go before the master and explain yourself."

The boy who spoke was about seventeen years of age.

He was of a lithe, athletic form, and with his dark hair, black piercing eyes, straight nose and olive complexion, he formed quite a type of Italian beauty.

He was known as The Barry of Barrymore.

Barrymore, the honoured seat of his ancestors, was now in the possession of an Englishman.

The Barrys had fallen upon bad times, and their estate had passed, by purchase, into the hands of strangers.

The elder Barry had died almost immediately after this disgrace; his wife followed him; and "The Barry," the only son, being left with a moderate competence, devoted a part of it to educating himself as an Irishman and a gentleman should be.

He lived on in the hope that he would one day be able to repurchase Barrymore, and re-establish the ancient family.

His face was flushed slightly now, as he advanced towards the defiant mountain lad.

"Come now," he said, "Master Hooligan, ye shall have the honour of a walk with The Barry of Barrymore. Will ye accept the honour of my arum? Ye won't? Then ye'll accept the honour in a different way."

And he raised his fist threateningly.

Dan's eyes flashed fire, and he raised his stick menacingly.

"Back," he cried, "or I'll brain ye. Divil a bit will a Hooligan be caught like a rat in a trap."

"You lie!" cried a voice, and ere he was aware of it, he felt himself pinioned from behind.

"Ah, then," said Pat O'Connor, "where are ye now, ye thieving, murderous rascal? Take his sprig of shillelagh from him, Barry, and we'll run him to the master."

The Barry, in spite of his struggles, had no difficulty in doing as he was bid.

In a few moments Hooligan was disarmed and a prisoner, for the whole of the boys crowded round him, and escape was impossible.

"Ye'll come quietly now," remarked The Barry.

"Lead the way. Shure, and myself 'ud rayther talk to a jintleman than a poor landless thing like you."

For an instant a gleam of anger shot from the eyes of The Barry.

But he speedily repressed it.

He knew that the unfortunate, wild, uneducated lad was not a subject for indiscriminate attack.

Just as they reached the summit of the lawn with their prisoner, the tall, commanding form of their schoolmaster was seen approaching.

"Why, what have we here?" cried he; "a prisoner, boys?"

"Yes, sir," said Pat O'Connor, as the circle of lads opened to allow the schoolmaster to pass; "yes, sir; I found him trying to murder Master Graham, and I pitched him into the river. Then I and The Barry brought him to you to explain himself."

A strange expression of pain crossed the face of Thaddeus O'Shaughnessy as he gazed on the wild-looking lad.

"Dan Hooligan—Dan the hunter, as I live," he said, as if half musing.

Then aloud he added—

"And pray, Master Hooligan, what have you to say to this?"

"Nothing," he replied, sullenly.

"Shure, and ye couldn't say less," cried the schoolmaster. "You confess the truth of what my bhoys say?"

"Yes."

"You murderous rascal; and pray, why did you do this deed?"

"I was tould to."

"By whom?"

"It's myself wouldn't till, if you'd put me on the rack," continued Dan, striking a theatrically defiant attitude.

"Never mind about the rack," returned O'Shaughnessy; "it's not that I'll try ye with. Forty-eight hours on bread and water's better than all the racks in the world."

The wild lad laughed.

"Hunger! Is that what you think will make me betray my friends?" he cried. "Hunger! What is hunger to me, who have lain for days on the mountain tops without a bite or sup? Lead on; take me where you think you'll starve me, and you'll find my body there one morning, stiff and stark, but you'll get no confission, as ye call it, out o' me."

"We'll try ye, my lad," said Thaddeus. "Pat, go and call O'Grady."

"Here he is, sir," exclaimed Pat; "coming across the lawn."

Sure enough, the Irish lad was hurrying along towards the scene.

"Here, O'Grady," said Thaddeus, "just help Master O'Connor and The Barry to take this fellow to the strong room beneath the west wing. We'll see how soon he'll alter his tune."

If the schoolmaster had not been so attentively observing the features of Dan Hooligan, he would have noticed that a peculiar look was on the face of Mat O'Grady, and that he shot a glance of intelligence at the prisoner.

The latter, schooled in a wild school truly, but one which taught its members to have confidence in one another, and never even at death's point to betray one another, kept his features perfectly motionless.

He suffered himself to be led quietly away, and within ten minutes he was the inmate of a dungeon with barred windows, such as must have been used in times gone by when the house was a stronghold.

He was soon forgotten by the merry, thoughtless boys outside.

A few remarks were made, a few circles formed, and then away they went once more to play and jest and row until three, which was dinner time.

Then another hour, and the guests would arrive.

Such a strange assemblage it was when once the gates of the academy were thrown open.

Young ladies and old ladies, young gentlemen and old, rich and poor, all had free access to the grounds of the academy.

It was not a time for distinctions, nor a place where they were thought of.

The strict precision of the school was forgotten for the time, and all was fun and jollity.

The great arrival of the evening was that of the fiddler.

He was received by the boys with a wild cry of welcome, and in the twinkling of a bed-post sets were formed on the green, and the joyous couples began to foot it gaily.

All went merry as a marriage bell, and as Reginald glanced round him and saw the happy ones dancing in the glow of the setting sun, and heard the chorus of music, he thought what a place of joy a school must be.

Little did he know what scenes of terror, anxiety and sorrow he would have to undergo on the banks of the fast-flowing Shannon.

It was but eight in the evening, and the company were dancing by the light of lamps, when a young fellow about seventeen years of age approached a tree, where a girl was leaning with her hands folded on her bosom and her eyes full of tears.

"What is the matter, Mary O'Rourke?" he said, in a gentle voice, as he took her right hand; "ye should not be sorrowful in such a scene as this."

"You would be sorrowful, too, if you had a bursting heart like mine," replied the girl, with sad eyes. "You, Master Marshall, the son of a fine English gentleman, can't tell what it is to be sad and weary."

The girl was eminently beautiful.

She had all the brightness of eye, the roundness of form, the *naïveté* which distinguish the Irish girl.

"My dearest Mary," said Harry Marshall, "you speak most unkindly to me. You know how I love you. You know how I have promised, in the days to come, that you shall be my wife, and yet——"

"And yet—let me finish your sentence, Mr. Marshall," said Mary O'Rourke, scorn and sorrow mingling in her bright blue eyes; "and yet the whole evening you have not bestowed a glance upon me, but kept your dances, your soft words and your looks for Miss Lizzie Stapleton."

The lad laughed.

"Really this is too bad, Mary," he said. "Here have you been hiding away behind these trees all the evening, in order that you may watch me unseen, and yet you complain of my not coming to you."

The girl's eyes flashed.

"It is false, Harry," she cried.

But she could say no more.

She had no sooner called him by his Christian name than he clasped her in his arms, and imprinted half a dozen kisses on her cherry lips.

"Come, Mary," he said; "don't let's quarrel. I want to tell you something most particularly. Let's get behind this tree."

As they did so, a dark form glided from among the shadows and took up its station near them, though unseen.

The moon shone on his face for an instant, as he crept serpent-like along.

Was it possible that it was the face of Dan Hooligan—Dan, who was safe under lock and key, and bolts and bars?

Whoever he was, there was a scowl of savage passion on his features, and he muttered oaths of vengeance on the head of the English boy, Harry Marshall.

He was close enough now to hear all they said.

"Mary, dear," said Harry, "I have bad news for you."

"Not worse than you gave me to-night, shure, when ye danced three dances running with Miss Lizzie Stapleton of Barrymore."

"And haven't I sealed all that with a kiss?" said Harry. "Never mind pouting your red lips, or I shall kiss you again. But, seriously, I have bad news for you."

"And what is it?"

"My uncle has returned to Harcourt Place."

The girl shuddered.

"That is indeed bad news," she said; "there'll be no more meetings at the ruins. You'll never teach me any more how to spake—speak I mane. Oh, there, you understand me, and you'll have plenty of time then to court Miss Stapleton."

And she fell to weeping again, and laid her head on his shoulder.

"There, don't be foolish," said Harry, kissing her brow fondly. "Don't be foolish. You know I love you; you know that The Barry has been dancing with Miss Stapleton nearly all the evening."

"The Barry—the Barry of Barrymore?" exclaimed the girl.

"Yes, look even now. See, in the dim light where the shadow of the elm-trees fall; they are whirling away now joyously."

The girl glanced in the direction indicated.

Surely enough The Barry was whirling round with Miss Lizzie.

"The daughter of his enemy. Bad luck to him," cried Mary O'Rourke.

"No worse than the son of the Saxon," exclaimed a thundering voice.

And in an instant the figure had sprung from behind the tree, a blow was dealt with such violence as to fell Marshall to the ground, and Mary O'Rourke, with a piercing scream, found herself carried quickly in the direction of the river's brink.

CHAPTER V.

THE PURSUIT ON THE SHANNON.

THE shriek which echoed from the lips of Mary O'Rourke along the broad avenue of lofty trees soon brought the merry dance to a full stop, and in an instant thronging crowds pressed forward to the spot whence the sound had proceeded.

They had no notion, of course, of the exact position of the person who had uttered the cry.

But as some of them bore flambeaux, they were not a moment in discovering Harry Marshall as he lay on the ground beneath the tree.

He was just recovering consciousness, when they neared him, and as he feebly raised himself, he exclaimed—

"Where is she?"

"Where is who?" exclaimed The Barry, earnestly, as he bent over his fallen friend.

"Mary O'Rourke," cried Harry, recovering fully now his scattered senses, and staggering to his feet; "she has been carried off by that ruffian, Dan Hooligan."

"Hooligan! Your senses are deserting you," cried The Barry; "the fellow is safe and sound in the dungeon of the west wing."

"There's no time for talking or doubting," cried Harry, as he leaped away. "I saw him as plainly as I see you now. Ah! there is the plash of his oars on the Shannon. He has got her in the boat. Come, Pat O'Connor, if no one else will help me, I know you will."

And off he dashed down to the brink of the fast-flowing stream.

The moon was now shedding a silver radiance over the bosom of the Shannon, and they could see plainly the dark form of the boat, as it skimmed away towards mid-stream.

"There—there they go," exclaimed Harry Marshall, excitedly, and he began at once to unfasten a light boat from its moorings.

Into this he leaped, and was joined in a moment by The Barry and Pat O'Connor.

"I'm the strongest rower, but I know the Shannon best," said Pat, "so I'll steer, and do you pull your hardest."

In a few moments they were in pursuit on the moonlit bosom of the river.

As they started, Thaddeus O'Shaughnessy came down to the Shannon's brink.

"Why, what on earth is all this about?" cried he. "Are all the bhoys gone mad to-night?"

"No, sir," exclaimed Reginald Graham. "No, sir, but that fellow Dan Hooligan has escaped from his cell, and has carried away Mary O'Rourke."

"Dan Hooligan escaped?" cried the schoolmaster. "If he has, there has been treachery at work. But what are the boys doing?"

"They've gone in pursoot, surr," said Terence McDermott, a tall, handsome fellow, about seventeen. "Shure and it's meself thinks them the brave bhoys for it. And it's wishing myself with them I am."

"Which of the bhoys is it?" demanded O'Shaughnessy.

"Harry Marshall, Pat O'Connor, and The Barry," returned Terence.

"Then, if anyone can catch the villain, they'll do it," said the schoolmaster. "Ah! what is that red light bobbing up and down in the centre of the river?"

"It's a warning to you that you ought to be quiet," said a voice.

Thaddeus started.

"Who was that spoke?" he cried.

"Not me, sir; not me, sir," was the quick but ungrammatical response that came from the circle of boys.

The schoolmaster did not doubt them, and walked thoughtfully away.

"Come and tell me, Terence, when the lads return," he said, and then he hastened into the house with a clouded brow

Meanwhile, the little skiff was rapidly gaining on the boat in which sat Dan Hooligan and his captive.

The latter had recovered now from her faint, and was gazing back eagerly in the direction of the school.

She uttered a cry of delight as she saw the boat put off.

"Oh, thank Heaven, they're after us," she cried, clasping her hands. "Sorra for you, Dan Hooligan, when they catch you, you murtherous thafe of the world."

"Sorra for you, mavourneen," he said, jeeringly, "sorra for you. The instant they catch us up, my knife'll be sheathed in your heart, alanna."

"'And shure it's meself'll be sitting here and letting ye do it, ma bouchal," returned Mary, in the same tone of banter; "no, Dan Hooligan, I'll be jumping in the river and then they'll pick me up, you ugly black-hearted thafe."

Dan Hooligan made no response to these compliments, but pulled away steadily at the oars.

He was making, as well as he could steer himself in his excitement, towards a point on the left bank of the river, where swung the red light which had attracted the attention of Thaddeus O'Shaughnessy.

As they neared it, Mary O'Rourke could see that it hung from the stern of a large vessel, whose black hull loomed up grimly against the blue and starlit sky.

A vague sensation of fear crept over her.

Why was he making for this ship?

What was the fate in store for her?

As this thought flashed through her mind, Mary gave one loud cry for help, and covered her face with her hands.

With a bitter curse, Dan Hooligan strained every nerve to distance his pursuers.

The lads in the pursuing boat were highly elated by what seemed undoubtedly their chance of success.

Guided steadily and well by Pat O'Connor, and propelled by the equally steady pulling of Harry Marshall and The Barry, the light skiff dashed after the heavier wherry manned only by the strong-armed villain.

"We're gaining on him!" cried Pat O'Connor, in a voice of delight.

"Yes, that we are," cried The Barry, as he took one glance round, and then quickly settled himself to his rowing.

Dan Hooligan muttered horrid oaths to himself, as he strove to drag the boat as it were through the water.

But steadily, certainly, he saw the pursuers overhauling him.

"Curse them!" he cried aloud. "But I won't be beaten."

And stopping his rowing for a minute, he drew from his pocket a whistle, and gave forth a long, shrill note.

In an instant it was answered from on board the ship, and in another moment lights were seen moving on the deck.

Then, as the girl gazed as if fascinated, her eyes distended, her bosom heaving, she saw plainly a boat being lowered.

"Heaven have mercy on me!" she murmured; "I am lost, I am lost."

She knew now that her idea of throwing herself into the stream, and swimming towards her friends would be utterly useless.

The crew of the boat from the ship would of course be armed, and she knew well that whatever party followed to save her would not be armed, and would most probably consist of boys from the school.

Just as the boat was put off from the ship, she heard a loud and familiar voice.

The voice of Harry Marshall.

"Cheer up, cheer up, Mary," he shouted, "we are coming."

She only clasped her hands.

"Oh, they will kill him! Brave boy, brave Harry."

Then she waited, gazing earnestly at the approaching boat.

Dan Hooligan rested on his oars.

Mary O'Rourke saw at once what was his plan.

He was leading the boys on into a trap.

She was ready to save them, if she anyhow could.

As they approached nearer, she exerted her voice to the utmost.

"Back—back! On your lives, put back!" she cried.

"No, no," exclaimed the voice of Pat O'Connor, "we are here to save you."

"No, vou must go back," exclaimed Mary, excitedly; "I will escape, but pray—pray, do not follow me! As you love me, Harry, turn back; there are those here, who——"

She could say no more.

Dan had scrambled along the boat, and seizing her in his arms, had soon stifled her cries.

"Silence!" he cried; "would you betray me?"

"Yes, to death, Dan Hooligan," she murmured, as well as she could, beneath the pressure of his hand.

He chuckled to himself.

"Ah, ah! my pretty one," he cried, "you'll find how I'll punish ye for these words. Wait till you're safe and snug in my shanty, up near the Black Gap, and then we'll see, alanna."

He could feel a shudder pass through the girl's frame, as he said these words, and in his black and cruel heart he triumphed.

Meanwhile, the crew of the boat came on with rapid strokes.

They paused as they came up to Dan Hooligan.

"What's up, mate?" asked a rather gruff voice.

"Stop that boat for me," cried Dan; "young spies from the school."

"Tonder and blitzen!" cried a second voice, "den it is you have been for meddlin' mit dem, or dey not for come here."

"There, and it's all as you like, captain," cried Dan, "if you're for letting them know——"

But the sentence was not finished, for the boat shot ahead, and in a few pulls was up with that containing the scholars.

"Vot 'ave ve here?" exclaimed the Dutch captain, for such he seemed to be.

"Boys from the Shannon school, out for a row," cried Pat O'Connor.

"Out for de row, at dis hour of de night! You 'ave got mit von fine master; but you cannot go no fader dis night."

"What's it got to do with you?" cried Pat. "Shure, has Queen Victoria sold the river Shannon to you?"

"Bah! talk not to me of queens," cried the Dutchman, snapping his fingers; "I care no more for your queen than I do for you. So go back, I say."

"And suppose we don't?" cried Pat.

"Lads, present!" cried the Dutchman, and in a moment the barrels of three muskets flashed brightly in the moonlight.

"Go home mit you now, like good poys," said the captain, "and I will not harm you—not von hair of your heads. But if you stop vaive minute, vile I count dree ondred, I vill blow your brains out mit the greatest of blezure."

"And, pray," cried Pat O'Connor, angrily, "pray by whose authority would you commit such an outrage?"

The Dutch captain, whose figure was plainly visible in the glow of the boat's lantern, made a gesture which would have done credit to a Frenchman.

He pressed his hands to his chest, bent forward and shrugged his shoulders.

"I should do this leetle act of shoostice, by de audoritee of de only berson I ever consoolts—meinself," he said. "So clear off, tonder and blitzen! or I vill blow all your brains aoud—as zure as mein name is Captain De Ruyter, of de goot sheep 'Silverhorn.'"

Pat O'Connor uttered a sharp cry of dismay.

He had heard often of De Ruyter, the famous smuggler of the Shannon; but he had never come face to face with him before.

He knew enough of him, however, to be quite aware that he was a man who would keep his word.

Reckless of all danger—utterly unprincipled, he set the law at defiance, and he would think no more of murdering them than he would of spearing a salmon.

"You murdering thafe of the world," cried Pat, in a furious passion, "we must obey you, since we have no arms; but, remember, the day shall come, when you and I'll meet hand to hand—face to face, and if you aid that villain Dan Hooligan to injure that innocent girl, I'll blow your brains out the first time I meet you—even if it's in the public fair."

The young Irish boy was half beside himself with rage, or he would never have given vent to such a desperate threat, but there was one near him who echoed it, and that was Harry Marshall.

"And if he misses fire, I'll do it myself," he said, as the boat was turned about.

"I am not very zure that I 'ave not bin von vool shoost to let those poys go," said the captain. "But vot for, no; they are poys and know no petter. And, den as for Misder O'Zonosee, ha, ha—he is our friend. Pull back, boys—tonder! I vont some schnapps after dis."

And so the reckless smuggler turned back to his ship.

As the boys rowed silently back, sorrowful and crestfallen, a wild, despairing shriek rent the air.

They knew—and they shuddered to know—that Mary O'Rourke had been dragged on board the "Silverhorn."

"'O GREEDY, THERE HAS BEEN TREACHERY HERE,' SAID THE SCHOOLMASTER."

CHAPTER VI.

THE TRAITOR.

MEANWHILE Thaddeus O'Shaughnessy, on entering the house, proceeded to his study, and sent for O'Grady.

The servant man entered the room, bold as brass, with all the assurance of innocence about him.

"O'Grady," said his master, "close that door."

The man did so.

"Dan Hooligan has escaped, O'Grady," said Thaddeus, quietly.

The man grinned incredulously, and shook his head.

"Shure, surr, and it's that that's impossible," he said; "it's myself that locked him in, and no human being but me, surr, has been anyways nigh to 'im, since."

"Then you're responsible to me for him," said Thaddeus.

"I'm not larned in the classics, sir, like Mooney Marrigan," returned Mat O'Grady; "and I don't know what 'sponsible manes, sure; but if yer honour manes that it's me as has got to give him up to ye safe and sound, it's your honour as is right and no mistake."

"Very well, I am glad to hear it," returned the schoolmaster, "for I have been assured by several persons that Dan Hooligan has been seen this night abroad in the grounds, and has even committed a disgraceful outrage on one of my guests."

The man shook his head.

"Unpossible, surr," he said; "it may have been his sper't, but not his own self, shure."

"I hope not," said Thaddeus; "however, I'm going to see if he's safe. Bring a lantern, and we'll proceed to the strong room."

O'Grady was in no way abashed.

"Very well, surr, though shure, surr," he said, "if ye wish to be with yer friends, there's never a bit of necessity; I can go myself, surr."

"I shall feel more easy if I go. Come, quick —no hesitation," said Thaddeus.

The man skipped nimbly away, and returning after a moment with a lantern, led the way down some broad stone steps to the basement story.

The house had once been a feudal residence, and beneath the basement there were several dark, vault-like chambers, where, doubtless, wretched prisoners had pined away their existence.

At the door of one of these they paused, and O'Grady knocked loudly.

"Dan Hooligan!" he shouted.

"Be silent, for a big fool!" cried the schoolmaster. "Open the door."

O'Grady did so, and advanced into the interior of the room, or rather vault.

All was quiet.

Evidently not a soul was in the place.

The brow of Thaddeus O'Shaughnessy grew dark with anger.

"O'Grady," he said, "there has been treachery here."

"Shure, and in very truth, sir, it sames like it," said Mat.

"This man could not have escaped by himself."

"Indade, then, sir, he must have escaped by himself, for he was all alone," said O'Grady.

"Now, understand me," said O'Shaughnessy, "I will not listen to any of your fooling. This man has escaped, and I am determined to discover by whose aid he has done so."

"Shure, and it's not myself you're suspecting, masther dear?" said O'Grady, with a sudden assumption of gravity.

"I say nothing," returned O'Shaughnessy, cautiously; "but whoever is guilty shall be punished severely. Ha! the bars are gone."

O'Grady rushed to the window, which looked out upon a slope of green.

He gave only one quick look at it.

Then he made a wild caper, and waving his hand above his head, he shouted aloud—

"Hurroo! hurroo!"

"Why, what is the matter?" cried his master.

"Shure, masther dear," exclaimed O'Grady, "I know you were after suspecting me, and here myself can prove it's not me at all, at all that's let the big blaggard out."

"Well, what is it?" asked his master.

"See here, masther," pursued O'Grady, excitedly, "see here. The bars have been removed from the outside, so there's an end of my part of the job."

O'Shaughnessy could not repress a smile.

"O'Grady," he said, "I never accused you of coming into the vault and letting him out, because I have had the key all the time. But you have the run of the grounds, and what is to prevent your pulling down the bars from the outside, when you know how they were fastened not two years ago?"

O'Grady looked terribly crestfallen.

"Shure, and it's no good argyfying wid a gintleman," he said, in a low voice, "but it's myself would die for your honour. Only let me get hold of that thafe of a Dan Hooligan, and——"

He paused suddenly.

Then he cried, excitedly—

"Oh, masther dear, look—look there!"

And he pointed as he spoke towards a piece of brick which lay beneath the window.

But it was not this (which of course proved nothing) that had excited his attention.

What his eyes had greedily devoured was a packet lying near the centre of the room, which Thaddeus O'Shaughnessy had entirely overlooked.

While the back of the schoolmaster was turned, he seized this parcel and eagerly placed it in the breast pocket of his coat.

Then, as Thaddeus rose, he said, drily—

"It's evident that someone has helped him from the outside, sir."

"Peace, fool!" cried O'Shaughnessy. "I shall keep a severe watch over you, and, by Heaven! if I find you have been playing me false, you shall remember this night as long as you live."

"Shure, and I shall, sir," said O'Grady; "this blessed night, when that thafe o' the world broke out of——"

But he was talking to empty air.

O'Shaughnessy had turned his back, and was already ascending the stairs.

He had left the lantern in the hands of

Mat O'Grady, and when Thaddeus had safely departed, the former indulged in a wild dance, accompanied by a broad grin.

"Ha, ha!" he muttered, "ha, ha! and it's the clever boy is the O'Grady. Whist! now, what's me treasure?"

He drew the packet from his coat and gave one rapid glance at it.

This one glance seemed to change him utterly.

He turned deadly pale, and all his merriment vanished.

"So soon—so soon?" he cried. "Well, well, it must come at last."

And so, locking up the vault, he hastened up the steps after his master.

When he reached the basement, he found by the voices that were proceeding from the master's little room that he was in earnest conversation with some of the boys.

He cautiously approached the stairs, and listened.

The sounds of music and laughter still floated in from the grounds, and so that his footsteps would not be heard, he began ascending stealthily.

Up, up, until he reached the master's bedroom.

Here he listened again, and then, as all was still, he hurried in and stuck into the table a little steel dagger about two inches long.

A dagger to which a piece of parchment was attached.

Then, as stealthily as before, he quitted the chamber and glided down.

That night, when all the revelry was over, when the guests had departed, when the weary boys had retired to rest, when the old house was wrapped in quiet, the schoolmaster, entering his room stern and full of thought, saw the strange emblem and started.

He seized it with feverish hands.

"Again—again!" he murmured.

And then he unfolded the parchment and read—

"*To* Thaddeus O'Shaughnessy.

"All who are not traitors to the good cause meet at the old place on the third night from this, at ten o'clock precisely. On the oath you have sworn, come.

"† LAURENCE RATURIER,
"Chief of the Fifth Section of United Irishmen."

Thaddeus O'Shaughnessy raised his eyes heavenwards, and clasped his hands.

"Poor Ireland," he cried, "poor Ireland! Once more the fatal fever is upon you. I go, but only that I may help to save you."

A pair of glaring eyes were upon him as he spoke.

The eyes of Mat O'Grady.

"Ha!" he muttered, as he glided from the half-open door, "you go to meet your doom, to be denounced as a traitor to your counthry."

CHAPTER VII.

FIGS VERSUS APPLES.

THE school settled down to its ordinary routine on the next day, though, conscious of the tiring time the "bhoys" had had of it, Thaddeus eased them off as much as possible.

The only person who seemed to be at all *distrait* was Timothy Finnigan, or "Figs," the usher.

Either his favourite dried fruit had disagreed with him, or else he was crossed in love.

Such was the verdict given unanimously by the big boys.

They were wrong in this instance, for it was neither.

"Figs" was truly in love, but his love smiled upon him, and there was no reason for him to be unhappy on this score.

The cause of his sorrow was of a different nature altogether.

He had received just before school hours a missive which we transcribe, *verbatim et literatim*, for the benefit of our readers.

"DEREST MISTUR FINNIGIN,—yore Last Kine lettur as retched men, and i will meat u at the plaise you naim. Sure, and it's miself ud be ongraitfull 2 yo saf i deed not koom. It's luvvin yo i am, ma beeshal, and and be art and sole. i wil bee in the awchard of the school at 9 o'clock 2 nite undre the red aple tre. So no maur from

"Your affecterate luvvur,
"KATHLEEN MORIARTY"

This exquisitely worded and spelt epistle lay as heavy on the chest of Figs as a cucumber on that of a dyspeptic subject.

The place was all right enough, but the apple-tree.

The favourite apple-tree of Thaddeus O'Shaughnessy, that overshadowed the window of his private study.

This was terrible.

He had no means whatever of communicating with Kathleen, and informing her the perilous spot she had chosen for her rendezvous.

Of late, great depredations had been made in the orchard, and the rosy apples of which O'Shaughnessy was so specially fond had formed a special object of attack.

Figs grew pale as he thought how he might be accused of being the thief.

But there was no help for it.

Go he must.

Kathleen Moriarty, ignorant as she might be, was a very pretty girl, and quite a catch for a poor Irish tutor.

So when evening approached, after a lengthened day of wretchedness, Figs darted out into the grounds, and made his way towards the orchard.

Of course it was forbidden ground.

The gardener and Thaddeus O'Shaughnessy himself were the only persons to whom the privilege of a key was afforded.

So Figs was absolutely going to commit an act of trespass.

To Kathleen, the ingress to the place of fruit was far easier than for him, for there was on the outer wall a series of projections at one spot, which would enable any young and active person to scramble over with the greatest ease.

Figs, on the other hand, had to make his

way as best he could over the high wall, by the assistance of a dilapidated old tree, which had been cut at, and hacked, and hewed, and burnt, and blown with gunpowder, from time immemorial.

However, faint heart never won fair lady, and so, regardless of the possibility of tearing his best "brogues," he made his way over, and was soon in the forbidden ground, which was redolent of the odour of delicious fruit.

He hurried as swiftly as he could in the direction of the apple-tree, and there, sure enough, was Kathleen.

She sprang towards him with a glad cry, and as Tim Finnigan folded her in his arms, he forgot all his peril, all about the proximity of the master's study, and only remembered that he held in his arms the being whom, of all others, he prized and loved.

For be it said, in spite of his peculiar ideas and peculiar appearance, Tim Finnigan had a good and trusty heart, and, in his own style, would have defended his ladylove from all comers.

"Arrah, Kathleen, alanna," he murmured, "it's yerself's the good girl to come and see me this blessed night."

"Shure, and it's me that'd be ungrateful to ye, Tim darling, if I'd not come when you sint me sich a lovely bundle of flowers," said Kathleen; "and the iligant verses too. I never knew you were a pôte, Tim."

"Oh, I've devoted a considerable time to pôtry," said Tim; "and some of my pômes shure have been printed in the 'Star of Ballinara.' But botherashun to the pôtry; it's yerself I'd rather be speaking about. Will ye be up at the fair the wake after next?"

"And it's there I'll be."

"And ye'll till me thin when you'll become Mrs. Finnigan?"

The girl blushed, only he couldn't see it, but he felt her hand tremble.

"Shure you're all in a hurry, Mr. Finnigan," she said, in a low voice.

"I am that same," returned Tim; "but where's there a bhoy on the banks of the Shannon that wouldn't be, if he'd such a darlint to love him as yourself, alanna?"

He was just about to imprint a loving kiss upon her lips, when the girl started, evidently in fear.

"Whisht! now," she murmured; "stand back there in the shadow. There's danger here."

Tim was no coward, but he fairly trembled as she spoke.

Not in bodily fear.

No.

His fear was of a different nature.

It was fear of encountering the eyes of Thaddeus O'Shaughnessy, when he was trespassing in his orchard.

The girl, as she retreated into the shadow, advanced a step or two, but she returned in an instant.

"Hide, hide!" she cried, "anywhere; up in the tree, shure. Don't be making bones about it. Up, on your life, or there'll be more let out o' your head, Tim darling, than you'll ever be able to put into it again."

Thus urged, though sorely against his in-clination, Tim scrambled up into the apple tree.

He had scarcely ensconced himself in the thick foliage, when a stealthy step was heard, and Kathleen was joined by a man.

As Tim saw him in the moonlight, he recognised him at once.

It was Rory O'Neil, one of the wildest, most desperate characters on the whole country-side.

Tim trembled now in earnest.

Rory O'Neil was a do-nothing, who lived upon his wits, and was suspected of being thief as well as poacher.

He was always in at a wake, a fight, or a wedding, and had set the law at defiance for years.

He was not an ill-looking fellow, and could flourish a shillelagh and dance a jig with the best boy on the hills or in the lowlands, and the special object of his affections was Kathleen.

It is wonderful that the handsome, high-spirited Irish girl, brought up without any special regard to the rights of property, should have preferred the quiet, little, ugly tutor to the reckless, dare-devil son of the mountains.

But she did, and was prepared now to fight for him, with woman's best weapon, her tongue.

"You here, Kathleen?" cried Rory O'Neil, in surprise; "shure, and it's the iligant time, for you to be out o' your father's cabin."

"It's yourself needn't throuble about it, Rory," said Kathleen; "it's my own legs brought me here, widout any help from you."

"And what are you doin' here?"

"I'm standin on my fate, Rory," said the girl, holding her clasped hands down in front of her, and looking up archly in his face.

Rory made a gesture of anger.

"Don't be answering me like that," he said. "What are ye doing in Mister O'Shaughnessy's orchard at this time of night?"

"I think I tould ye onst."

"Ah, bad cess to the hour," cried Rory, stamping his foot; "you've been here after that snivellin' bit of flesh and bones, Tim Finnigan?"

"And what wud ye have him made of if not flesh and bones, Mr. O'Neil?" asked the girl, provokingly.

The man seized her by the arm.

"Don't thrifle wid me," he cried. "I didn't come here to seek ye, but I've found ye, and I'll be afther telling ye a piece o' my mind. The third Sunday after the fair ye'll be Mrs. O'Neil—it's arranged wid yer father, and so yer voice won't be heard."

"Faith, and I'm thinking I won't be in chapel that blessed morn," cried Kathleen. "And so I'm to be Mrs. O'Neil, and we'll be as happy as Dan Hooligan when he weds Mary O'Rourke, and you'll keep me on the palings of the praties that the English squire gives to his pigs."

These allusions to the well-known hatred of Mary for Dan, and the poverty of the peasantry during the terrible potato famine then raging through Ireland, stung Rory to the quick.

"Ah, ye'll sing a different tune, alanna," he cried, "when yer father tells the praist to tie us up. Come home wid ye now—it's time."

" I'll be spoiling yer little business, Rory," said Kathleen ; " stop and stale the apples, if that's yer game, but Kathleen Moriarty can take care of herself, as she's been after doin' for years."

But she didn't stir to go.

"Look here !" cried Rory.

"I'm looking," said Kathleen, "and I'm thinking I don't see much but a desperate, wrong-headed thafe, who'd want a girl to marry him against her will, and 'ud bring misery and starvation on her, and perhaps the name of disgrace on her when ye dance on nothing at the gaol.

" Don't spake to me, Rory," she added, as she moved away ; " the praist isn't born that'll make me yer wife, so lave me to myself, and mate with yer likes."

She moved away rapidly towards the wall, and Rory O'Neil, with a curse, followed in her footsteps. Poor Figs.

What was he to do ?

His brave little heart beat high with rage, yet he knew well that if he disclosed himself to Rory, ensconced up in the apple tree—it would not only expose him to the ridicule of the whole countryside, but be bad also for Kathleen.

He was sure that on this occasion Rory would do her no harm, and so waiting until the two had disappeared, he was just about to descend, when he heard a voice.

A dread voice.

That of Thaddeus O'Shaughnessy.

"Surely," he cried, "surely I heard a voice near the apple-tree."

He came under it and looked up, and as he did so an apple fell full upon his nose.

"Dear me, bless me !" he cried, "this is very strange ! There is no wind, and apples don't fall suddenly like this, and gracious," he added, as he stooped and picked it up, "this is sound and unripe too."

As he rose again to an upright position, he saw the black form of the tutor, in the heart, as it were, of the tree.

Thaddeus smacked his lips, and grasped his heavy stick.

"Ah," he murmured, "I've discovered the blackguard at last. Come down, ye thafe, come down."

"Yes, sir," said Figs, in a feeble voice.

His doom was at length approaching.

As he descended slowly, Thaddeus raised his stick, and whack ! it came, full on the rear of Figs' tight breeches.

A howl of pain followed, and Figs dropped quickly to the ground.

Thaddeus O'Shaughnessy seized him by the collar and dragged him out of the shadow, and there master and tutor stood, the one in fear, the other in utter amazement, facing each other in the moonlight.

CHAPTER VIII.
THE GAP.

FOR a moment the schoolmaster and the usher stood facing one another in utter astonishment. At length Thaddeus spoke.

"Why, what on earth is the meaning of this ?" said he. "What are you doing here ?"

Figs was at a nonplus.

If he told the truth, it would be very likely that he would get dismissed—if he did not, it would make him appear a thief.

"And sure, Mr. O'Shaughnessy," he said, "I'm sorry that you should find me here."

"Sorry I did find you, you mean," said the schoolmaster. "Will you do me the kindness of stepping into my room ?"

"Certainly, sir," said Figs, meekly.

And he followed the schoolmaster into his study.

"Sit down," said O'Shaughnessy, in a mild voice.

Figs did so.

But in his nervousness and dread of what was coming, he did not notice what he was doing.

The consequences were disastrous.

Sitting on the very edge of a light chair, he fell headlong over, and came sprawling on the floor at the feet of the master.

"Ah, I see it all now," said Thaddeus ; " it is as plain as a pikestaff. You're drunk."

Figs, red and aghast, picked himself up and sat down again.

If there was one vice more than another that Figs was not addicted to, it was drink.

"It's very hurtful to my feelings, sir," he said, "that you should think that I have been drinking. It's not a thing that I indulge in, sir."

" It has certainly not been my misfortune to have to speak to you on such a subject before," said the master ; "but if you are not intoxicated, what is the meaning of your extraordinary behaviour ?"

Figs thought for a moment, and then said—

"Well, sir, it's best, I suppose, to make a clean breast of it."

"Certainly, if you wish to remain here," cried Thaddeus, "that is the only course to pursue."

Figs took a galp, and then began his story.

O'Shaughnessy, in spite of all, could not help laughing.

"You have taken a great liberty," he said, " and if you had not come down from the tree, you might have suffered severely."

Figs looked very sheepish.

"Well, sir, I trust you will pass it over," he said.

"Yes, I will on this occasion," returned Thaddeus, "especially when I understand that you wish to marry this person. But you will have to live out of the house, as you know I make it a rule to have only unmarried tutors."

"Very well, sir," said Figs, "very well."

But he didn't seem pleased.

Thaddeus saw at once that Kathleen's lover was crestfallen.

"Well, well," said he, "you can stop if you think your wife would not mind doing some little thing about the house for me ; she would be very useful in the school, and you can have a couple of rooms for yourselves."

And so this arrangement was agreed on.

Little did they know the consequences which would ensue through this simple thing.

They saw not the black cloud closing around them like a funereal pall.

The night came at length, when Thaddeus

O'Shaughnessy was to proceed to the Black Gap, and meet the United Irishmen.

It may seem strange indeed, that O'Shaughnessy should have joined such a society.

But the truth was, that he had been led into it.

The potato famine had been the means of rousing up again the angry feelings of the Irish against the English.

The old wound which had been opened in the latter part of the last century, had burst forth afresh, and again the rebellious factions were at work.

Once more the foolish hope had arisen in the minds of the Irish, that the French would aid them.

Interested men persuaded the poor deluded peasantry that the "French were coming," and none of the disasters which had occurred when this foolish vision had been presented to them before, had any effect in dispelling the illusion.

To this day there are thousands who believe that Napoleon I., when he assembled his vast armament on the French coast, was preparing to invade England, when in reality he was doing nothing more than planning the erection of an Egyptian empire.

The night arrived then, and as soon as darkness had overspread the country, Thaddeus O'Shaughnessy wrapped himself in a large cloak, and made his way towards the narrow mountain path, which led in the direction of Terence O'Rafferty's cabin.

It was not to this point, however, that he directed his steps.

As soon as he had proceeded half-way, he turned sharply to the right, leaving the path, and clambered up the rocky and precipitous side of the hill.

His heart was very heavy within him.

As I have said, it was not by his own desire that he had anything to do with a society which, as he knew well, was only doing harm to his fellow countrymen, by stirring up mad and foolish passions.

Caught in a terrible storm on the hills one night, he had overheard accidentally a conversation which was not meant for his ears.

Discovered, while he was in the very act of escaping from such company, he had been dragged into a cavern, and there he had been initiated into the mysteries of the society.

The oath he had been forced to take was such a terrible one that he dared not break it, and now unwilling, dragged as it were like a victim to the slaughter, he was hastening on to take part in a scene which he hated the thought of as he would have done a Bacchanalian orgie.

On passing up the mountain side, he paused for a moment on the summit of a rocky ledge, and gave a long whistle.

It was at once answered from above, and in a few moments a light appeared, waving to and fro.

With a sigh, Thaddeus O'Shaughnessy hurried up, and in a short time he was standing in the haunt of the United Irishmen.

It was a strange scene.

The huge cavern was lighted by torches stuck in niches, and their glow fell upon the faces of about thirty or forty men of all ages and all kinds of countenances.

There was scarcely one, however, except the leader, who was of a gentlemanly exterior.

All were of the humble and middle class, but while some were evidently of the reckless and desperate type, others were of the ignorant and enthusiastic sort, persuaded by the demagogue to believe in the regeneration of their country by means of fire and bloodshed.

A murmur ran round the cavern as Thaddeus O'Shaughnessy entered.

His noble mien and stately presence made an impression at once upon all.

But still they all recognised in him an enemy to their cause; and the sounds which for an instant had been those of welcome, were changed at once into sounds of anger.

Laurence Raturier, however, raised his hand in token that he wished for silence.

" Stay, my friends," he said, "do not prejudge anyone. Thaddeus O'Shaughnessy, you are welcome."

A strange smile wreathed itself over the lips of the schoolmaster.

He knew well why he was welcome.

With a slight bow, he took his seat at the table, saying—

" I am glad that I am welcome, but I regret that I have been called hither."

" And why ?" asked Laurence.

" Because," returned Thaddeus, " although I have sworn never to betray your secrets, I wish to have nothing to do with this movement, which will be the ruin of my country."

" Those who are not with us are against us," returned Laurence, " so let us not speak of that."

Then, turning to Terence O'Rafferty, he added—

" Bring in our prisoner."

Terence rose at once to perform the bidding of his leader, and, in a few moments, he brought out of an inner cave a tall, cadaverous man, who looked as if he had gone through a long period of starvation.

Anyone who knew him, however, could tell it was the lean man who had come down on the coach with Pat O'Connor.

He had evidently, since then, gone through a deal of suffering.

Yet he drew himself up proudly, as he was led into the presence of his captors.

" Well, Thomas Macartney," said Laurence, in a tone of authority, " have you resolved yet to confess what brought you to Ireland ?"

" No ! I decline."

" Then, as you decline, we will tell you ourselves," replied Laurence. " You are a spy !"

" It is false !"

" Who are you, then ?"

" I have already declined to tell, but I am no spy."

" I can prove that you are telling a falsehood," said the leader.

" Why have you not denounced me before, then ?" said Macartney.

" Because we have been waiting for proofs," returned Laurence ; " and these now we possess."

The tall man turned deadly pale ; but he made no reply.

Standing erect, with his arms folded, he calmly awaited the verdict of his self-appointed judge.

"Yes," pursued Laurence, in a louder voice, as he glanced round upon the eager crowd, "yes, we possess the proofs, and we will delay no longer in giving our judgment. You came over here, from England, for the purpose of discovering the movements of the United Irishmen. You were placed in communication with another traitor, who, unfortunately, belongs to our country—Thaddeus O'Shaughnessy!"

"It is false!" exclaimed the schoolmaster, in a loud voice.

"Beware!" thundered Laurence, as he brought his clenched hand down upon the table with a force that made the cavern echo again. "I have here, in my hands, the papers that prove the truth of what I say. I will now read them," he said, eyeing Macartney with a severe glance.

Then, taking up one of them, he began to read, in a clear voice, as follows—

"'To Thomas Macartney.

"'Proceed at once to the school on the Shannon, near the hill of Barydare, and give the enclosed to Thaddeus O'Shaughnessy. He can be trusted in every way. The watchword you can give him, to prove that you are his friend, is 'From England.'

"'Kingsford.'"

"Kingsford," said Laurence, "is an agent of the English Government. And now this man, who says he is not a traitor, receives the following letter for Thaddeus O'Shaughnessy—

"'To Thaddeus O Shaughnessy.

"'Schoolmaster, Barydare.

"'The bearer of this letter is a trusted servant of the English Government. You can give him all the information you can glean. Be careful, as in your last, to write in cypher. The information you gave us when you last wrote has been of great service, and the Black Gap cavern will soon be visited by the military. The money which you may require for the purposes of bribes to those you think will be of use to you, is in the bank at Barydare to your credit. Destroy this as soon as you have read and understood it.

"'Kingsford.'"

A groan of anger burst from the lips of everyone of those present, as Laurence finished reading.

A flash of triumph sparkled in his eyes, as he heard the threats and saw the scowling faces of his companions.

"What is your verdict, my friends?" he said. "What is best to be done to these traitors?"

"Death to the Saxon!" was the immediate answer.

"And what is to be the fate of our countryman, who has helped this Saxon to betray us?"

A whisper ran round the room, and then Terence O'Rafferty rose.

"Shure, and if yez let me say a word, it's myself has got the plan for 'im," he said.

"And what if I let you speak," said Laurence; "are you speaking for all the rest as well?"

"It is myself that'll be doing that same," said O'Rafferty.

"Speak then."

"It's ourselves that say, thin," said Terence, "that if we were to put Thaddeus O'Shaughnessy out of the way, we might lose a great deal of information. Let the thraitor be taken to the island on the river, and left in the subterranean cavern till we've found out more about 'un; and then we can confabulate as to what to do with him."

"A good suggestion," said Laurence; "let him be taken there at once."

Thaddeus O'Shaughnessy, during this conversation, had stood with folded arms, eyeing the assembly with an expression of supreme contempt.

When, however, Laurence Raturier had finished speaking, he said—

"I do not hold myself to be one of you, though I have sworn never to betray your secrets; but I will say this, that the letters you have produced are forgeries. Much as I dread the result to my country of these foolish conspiracies, I can never break my oath; and never shall I be found a traitor. Do as you please, therefore, but remember this accusation is false, and founded upon a detestable forgery."

These words were listened to with eager attention; but they failed to bring conviction to the hearts of anyone, apparently.

All were still stern and pale.

"It's myself will take the O'Shaughnessy to the island," said O'Rafferty, "if you will tell off some of the bhoys to help me."

"You can have six of them," said Laurence, "and then, when you have done that duty, we must certainly decide upon the fate of Macartney."

"Death to the Saxon!" was the cry that at once followed these words.

Macartney stood very pale during this conversation.

But when this second cry resounded through the cavern, a flush of indignation rose to his brow.

"Whoever has done this thing is a false and treacherous liar," he cried. "I never saw this Thaddeus O'Shaughnessy in my life before, and never brought a letter to him. Neither is this letter which your leader has produced from Kingsford. The watchword is an absurdity, and the whole thing has been concocted to ruin two innocent men."

"We cannot believe this," said Laurence Raturier; "we have reason to know you are an English agent."

"I never denied it."

"Then you are here to betray us," returned the leader, "and if we do not take your life, not one life that is here is safe. Away with him, O'Rafferty; let him have an hour to prepare for his doom, and then—let justice be done."

"A WILD, DESPAIRING CRY BROKE FROM THE LIPS OF THE SPY."

"A cruel and deliberate murder," said Thaddeus O'Shaughnessy, "for which Heaven will punish you."

In a few minutes both Thaddeus and Macartney had left the cavern, the one to the inner cave, the other, bound and gagged. along the mountain path towards the banks of the Shannon.

As they descended rapidly, Terence O'Rafferty pressed up to the side of the captive.

"Whisht, now," he said, in a low whisper, "if I loosen away your gag, will you promise me not to cry out?"

Thaddeus being utterly speechless, this was a strange question to ask.

But he nodded his head, and in an instant Terence had partially freed his prisoner's mouth from the gag.

"You must listen with all your ears, shure," cried Terence, bending down close to him.

"I'm listening."

"Do you remember ten years agone, shure," said Terence, "when there was a little ignorant lad a-running about the place, called Tim O'Callaghan?"

"I do," said Thaddeus; "what has become of him?"

"He's in America, the darling boy, Heaven bless 'im, and doin' well," cried Terence, with pride; "he was the only child of my darter, who died and left 'im to me to take care of. That poor boy was taken in hand by Thaddeus O'Shaughnessy, and made a gentleman of, and do you think I'd be ever after forgetting it? I'll save you for the sake of my dead child's darlin', and that soon too, but you must have patience."

Thaddeus was walking quite in advance of all except Terence.

The others were marching on behind, walking like soldiers, and keeping strict watch upon their prisoner.

"Do not compromise yourself for me," said Thaddeus; "your life will pay the forfeit if you save mine."

"Not so, if you do not bethray me; I shall be safe—safe as iggs, Masther Thaddeus," returned Terence, "only you must do exactuly what I till you."

"I will, you may be assured of that," said the schoolmaster.

"Well, thin," said Terence, dropping his voice into a still lower key, "well, thin, I shall leave you on the island, and thin I shall till those that'll save you, but you've got a big inemy in your house, and you must mind how you thrate him, or he'll destroy us both."

"And who is he?"

"Mat O'Grady."

"Then it was he who assisted Dan Hooligan to escape."

"Yes, and thin summoned you to the Black Gap. It's a black heart, too, who has forged those letters, masther, but I don't know who it can be. It can't be one of them, shure, by the token that they can neither rade nor write. Whisht! now, we mustn't spake any more, or we'll be afther being suspected."

In a few minutes they were in the boat, and being rowed over to the island, whose dark outlines could be seen from the shore.

Nothing was said by anyone during the voyage.

Thaddeus sat quiet, as if his gag was still within his mouth, and presently they landed on the banks of the little island.

CHAPTER IX.
PAT O'CONNOR TO THE RESCUE.

IN the centre of the island there was a strange place which was used by the conspirators to hide away some of the firearms, and so forth, which were supposed to be destined to drive the English from Ireland.

It was nothing more nor less than a huge pit, which had been dug out by stealth, and then boarded round to render it damp-proof.

Of course it was never intended to be used for any human being to dwell in, but now and then, when any suspicion was excited of treachery, one of the United Irishmen slept there for a night or two.

On this occasion, however, all was still upon the island.

Leaving two men in charge of the boat, Terence O'Rafferty made his way to its centre, and, passing through a clump of trees among which the brushwood had evidently been trained artificially, he paused at a spot where a piece of level turf spread out bright and green.

Here he knelt down, and after fumbling for a moment among the high grass, he pulled at a large iron ring.

In an instant he had inserted a key, raised a trap-door, and taking a lantern from his pocket, disclosed a set of steps.

"Now, thin, Misther O'Shaughnessy, I will take you down myself," he said; "come on."

With great difficulty, bound as he was, Thaddeus descended the steps, and in a few moments they were standing together in the immense underground chamber where the firearms, cutlasses and pikes were piled and ranged round the walls.

"Shure and you'll have to be careful, masther," said Terence, "for thim barrels are chock full of powther, and if you sit fire to anythin', you'd be sent across the river in half the twinkling of an oye."

All this time he had been undoing the cords which bound the schoolmaster, and after hanging the lantern up in a convenient place, he whispered—

"Before the mornin', Masther Pat O' Connor shall knaw all."

"Why not tell one of the ushers?"

"Because they're both United Irishmen, and though they may be friendly enough to ye and respect ye, surr, they daren't hilp you to escape. Good-night, surr, and kape up your courage."

Then he disappeared up the steps, and Thaddeus O'Shaughnessy was alone.

Meanwhile, as he threw himself on a heap of sacking which was piled in one corner of the place, Terence passed again into the boat, and the seven men made their way once more across the broad bosom of the Shannon.

They were soon ashore, and making their way to the cave of the Black Gap.

They had been absent now about one hour and a half, and the doom of the spy was therefore sealed.

As O'Rafferty made his way into the cave, he found six of his companions, grasping heavy bludgeons, ready for their murderous work.

"Now, then, O'Rafferty," said Laurence Raturier, "I will give you the charge of this party. You know what to do to avert suspicion."

"Yes. I do—will, masther," cried Terence, as he too took down a large shillelagh from the wall.

"Have you your pistols?" asked Laurence.

"Yes, all."

"Then bring out the prisoner, and let us get this job over."

It was not long before the supposed spy was brought out, bound and gagged, and borne out into the open air.

Their destination was a high rock which towered some distance above the Black Gap.

On one side it descended sheer for full a hundred feet.

It was a dangerous place, and many a terrible accident had happened there.

It was, therefore, with a deep design that he was led hither.

Of course, if he were found dashed to pieces on the rocks beneath this spot, it would be attributed to an accident.

There would be no evidence of foul play, and the record of murder would only be impressed on the minds of those who had done the hideous deed.

The moon had risen when they reached the top of the crags, and the wretched man who was doomed to so horrible a death could see the terrific abyss before his very feet.

"If you've got any prayers to say, you'd bether be afther saying thim," said Terence; "we'll wait for five minutes."

The gag was removed from the mouth of the spy, and he knelt at once on the edge of the cliff, with the moonlight falling on his ghastly face.

He made no sound, but the movement of his lips showed that he was uttering a prayer.

When he had concluded, he rose to his feet.

"Now, do your worst," he cried, "do your worst; and may the curse of Heaven fall upon you for taking an innocent life."

"Lape," said Terence; "it'll be betther."

"I shall not commit a crime, to please you or anyone else," said Thomas Macartney. "Let my blood be on your heads."

The merest sign passed between Terence and a tall, broad-shouldered man who stood near at hand.

Then, in an instant, there was a spring forward; a heavy bludgeon was raised, and brought down with a crash upon the head of the spy, and he fell over the edge of the cliff.

In spite of his stolid courage, a wild, despairing cry broke from the lips of the spy, and then all was over.

The seven men, coolly as they had done the deed, were silent for a few moments.

Then O'Rafferty said—

"We'd bether disperse now, bhoys. I'm going down to Ted Dennis' cabun."

"And shure, ain't ye coming back to the Black Gap to drink the health of ould Ireland?" asked one of the men.

"No. I must see Dennis to-night," returned Terence; "besides, I've not the heart to go drinking and fasteing when we've just done justice on that villanous spy."

And so he went slowly away down the mountain path.

He walked along quickly, and full of thought, until he had reached the schoolhouse.

Then he made his way to the same spot where Kathleen Moriarty had climbed over into the orchard.

Here he got over without hesitation, and was proceeding to hurry across between the trees, when he found his leg seized in a grip, which he knew to be that of a dog.

To tell the truth, since the extraordinary meeting between Figs and the schoolmaster under the apple-tree, he had let loose in the orchard a large dog, which he had usually kept in the front of the house.

The animal was not a ferocious one, but he was a faithful watchdog, and as he held on like grim death, he began to growl loudly.

Terence only laughed.

"Shure, and it's yerself will do me a good sarvice," he said; "you'll save me the throuble of waking the people up. But as you might make a mistake, and put yer teeth too near the calf of my leg, I'll serve yer the same thrick that I did to Paddy Mahoney's black and tan."

So saying he drew his lantern from his pocket and suddenly flashed it in the dog's eyes.

The animal, frightened out of his senses for an instant, sprang away with a cry, and Terence, taking advantage of this, struck him with his bludgeon a heavy blow on the head.

The animal staggered to its knees, and then as it got up again, it went howling away.

"Arrah, it's myself'll sind you a plaisther for your sconce when I've saved the masther," said Terence, with a laugh, and then, leaving the dog to its howlings, he hurried to the back window. Here he tapped.

For an instant there was perfect silence.

Then a tap was given from within.

"Now then, who's there?" exclaimed a woman's voice.

"It's Terence O'Rafferty, shure," said Terence.

"Wait a mawment," cried the voice again.

In another minute the shutters were opened, and the window was thrown up.

"What's the mather wid ye, Terence, that ye come here in the middle of the night?"

The speaker was a tall, broad-shouldered woman of about forty years, a regular type of the Irish women of the lower order.

She had small, twinkling blue eyes, deep-set in her head, a little pug nose, and a wide, grinning mouth.

Terence was full twenty years older than she was, but, nevertheless, when the rebellion was over, it was understood that they were to be man and wife.

"It's Pat O'Connor I'm wanting to say," said Terence; "will ye be afther calling him for me?"

The woman raised her hands in mute amazement.

"Shure and it's mad ye are, Terence," she cried.

"Why not—why shouldn't I see the lad" said Terence; "whisht now, Katie, and listen to me."

He leaned in at the window, and whispered—

"Katie, darlin', the masther's in trouble."

"What, Master O'Shaughnessy?"

"Shure and it's himself's in great danger, but if ye love me, Katie, ye must never breathe to a livin' sowl that I came here to tell inyone of it."

"And shure you're not thinking it's myself would betray you?" said the woman; "but what good can the young O'Connor do for the masther?"

"That's exactly what I mustn't be telling," he said. "If ye want to save the masther, go and tell Masther Pat to be down dirictly."

Katie hesitated no longer.

She hurried out of the room, and within ten minutes Pat O'Connor was dressed and down.

"Will ye come out inte the awchard?" said Terence. "I've come to bring ye a message from the masther."

Pat did not hesitate.

He scrambled out of the window, and stood by the side of Terence beneath the apple tree.

Quickly Terence told his story.

Pat listened in surprise.

What on earth could he have been chosen for? He, who had only been in the school such a short time?

His heart, however, bounded with pleasure.

"And who else am I to take with me?"

"No one," said Terence. "There's no one to molest ye on the island. Here's the kay that opens the iron ring. Take a bote and row there yerself, and Heaven will reward ye."

For an instant a suspicion crossed Pat O'Connor's brain.

Could any treachery be intended to him?

But the suspicion did not rest long in his mind.

"I'll go," he said; "only give me a pistol."

Terence put his hand into his pocket, and drew forth a great horse-pistol.

"Here ye are," he said, "and be quick, for some of the bhoys may be prowling abhout."

Pat ran into the house, got his hat, clambered over the wall, and was soon on the banks of the river, by the boat-house.

In a few minutes, the brave boy had commenced moving along the broad bosom of the Shannon in the direction of the little island.

It was very still on the river, and the plash of the oars echoed even up the distant hills.

Remembering the night when he had rowed up the Shannon in pursuit of Dan Hooligan, he looked with eagerness to see if he could again discover the red light of the Dutch lugger.

There sure enough it was, but no one among those on board noticed Pat as he pulled by the ship in the direction of the island.

Indeed, had they done so, they would not have thought of challenging him.

The lugger was itself there on no good errand, and this solitary figure in the boat might be an officer of excise.

So Pat hastened on, and in the course of half an hour, after passing under the shadow of the lugger, he reached the island and leaped ashore.

He moored his boat there to a stunted tree that dipped its branches into the water, and then hurried with an anxious heart to the centre of the island.

With the scanty directions which Terence O'Rafferty had afforded him, it was difficult to find the exact spot.

But at length the locked ring was found and raised, and by the feeble light of the lantern below, Pat O'Connor descended.

"Who is there?" cried Thaddeus O'Shaughnessy.

Naturally, he imagined it might be some assassin, and he at once seized a musket and watched.

"A friend," exclaimed our hero. "It's me—Pat O'Connor."

The schoolmaster uttered an exclamation of joy, and advanced eagerly as he saw the form of the lad issue from the shadow of the dark staircase.

"Brave boy!" cried he, as he grasped Pat by the hand. "Who is with you?"

"No one," exclaimed Pat O'Connor. "I'm alone."

"Alone! Ye have come all the way by yourself?"

"Yes. Terence O'Rafferty told me not to trust anyone, and so I didn't."

"Well, my lad," said the schoolmaster, with great emotion, "such a courage as this I have never seen. It is a courage which will bring you through the world in triumph, Pat O'Connor, and if the blessings of an honest and grateful heart can do you any good, you have mine."

Pat O'Connor flushed pleasurably.

"I've only done my duty, sir," exclaimed he, "to one who has always been kind and good to me. But come, sir; we must hasten, or perhaps some of those devils in human form will return."

"You are right," said Thaddeus, "and since we may be attacked on our way, I will take the liberty of appropriating a couple of these muskets and two pairs of pistols. Here, Pat."

Our hero received from the schoolmaster a musket and a pair of pistols, and then they prepared to ascend.

In a few moments they were standing above on the greensward.

"Let us leave the trap open," said Pat, "and let the villains be found out by the authorities."

"No, no; it must not be," exclaimed the schoolmaster. "I have sworn an oath, and I must keep it, even though they have this night attempted my life. No; close the aperture; think not of betraying them. Let them go their own way to destruction."

The ring was accordingly locked and hidden away among the long grass, and then master and pupil took their way to the boat and were soon pulling towards the schoolhouse.

"The Dutch lugger is yonder still, I see," said Thaddeus, presently. "Did they notice you in passing?"

"No, I think not," said Pat; "but have they anything to do with the wretches who placed you on the island?"

"Yes, they are in league with them," said Thaddeus, in a low voice, "and if they knew I was in the boat here with you, they'd fire on us and sink us."

They were now nearing the ship.

"Pat," cried Thaddeus, "Pat, you pull, and I will keep a musket ready. If anyone interferes with us, I shall fire."

Pat now took both oars, and the schoolmaster sat in the stern of the boat eagerly watching.

Presently, just as the great hull of the Dutch lugger loomed up above them, Thaddeus exclaimed—

"Pull more slowly, Pat; there is someone in white on the deck and beckoning to us."

Pat lay upon his oars and glanced round.

A wild joy entered his heart.

It might be Mary O'Rourke.

Here, then, was a chance of doing his friend Marshall a service.

"Let us pull in closer to the ship," he said; "perhaps it may be someone desirous to escape."

Nearer and nearer Pat pulled to the lugger, the schoolmaster still on the alert, stern and watchful, and musket in hand.

As they came close to the ship, they could see plainly that it was a female figure that stood upon the deck.

Suddenly she uttered a piercing cry of—

"Help!"

Then, throwing up her arms, she plunged headlong into the water.

Pat rested once more upon his oars, and as the figure came to the surface of the river, he leaped in.

He was not aware of the fact that Mary O'Rourke was such a splendid swimmer.

She at once began to strike out for the boat.

"Never mind me," she cried; "get back to the wherry quickly, or you'll never save me."

Pat saw at once that his services were not required, and swam as quickly as possible back to the boat.

In an instant he was once more at the oars and ready to start.

Thaddeus O'Shaughnessy leaned over the side, and waited.

In a few moments the young girl had swam up, and was helped in.

Of course during this time the schoolmaster could keep a look-out only on the water.

Pat, however, kept his eyes fixed upon the lugger, and as Mary O'Rourke sat down in the boat, he cried loudly—

"Now, Mr. O'Shaughnessy, I'm going to pull like Tom Morissey did when he was running away from the devil. I'm going to close my teeth, shut my eyes, and let St. Patrick guide me."

"Why, what's the matter, then?" asked Thaddeus.

"Matter enough, sir," cried Pat; "they have lowered a boat, and are after us."

"Pull then," said Thaddeus with set lips, "and I'll watch."

With his finger on the trigger of his musket, the schoolmaster waited.

The boat which had put off from the lugger was manned by six stalwart rowers, and it came on hand over hand.

They were soon in close hailing distance.

"What do you want?" cried Thaddeus in a loud tone.

"You've a young girl aboard," shouted a voice in reply.

"Yes."

"She has escaped from the ship yonder."

"Yes."

"Well then, give her up to us, or we will sink you."

"And if we change the game and sink you?" said Thaddeus.

A loud cry was the answer to this.

"Ha! ha!" cried the voice of the Dutch skipper, "ha! ha! dat is shoost the best choke of te day! Pull up, or ve vill fire into you, mein friend."

"Fire! and on your head be it!" thundered Thaddeus; "Mary O'Rourke, lie down in the boat."

"No," cried the girl; "is it myself that's going to let two brave hearts be shot at like nuts at a fair, when I can fire a musket as well as any bhoy in Ballynara? Pull away, Master O'Connor, and Heaven's blissings on ye."

Pat wanted no incentive to exertion.

He had been pulling away before at a long, steady pace, and he now never altered his stroke.

"All right, Mary dear," he said, "we'll be right enough, never fear. Before night is up, you will see Harry Marshall."

At this instant, the voice of the Dutch captain was heard once more.

"Vill you shtop or shall I shoost put a bullet through your head?"

"You must please yourself," said Thaddeus; "if you fire, your blood be upon your own guilty head."

"You refuse then?"

"Yes."

"Martin Curtis, pe goot enough shoost to fire."

The man addressed at once raised his musket and fired.

But the ball missed its aim, and buried itself with a fizz in the water.

Then Thaddeus slowly, and with stern determination, raised his weapon.

Only an instant, and then there was a flash, followed by a cry of agony.

O'Shaughnessy's bullet had sped home, and Martin Curtis lay dead over the boat's edge.

"By tonder! ve vill kill dem—every von," shouted De Ruyter, in a voice hoarse with passion. "Pull hard, mein friends, pull hard, and ve vill kill dem close at hand."

Thaddeus knew well what the Dutchman meant by his roundabout talk, and he answered quickly—

"Keep back, or I shall fire, and my companion too, and two of your crew will go to keep Martin Curtis company."

"Fire again, mein phoys," exclaimed De Ruyter.

Then two shining barrels gleamed in the moonlight, dim and uncertain as it was.

But again, by a strange luck, the bullets missed their aim.

"Now, Mary," said Thaddeus, "keep your nerves steady and fire. Remember—it is for life we do it."

The young girl raised the musket, and she and the schoolmaster fired together.

Two of the rowers fell again, one mortally wounded.

"Tamnation!" cried the Dutch skipper, "dis is too pad!"

And seizing a musket from one of his men, he took steady aim at the schoolmaster.

But Thaddeus was not thus to be sent out of the world which he so graced by his presence.

Mary O'Rourke had quickly reloaded; and as De Ruyter and his men approached, she fired.

The shot was not mortal; but it caught him on the shoulder, and extorted from him a howl of agony.

A volley of curses followed, but the boat was stopped for a moment.

And during that short time Pat O'Connor had pulled with all his strength, and brought his boat nearly level with the school.

As they neared it, they saw that there were lights in nearly all the windows.

The boys, in fact, and all the household had been aroused by the firing on the river; and some of the bigger lads, with the two ushers, had even ventured down to the river's bank.

The crew of the lugger's boat were nowhere now.

With a long and strong pull Pat O'Connor shot the boat clear up to the shore, and the disappointed smugglers, after a moment's hesitation, turned their skiff about and rowed away.,

"Tonder!" growled the Dutchman, as one of the men busied himself in binding up his wound, "those poys are the very tevil! But—hein—ve must have shoost a little revenge! Carl!"

"Yes, cabtain," cried a gruff voice; "I'm here."

"Vell den, shoost listen to me one leetle moment," said the Dutch skipper; "some other night ve vill have our revenge."

"Yes, cabtain."

"You must get ready a boat's crew, and ve vill run up de river to this boint. Den ve vill set fire to this tamned vellow's house, and shoost burn the lot oop; oh! tonder and blitzen, M'Carthy, mein jolder is not made of iron!"

A groan of agony burst from his lips as the man dragged out the ball, which had not penetrated far.

"Vell, vell," he said, "Mister O'Zonessy has had a game mit me to-night—to-morrow he vill be grilled like the swinefleish."

But De Ruyter forgot one motto, which says—

"Man proposes, but Heaven disposes."

Very little explanation was given by Thaddeus O'Shaughnessy to his anxious pupils in regard to the events of the night.

He said simply that he and Pat O'Connor had rowed down the river on business, and been attacked by these men; and with this explanation they had all to be content.

Mary O'Rourke was given over to the care of the servants, and soon the whole household was once more asleep.

CHAPTER X.

THE FAIR OF BALLYNARA.

THE next morning was the day of the grand fair, to which "Figs" looked forward with such pleasure, because then Kathleen was to name the hour when she would make him a happy man.

To a stranger suddenly coming into the neighbourhood it would have certainly seemed as if everyone had gone mad.

For from an early hour in the morning every cabin on the countryside began to vomit forth its occupants.

The dread famine was for the time forgotten by the women and the children, and if it was remembered by the men, it was also remembered that the fair would be a good excuse for them to assemble and talk without fear of the dreaded "informers."

Along the road that led from Shannon's banks to the great open space where the fair was to be held, it was a glorious sight to see people streaming along on foot, or on crazy cars, or on donkey back, or what we call here in England the "costermonger's brougham."

Women with babies strapped on their backs, or hanging like heavy bundles by their sides, accompanied by strong, burly fellows who thought more of their shillelaghs than their offspring; trim wenches in short red petticoats and variegated bodices, and perhaps no shoes or stockings; dapper young fellows bent on mischief, thieves, vagrants, honest people, full and starving, all mingled in one vast moving crowd.

Among that crowd—among the laughing faces, were those who scowled and darkened as they went on; becoming worse and worse as each "poteen" shop was passed.

Mat O'Grady, Dan Hooligan, and Terence O'Rafferty were to be seen there, and women trembled and clutched their babies closer to their breasts as they saw them.

There was not an Irish heart among them that did not beat high for the chance of the "liberashon" of the "ould counthry."

But yet the women knew that that time of liberation would begin and end in blood; and they looked with awe upon the stern, brave, resolute men whom they knew would be the leaders of the movement.

The men to lure their husbands, brothers and sweethearts into the heat and thick of the fight.

Noticeable among all others, was a man who rode on top of a tub which was standing on a barrow, drawn by two donkeys, tandem fashion.

He was attired in a red coat, covered all over with curious devices.

His hat was about four feet high, and of a conical shape.

Over his eyes were a huge pair of spectacles, while his beard, which was of a sandy grey colour, hung down below his waist.

By his side was a little negro dwarf, with only a waist cloth and a turban.

He was about the size of a boy of six or seven, but he had a moustache and beard, and looked altogether like a man between thirty and forty.

He kept continually banging on a little drum, and uttering snatches of strange songs in a guttural voice.

And all the while his little, round, malevolent eyes kept rolling hither and thither among the crowd.

By the time the vast multitude had reached the great open space, or, rather, what had been a great open space the day before, the man in the tall hat and the red coat was the hero of the day.

"Who can he be?" was the question asked by everyone.

And as no one seemed to be able to give the least clue to the matter, curiosity became at last at fever heat.

Oh, what a scene was there that morning at Ballynara fair!

With the bright sun glittering on the mountain tops and slopes, and thousands of merry faces, whose owners had forgotten their troubles for the hour, and resolved to make themselves happy while they could.

White tents glistened everywhere, and the roar of voices was like a second Babel.

"Shure, and here's the lively dog with three tails, that's got more bark in 'm than a beech tray, and can bite so soft, that he's employed to carry iggs to markut in his mouth," shouted a tall Hibernian, at the door of a wretched little booth.

He was full six feet in height, and about as fat as his own shillelagh, so that what tattered clothes he wore, hung about him with as much grace as a bundle of rags on a prop.

His hungry eyes gazed eagerly round upon the crowd, as if anxiously watching for a penny.

"Shure and it's few iggs he brought ye, I'm thinking, Dennis Mannigan," cried a man in the crowd, "for you're looking like a half-starved informer."

"No, shure, and the raison is, that you met the dog and stole 'em on the way, you thafe of the world," returned the showman; "take no notice of 'im, ladies and gentlemen, but walk in and see the dog with the three tails, that was robbed on his way from market by a dog without any tail at all—at all!"

"Now then, ladies and gentlemen," exclaimed another man, on a pair of steps, leading up to a booth standing upon piles. "I'd show you an ilephant if I could, but as he was taken with the maisles, on his voyage from Injy, I'm obloiged to put ye off with the grandest and most gorgeous, most surprising panyrammy that iver fell to mortial man to say. Here's the place to spind your money."

"I say, Marshall," said the voice of Pat O'Connor (for all the school were there), "let's go in for a lark, and see the 'panyrammy.'"

"All right," said Marshall, and the two boys at once advanced up the steps.

The showman in this case was just as gaunt, as hungry-looking as the other, and a light leaped up into his eyes, as the two lads paid their pennies.

"Now then, shure, my ladies and jintlemen," he shouted in a louder key, as if a new life had been awakened within him, "here's two illigant young jintlemen from the acâdemy, coming in to see my panyrammy. And if the educâted classes can come and see it, it shows the charâcther of the exhibishun. What! no one coming up! Not aven that purty girl with the blue eyes, whose golden hair looks like a living piece of po'try. Well—well! shure and the young jintlemen shall see it all to thimselves."

And so, with a disdainful look at the crowd, he led the way into the booth, which was in fact nothing but a few uprights, covered with some tattered tarpaulin and canvas.

On entering it, Pat O'Connor saw, huddled in a corner, hidden away as much as possible from view, a woman and two children.

They were evidently in the last stage of starvation, and their hungry eyes gazed wistfully at the two well-dressed lads as they entered.

The one child was not more than six months old, and the woman was vainly seeking to give it nourishment from her empty breast.

"I knaw ye'll be afther excusing me, jintlemen, just for one mawment," said the showman, still keeping up his voice as well as he could, but looking wistfully at the wretched group in the corner, "but ye see, sirs, business being slack lately, and the praties having been blighted, my wife and little ones" (here he nearly broke down) "have scarce had a bite or a sup, young jintlemen, and I'll be giving them these halfpence jist to git a bit of bread."

Pat O'Connor's hand had been in his pocket some time, and he drew out now a couple of shillings, as did Marshall also.

When the money was placed in the hands of the man, he glanced at it for a moment as if spellbound.

Then he suddenly fell upon his knees, and clasping his hands, looked upwards earnestly to a spot where a rent in the ragged canvas permitted him to catch one glimpse of the bright blue vault of heaven.

"Holy Mother! Holy Virgin!" he cried, as the tears coursed down his cheeks; "keep these bhoys in your care, for saving me Kathleen and my darlin's from the grave, when they were totterin' on the brink of it."

"I am sure you're welcome," said Pat with some emotion; "go and send for some food for your wife and children, and then we'll see the panorama, just to cheer us up a bit."

With the brightness and vivacity of his nation, the showman sprang up, took the money to his wife, and then said—

"Shure and it's myself was as hungry as the praist's pig jest now, and bedad, if I don't fale as full and as hearty as if I'd been ating all the praties and butter milk in the counthry. Faith, and it's small fun ye'll get, young jintlemen, from seeing my panyrammy, save and except 'tis to make fun of it. But here goes, now."

But we will save our readers a description of all the monstrous absurdities of which the showman was guilty.

It is enough to say that the "panyrammy" consisted of a number of wretched daubs, on "holey" canvas, glued together anyhow, and represented scenes from every imaginable spot in the world.

The boys laughed at it, and knew it to be a miserable imposition.

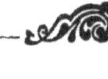

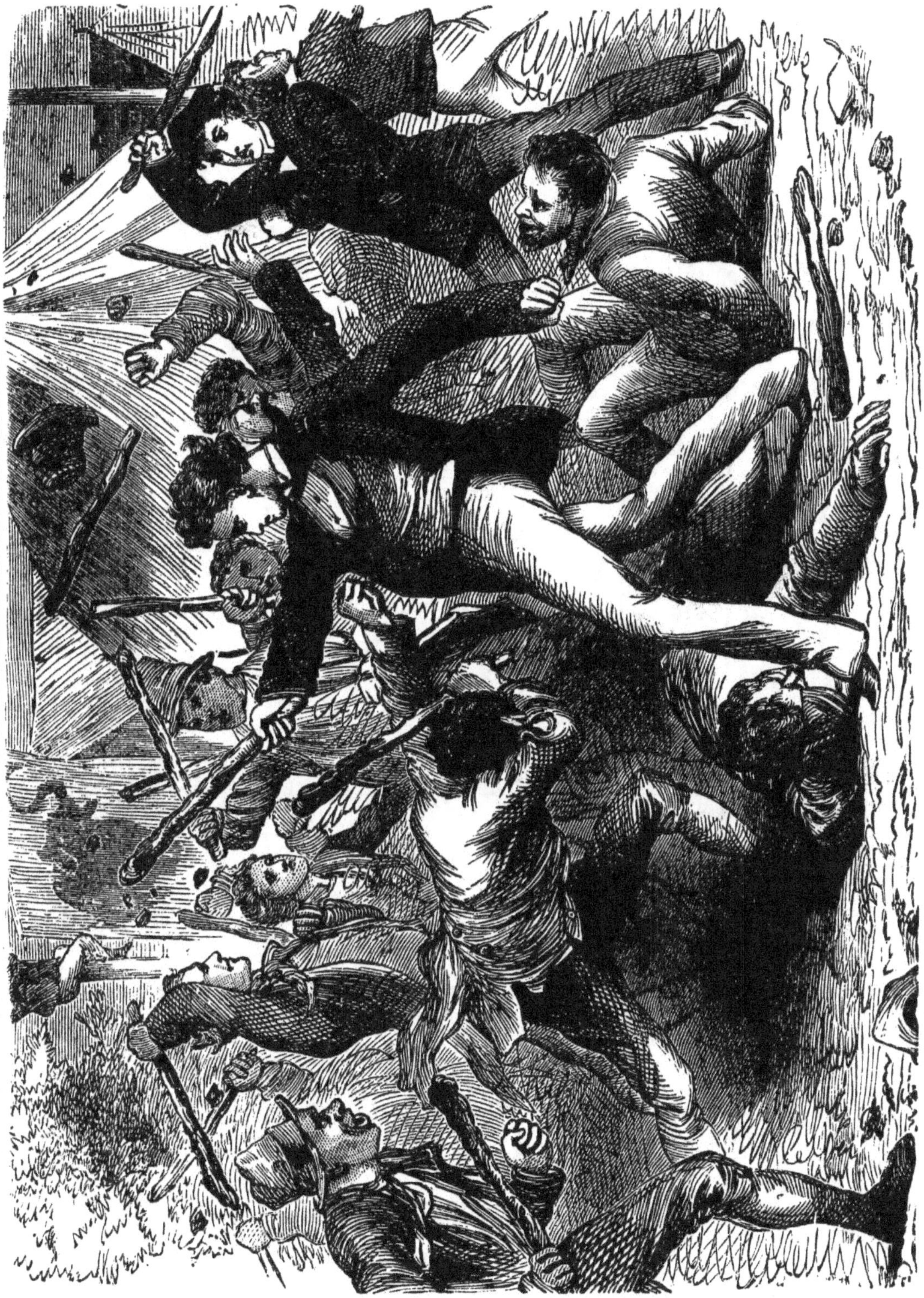

"THE BRAVE BOYS OF THE SHANNON DASHED UPON THEIR FOES."

PRICE ONE HALFPENNY.
[PUBLISHED EVERY FRIDAY.]

But then, what was the imposition for, but to find a wretched wife and children something to eat?

And so—when, pursued by the thanks of the family, they quitted the booth—Pat O'Connor said—

"By Jove, Marshall, we must go and have a spree now—something desperate, for I feel choking. Oh! here's a man with a hat four feet high, and a dwarf not so tall as his hat. Come on—here's fun."

CHAPTER XI.

BALLYNARA FAIR (CONTINUED).

THE man in the tall, conical hat had by this time assembled an immense crowd, and the negro kept "tum-tumming," rolling his little eyes round, and grinning so as to show his horse-like teeth.

The fellow was exhibiting a quantity of conjuring tricks, and his restless eyes were ever glancing hither and thither among the crowd, as if in search of someone.

Just as Pat O'Connor and Marshall arrived at the barrow and tub, which constituted his equipage, he was haranguing the crowd.

"Now den, ladish and shentlemansh," he said, "shoost look at dis leetle ball. You places it in the cup, shoost so—den you covers it up, shoost so—and den—tonder and blitzen!—it is gone—shoost so! Ha, ha! mein friends! De leetle ball and me, ve understand one anoder. And now—now dat I have shown you de magic trick, I will show you de magic medicine. I am not going to sell de medicine—I am going to give it away. No one must open de leetle parcel I gives to him until he reaches his home, and den, ven he opens it, he will find someting dat will make his hair curl and his eyes glisten—make him a new man—make praties grow again in Ireland, and if taken in proper quantities, will make every man a free man."

A roar of applause, mingled with groans, followed this speech.

And then the crowd pressed anxiously forward, to receive the magic powders.

"Marshall!" whispered Pat O'Connor.

"Yes."

"Do you know who that is?"

"No."

"It is the Dutchman, the captain of the lugger," replied Pat, "the one who shot at us last night when we were saving Mary O'Rourke."

"Oughtn't we to give him up to the constables or to the soldiers? There are lots about."

"I don't know what we could charge him with," cried Pat. "Oh, yes; we can charge him with aiding Dan Hooligan in abducting Mary O'Rourke from the school grounds, and in detaining her against her will on board the lugger."

"Good! then let us go at once; only let us get one of these mysterious little packets first," said Marshall. "This is part of the conspiracy, I believe."

The two boys at once pressed forward through the crowd, and held up their hands to receive some of the "magic medicine," which the man in the tall hat, and the little negro, were distributing.

But in an instant the former uttered some words in a low whisper.

The negro resumed his drum, and "tum-tummed" right in the face of the two schoolboys.

The magician indulged in a loud laugh as a forest of hands—large, and small, and middling, but all dirty—were stretched forward to receive the magic powders.

"No more powders to-day," he said. "I have only shoost one left, and that is for mein own self."

"Won't you give me one, Mr. De Ruyter?" cried Pat O'Connor, boldly.

There was just the least suspicion of a start on the part of the conjuror.

Then he said, as if not noticing the lad's words—

"Shoost now the exhibition is over. Presently, ven I have partaken of a boiled monkey, ten pounds of fried shark, and de tail of a hippopotamus, washed down by a pailful of alligator's blood, I will show ye some more tricks."

"Vengeance for Mary O'Rourke!" shouted Pat O'Connor.

In an instant the man in the tall hat waved his hand, and a wall of living beings formed around him.

"We must away," said Marshall, in a whisper. "To stop here means a row and—death."

"Let us go up the hill yonder, then," said Pat, "and tell the officer. To let such a wretch as this go loose would be a crime."

"Come on, then," cried Marshall, whose heart, of course, was full of anger; "come on, then. I am all impatience."

Hurrying away from the crowd, whose scowling looks portended no good, they hastened up the slope of the hill, towards a point where a regiment of dragoons had stationed themselves, as if resting on a journey.

No one believed this pretence, of course.

But it was endeavoured to keep up the pleasant fiction as far as possible.

The enthusiastic schoolboys little thought of the dread tempest they might be raising.

The peasants had, as I have said, turned out to enjoy themselves in spite of all.

But whisky had already begun to do its work, and the least spark only would have been required to kindle a terrible conflagration.

But Pat thought not of it.

He and Marshall pressed eagerly up the slope until they were challenged by the sentry.

"Who goes there?"

"Friends," said Pat O'Connor. "I wish to see the colonel."

The sentry frowned upon him.

He was an Englishman, and knowing well how every Saxon was at this time hated, he looked upon Pat O'Connor as an enemy, young and frank-looking as he was.

"What about?" he growled.

"Sir," returned Pat, earnestly, "sir, I have come here to ask you to capture a villain who is in yonder crowd, exciting the unfortunate people to rebellion. I can make a charge against him which will enable you to take him at once."

The man's face relaxed.

"I will go and tell the colonel," he said. "Remain here."

Within ten minutes the two boys stood in the centre of a tent, in the presence of one of those fine, military-looking men who are the pride of the English army.

He smiled graciously upon them.

"Well, my lads," he said, "I hope this is not a storm in a teapot, because, unless there is something very serious, I can't order my men to move."

"I'll tell you all, sir," said Pat.

And in a few words he told his story.

The colonel eyed him with curiosity and admiration.

"Do you know, my boy," he said, "the risk you're running? Do you know that if they got wind of this, they'll tear you in pieces?"

"Yes," returned Pat, "I do know; but I never shrink from my duty. If that wretched villain were only removed from among them, they would be peaceful as lambs."

"You are an extraordinary lad," said the colonel, "and I will act upon your instructions. But you had better go now. Be in readiness, though; wherever you see this mountebank, stay near him. I know the danger; but as you have braved so much, I am certain you will not shrink from this."

"No, colonel," said Pat O'Connor; "we will be there. But you do not think me a traitor."

"A traitor, my boy?"

"Yes, for going against these people who hope to set Ireland free," said Pat, looking earnestly at him.

There was something so earnest, so wistful, so searching in the boy's look that the colonel averted his head.

"My lad, you are brave and honest," he said; "I will say no more. I am a soldier, and have to do my duty, but remember, in taking advantage of the information you have given me, I will see that no blood is shed. I can depend on my men, and if that fellow is to be captured, I will capture him."

He shook hands with them both, and they were just about to depart, when he said—

"You have done well for your country. Here comes a double-dyed traitor, if you wish to see one. But, remember, I demand secrecy."

As he spoke, Dan Hooligan entered, and stood before them.

He turned ashen pale as he saw the two lads.

Then, recovering himself, he bowed low to the colonel, saying—

"Your sojers, colonel, have taken me by a mistake, shure, and I come for a free pass."

"Good day," said the colonel to Pat and Marshall, not even answering the spy. "Remember the place and your duty."

CHAPTER XII.

THE DONKEY AUCTION.

PAT O'CONNOR and Harry Marshall lost no time in making their way back to the thick of the fair, where they at once sought for the man in the tall hat.

For a long time they sought in vain.

But at length, in the centre of a large crowd, they espied the little negro and the flaming red coat and immense hat which had so attracted their attention.

They at once withdrew a little distance and waited.

Anxiously they looked in the direction of the slope where the dragoons would have to descend, and presently they saw the glittering squadron approaching at a trot.

A scowl was on every brow, and a cry of anger escaped every lip, as they came.

But they advanced quietly and easily, as if not on duty.

The colonel was at their head; and, as they neared the spot where the man in the tall hat was showing some fresh conjuring tricks, he made a sign to Pat to draw nearer.

With beating hearts both Pat O'Connor and Harry Marshall approached.

The dragoons, at a sign from their commander, urged their horses gently forward, until they had pressed the people away from around the conjuror.

Then the colonel said, addressing him in a firm though gentle voice—

"Will you do me the kindness to remove your hat and disguise a moment? I have no wish to interfere with your amusement, nor would I for the world spoil the fun of the fair, but a soldier must do his duty."

The way in which these words were spoken greatly mollified the crowd; while the man with the tall hat at once removed it, and cast aside also the false spectacles and beard which disguised his face.

As he did so, he disclosed the features of a man of about twenty, a pleasant-looking Irishman.

Pat O'Connor, aghast with utter amazement, was beckoned forward by the colonel.

"Is that Captain De Ruyter?" he asked.

"No, colonel."

The colonel frowned.

"Have you played me a trick, young sir?" he said; "if you have, you shall have two dozen."

A malevolent grin spread over the features of the Irishman, while a titter passed through the crowd.

"Shure, and he desarves two dozen, sirr, for thrying to desave yer honour," cried the conjuror; "it's meself that's thinking he's a false informer and shpy thrying to make money out o' yer honour."

"You lie!" cried Pat O'Connor; "I know you not; but I know this, that not half an hour ago that dress was worn by Captain De Ruyter, of the 'Silverhorn,' now in the Shannon, the man who carried off an innocent girl and then tried to murder my master. How you changed clothes I don't know, but you've done it."

The way in which Pat delivered his speech impressed the colonel with the truth of what he said.

And more than that, he had seen something in the man's eyes, which told that he was in terrible anger, and he had caught, too, a sign made by the negro to someone in the crowd.

"There has been some mistake here," said

the colonel. "I quite believe what I have been told, and I shall keep a sharp look-out, you may depend on it."

Then, addressing the conjuror, he added—

"Pray do you intend me to understand that you know nothing of this De Ruyter?"

"Shure and it's meself means that same," said the Irishman.

"This is all false," cried Pat O'Connor; "the man who wore this dress before spoke bad English and had a strong Dutch accent."

"Shoosht as I speak now, mein friend," said a voice, which seemed certainly to come from the spot where the Irishman stood.

But his lips never moved.

"There is some juggling here," muttered Pat.

"Yes; and you will faind, mein friend, that you will be choogled away altogeder," said the voice of De Ruyter again.

The colonel looked very angry.

But what could he do?

He was under special orders not to stir up the angry passions of the peasantry, and here he was decidedly in a dilemma.

However, he felt certain that Pat O'Connor was in the right; and, as he made a sign to his men to reform and march up the slope, he said—

"Mr. O'Connor, you have either been mistaken or imposed upon. I feel certain you have not deceived me. I shall take measures to secure this De Ruyter."

Pat bowed, and was soon moving away from among the angry crowd.

"Isn't it rather dangerous to remain here?" said Harry Marshall; "if any of these people get hold of you, they'll attack you, I'm certain."

"Oh! then I'll be taking the chance of that," said Pat O'Connor, in his usual light-hearted way; "let's have a bit of fun; it's been dismal enough up to this."

The fair in other parts was at its height.

It was not everyone present at Ballynara Fair that was going to let "politics" and the "murthering Saxon" spoil their chances of enjoying himself.

Every imaginable kind of fun was going on, including stand-up fights, climbing greasy poles, drinking whisky for wagers, and so forth.

Pat had had his fill of nearly all these, when suddenly he saw a man standing by a tent with a rope in his hand.

The other end of it was inside, the rope passing between the canvas of the doorway.

"Here's a lark," whispered Pat O'Connor to Harry Marshall. "Come along with me."

Meanwhile, the man with the rope was haranguing a laughing mob, among whom was a Catholic priest, who joined heartily in the merriment of the crowd.

With his eyes sparkling with fun and mischief, Pat O'Connor suddenly darted behind the tent.

The man who held the rope did not observe the movements of Pat, and continued his address to the crowd.

"Ye see, jintlemen and ladies," the man said, "ye've come all the way from—you know where—to buy a donkey at Ballynara Fair. Ye

might ha' seen many a donkey, ladies and jintlemen, by lookin' into yer own lookin'-glasses; but ye never in yer life saw sich a donkey as this."

"But look here, Mike Mannigan," cried one of the crowd, "do you think we'll buy a pig in a poke? Show us the donkey."

"Ye may say what ye like, Tim O'Callaghan," cried Mannigan; "but d'ye know the raison why I don't show him?"

"Yes; bekase ye're afraid we shall see his sprained leg."

"And his blind eye."

"And his lopped tail."

"And the marks where you whipped him to markut."

These and other cries greeted the unfortunate dealer.

But he took it all in good part.

"Shure and it's all wrong ye are," cried he. "Now the raison is that he's sich a beauty—such a purty donkey—that if I showed 'm—or rather her, for she's been the mother of three—the whole fair would ha' bin here to buy, and I'd ha' spoilt thrade for iveryone, and got myself mobbed into the bargan. Now," he said, after a round of laughter had followed his absurdities, "now thin, who's goin' to bid twinty pounds for the unrivalled donkey?"

"Five shillings," cried the priest.

"Long life to yer honour, and may praties in your garden never be dug up by Saxon spades. But, yet, surr, I'll bid tin against ye."

"Tin," said another.

"Fifteen."

"Twenty," said the priest.

"No offince," cried Mike Mannigan, "but I'll bid twinty-five."

"Thirty," said another.

And so it went on, until the priest had bid two pounds ten.

Nothing could induce anyone to go beyond that sum; and so Mike, with tears in his eyes, consented to let his ass go for that, though "shure and I'm the biggest ass," he said, "for partin' with it."

"But, there," he added, "there; you'll be after taking her, with all her infirmities, Father Prout, won't ye, and not be bringing her back to me to sadden my eyes with the look of her?"

"I'll take her as she is, and chance what mischief ye've been up to, Mike Mannigan," said the priest, laughing; "but, mind ye, if ye chate me, ye'll have to do penance, and that a heavy one, too."

"And it's happy I'll be to do that same," returned Mike.

Then, turning towards the tent, he added—

"Now then, Kathleen, my jewel, come out and glad the eyes of Ballynara by a sight of the biggest donkey in the whole place. Shure and it's lying down she must be, or else she's a bad Catholic, and doesn't like her new masther. Ah, here she comes."

As he said this, and gave an extra and strong tug at the rope, the canvas which formed the door of the tent was pushed open, and there appeared—

Not the donkey! Oh, no.

Pat O'Connor was at this moment comfortably riding on her back.

It was not the donkey, but the wife of Mike—Mistress Bridget Mannigan—with the rope round her waist, and as drunk as Chloe.

The priest looked aghast.

The crowd shouted.

Mike grinned and slapped his thighs.

Bridget swayed to and fro, with an idiotic stare upon her face.

"Shure and I'm thinking I tould the thruth when I tould yer honour," cried Mike, "that ye'd bought the biggest donkey in Ballynara."

"You have cheated me," said the priest.

"And I've not done that same," cried Mike, indignantly. "Do ye think I'd be wishing yer rivirence to serve me the same thrick by chargin' double for masses for my soul, shure. Hurroo! hurroo! pay me your silver, Father Prout. See, here comes my donkey with another ass on his back."

Pat O'Connor, having just arrived in time to see the fun, drove the donkey to the tent door, jumped off, and giving it a kick, sent it flying with such a rush that it knocked Bridge Mannigan clean on her back.

"Oh, you thafe o' the world!" cried Mike, as he gave his wife a kick, "shure and it's myself 'ud wish the praste would take you in with the donkey, and I'd give him five shillings for the bargun."

"Come on," said Pat O'Connor to Harry Marshall, "come on. Mother Bridget yonder is recovering a bit, and the place'll be too hot to hold us."

CHAPTER XIII.

"THE BOYS OF THE SHANNON" TO THE RESCUE.

THE peasants seemed to have subsided into their ordinary routine of fun now, and to have forgotten the man in the tall hat, the mysterious voice, the presence of the military, and everything, in fact, but jollity.

As evening approached, the dancing booths became full, the whisky tents also, and the outer part of the fair was given up to the younger portion of the community.

"I say, Pat," said Harry Marshall, as they passed along, amusing themselves with gazing at the motley, merry crowds, "what was the meaning of that voice which seemed to come from the Irishman with the tall hat, when his lips never moved?"

"It was the voice of the Dutchman, no doubt," said Pat.

"But what was the mystery?"

"Why, it must have been done by ventriloquism," said our hero. "The skipper must have been present in the crowd in some disguise. But, I say, Harry, I've an idea."

"What's that?"

"Have you ever read a description of Donnybrook fair?"

"That I have," returned Harry, "in several books."

"Well, then, let's buy two shillelaghs from the lad yonder, and then 'go feeling for heads.'"

"Feeling for heads! Oh, oh! I remember; go groping round the tents and find the biggest head, then whack it hard and bolt."

Pat laughed.

"Well," he said, "that's what *we* should have to do; but the object of the men in Lever's story was to get up a good row."

"Come on, then; the boy yonder's got some capital head-breakers," said Marshall.

The Irish lad who was selling the bludgeons was a laughing, merry fellow about fourteen.

He was twisting about on one leg, and whisking the sticks round his head, while he kept shouting—

"Here's the shticks for a spree! Shure, and it's the very shillelagh I have here with which Dan Artigan held back a whole rigiment of ridcoats at Ballinasloe Gap. Who's the bhoy to buy one? Hard as iron; chape as dirt."

The two school chums had soon made their purchases, and started on their somewhat dangerous errand.

It happened that not far from the spot was a large booth, where men, and women too, were lolling on the ground, the shape of their heads showing plainly through the canvas.

Pat, scarcely able to contain his laughter, selected at last a good round bump and delivered a wholesome crack upon it.

It was not a savage crack, but quite enough to rouse the owner, who after a moment sprang up with an oath.

Pat O'Connor and Harry Marshall at once sought the shelter of a neighbouring booth, and in a minute after they saw issuing forth from the whisky tent Dan Hooligan.

His face was red with drink, and he flourished in his hand a most murderous-looking bludgeon.

He glanced round him savagely.

For an instant he saw no one near who was at all likely to have done the trick.

But presently he espied a man sitting on a fallen tree, and apparently half asleep, for his shillelagh was gradually dropping from his hand.

Dan Hooligan rushed up to him and shook him by the shoulder.

"Arrah, wake up here, ye murtherin' villain!" he cried.

The man looked up at first with an idiotic stare upon his face.

Then he rose to his feet.

"What in the wurold are ye afther?" he said. "I was slaping off me last quart of whisky."

"Have ye had a crack on the head yet to-day?" asked Hooligan.

"I have not had that same," exclaimed the man.

"Then it's time that ye had," said Dan.

And before the other could ward off the blow, he brought his bludgeon down with terrific violence full on the head of the half-awakened man.

The latter staggered away, but quickly recovered his equilibrium.

Then he shouted—

"O'Connell! O'Connell! To the riscue! Quick, bhoys, quick."

"A Hooligan! a Hooligan!" shouted the other.

And before the echoes had scarcely died away, a crowd rushed out from the various tents like a swarm of bees.

"I say, Harry," cried Pat O'Connor, in an undertone, "I think we've done too much; I'm afraid we've raised a storm that we cannot quell."

By this time a crowd had collected, the Hooligans and the O'Connells ranging themselves upon opposite sides.

Dan Hooligan and the other man, who rejoiced in the cognomen of David O'Connell, advanced to the centre.

"It's faling heads ye've been afther, Mister O'Connell, this morning," said Hooligan, with a jeer.

"I have not that same," returned the other, "but as ye've had the kindness to knock a fly off my head with your little stick there, maybe I'll be afther doing the likes by you. So the top of the marning to ye, and take that."

And with the words he aimed a tremendous blow at his foe.

It took effect on Dan Hooligan's shoulder.

He staggered, and was about to recommence the attack, when Pat O'Connor burst through the throng and rushed between them with uplifted shillelagh.

"Stop, stop," he cried; "this is all my fault."

The vociferous crowd stopped their cries in very amazement.

Dan Hooligan scowled darkly on the boy, whom he recognised as the one who had capsized him into the Shannon.

"What are ye afther, interfering here?" exclaimed he. "Is it a broken scance ye're wantin'?"

"I'm not minding that," said Pat, "but I came to say that it was I that hit you on the head for a lark, and Mr. O'Connell has nothing to do with it."

"Hurroo, hurroo, for the brave boy!" cried the crowd.

Dan Hooligan scowled.

"Then if ye're big enough to fale for heads and wield a shillelagh," cried he, "shtand and get such a thrashin' that when I've done wid ye, your own mother won't know ye."

At this moment a tall, stalwart figure pushed its way through the throng and stood before Dan Hooligan.

It was Thaddeus O'Shaughnessy, the brave old master of Shannon Academy.

"You're a coward if you fight that boy, Hooligan," he said.

"Shure and is it yerself as his masther that'll tache him to fale for heads and crack people wid his shillelagh, and then expict him to be let off widout a crack for himself?" remarked Dan.

"No; I can punish him if there is any punishment due," replied Thaddeus.

"Maybe ye'd like to take his plaice and fight for 'm," said Dan, with a sneer.

Thaddeus O'Shaughnessy turned for an instant very pale.

Then he quietly took the shillelagh from the hands of Pat O'Connor.

"I'll oblige ye with great pleasure, Dan Hooligan," he said, "and if my eye is only as true and my arm as strong as it was when I was a student in Dublin, I'll give you as perfect and elegant a thrashing as ever ye've had, or ever will wish for."

Dan Hooligan paused for an instant in doubt.

The schoolmaster was old, but there was a grandeur and a firmness about him that told that youth was only concealed by the outward garb of age.

But there was not much time to hesitate.

"Hurroo for the schoolmaster!"

"Hurroo for the Hooligan!"

And then yells of every kind resounded from the rival factions.

Hooligan saw that he was in for it, and so he made the best of it.

Eyeing the schoolmaster steadfastly, he waited for the attack.

It was not long in coming.

With a skill and a quickness for which few would have dreamed of giving him credit, Thaddeus O'Shaughnessy gave his shillelagh a twist, and avoiding the weapon of his adversary, brought it down with tremendous effect on the sconce of Dan Hooligan.

Then there rained in a perfect storm of blows.

Hooligan was no coward, and he bore himself bravely enough.

But he had found his match.

Now and then he succeeded in catching his adversary a goodly crack on the arm or shoulder.

Yet it was all in vain.

Struggle as he would, he rapidly became exhausted, and, at length, stunned and bleeding, he fell on the green sward.

"Have ye had enough, Dan Hooligan?" said the schoolmaster, calm and collected as ever.

"Yes; this onst," said Dan.

And then he made a peculiar sign to one of the crowd.

In an instant the throng began forming in a compact circle round Thaddeus O'Shaughnessy, Pat O'Connor, and Harry Marshall, and ominous groans and whispers were heard.

"Spy!"

"Infarmer!"

"Let's give him a little stick-larning to kape his hand in."

"Who put Dan in the dark vaults by the Shannon?"

"Who broke his oath?"

"Let's brake his bones and sind him home on a car for his last ride."

Thaddeus stood stern, pale, and resolute, and gazed round at the crowd.

"Are ye Irishmen, that ye all talk of attacking one man," he said, "because I can thrash one of ye in fair fight?"

"A man! A shpy and an infarmer isn't a man," cried a voice. "Let's give it to 'm."

But yet they hesitated, as everyone does hesitate, to break the laws.

Harry Marshall had had his eyes fixed for a moment on the slope of a hill close at hand, where a crowd was congregated.

"Here, take my shillelagh, Pat," he cried, "you may want it. I'm off."

Before Pat could divine his meaning, he was elbowing his way through the crowd, and was soon seen dashing away at full speed.

"Ha, ha! look at the Saxon coward."

"See how he runs."

"Ah! when the Frinch come, we'll make the murthering Saxons run for their lives like that."

Pat himself was mystified.

But he had not much time for thought.

The crowd was closing in, and he was by the side of the beloved master who had risked his own life for him.

So back to back master and pupil prepared to keep off the crowd.

"Irishmen!" cried Thaddeus O'Shaughnessy (for he too had noticed the flight of Harry Marshall, and guessed its purport), "Irishmen, are ye mad, that ye are going to commit murder in the broad daylight, because this villain has told you that I am a spy. Beware! There is no proof that I have ever wronged anyone, or ever broken an oath. If you attack me, I will break as many sconces as I can, so if you are coming on, come on at once.

"Keep close, Pat," he added to our hero. "Keep close, and fight for yourself and the honour of your school."

Dan Hooligan had by this time risen from the ground, and had spoken a few words to one or two in the crowd, who had spread about the passion-stirring sentences he had uttered.

And so the men began to advance.

In a few moments the attack had commenced.

With a brutality which they would not have indulged in had it not been for the drink they had imbibed, the mob flung sticks at the two heroes, and then assaulted them savagely.

It was a fight which could not have lasted long.

The numbers would have been enough to overwhelm them, even had the Hooligans alone been their foes.

But in this the O'Connells made common cause with their enemies.

And on both sides the two found themselves assaulted.

But it was only for a moment.

There was a sudden rush down the hill side, a sudden roar of voices, and then every boy in Shannon Academy, headed by Tim Finnigan and Laurence McMahon, the ushers, dashed down upon the infuriated crowd.

So sudden and so resolute was the onslaught that the boys had burst through the throng, and formed a circle round the schoolmaster and Pat, before the peasants were aware of it.

"Now then, ye devils," cried Figs, who had been indulging a little, and besides that, was desperately fond now of the schoolmaster for his kindness to himself and Kathleen, "away ye go, or there'll be more broken heads than were ever seen at one time in Ballynara."

The crowd took no notice whatever of all this.

Their blood was up, and so, forming themselves in as compact a manner as possible, they took counsel and then charged upon the scholars.

The latter, however, were in no way dismayed.

Everyone of them had purchased shillelaghs, and now, as the mob came on, helter-skelter, they fought like drilled scholars as they were.

Dan Hooligan and his men were repulsed, and many a face streaming with blood testified to the heavy blows that had been struck.

But the sight of blood only infuriated them.

"Keep close, bhoys, keep close," cried Thaddeus O'Shaughnessy, forcing his way to the front. "Mr. McMahon and Mr. Finnigan, get your forces into two divisions. Pat O'Connor, come with me and twenty more; we'll rout these rascals."

Laurence McMahon at this moment turned very pale.

"See, sir," he said. "This will be very serious. They are picking up the flint stones."

It was true.

At the back of the mob, the women and the men were gathering piles of large, jagged stones.

"We must charge and disperse them if we can," said Thaddeus; "that's our only chance. Two divisions can attack, the third can be in reserve."

In another moment the necessary orders had been given, and the brave boys of the Shannon dashed at two points upon their foes.

The mob was all very well while it had only another mob like itself to deal with.

But attacked by a lot of enemies—even though they were boys—who advanced in regular order, they felt lost.

As soon as they began to retreat, the third or reserve division of boys under Figs, and with The Barry of Barrymore in the front ranks charged in upon them.

The rout of the peasants was now complete.

They gave way in all directions, and huddled away down into the valley, while the scholars hurried up the slope and reformed.

It was now dusk.

The sun had set behind the mountains, and the shadows of the great hills were falling on the valleys.

"There'll be murder done, Mr. O'Shaughnessy," said Laurence McMahon, "unless something is done towards getting the boys home. These men will never stand being beaten by a parcel of lads."

"Very well," said the schoolmaster, pale and stern, as he saw the peasants reforming below, "we will march home in three divisions as before. Keep a sharp look-out, boys, and remember that Thaddeus O'Shaughnessy will never forget the day when his lads stood round him to save him from the rabble."

They began slowly and in order, now to retreat down the mountain path which led into the road towards the school.

As they reached the corner of the rocky pass a man suddenly darted out from the shadows.

Thaddeus paused, and gave the word to his boys to halt.

"Whom have we here?" he cried, in stern tones.

"Hush! masther dear," said a whispering voice, "it's me, Terence O'Rafferty."

"What brings you here?" said Thaddeus. "I dare not pause. My lads are in danger."

"Shure, and it's that same that I wish to spake about," said Terence; "if ye take my advice, ye'll be afther stoppin' at the mountain inn to-night."

"'SHURE, NOW, AND WHAT'S THAT?' CRIED MAT O'GRADY."

"Why ?"

"The bhoys'll all be up at the gap, and they'll stop at nothing," said Terence ; "they're as mad as a praste without a pinch of snuff, because ye've escaped, and because they've been licked by a parcel of gossoons. So, masther darlin', don't go. Rist up at the inn."

"It won't hold us, if it is the one I think of," said Thaddeus.

"And which is that, masther ?"

"The 'Emerald.'"

Terence burst out laughing.

"And is that the little barn that the masther will be after thinkin' I'd send him to ?" said Terence ; "no, it's the 'Who'd-ha'-thought-it ?' the snug little place that lies back among the trees, so that it's a surprise to anyone to find such a place of refreshment."

"And Darby McDermot, the landlord, can he be depended on ?" asked Thaddeus O'Shaughnessy.

"To the death."

"And there is room for all ?"

"Yes, for every man Jack of ye."

"Well, I think your advice is good," said Thaddeus, "and I'll take it. Come on, boys, we'll turn aside here."

"Which way, sir ?" said McMahon.

"Up the path to the left," returned Thaddeus.

Hurrying as well as they could up the rugged ascent, they presently came in view of a large clump of trees.

Not a sign of any public house was to be seen.

But, on reaching a clump of poplars, they came suddenly in view of an inn, standing back about twenty yards from the roadway.

As may be imagined, the landlord stared in utter astonishment when he saw the sixty boys and the three masters.

"Shure and it's hoping I am that all your honours are thirsty," he said ; "will ye be afther walkin' into me back room ?"

"Yes," said Thaddeus, "and when you have served up some refreshment, let us speak with you a moment."

It was not long before the boys were seated in a huge barn at tables where bread and cheese and ale were served.

Then Thaddeus O'Shaughnessy called the landlord, Darby McDermot, aside.

"My boys and I are in danger," he said. "I dare not take them by the gap. They had a row up in the fair, and the mob have sworn vengeance."

Darby scratched his head.

"Well, yer honour, and what is it ye're afther wishing me to do ?" said he ; "is it helping yer honour to foight 'em ?"

Thaddeus smiled.

"No, not that, Darby," he said. "I want ye to give my lads shelter till the morning, that is all, and I will pay you well."

"And who," said Darby, with a slightly suspicious air, "who was it tould yer honour that I had room for ye ?"

"Shure, and it was myself did that same, Darby," said Terence O'Rafferty ; "I'll be bound for the schoolmaster wid my life."

"Oh ! then if it's you, Terence, my bouchal," cried Darby, "it's all right. And be sure I'd

thrust the schoolmasther himself, but the times are so strange, and so forth——"

"Don't apologise, Darby," cried Thaddeus, with a smile ; "my lads can sleep in the barn anyhow, and we shall be grateful enough for the shelter. As for me, I shall rough it as they do."

"And shure, sir, it's an iligant bed I can give your 'onour," began Darby.

But Thaddeus raised his hands deprecatingly.

"No, no," he said, "I'll be with the rest. If the place is good enough for my boys, it's good enough for me. Bring me in some hot whisky, Darby, for me and my two teachers, and yerself, and Terence O'Rafferty here, and we'll talk over the fun of the fair."

"Oh ! then, Nora alanna," cried Darby to his wife, as he was mixing the grog, "it's the illigant jintleman that the schoolmasther is, to be shure. He trates me for all the world as if I was his aqual."

"And drinks up all the blessed beer in the cellar," cried Nora, laughing ; "it's glad I am he showed his face here this night."

Glad !

Had she only known what was coming !

It was not long before the schoolmaster, the two teachers, the landlord, and Terence, were indulging in strong glasses of grog, while the tired schoolboys flung themselves on tables and benches, and were soon fast asleep.

It was about midnight that Nora came in with a pale face and beckoned Darby.

He went out, but returned in a few minutes, more pale than his wife.

"Whisht ! masther," he said, "wake the bhoys, and let them be riddy. The United Irishmen are upon ye."

"Is this really true? Are you certain ?" asked Thaddeus, in real alarm.

"Arrah, and it's myself wouldn't be after desaving you," he said ; "they're coming up the road with tarches and their rifles too."

At this moment a loud yell rent the air, and a hundred voices shrieked in chorus—

"Bring out the spies ! Death to the traitors !"

CHAPTER XIV.
THE ATTACK.

FOR an instant a chill went to the heart of the schoolmaster, as he heard the shouted threats of the excited men outside the inn.

"There must have been deadly treachery here," he said, "or else how would they have known that I was here with my boys ?"

"I don't know," said Dennis, "I don't know, and it's meself would brake his head wid a poker if I did know. But what's to be done ?"

"That's a thing I can't tell ye," exclaimed Thaddeus O'Shaughnessy ; "how many of them are there ?"

"Nearly a hundred," said Dennis.

"And they are armed with rifles, ye say ?"

"Shure, and they are that same," replied Dennis.

"Well, I will go to one of your front windows, and try to temporise with them," said Thaddeus.

"You must be careful thin, masther, that they don't pop ye off," cried the landlord.

"Arrah, but it's the brave man ye are to go in front of 'em, and face 'em when they've got firearms."

The schoolmaster paid no attention to these words.

His mind was, in fact, entirely occupied with the question—

"How was he to extricate his lads from the dilemma?"

But just as he was going to face the United Irishmen, where he might have been shot at and killed on the spot, Terence O' Rafferty came forward.

"Shure, and it's not meself will let you go, masther. I understand 'em, and will be able to talk to 'em betther than you can."

"But they will shoot you for a traitor if you protect me," cried Thaddeus.

"Not them; they know a thrick worth two of that. It would not be good for a good many of 'em if they shed the blood of O'Rafferty. Annyways, I'm goin'."

And so, without another word, he loosened his pistols in his belt, and hurried from the room.

When he reached the front of the house, an extraordinary scene presented itself.

The United Irishmen were, of course, excited with drink, and they were whooping and yelling in a manner worthy of Red Indians.

They waved their torches about in the most frantic manner, and sent a red glow of light everywhere around them.

Some of them were quite close to the windows, and Terence O'Rafferty, leaning out, addressed them—

"Shure, bhoys, what's the mather?" he cried. "What is it ye're wantin' in the middle of the blissed night?"

A tall, burly Irishman, with deep-set eyes, a pug nose, and a mouth like a gash, whirled his torch round his head as he shouted—

"Hurroo! then it's the O'Shaughnessy we want, the murthering traithor."

"What are ye afther wantin' him for?" asked Terence.

"Shure, and it's to hang him up to the furrust tree there," cried the same ruffian, who had spoken before.

"Then I think it's Mr. O'Shaughnessy himself'll objict to that same," said Terence; "and, in fact, I objict to it mesilf, becase Mr. O'Shaughnessy is no traithor. I tell ye what, bhoys, the poteen's been a thrifle too sthrong, and has got into your hids. Think of it till the mornin', lads, jist till the mornin'."

A groan was the answer to this speech.

Evidently Terence O'Rafferty was not saying what was popular among the throng of conspirators.

"What's the matther, lads?" exclaimed Terence; "has what you've had to ate disagreed wid ye?"

One of the men, more sober than the rest, raised his rifle, and took steady aim at the head of Terence O'Rafferty.

"We want none o' this nonsense, Misther O'Rafferty," said he; "if ye don't give a proper explanashun of yourself, I'll put a bullet through your brain."

"And pray, Misther McCarthy," said Terence, in a jeering voice, "pray, Misther McCarthy, what is the explanashun ye desire?"

"We want to know who let Thaddeus O'Shaughnessy out of the cave on the island. We want to know why ye're after pertectin' him when he was adjudged a traithor by the United Irishmen, and we——"

"Well, then, sthop; I'll come out to ye," cried Terence; "for I don't like to be bawlin' out of winder to ye, like an old ox out of a shtall."

And he moved away.

As he did so, Thaddeus O'Shaughnessy caught him by the arm.

"Terence O'Rafferty," he said, in a low voice, "you shall not run this risk for me."

"What risk, masther dear?" said the man, laughing. "Shure, and it's no risk I'm runnin' at all, at all. The bhoys won't hurt me, and they would be sartain to hurt you."

He pulled himself away from Thaddeus, and sprang out through the window.

On the instant, the schoolmaster saw him coolly and defiantly facing the throng of resolute and desperate men.

A growl of fury greeted Terence O'Rafferty.

"Now look here, Master McCarthy," he said, to the man who had threatened him with the rifle. "Look here, I am not one o' those omadhauns who are to be hounded down for nothin'. Mr. O'Shaughnessy is one of us, or at iny rate, he's taken the oath; and he'll never break it, no matter what ye may do to 'im."

The men were thirsting for the blood of the schoolmaster, and nothing they heard in his favour would they listen to.

"We don't want any prachin here," cried another big, burly Irishman; "we want Thaddeus O'Shaughnessy and his cubs, and, by the same token, we'll take 'im, if he doesn't come out. We'll burn the place down about his hid, so if he doesn't want to do harum to innocent paple, he'll face us."

Another angry groan followed.

But Terence was not dismayed.

He had that chivalry implanted in his heart which forbade him to give way.

"Will thin, to pacify ye all," he said, "I'll go with ye as a 'hostage,' or whatever you call it, I'll be bail for 'im till the mornin', and then if ye don't hang me in the manetime, I'll be able to explain."

"Take 'im at his word," cried McCarthy, "that's the best way. Give up your arums."

Terence did so at once.

Then they bound his hands behind him, and led him away.

As he went, Thaddeus heard plainly the words—

"We'll hang the traithor, and then we'll come back."

"Will ye?" thought Thaddeus. "Perhaps we'll be there among ye, before ye know it."

Without any delay he hurried back to the barn, where he had left the boys from the Academy.

As he entered it, he saw Pat O'Connor scrambling in through a window.

In his hand was a rifle.

"Why, what's that?" he cried; "what's that? Where did you get it?"

Pat put his finger on his lip.

"Hush, master dear," said Pat; "we're in trouble, are we not, sir?"

"Yes; well?"

"We should be safer if we were up at Shannon Academy."

"Certainly, my boy, but don't beat about the bush, for we've strange work to do to-night."

Pat approached nearer the schoolmaster, and took his hand.

"Mr. O'Shaughnessy," he went on, "while you've been away with Mister O'Rafferty, we've been having a talk."

"Yes, my boy."

"And if you will trust us, sir, we'll fight our way back to Shannon School," said Pat. "We won't disgrace you."

Thaddeus' face glowed with the emotion which pervaded him.

"My lads," he said, "in the first place, you have no arms."

"Yes," cried Pat, "we have. I've been out in the stables, and found enough rifles for all."

"But then, my lads," said Thaddeus, "remember that I did not take you into my care to place you in peril like this. I have taken you to protect you and act as guardian——"

Crash!

And a loud report.

A pistol shot or a rifle shot had been fired at one of the windows of the house and smashed it.

"They're going to begin the attack," cried Dennis, rushing in. "What's to be done?"

Thaddeus thought for a moment.

If he remained where he was, his boys stood the chance of being killed in a huddled crowd, whereas, if they fought, they would have a chance of victory, and of vindicating their honour.

"Boys," he cried, "do as ye like. Arm yourselves, and may Heaven defend ye. We'll save Terence O'Rafferty if we can, and we'll fight our way to Shannon School."

Despite all the circumstances, the boys burst into a loud cheer, and in a few moments some of them had scrambled out of the window, and brought in the rifles from the stables.

In a short time they had passed out on the mountain path, towards the spot where the United Irishmen had hurried away with Terence O'Rafferty.

As they passed down the road, they saw in the distance a sight which curdled their blood.

The men had lighted a huge bonfire, and in the glow of this they could all see Terence O'Rafferty with a rope round his neck, and a man standing as an executioner by his side.

"We're wanted there quickly, bhoys," cried Thaddeus. "See, they're going to murder him."

The boys, though some of them, of course, being young, felt a slight tremor of the heart, were all sufficiently drilled to advance calmly towards the spot where danger threatened them.

The younger ones, in fact, were stimulated by the example of the elder ones, and as they neared the point of action, they advanced with the regular tread of soldiers.

The sound of their advance gave an idea to Thaddeus.

What if he suffered the rebels to think that the soldiers were advancing?

But no.

The blood of the peasantry was up, and if they only thought that they were the hated "rid coats," a terrible scene of bloodshed might ensue.

So, desiring his boys to halt for a moment, Thaddeus O'Shaughnessy advanced in the direction of the place of execution.

He went far in advance of the boys, and said in a loud voice—

"Is Mr. McCarthy here?"

"Here I am, at your sarvice, sirr," said the man with the rope, in a jeering voice.

"Release that man," exclaimed Thaddeus, sternly.

McCarthy made a mock bow.

"And is it yerself, Master O'Shaughnessy, that is the masther here now? Shure and we haven't all gone to school ag'in."

"Release that man!" cried the schoolmaster again.

"Bhoys, we've traithors here; look out," exclaimed McCarthy, and held more tightly on to the rope the end of which was around Terence O'Rafferty's neck.

Thaddeus, however, was prepared for emergencies.

He beckoned to Pat O'Connor, and whispered to him quickly.

Then he made a sudden dash, seized McCarthy by the waist, and flung him into the midst of the bonfire.

Then there came a rattle of firearms, fired by design over the heads of the crowd.

The United Irishmen were, for the instant, scared by this, not knowing whether any of their party had or had not been injured by the volley.

And, before they could recover from the momentary panic into which it had thrown them, the boys of the academy charged down upon them.

It succeeded admirably for the moment.

McCarthy, in his utter surprise, of course left his hold upon the rope, and Terence O'Rafferty, snatching a rifle from the hands of one of the men, cracked him on the head with the butt end of it, and joined the ranks of the scholars.

The half-drunk and excited throng gave way on all sides, and the boys were in possession of the mountain pass.

"Now then, bhoys!" exclaimed Thaddeus, "quick, retreat. We must not expose ourselves without necessity."

The boys in the rear of the party retreated with their faces to the foe, and their bayonets gleaming in the moonlight.

For a moment Thaddeus O'Shaughnessy hoped that he would be able to pass on to the academy without a fight.

But not so.

The United Irishmen, in spite of the drink, and in spite of the bloodthirstiness which characterised everyone of them, were brave men.

And so they soon righted themselves, and with a rush they dashed down upon the scholars, firing a terrific heavy volley as they came.

Several cries of pain told the schoolmaster that some of his scholars were struck, and he bit his lip with an agony worse than that suffered by those who had received the wounds.

"What will their friends say to me?" was his thought.

But still this was no time for thinking, but for action.

So he turned at once to them, saying—

"Fire!"

The scholars took deliberate aim, and, as they fired, several of the United Irishmen fell.

This huddled them together for an instant, but they soon re-formed, and came rushing down impetuously.

At this instant, when Thaddeus O'Shaughnessy thought that his school would be annihilated, the heavens on either side of the pass seemed to open.

A red glow illumined the road, and a double volley of musketry was poured into the thronging crowd.

The "red coats" were upon them at last!

There was an end to the battle now.

The soldiers, after the two deadly volleys which they had poured in, swarmed down the sides of the mountain pass, and, man to man, bayonet to bayonet, drove the deluded peasants away.

Thaddeus O'Shaughnessy waited for no more.

His boys had asserted their honour, had proved their manliness, and now it was his duty to lead them home.

So, within another hour, they had once more lain down in their comfortable beds, after as exciting a day as ever it had been their lot to pass through.

CHAPTER XV.

A SEARCH FOR RIGHT.

IN spite of the fact that several of the men were wounded, and one killed, while two of the academy lads were also hurt, little notice was taken of the affair of Ballynara.

Riots at fairs were of common occurrence in Ireland, and the interference of the soldiery was a thing not out of the usual.

So outwardly all was calm.

And, with the exception of the sudden disappearance of the Dutch skipper and his ship, everything went on as usual.

As all believed, however, it was but the lull before the tempest.

No one could believe that Dan Hooligan and Rory O'Neil and McCarthy, and all their set would long sit down quietly under what they would consider deadly wrongs.

They were, of course, only biding their time.

But the scholars, although naturally proud of the name they had made for themselves on the countryside, soon forgot to think of the dangers which might accrue to them from it, and lapsed once more into study and play.

It was about a month after the fair, and Figs was looking forward to the day, not far distant, when he would be the happy husband of Kathleen, when The Barry of Barrymore met Pat O'Connor in the grounds.

It was just after dark, and our hero was taking the stroll which was allowed to those boys who liked it, before retiring to rest.

The Barry was evidently in a great state of excitement.

He seized Pat by the arm.

"I say, Pat," he said, "can you spare me a few moments?"

Pat passed his arm through that of his friend.

"Of course I can," he said, "fire away. What's up?"

"Something serious, I can tell you," returned The Barry; "I've found my clue to the recovery of my estates."

Pat pressed his hand.

"I'm glad of that, old fellow," he cried, "but do not be deluded by false hopes."

"Never fear," said The Barry. "I have been too often deceived to permit myself now to be led away. I shall soon be able to find out the meaning of this, if you will only assist me."

"That you know I will," cried Pat; "anything for you."

"Well, then, listen, and I will tell you."

It seemed that on the preceding night The Barry, who from his age was permitted a trifle more liberty than the others, was out on the mountain path.

He had paused at his favourite spot, where he could gaze in melancholy longing on the home of his ancestors, when he heard two people approaching.

They were talking earnestly.

The Barry drew back into the shadows.

He meant, of course, as soon as they passed, to hurry away.

But it was not to be.

Fate had ordained that he should hear all they said.

The two men stopped as they came to the spot where he stood.

"Shure and it's here we'll shtand, Mat O'Grady," said a voice; "divil a bit of a sowl will hear us."

"All right, Rory O'Neil," said O'Grady (pronouncing it "O'Nale" by the way).

"Then out wid it."

"Ye'll nivir tell?"

"Nivir."

"You'll swear it?"

"Aye, by the freedom of ould Ireland," cried Rory.

"Whisht, then," said Mat, lowering his voice.

In vain as regarded The Barry.

The mountains were as still as a city of the dead, and every word could be heard distinctly.

"Whisht, then," said Mat, "it's after making my fortune I'll be."

"I hope so, for my sake," chuckled Rory O'Neil.

"Shure and it's yerself shall share," said Mat, "but listen. I've got in my black box at home the papers that relate to the property of the Barrymores."

"And how were you afther gitting them?" said Rory.

"It was an accident, ma bouchal," returned O'Shaughnessy's serving-man; "I was coming across the hills when there was a storum, and I went into ould Callaghan's Folly—ye know the ruins up by Crogan's hut."

"Yes."

"Well, thin, when I got into the only place where a pig could hide to keep himself dhry, I saw Mr. Osborne, old Stapleton's agent, a-lying us comfortably aslape in a corner, as if he'd robbed all the poor bhoys for miles around."

"Bad cess to the baste!" muttered Rory O'Neil.

"Well, thinks I, it's no harum jist to have a pape into yer pockets, Misther Osborne, and so I knales down by the side of 'm, and gets my bit of a knife in my hand, shure, for fear he might wake. But good luck to the poteen up at the shanty yonder, he was as thrunk as a praste at a fair. So I gets out his papers, and I thinks I'll kape 'em at iny rate, and bad luck to the day that I didn't. When the storum was over, I gets away to the school, and there I finds all the papers that Misther Stapleton 'ud give thousands for, but the Barry'd give more."

"Then it's the best markut I'd be afther takin'," said Rory.

Mat uttered a low curse.

"What! when The Barry was one of 'em as put me bist frind into the dark cell? No; if The Barry offered me three times as much as the Saxon, murtherin' thafe as he is, the Saxon should have 'em."

"Then, why don't you sell 'em, and be quick then?" said Rory. "Oh! the iligant day when ye get yer money! I can fale the whisky thrickling out o' the chorners of me mouth; but till me, Mat," he added, "what did ye put me in your confidence for?"

"Because I want yer help, shure."

"And how would that be?"

"Oh! it's aisy enough, as O'Connor said when he broke his wife's hid with the poker," returned Mat: "it's goin' to the Hall ye'll be, and telling Masther Stapleton that a frind of yours has by accident found the papers."

"Shure, and it'll be putting me hid into the lion's mouth I'll be. Perhaps ye'll be after doin' it yerself, as the man said to his best frind, who wanted him to be hanged for 'im."

"Oh! and it's the coward ye are, Rory; it'll be ashamed of ye I'll be," cried Mat. "And what'll I be givin' money for, if ye do nothing to hilp me?"

"But why don't ye go to the Hall yerself?"

"And it's myself's not got yer tongue, Rory," said Mat, "and saving yer presence, Rory, I've not got yer imperdence. I'd be after flushing up like a colleen, and stammerin' and stootherin' like old Father Prout at a christenin', after he's wet the baby's head tin times."

"And what'll ye be afther givin' me for gettin' my head broke?" said Rory.

"A third of what I git, Rory."

"And where'll ye be keeping the papers?"

"Safe and sound in my box, in my room at the school yonder," said Mat.

"And whin am I to go up to the Hall?"

"The day afther to-morrow, if you loike."

"Very well," said Rory, "I'll go, and I'll be caushious too. Meet me ag'in here at eleven, on the third night from this."

And then, after a grip, they parted.

"What do ye think?" asked The Barry, when he had finished his story. "Isn't this something, Pat?"

"It is indeed," returned Pat O'Connor. "Hadn't ye better tell Mr. O'Shaughnessy?"

"No; not till I've read the papers, and seen how far they will aid me in recovering my inheritance," returned The Barry.

"And, as to that, how is it possible to get hold of them?"

"That's exactly where I want you to help me, Pat O'Connor," said The Barry; "we must get into his bedroom somehow, and open his box."

"That's dangerous."

"But it's no harm."

"No; you're looking for your own property."

Pat O'Connor mused a moment.

Then a bright idea seemed to leap into his brain.

"I think I've got it, Barry," he said.

"What is it?"

"You know O'Grady has got a wife?"

"He had one, but she bolted away to America."

"Yes; but that was a long time ago, and I heard that O'Grady was going to be married again."

"He won't this time, then," said Pat, "for she's coming home."

"And what's that got to do with me?" asked The Barry, with a smile.

"Much," said Pat O'Connor; "much, if you'll only listen."

"Fire away, then."

"Well, Mat expects his wife home directly," said Pat, "and upon this fact we must build up a plan by which to get the papers. Thaddeus O'Shaughnessy has bought a pig, and it's hanging up now in the pantry."

"Sh'are, and it's mad you're going entirely," said The Barry; "as Mat would say; what can the pig have to do with us?"

"Everything," said Pat, "only be listening. I'll get the pig, and I'll carry it up into Mat's bedroom, and put it to bed. Then I'll turn his back to the outside of the bed, and I'll put him on a nightcap. Then Mat will go up, and think that it's Biddy, and he'll be frightened and bolt. We must watch our chance then, and run in quickly."

The Barry laughed.

"Well, we'll try it, at any rate," said he, "for it will be a lark, even if we don't succeed."

"But when is it to be?" he added, after a short pause.

"Oh! let's do it to-night."

"Yes," said The Barry; "and, to make things better, I'll give Mat some silver to fetch me something from the town."

A few preliminaries were arranged, and then The Barry went in search of O'Grady.

He was not long in finding him; and truth to say, he was not sorry to discover that he had been slightly indulging.

"Mat," he said, "can ye go to the town for me?"

"If the masther will be letting me."

"I'll ask him," said The Barry; "it will be

all right. If there's a row, I'll take it on my own shoulders."

"Very well, surr," said Mat, unsuspectingly; "I'll be going; and what will ye be ahfter wantin'?"

The Barry gave him a list of things; and, never dreaming of anything, the O'Grady put down an extra glass of poteen, and started.

When he was safely out of the precincts of the school, The Barry hurried to find Pat O'Connor.

"Now then, Pat," he cried, "all's well."

"Has he gone?"

"Like a lamb. Where's the pig?"

"Down in the larder; we'll have to be very careful."

But the servants were very busy; and as Mat O'Grady, the "Paul Pry" of the place, was absent, they contrived to pass unnoticed to the pantry. The pig was heavy.

The peril, therefore, lay in carrying it upstairs.

But, as good luck, or ill luck would have it, they met no one; and, in the space of a quarter of an hour, the pig lay pleasantly reposing in the bed with a nightcap on.

"I wish we could have persuaded a live one to lie quiet," said The Barry; "wouldn't Mat jump when it squeaked?"

"Oh! it's good enough as it is," said Pat, laughing; "now for the cupboard."

"That won't be very amusing," said the Barry, "without anything to do."

"I've got some cakes and apples," said Pat, "but I tell ye what, we'll keep in the room till we hear him coming."

It was about half an hour after this that they heard a hoarse voice shouting outside the school.

"Whisht," said The Barry, "listen; there's O'Grady drunk and singing."

Pat listened. And, sure enough, it was so.

"'Twas a fine summer's morn. about eight in the day,
When the birds fell to sing, and the asses to bray,
When Patrick, the bridegroom, and Onoch, the bride,
In their best bib and tucker set out side by side.
Oh! the pipers played first in the rear, sirs,
Good luck! how the spalpeens did stare, sirs,
At this wedding of Ballyporeen."

"And it's a lark we'll be having now," said Pat O'Connor. "Quick, come into the cupboard. Turn down the lamp—never mind the crumbs."

"There's no such hurry as this, Pat," said The Barry; "he'll be looking for me."

"Not he," said Pat; "he will bring all the things up here first and overhaul them."

Pat was right.

In a few moments, Mat O'Grady staggered into the room.

He was still singing under his voice—

"There was pudding, hot dumplings, cod, cowheel and tripe,
And praties and all, but the praste got the snipe."

Then he paused.

"I'm wonderin' now," he said, as he pushed the door to, "what these little iligant parcels contain. He never told me a word at all, at all; and divil a bit of the list could I read. But shure the man as kapes the shop is a proper scholar. Hurroo! What's this?"

He opened one parcel and saw some figs.

"Shure, and this must be for Mr. Finnigan,"

he said. "I'll taste them, to see if they're dacent."

"Thief!" murmured the voice of The Barry solemnly, in the cupboard.

"Who was that called me by my name?" cried Mat, looking round in terror.

But all was again quiet.

"Then the bridegroom got up, and he made an orashun,
And he bothered them all with his fine botherashun."

"Hullo!" pursued Mat, "what's this? Swates; ah! and that's proper."

"Ugh! ugh!" groaned Pat.

O'Grady turned, and for the first time he saw that his bed was occupied.

"Shure now, and what's that? Holy Vargin presarve us!" he cried.

He took the lamp, and approached the bed with trembling steps.

"Oh! merciful Heaven!" he cried, as he saw the huge nightcap, "sorra, sorra for me, if it ain't Biddy come back jist as I was going to marry the Widdy Mulligan. But there, afther all, it's the ould woman. Biddy! Biddy!" he added, "wake up, wake up. It's yer Mat that's callin' ye."

And then he leaned over to embrace her.

But in an instant he had touched the pig's face, as cold as that of a corpse; and, with a shriek of terror and a wild leap, he fled from the room.

"It's as I thought," said Pat; "he's put his keys on the table. Now for the papers."

CHAPTER XVI.
WHO IS THE THIEF?

THE boys lost no time in opening the box.

Within it was a most heterogeneous mass of articles; but it was not long before they arrived at the object of their search.

It was a small parcel of blue paper, tied with red tape, and endorsed in a bold hand—

"Documents relating to the Barrymore Estates."

"Here they are," cried The Barry; "let's read them."

But at this moment there was a creaking on the stairs.

"Be careful," said Pat O'Connor, "put them back. It is enough that we know that they are here. We can tell Mr. Thaddeus O'Shaughnessy, and he'll make Mat O'Grady produce them."

"True, true; we mustn't be caught here like rats in a trap," said The Barry. "We'll lock the box and go."

They little thought who at this moment was watching them.

Little dreamed that the lynx eyes of Mat O'Grady were upon them.

In fact, it was not long before he recovered from his fright.

He would not, of course, have been fool enough to be alarmed at all if he had been quite sober.

And now that the fright had somehow cleared his brain for the moment, he had thought, as he reached the bottom of the stairs, that he would be making an ass of himself to expose to Thaddeus O'Shaughnessy the fact of his wife's presence in the academy.

"AS THE DARKNESS FELL, THE MEN BEGAN TO GATHER."

He determined, therefore, to return to his room, and if, as he feared, his wife was dead, he must confess in the morning.

If not, he must remain quietly with his spouse, and get her out as best he could on the following day.

On reaching the door he saw the two boys.

For the first moment his impulse prompted him to rush in and seize them.

But then his cunning came to his aid.

"No," he thought, "no, I won't. I'll be afther watchin' 'em, and listening to their conversashun, and then I'll be knowin' what to do to rivinge meself."

And so when Pat O'Connor heard the creak on the stairs, and the two friends determined to quit the room, he heard all, and hid away in the big doorway near at hand.

"Ah! ye young blaggards," he said, "I'll be even wid you. It'll be a dark hour for ye both when ye thried to git the best of Mat O'Grady."

On the following morning, just as Mr. Thaddeus O'Shaughnessy was going into the schoolroom, Mat O'Grady asked for an interview.

Knowing the treacherous character of his serving-man, the schoolmaster did not feel very well disposed to grant it.

"What do you wish to speak of?" asked he, sternly.

"I wish, surr, to lay a complaint against two of the scholars," replied O'Grady, "which it's against my heart to do it, surr, only——"

"Well, well," said O'Shaughnessy, raising his hand to interrupt him; "well, well, if that's the case I should prefer its being done in open school."

"I will do that same thin," returned O'Grady, "for it's thrue what I'm goin' to till ye, masther dear."

"Very good, then, follow me."

With a serious face, but eyes twinkling with malice, the serving-man followed the schoolmaster.

The pupils stared in astonishment as they saw him.

The Barry and Pat O'Connor took one rapid glance at each other, and then waited.

"Now," said O'Shaughnessy, as he took a seat at his desk, "now, Mat O'Grady, what is this that you have to say against my scholars?"

"Well, surr," said the man, "it's yer honour's self is after knowin' that tin years ago my wife, Biddy, that was Biddy McGorregan afore, ran away with Patrick McConnell to Ameriky."

"Yes," said O'Shaughnessy, impatiently, "yes, but come to the point."

"I will, surr. Will, thin, I got a letter the other day; I mane by token, it was brought to me by the postman, as tould me that me wife was comin' hoam again. So, when I sees a person a-lying in my bed, wid a nightcap on, shure and I thought it was her. And thin I catches hould of her, and goes to kiss her, when I find she's as could as a shtone."

The master frowned.

"What on earth has this to do with my boys?" he said.

"Everythin' surr; if yer honour will only have the paishence to listen," said O'Grady. "I thinks, on course, that she's dead, and I rushes out o' the room like mad to call someone up to her assistance."

At this a loud titter passed through the crowd of boys.

The schoolmaster could hardly help joining in their laughter at Mat's "bull"; but he contrived to put on a stern look, and exclaimed—

"Silence!"

Mat O'Grady scowled heavily at the boys.

"Will, surr, whin I gits half way down the stairs, I thinks to meself, what's the use o' bringing up anyone to a did corpse? So I shtops, and, after a moment, I goes upshtairs, and there, shure if there weren't two of the young jintlemen" (and he put a jeering emphasis on the word) "a-overhauling me box."

Thaddeus looked grave.

"I suppose, O'Grady, you're able to prove what you say?"

"Oh, yis, surr, I hope to be aible to do that same," he said, sturdily.

"And pray," said O'Shaughnessy, "pray, who are the two whom you accuse?"

"The Barry, surr, and Masther Pat O'Connor."

His two favourites!

He turned deadly pale.

"And pray have you lost anything?" he said.

"Yes, surr."

"And what is it?"

"Somethin', surr, which I would not have lost for the world, surr. Ye know that golden horseshoe that was given me by the English thraveller that I saived on the mountains?"

"Yes."

"Will, thin, that's gone."

"And you accuse them of stealing it?"

"Will, thin, shure, surr," said O'Grady, with a look which was meant to be one of deep concern, "you see, I can't accuse them without proof. But I know this, that the horseshoe was in my box before I wint out to get some things for The Barry."

"You went out for him?"

"Yes, surr, and it's my opinion that he sint me out to get rid of me, that he might stale out o' my box the thing that 'ud get me ten goulden sovereigns directly the Englishman comes this way ag'in."

And he spoke this in a voice, as if he had been suddenly roused to furious indignation.

The schoolmaster fixed a stern look on O'Grady as he asked—

"And what proof have you of this?"

"Shure, and I'll ask your honour to search the bhoys' boxes; excuse me, masther dear, the young jintlemen's boxes, and then you'll find I've not been tilling an ontroth."

Thaddeus O'Shaughnessy, very stern and pale, turned to Pat O'Connor and The Barry.

"Now, then, Masters O'Connor and Barry, what have you to say to this?"

The Barry and his friend at once advanced.

"I think I can explain all the first part of the accusation," said the former, "but as to what he has told you about the golden horseshoe, I know not what it means."

"Speak, then," said O'Shaughnessy, "and,

for the honour of the school, let me hear you disprove this terrible accusation."

The Barry thought a moment.

"Why do you hesitate?" said O'Shaughnessy, nervously.

"Because, sir," he said, "because I was considering whether I should tell you before the whole school, or whether I should ask a private interview."

"And which do you desire?"

"Well, sir," replied The Barry, "as Mat O'Grady has made the accusation before my schoolmates, I'll answer him before them, both for myself and Pat O'Connor."

A murmur of approbation rose from the assembled scholars.

A murmur which the schoolmaster did not attempt to repress.

"I am glad to hear you speak so," said he; "come, tell me all, and keep back nothing."

With pale face and beating heart, but with a loud, clear voice, The Barry told his story.

The accidental meeting on the mountains —the conversation he had overheard between O'Grady and Rory O'Neil—the search for the papers in the serving-man's room—all was told with a truthfulness which could not but impress itself on the mind of Thaddeus O'Shaughnessy.

However, he could not avoid being struck with one thing.

Whatever was the truth, he saw that The Barry and Pat O'Connor had placed themselves in a most cruel position.

"You have acted most imprudently, to say nothing more," he said, "but, in regard to this golden horseshoe, I know it well. Did you take it?"

"We never heard of it before," chorussed the two lads.

"Then, of course, you don't mind your boxes being searched?"

"Certainly not," replied The Barry, in some indignation.

"Very well, then," said Thaddeus, "come both of you with me; and you, O'Grady, also."

The latter, as the schoolmaster spoke, could scarcely repress the malignant smile of satisfaction which forced itself upon his face; but, with hung head, as if he was going to do some wrong deed to the "young jintlemen" of the academy against his will, he followed the schoolmaster and the two scholars.

On reaching the bedroom where both the friends slept, Thaddeus directed Pat to open his box first.

Then, with hands trembling more than the schoolboys' would have done, he began turning over the things.

At length, with a gasping cry—a cry which seemed to come from his very heart, he leaped up.

"Heaven!" he cried, "what is the meaning of this, Master O'Connor? Here is the golden horseshoe."

Pat O'Connor naturally turned deadly pale at this.

But, in an instant, the red flush of indignation succeeded.

"This is a disgraceful and infamous conspiracy to ruin me," he cried.

"We'll say no more about it now," said the schoolmaster; "let us go to the schoolroom, or rather to your room, O'Grady."

The Barry, before he quitted the bedchamber, grasped O'Connor by the hand.

"You know that I believe you innocent—in fact, you are innocent," he cried, aloud, "and come what may, I will stand by you."

On reaching the room of the serving-man, O'Shaughnessy said—

"Now then, O'Grady, where are these papers?"

O'Grady was dumbfounded.

He had not expected this.

His cunning had failed him after all.

"Shure, and if there are papers here, that makes no difference at all, at all," he said; "the papers may have been the excuse; but sartin it is, surr, that the horseshoe has bin stolen, and it has been found in Masther O'Connor's box."

"Yes; but let us see these papers, that I may know you have them."

O'Grady thought a moment.

Then he said, firmly—

"I refuse to show them, surr."

"Very well," returned Thaddeus O'Shaughnessy, quietly, "let us return to the schoolroom."

O'Grady, cunning as he was, had not even yet studied his master sufficiently.

If he had, he would have known that he meant a great deal by his quiet manner.

On reaching the room, he reseated himself at his desk, and said—

"Well, it seems that the horseshoe——"

As he spoke, there was a rush of feet, and Reginald Graham came up to his master, breathless and half frightened.

"Pray excuse me, sir, for being so rude as to interrupt you; but, if I didn't speak now, you'd think that I had spoken because of what you said yourself. If you have found the horseshoe in the box of either Pat O'Connor or The Barry, I can tell you how it came there."

Mat O'Grady gave a slight start as he heard this.

A start which was not lost upon the schoolmaster.

"Pray tell me then," he said to the young English boy; "pray tell me, for I shall be glad indeed to be sure that none of my young gentlemen would be guilty of such an action."

"Well, sir," said Reginald Graham, "I must confess that I and Tim Desmond have no business to be in the dormitory where Pat O'Connor and The Barry sleep; but I don't mind being punished for that now, for it seems as if Providence had sent us there for a purpose."

"Go on, my boy," said Thaddeus O'Shaughnessy, kindly.

"We went into the room," pursued Graham, "because somebody there—I can't tell who, sir, if you don't mind—asked us in to take some cake and ginger wine. While we were having this, we heard someone coming along the corridor, and so we put out the light, and we two hid under the bed. Presently the door opened, and O'Grady came in. He stood listening a few moments, to hear if we were all asleep, and then, going to Pat O'Connor's box, he opened it with a false key. Then he took something shining from the pocket of his waistcoat, and placed it in the box. This both I and Tim Desmond saw plainly."

"This is a most extraordinary story," said Thaddeus O'Shaughnessy; "is this correct, Tim Desmond?"

"Yes, sir," said the boy.

"And how can you prove that you are correct?" asked their master.

"In the first place, sir," said Reginald Graham, proudly, "I have given my word that it is true; in the second place, in his hurry, when he heard one of the boys move in his bed, he dropped from his pocket this paper."

As Reginald spoke, and handed a document to the master, Mat O'Grady eyed it with a greedy look as if he would have pounced upon it.

But Thaddeus took it quickly though quietly, and held it in an iron grip.

"Hold the door," said he, loudly. "Pat O'Connor and Barry, see that no one leaves the schoolroom."

The two boys leaped to do his bidding.

They saw, and at any rate felt convinced that Mat O'Grady's game was up.

Thaddeus quickly glanced over the document.

"With this paper and its contents," he said, "I have nothing to do. But this I do say, that with this as a corollary, the evidence of Reginald Graham and Timothy Desmond enables me to say that I believe both. Pat O'Connor and The Barry entirely innocent of this foul charge. And more than this," he added, turning to Mat O'Grady, "I believe you to be guilty of a theft; and, by this letter, you are preparing for a murder."

Mat made violent efforts to repress his emotion.

"You are prejudiced, masther dear," said he. "Shure, and I thought, surr, you'd be afther takin' a poor bhoy's part when he's wronged."

Thaddeus rose to his full height.

His eyes were ablaze with rage, and Mat saw plainly that he was determined to throw off the thraldom to which his unwilling oath had doomed him for a time.

"Mat O'Grady," he said, "I shall deliver you now into the power of the law. Whatever you may imagine may be the reasons which will prevent me from appearing against you, you will find yourself mistaken. Pat O'Connor," he added, turning to our hero, "go fetch me a constable."

"And me papers, surr," cried Mike, "I hope I may have them?"

"Your box will be delivered over to the authorities just as it is," returned the schoolmaster as Pat quitted the room. "I have no further power over that or you."

As luck would have it, Pat, as he quitted the school, met two of the police descending the mountain side.

In a few minutes, therefore, they were within the schoolroom.

They bowed as they entered.

Everyone near Ballynara respected Thaddeus O'Shaughnessy.

"What is it, sir?" asked one.

"Well, Mr. Callaghan," said Thaddeus, "I charge this man, O'Grady, my serving-man, with the theft of certain papers, contained at this moment in his box, and also with being in possession of a document which proves that he is accessory before the fact to a hideous murder."

"What have you to say to this, Mat O'Grady?" said Callaghan; "of coorse ye need say nothing unless ye like."

"Then I'll just say nothing, shure, but this," said Mat O'Grady, "that I've no papers at all, and that ye can see by going up and inspecting me box. And as for the paper that the masther there houlds in his hand, shure no one ever saw it in my possession. And it's a lie, sir, altogether that I ivir drimt of doing anyone any harum."

And he made a most ridiculous gesture, which he thought represented a bow.

Thaddeus O'Shaughnessy was now utterly amazed by the fellow's impudence.

He would not have been so, however, had he seen the extraordinary glance of intelligence which passed between him and Figs.

The latter had caught the eye of the serving-man, and he had at once quitted the room.

And now, as Thaddeus looked at the cool assurance of the man, he for a moment felt staggered.

"Very well," he said, "as you say there are no papers in your box, we will have an examination."

They were absent only a few moments.

Then Thaddeus returned with a puzzled air.

"Pat O'Connor, and you, Barry," he said, "I can't help believing the truth of what you say, but there are no papers there now."

"I can solemnly swear," said Pat O'Connor, "and so also can The Barry, that they were there last night. We had them in our hands."

"I do not disbelieve you," returned Thaddeus; "but there is some mysterious and evil influence at work in the school."

"Well, what say ye, sir?" asked Constable Callaghan, "shall we still take this man into custody?"

"Yes; I will be responsible for the charge; take him away. Here is the letter which two of my boys saw him drop from his pocket in one of the dormitories, while he was opening Master O'Connor's box with a false key."

"Very well, sir," said the constable, "I will take him."

"Shure, and it's meself will go wid a light heart," cried O'Grady, "and I reckon that I'll not be in gaol four-and-twenty hours."

"Yes; and if I'd my way, you shouldn't have the time given ye to get there," replied the constable. "I believe you're about the most sneaking, underhanded, treacherous rascal on the whole of the countryside. Come on."

With a wild jig, the daring fellow prepared to quit the room.

"Good-bye, Mr. O'Shaughnessy," he said, "good-bye, surr. It'll not be long before we meet in Ballynara gaol."

O'Shaughnessy knew well what O'Grady meant.

So also did Figs and Laurence McMahon.

All three turned slightly pale, but the constables observed it not.

They were busy handcuffing their prisoner.

"It will be necessary for you, Mr. O'Shaughnessy," said Callaghan, "to come with us, and also the two young gentlemen who saw the paper fall. We shall just have time now to reach the courthouse, and the magistrates can take the depositions at once."

"Very well," said O'Shaughnessy, "I will leave you, Mr. Finnigan, and you, Mr. McMahon, in charge of the school. Come, Master Desmond, and Master Graham, we'll start at once."

As the prisoner passed out, and Thaddeus followed, Figs touched the schoolmaster on the arm, and beckoned him aside, to where McMahon was standing.

Here the two ushers made a peculiar sign.

A sign which was quite understood by O'Shaughnessy.

It was that of the United Irishmen.

"I knew this before," he said, in a low tone, "but what do you wish ?"

"I merely say that this blaggard will betray the whole society," said Figs.

"Which means death," said McMahon.

"It does," said O'Shaughnessy; "but what then ? I will never break my oath, even to save my life."

"Mr. O'Shaughnessy, you've been a kind and good masther to me," said the Irish tutor, "and I will save ye."

Thaddeus shook him by the hand, and quickly passed out with the constables.

"How will you do this, Finnigan ?" asked McMahon.

"Never mind, depend upon *me*," cried the brave little man; and his face lighted up with a radiance of courage which made his ugly features look handsome.

"When will you do this?"

"To-night; after school, I'll be off to the village, and give the word."

CHAPTER XVII

THE RESCUE AND THE DEATH.

As soon as darkness had begun to fall over the hills of Ballynara, Figs quitted the school, and hastened up the mountain path.

His first destination was the cabin of Terence O'Rafferty.

He whispered only two words through the open cabin-door; and yet Terence, who was enjoying his "potteen" and his "dhudeen," by his peat fire, at once jumped up, put on his caubeen, took his shillelagh and his great horse-pistol, and passed out into the misty night.

And yet the words which had produced this effect were but simple.

They were merely—"Landress Green."

But he well knew their significance, and he hurried away.

In like manner Figs visited all the cabins on the countryside, and from every one of them there issued a hale and hearty man, ready for the fight.

Landress Green was a spot in the valley, just beyond the place where the fair of Ballynara had been held.

It was a wide piece of exquisitely green turf, and in the centre was a huge tree, whose wide-spreading branches would have sheltered a hundred people from the rain.

Here, as the darkness fell, the men began to gather; and, in a wondrously short space of time, the place was covered with figures, clad in the odd-looking cloaks which distinguished the Irish peasantry.

Figs and McMahon were there, and so were Terence O'Rafferty and Laurence Raturier, the leader of the movement.

A few words were exchanged between the head men.

Then a whisper was sent round the crowd, and the men began to move rapidly away in the direction of the town.

They did not go, however, in large bodies, but in twos and threes, and sometimes sixes.

Meanwhile, while this strange multitude was advancing—resolute and silent—silent as a throng of shades—Mat O'Grady was sitting in his cell in "Longworth's Cage," as the peasantry had named the gaol, in "honour" of its governor.

He had appeared before the magistrate, and a short half-hour's examination had resulted in a remand.

He was not alone in his place of confinement.

A thick, burly man sat opposite to him, on the bench, at the middle table.

He had a shock head of red hair, and a bullet head, and his mouth and his eyes showed plainly by their expression that he had made up his mind resolutely for the worst.

"You're taking it mighty easy, Mister O'Grady," he said, presently; "I'm thinking that ye'll be less light-hearted when ye're jist about to dance on nothing up at the top of the gaol."

Mat O'Grady responded with a loud laugh.

"Are ye thinkin' that I'm goin' to swing for it ?" he asked.

"Well, it seems extremely loikely, in the style that you're going on," said the man; "why, you haven't a ghost of a defince."

"Defince ! to what ?"

"Why, to the litther as was produced aginst ye," said the other, "where you plainly say that you're willing to lead Henry Ramsden into a trap, that he may be murdered."

"Ah' shure, and that's not a swinging matther at all, at all," cried O'Grady; "and, if it was, I'm not afrade."

"Why ?"

"Becos, shure, the bhoys will save me, or I'll turn Queen's evidence on the lot."

"And be shot like a cur, as ye'd be, the instant you come out o' the cage," said the other; "and bad luck to ye, for a coward, I'd be the one to do it !"

"Ah, will," laughed O'Grady, "bitther run the risk of a bullet than be shure of the rope. But whisht, now, Mahoney, for a fool !"

He beckoned to his companion, who at once leant over the table.

"Can I thrust ye ?" he said.

"Shure, and ye can be afther doing jist as ye plase," returned the other.

"Well, and bad luck to ye, if ye bethray me !" said O'Grady; "the bhoys will be here to-night."

"Well, and what then ?"

"They'll brake open the gaol, and set us free."

"And it's meself'll be glad to step out in the fresh air again," said Mahoney; "but I'm thinking, while they're breaking in, they'll be taking us out some other way."

"Ah, ye were always a croaker!" cried O'Grady. "Hark! ah, good luck to the sound!"

A voice, in a low and melancholy tone, began chanting, below the window—

"The harp that once in Tara's halls
The soul of music shed."

O'Grady leaped up, and began dancing a jig.

"Hurroo! hurroo!" he cried, with suppressed excitement, "it's Figs!"

"Are ye mad?" exclaimed Mahoney, never altering his position. "Who's Figs?"

"Shure, and ain't he the usher up at the academy?" cried O'Grady.

"And what thin?"

"He's one of us."

"Well?"

"And he's sworn to save me—he tould me so in the coort."

What could he mean?

Was not Figs pledged to save O'Shaughnessy against O'Grady?

"Oh, will, then," said Mahoney, whom it took a great deal to rouse, "will, then, if the bhoys arc comin', I'm glad, and'll help to the utmost. But—bad cess to them all, nowadays!—they don't seem to have any sperit in them."

At this moment, a blue rocket shot upwards towards the sky, casting a lurid light into the cell.

"There's the signal!" cried Mat O'Grady; and rushing to the window, he gave a long, shrill whistle, and waited anxiously for some answering sound.

The window had no glass in it, being only a hole, crossed by iron bars, and the sound echoed out loudly across the open space in front of the gaol.

It was answered at once; and then Mat O'Grady and Mahoney waited and watched with wildly-beating hearts.

Meanwhile, the Men of the Mountain, as the society sometimes called themselves, had descended from Landress Green, and slowly gathered round the gaol.

Their approach was not noticed.

Though—in consequence of the irritable state of the mind of the peasantry—an extra watchfulness was supposed to be observed, the garrison of Longworth's Cage had dozed, as it were.

And so the Men of the Mountain had descended, and hidden themselves in the shadows of the doorways near, and even behind the buttresses of the prison itself.

Suddenly a roar of voices rent the air.

"Hurroo! hurroo!"

"Owld Ireland for iver!"

"Bring out the prisoner!"

And then Figs advanced and rang the great bell.

Hardly had the echoes died away when a little wicket—or judas, as the French call it—was opened in the gate.

"What are ye afther wantin'?" asked a gruff voice.

"We want the O'Grady. Bring him out at onst!" shouted Terence O'Rafferty.

"Shure and I won't be afther dishturbing the gentleman," said the man, in a voice of irony. "He's in his private room, and he's fast aslape, I'm thinkin'."

It was at this moment that Figs struck up the first verse of "Tara's Halls."

Then followed the rocket.

And then, when O'Grady's whistle had echoed out into the night, there arose one universal shout of anger.

"Will ye bring him out?" cried Figs, in a loud voice.

"No; go away."

"Then we'll take him! and that'll save ye a grate dale o' thruble!" exclaimed Terence O'Rafferty. "Come on, bhoys; bring up the pole."

The men addressed were at the back, and, the rest of the crowd parting to give them room, they advanced to the front, and stood in readiness.

Terence O'Rafferty drew his great pistol from his pocket, and placed the muzzle to the lock.

Then, firing suddenly, he shivered the lock into fragments.

This obstacle removed, there were still formidable bolts, and these it remained for the battering-ram to remove.

The log was of huge dimensions, but the twenty men who held it began to swing it gradually to and fro, until it had attained a momentum.

Then they brought it with a terrific crash against the portal.

The gate was a strong one, and resisted; but from the way in which it creaked and shivered, it was evident that it would soon give way.

Just as the men had begun to swing their missile once more for another terrific blow, a loud voice from within caused them to pause for a few moments.

It was not the voice of the man who had first spoken, but that of Longworth, the governor of the gaol.

"Hold, there!" he cried, in tones which resounded above the din. "What is it ye want?"

"You know well. The release of Mat O'Grady!" cried Laurence Raturier.

"It is impossible. He is left in my charge, and I will die sooner than betray my trust," returned Captain Longworth. "Let me entreat of you to go away quietly. If your friend is innocent, he will have every fairness and justice."

"Aye, Saxon justice!" yelled the crowd. "On to it, my bhoys! Brake it down—burn the cage to the ground!"

The men at once began to swing the huge beam, and again it came with a crash against the door.

In answer, a volley of musketry was fired from the loopholes of the gaol.

But in vain.

Though two or three of the Irishmen were wounded, the blood of the crowd was up, and willing hands were ever ready to take the post of those who were disabled.

Again and again, crash went the huge beam against the door, and at last it gave way with a thundering noise, and rushing in like a mad torrent, the Irishmen dashed into the gaol-yard.

Of course there was a second obstacle here, in the shape of a second door.

But here they were enabled, by keeping well under the wall, to conceal themselves so as to prevent the possibility of their being wounded.

So they could work without being fired on, and the consequence was that in a short space of time the triumphant mob swarmed into the passage of the prison.

CHAPTER XVIII.
SAVED—FOR WHAT?

WHEN once the rushing tide of human beings had entered the gaol, there was no withstanding it.

Up and down the great corridors they swarmed, peering here and there and everywhere in search of Mat O'Grady.

At length, finding that amid the din it was quite impossible to hear any signal that might be given, Terence O'Rafferty gave a long shrill whistle and waited.

"Silence there, bhoys," cried he; "some of ye keep orther there. How the dhevil can I till where Mat O'Grady is, if ye don't let me hear his voice."

The men, who a moment before had been so turbulent, were hushed in a moment.

Terence then gave some whispered directions, and those in the rear formed themselves into a solid mass.

Then the half who were on the stairs following the guidance of Terence, passed up into the second corridor, and there with Figs and their rough leader, they waited.

Then the latter began whistling in a plaintive tone, "The Harp that once in Tara's Halls."

The tune was at once taken up by Mat O'Grady in his cell.

"This way, this way. Hurroo, hurroo!" exclaimed Terence, and with a wild leap he led the way up to the third corridor.

The plaintive notes of the exquisite melody still floated on the air, and in a few moments the cell of the O'Grady was reached.

"At it, bhoys, batther it down," cried O'Rafferty, and Figs, seizing a crowbar from one of the men, commenced operations by hammering away at the door.

Wild with excitement, the crowd soon succeeded in their wish.

The French crowd pulled the Bastille down almost with their hands.

What then was a door in an old gaol, when a wild and excited throng was there to bash it in?

In a few minutes, as it were, Mat O'Grady was standing amid his comrades, smiling and free.

He shook hands with all, and was vociferous in his thanks.

"Come; our task is over," exclaimed Terence; "we'd better be afther makin' off as quickly as possible. Come, Mat, and you, too,

his frind, and get into the middle of the crowd, and there you'll be safe."

Mat and his fellow prisoner at once did as they were directed, and in this manner they began descending the staircase.

There seemed now indeed every chance of their retreat being a triumphant progress.

But it was not to be.

Hardly had they forced their way back into the courtyard when an ominous sound was heard.

The sound of approaching cavalry.

While the crowd was outside and an iron gate and a stone wall interposed between them and the object of their search, the governor spoke big words, but when they had burst into the interior of the gaol, and armed and in numbers, threatened its few defenders, it was another thing.

He was compelled to acknowledge his own inability to check their progress, and he as quickly, therefore, as possible sent off to the neighbouring station to summon the military to his assistance.

The cavalry barracks were at no great distance, and had O'Rafferty and his men been a moment or two later, all would have been up with Mat O'Grady and his friends.

As it was, the tramp of the coming cavalry was not heard until the triumphant mob had reached the door of the prison.

The outer door or gate which led out upon the square.

There was just time now, with skilful arrangement, to escape a conflict with the military.

"Now, lads," cried Terence, "the time for fighting the murtherin' Saxons is not yet come. Don't waste any pricious blood. You there with the prisoners take the nighest road to the mountains, and then, 'iviryone for himself,' as the man said as he ate his neighbour's dish o' praties."

The men lost no time in obeying the orders of the man, who in this daring exploit had placed himself in the position of their leader.

As soon as they reached the gate, they divided themselves into three parties.

Two of these formed lines across the square in the direction of a spot where a narrow thoroughfare led upwards towards the hills.

The third, consisting of six men with Figs at their head, and Mat O'Grady in their midst, passed through the lines, and were soon hastening up towards the mountains.

When these had, as it were, secured their safety, the men in the square broke up everywhere, and in spite of all the efforts of the dragoons to take them, they escaped completely by means of the narrow lanes and alleys, which abounded everywhere.

On reaching a spot about half way up the hills, Figs called a halt.

"It'll not be safe for you to be seen anywhere near at hand, O'Grady," he said, addressing the serving man.

"Shure, and it's thrue for you, Mister Figs," said O'Grady; "the dhivil a bit should I like Mister O'Shaughnessy, or any of his people to see me afore the day comes."

"Well, then," said Figs, who spoke with an eagerness which was quite astonishing, "I

"FIGS STOOD GAZING AT THE MAN HE HAD SLAIN."

think I know a mode of protectin' ye, one better far than hiding away in holes and corners which everyone knows everything about."

"Thrue again for you, Mister Figs," said Mat O'Grady.

"Well, then, dismiss your friends," said the usher; "not even to them will I reveal my secret. Let one of them give you some arms, for we may be molested."

One of the men at once handed over to Mike O'Grady a pistol, and thus armed, he said adieu to his companions, and followed Figs up the hill.

Little did he imagine the terrible fate he was hurrying to meet.

Tim Finnigan spoke not a word.

His mind apparently was intent upon one thing, and though now and again Mat O'Grady asked him a question in regard to their destination, he answered never a syllable

Presently they reached a drear and lonely place—a wide expanse on the very edge of a precipice—on the other side of which there glimmered a faint uncertain light.

Here Tim Finnigan paused.

Turning to Mat O'Grady, he pointed towards the light.

"Do you see yonder lamp," he said, "in the window of a far-off cottage?"

"Yes; shure, and it 'ud be blind I'd be if I didn't," said O'Grady.

"That," said Figs, in a stern, sedate voice, which made Mat somewhat uneasy, "that is the cabin of Mat Burke, one of the honestest lads on the countryside."

"Shure, and I know him well," said O'Grady, "but I am fancyin' it's not likin' me much he is just at this toime."

"Why?"

"Well, I once borrowed a pig of 'im in the noight toime, and he never forguv' me," said Mat, laughing.

"Oh, no matter," said Figs; "if ye say ye come from me, it'll be all right. But before ye go, I've got something to say to ye."

"Somethin' to say to me! Arrah; then talk away till mornin', Mr. Finnigan. Shure, I'd be ongrateful if I didn't listen, when you're the brave boy that helped to save me life."

"Yes, for a purpose," said Figs. "I did'n't save ye because I liked you. I think you're about the most sneaking, black-hearted, treacherous thief that ever disgraced the dear old land of Erin."

"Then why did ye save me, Mister Driedfruit?" said Mat, jeeringly.

"Because," said Tim Finnigan, "I thought I'd like to have the chance of ridding the world of such a villain and deceiver as you. So out with your pistol, step back twelve paces, and we'll take our chance."

"I might have shot ye like a dog, Mr. Finnigan," said Mat, "as we came up the hills, and sorra for me now that I didn't; tell me now though, what do ye want me life for?"

"Because you would betray Thaddeus O'Shaughnessy; because you would cast a blight and a curse on everything you came near," cried Tim Finnigan; "so prepare, for before I can count five, I'll fire."

Mat waited for no more.

He didn't mind a good fight; a good rough and tumble; a good hand-to-hand encounter with a shillelagh.

But to stand here in cold blood, to be popped at like a gentleman in a duel, was not at all after his heart.

So without waiting a moment for Tim Finnigan, he fired straight at the usher's head.

But in his haste and nervousness, he was unable to take a good aim, and the ball whistled past Tim's ear.

"Cowardly murderer!" exclaimed Figs, and taking deliberate aim, before the horror-stricken wretch could fly, he pulled the trigger.

The ball took effect.

But not in a place where a wound would be mortal.

"Ah, I've shtrength now to pay ye for this," yelled Mat, and dashing forward, after the first staggering step he took after the blow in the left shoulder, he raised his shillelagh.

Figs had no time to reload his pistol.

He therefore clubbed it, and awaited as calmly as he could, the onslaught of the man, whose eyes now gleamed with fury.

Mat felt, indeed, like an enraged wild beast.

The pain of his wound maddened him; and the first blow, if it had struck his foe, would have ended all his woes in this world.

But Tim's agility saved him, and as Mat O'Grady staggered forward, after missing his aim, he caught him a blow on the side of his head, which sent him reeling.

Then Figs closed.

He was, as I have said before, a little wiry man.

But it would certainly have seemed to any one that it was madness to risk a close contest with a person of O'Grady's strength.

But his blood was up now.

The brave little man had taken an oath to himself that either he or O'Grady should die that night in a fair fight.

He knew the inestimable injury that this man had it in his power to do the O'Shaughnessy; and he had resolved to risk his own life in the trial.

Urged to the fight by a superhuman influence, as it were, he grasped Mat O'Grady by the waist and tried to throw him.

In this he failed.

And, as Mat regained a firm position on his feet, he saw that the man was endeavouring to draw a knife from his pocket.

There was nothing now to be done but to fight for dear life.

Figs was by no means a cold-blooded man.

But in this instant a thought flashed across his mind.

He remembered that in his breast pocket was a clasped knife which had been given him by Kathleen.

Here then would be the means of putting him on an equality with his adversary.

Suddenly starting back, and releasing his foe from his grasp, he drew his knife, just as the blade of O'Grady's weapon flashed in the moonlight.

"Ha, villain, I am even with ye!" he shouted.

Mat uttered a loud curse, and raised his weapon.

Tim Finnigan did the same.

For an instant the two men stood facing one another with a terrific and deadly determination written in their faces.

Then there was a sudden rush; and anyone who had seen the conflict would have beheld nothing but a writhing mass, and the flash, flash of the knives.

They were on the edge of the precipice, and a false step at any moment might be their death.

But in spite of this—in spite of the fate which stared them in the face, Tim still grappled his foe.

Bloodstained, wounded, stabbed in every part, the two men fought on their ghastly fight.

At length, an accident gave Figs the supremacy.

Just as they were tottering on the very brink of the abyss, Mat O'Grady drew back an instant; and quick as a flash of lightning the blade, which Kathleen had given her lover, was buried in O'Grady's heart.

Not one sound gave he.

Not a groan.

Down he fell like a bullock beneath the pole-axe of the slaughterman, and lay still on the chalk cliff.

Tim Figs stood for a moment gazing at the man he had slain.

With a shudder he dropped his knife on the body of O'Grady. Then he took out his handkerchief, wiped his bloodstained hands, and took his way slowly down the mountain.

"Let him lie there," he cried, "till some of the fellows find him. They'll know it was done in fair fight."

That might be, brave little Tim Finnigan; but you forget that the knife inscribed with your name is sticking in the dead man's breast.

CHAPTER XIX.

THE NEW SERVING-MAN—A CONFESSION.

OUR readers will, of course, remember that when Mat O'Grady accused Pat O'Connor and The Barry of theft, and the papers were mentioned, he had cast a sidelong look at Figs, who had at once quitted the room.

It was not in the interest of O'Grady, however, that he did this.

It was in the interest of the terrible society, which was known as the "Men of the Mountain—the Brotherhood of the United Irishmen."

Great was the consternation of The Barry when he heard that the papers were gone.

But greater still was the alarm of both him and his friend, Pat O'Connor, when they heard of the O'Grady's escape and death.

"Fate, indeed, seems to fight against us," he said, as he passed down the grounds with his friend towards the Shannon's banks. "I had, as it were, Fortune within my grasp, and now—all—all has again gone."

"Fear not," said Pat, "the papers cannot have been destroyed. Mat O'Grady had not the chance."

"But others may have done so," said The Barry, sadly, "and those others may have an interest in my destruction. Remember Rory O'Neil."

"I do remember him, and his conversation with O'Grady," said Pat, "and I know this, also, Mat had no chance of communicating with Rory."

"Then the papers——"

"Must have been taken by someone in this house," said Pat, "and, as they are of value, do not fear that they will be destroyed."

"Perhaps you are right," said The Barry. "I will bide my time."

About a week after the death of Mat O'Grady, a new serving-man entered upon his situation at the Shannon Academy.

He was just eighteen, stood six feet in height, with low, sloping shoulders and a lanky form, as if he had grown out of his strength.

He had light, wavy hair, a soft, insipid face, and a sort of shambling walk, which was made worse by a way he had of drooping his head forward.

"Well," said Thaddeus, when he had set eyes on this peculiar specimen of humanity, "well, and what is your name?"

"Willie, surr."

"Willie what?"

"Me name's not Willie Watt, surr."

"Oh, don't be foolish if ye can help it," said the schoolmaster; "what other name have ye got?"

"Well, surr, I'm not able to say how far I'm entitled to it," said the lad, "but to the bist of my belief, the godmothers and godfathers, at me baptism, christened me Willie Curtis."

"Willie Curtis, then, what's your age?"

"It's about aiteen, I'm thinking, but the parish clerk of——"

"That will do. I've read the letter of recommendation which you sent me from Father Clarry, and it is in every way satisfactory. When can you come?"

"I'm here at the prisint moment, surr," said Willie Curtis, smiling.

"But haven't you any clothes to bring?" asked Thaddeus.

"Well, surr, you see there was a fire not long ago——"

Thaddeus laughed.

"There, that will do," said he, "I'm quite used to stories of fires. I'll provide ye with clothes. Be honest and industrious, and ye'll find this a good home."

On the evening on which this new specimen arrived, Thaddeus O'Shaughnessy dismissed him to bed early, for he seemed tired out by his long walk from Dartpoint.

He had not been absent many minutes when he returned with a doleful look in his face.

"Shure, masther, may I be afther spaking to ye a moment?" he said.

Pat O'Connor and Harry Marshall were saying "good night," when the Irish lad came down, and they could scarcely help bursting with laughter as they saw his woebegone visage.

"Why, what is the matter, Willie?" asked the schoolmaster, keeping down his laughter with difficulty.

"Shure, surr, I wint up to the corridor. as ye call it," said the Irish boy, "and dhivil a bit of a room could I find that wasn't full of bhoys a-grinning at me."

Thaddeus smiled.

"Pat," he said, "you're going to bed; just see this fellow to his room. I'm afraid the lads have been having some fun with him."

The Irish lad pulled his forelock, and, preceded by Pat and Harry Marshall, he ascended the stairs.

On reaching the corridor Pat said—

"Stop here a moment, Willie; I'll go and see which is your room. Don't move away from here, for you may lose your way. There are a hundred ways from this place. Come, Harry."

Marshall followed his companion at once.

"What are ye up to, Pat?" said he.

"A lark, of course."

"With Willie?"

"Yes; see here's the bath room," said our hero; "now then, get some sheets and blankets, and if we don't have a spree with him this time, my name isn't Pat O'Connor."

And so, leaving the greenhorn to wait at the head of the stairs, they crept on to the end of the corridor.

Meanwhile, Thaddeus O'Shaughnessy, as soon as the two scholars had gone, called Tim Finnigan.

"Mr. Finnigan," he said, "I have heard to-night something which has distressed me sorely."

Figs looked conscious.

He thought he was about to speak of Kathleen.

"What is it, sir?" he asked.

"I mean in regard to O'Grady's death," said Thaddeus.

Figs turned pale now.

"In regard to that," said he, "I have kept silent up to this; but if it is necessary, for my own reputation, to tell you, I must."

"Listen then," said O'Shaughnessy, as he closed the door, "listen, and I will explain. Sit down, and we will have a glass of grog together."

It was the pale visage of the usher that made him say this.

When the grog had been mixed, which was a matter of only a few moments, Thaddeus O'Shaughnessy leaned over and said—

"Finnigan, I have in my mind a strange suspicion."

"What is it, sir?"

"That you killed O'Grady."

A sad smile illumined the face of the usher.

"I know you wouldn't say that, sir, if you thought me guilty of unfair play," said Tim Finnigan.

"Then you confess you did kill him."

"Yes, I did; but, listen, and I'll tell you how and why."

The schoolmaster listened attentively.

When the brave little man had finished speaking, Thaddeus grasped him warmly by the hand.

"You are a good and courageous fellow," he said, "and what you have done is not only for my good, but for the good of all."

"But, tell me, sir," said Figs, "now that I have confessed, how did such news reach you?"

"Your knife was found sticking in his heart."

"Great Heaven!" exclaimed Tim Finnigan, "what a fool I was. But, tell me, was it found by the police?"

"No; only by the United Irishmen. They won't tell tales on one of their number; but, as sure as fate, they will look after you."

"They will, I suppose," said Tim Finnigan gloomily.

"You will be cited before their tribunal," said the schoolmaster; "if you are, will you take my advice?"

"What is that?"

"Refuse to appear."

"And be shot down the first time I appear beyond the walls of the school."

"Not so; they will not dare to shoot you in daylight, and they will not dare either to come to the school to attack you," said Thaddeus, "so all you have to do is never to show yourself at night."

Figs made a rueful face.

"And never see my Kathleen, sir," he said; "that's a thing I'd rather risk my life than do."

The schoolmaster laughed outright at the woebegone expression on the face of the tutor.

"Why, if that is the only matter that's troubling you, Finnigan," he said, "I fancy I see an easy way out of the difficulty."

"And what's that, sir?" said Figs, brightening up at once.

"You're going to marry Kathleen Moriarty, are ye not?" asked Thaddeus.

"I hope I am that same," said Figs enthusiastically.

"And when?"

"Kathleen told me it was for the thirtieth of next month, sir, when I met her up at Ballynara fair."

"Very well, and I'll give her away, and dance at your wedding too, Finnigan," cried O'Shaughnessy; "so, if it's sighing for Kathleen you'll be during this and the thirtieth, why, let her come and see ye as often as ye likes, and she'll be welcome."

Just at this instant, as Figs was about to express his gratitude in fervent terms, a cry echoed through the big house.

A wild and unearthly cry, such as would have startled the Seven Sleepers.

"Why, what on earth can that be?" cried O'Shaughnessy, as he leaped up. "I hope there is not another upset in store for me and the school."

CHAPTER XX.

COLD WATER CURE.

To explain the shout that rang through the house, we must return for a time to the moment when Harry Marshall and Pat O'Connor left the new serving man on the top of the stairs, while they went to look to his bedroom.

As soon as they reached the end of the corridor, Pat leaned over towards Marshall, saying in a low voice—

"I say, Harry, I'm going to fit up the bathroom for him."

"But what's the use of these sheets and blankets when there's no bed?"

"Ye'll find there will be a bed, and a jolly

soft one too," said Pat ; "come, be quick, or you'll excite suspicion."

The bath-room was an apartment not by any means badly furnished.

If it had a bedstead in it, it would have passed well for one of the dormitories.

In the centre was a bath, a large and long one, capable of containing even the form of Thaddeus O'Shaughnessy himself.

"Come on, Harry, be quick," cried Pat O'Connor ; "put the lamp down, and help me to put the bath on these chairs."

"Well, what you're up to I don't know," said Harry, laughing, "but, whatever it is, I'm in for it."

He placed the lamp down upon the table ; and then assisted his friend to raise the large and heavy bath upon the top of the chairs.

"Now, then," said Pat, "turn on the hose."

In a few minutes the bath was filled.

"Now for the sheets," said Pat.

Harry could not help him.

He simply looked on in wonder.

Pat took one sheet, laid it carefully over the bath so that it did not touch the water, and then secured it carefully with pins, so that it should not become wet.

Then he arranged a feather pillow, by fastening it with strong pins also.

Then the other sheet, and the blanket and the counterpane were disposed carefully, and turned down comfortably.

"There, doesn't that look jolly ?" cried Pat.

Harry Marshall could not answer.

He was too suffocating with laughter to utter a sound.

"I'm sure," continued Pat, as he gave the bed an extra pat down to make it look level "I'm sure now he'll find that beautiful and soft."

In a few moments the boys quitted the room, and hastened to the spot where they had left the serving-man.

"Now, then, Willie Curtis," cried Pat, "you'll have to stand such a roaring lot of the 'crater' to-morrow, for I've had to turn out a lot of bhoys for ye. Good night—there—the third door on the left—that's your room."

"And it's myself will be always grateful to yer honour," said Willie, pulling his forelock and bowing as low as he could, "and if a small dhrop——"

He had his hands in his pocket as he spoke.

But the "bhoys" were gone.

They slunk away as if they were afraid of the schoolmaster, and Willie Curtis, quite satisfied now, retired to the bath-room.

"Shure, then," he cried, "it's me mother's heart would be glad if she only saw me in sich a place."

"And this is illigant, then," he said, "sich purty chairs, and sich purty tables, and curtains and all. Shure, and a bed, too, fit for a saint."

As his eyes wandered to the snow-white bed linen, he rose from his chair and touched them daintily with his hand.

"Arrah ! now," he murmured, as he folded back the clothes, "arrah, now, if the masther isn't the best bhoy on all Shannon-side. To think now that he'd plaice a poor gossoon like me in sich an illigant bed. Ah ! shure, and

I'll have a small porshun of the crater before I enter sich a proper plaice as that."

Though only eighteen years of age, Willie could take his glass with the oldest of the "bhoys" that frequented the dram shops in Dublin.

But he knew nothing of the whisky down Shannon-way.

What he had drunk, even in the best of "poteen shops" in the "fair city," had been tortured, and twisted, and bedevilled until it tasted more like a mixture of pepper, bad gin, weak brandy, and Cape sherry, than the true stuff from up the mountains.

And now, having obtained "a dhrop of the rale crater" from a friend on the road, he drew out a glass without a stem and prepared to enjoy himself.

"Ah ! shure," he cried, as he surveyed the glass, "this is a true Irishman's friend. He can't stand him down for fear of upsettin' him, and so he must tip it up wid the little finger."

And, suiting the action to the word, he tossed off a brimming glass of the golden fluid.

He staggered back in his chair, as he drank it, and spluttered violently.

"Oh ! and it's the land of whisky I must be in, shure," he stammered ; "oh ! and it's enough to choke all the Dublin bhoys that ever existed."

But it didn't seem to have any choking effect on him.

Having paved the way, or, in other words, made it fireproof, he gave a second gulp, and swallowed number two glass without any trouble.

Then a smile of idiotic pleasure beamed over his face.

The whisky, in fact, was taking its accustomed effect.

"Ah ! if I'd only the chake now, I'd sing a good shong," he cried, "and it 'ud be a jolly one too.

"'It's just the proper song.
That is the size of it.'

"Ah ! there, there, if I ain't singin' afther all, and me only a few hours in the pla-ace. Oh ! Willie Curtis, Willie Curtis, if ye only knew what a silly, long-legged, empty-headed omadhaun you looked just at this prisint moment, ye'd never be sinding your powtrat to all the gyurls, and a-thinkin' they were in love wid ye."

These last remarks were called forth by his catching sight of his pale face in the mirror opposite to him.

And sure enough it was no pleasant sight.

His face was white, his hair looked limp, his eyes were fishy.

"And it's time that ye were goin' to bid, I'm thinking, Willie," he said ; "ye're looking for from graiceful, and—yes—a little wee dhrap more of comfort, and then hey for bid, before old Father Clarry can count Peter's pence on a Saturday."

He staggered to his feet ; but, quickly recovering himself, and having before him a dim idea of the position in which he stood in the academy, he approached with some degree of quietude "the bed" in which he was to lie.

As he did so he started back in horror.

It had never struck him before what a terrible resemblance the bath bore to a coffin, now that it was covered with the white counterpane.

"Arrah! thin," he cried. as he reeled back, "is it a coffin they've been after givin' me to slape in? Shure, and there will be toime enough for that by-and-bye, I'm hoping, when I've had a saison of good luck and so forth. Bad cess to the man that put this thrick upon me."

Then, gathering courage, he approached the bed once more.

"Ah! thin, the thick-headed ass that I am, the stoopid, moony omadhaun, when it's an illigant round hid the bid's got," he cried; "here goes."

He began at once to undress, and was soon reduced to his shirt.

Now, unless Pat O'Connor had taken due precautions, all would have been spoiled; for, in his drunken folly, the new serving-man would have upset the bath.

However, he had so arranged that the man could step on a low stool, then on a chair, and then into the bath.

Impatient indeed were the boys for the *dénouement*.

As they lay in the dormitory adjoining, it seemed hours upon hours before the unfortunate fellow went to bed.

But at last the time arrived.

Steadying himself gradually, Willie Curtis got upon the stool, then stepped on the chair, and then, with a kind of luxurious roll, got into bed.

Of course what followed was only of an instant's duration.

He fell, sheet and all, into the bath of icy water, and there, with his feet kicking, and his hands wildly clutching at the air, he lay and yelled.

"Arrah! save us. Oh! and it's drownded altogether I am," he shouted. "Oh! ochone! ochone! Mr. O'Shaughnessy, have mercy—have——"

"Mercy! have we a madman here?" cried the schoolmaster, in a stern voice, as he entered. "What the devil, sir, are you doing in my bath-room?"

"Oh! save me, save me, Mr. O'Shaughnessy," cried Willie, still buffeting imaginary waves, and fighting imaginary enemies. "Oh! is it lookin' on ye're goin' to be, whin a poor bhoy's drownდin' fast?"

"Here, Mr. Finnigan," said Thaddeus, to the usher, who was bursting with laughter behind him, "help me to get this madman out of the bath, and then we'll leave him to do the best he can in his own bedroom. He's drunk."

They immediately proceeded to drag the wretched man out of the cold water, and stood him shivering, and with a shirt clinging to him like a skin, on the floor.

The shock, or rather the combined effect of the two shocks, sobered him.

He glanced vacantly from Figs to Thaddeus O'Shaughnessy, and from Thaddeus O'Shaughnessy to Figs.

"Will—will then; sorra, sorra for me," he cried, and dropped on his knees.

"Rise up," cried Thaddeus; "don't kneel to me."

Willie staggered to his feet.

"Oh! shure, and it's the great shame," said he, "to sarve a poor bhoy like this."

"I don't think anyone's to blame but yourself," said Thaddeus, still laughing, as he saw the whisky bottle on the table; "it seems to me you have been drinking yourself stupid, and have made your bed in the bath."

"Is it a bath you call this thing, surr?" said the shivering lad; "shure, and I don't know how it comes to have shates and blankets on it, thin; it's half dead I am, surr."

The cold bath had somewhat sobered him; and now, for the first time, he remembered that Pat O'Connor and Harry Marshall had been the ones to conduct him to his room.

"Ah! shure I've hit the right nail on the head now, Mister O'Shaughnessy," said he; "it's the young jintlemen that brought me here. They've been up to their little larks wid me."

A look of intelligence passed between Figs and the schoolmaster.

"If it is so, I will inquire into it," said Thaddeus; "but, come, slip something on, and then I'll show you your room."

The Irish lad soon divested himself of his shirt, and placed on his waistcoat and breeches.

Then he was conducted along the corridor, and shown his room.

Arrived here he pretended to have entirely recovered his temper, and his face beamed with smiles as he saw the comfortable bed prepared for him.

"Ah! thin, it's thankful I am that I came to this same pla-ace, surr," he said, "and I dare say the young jintlemen did it for a lark, and I hope you won't be after saying anything about it, surr."

"I will see; I will see," said O'Shaughnessy, "and now that you are in a comfortable room, I trust I shall hear no more disturbance."

"Not from me, surr," he said, humbly; "it's meself that is grateful to ye, Mr. O'Shaughnessy, and I'll do my best to sarve ye, surr."

As soon as the schoolmaster and the tutor had taken their departure, Willie closed his door and slid into bed.

"Bad cess to the murtherin' young varmints," he said, as he snuggled himself under the warm clothes; "it's even I'll be wid 'em yet; and the masther thinks I'd be afther forgivin' 'em. I'll pay 'em out before I've been here a wake."

On the next day he looked for his opportunity.

But it did not come.

Of course his idea of revenge did not take the form of a lark.

It was to be a real revenge—something that would do them injury.

On the third day an idea struck him, and in the grey of the morning he went down to the boat-house.

It was a half holiday, and he knew that Pat O'Connor and his friend Marshall would be sure to go out for a row.

Carefully watching to see that nobody was about, he entered with the key, which he had abstracted from the room of Joe Cronin, the gardener; and, having locked himself in, he hauled on one side the skiff that the two boys invariably used.

It was called "The Little Mermaid," and was certainly one of the prettiest of the school-boats.

Turning it bottom upwards, he carefully, with a large gimlet, bored three or four holes sufficiently big to admit the water rapidly, but, not with a rush.

Then he replaced the boat as nearly as possible as he found it, and quitted the shed.

He imagined he was unwatched.

But he was wrong.

As he entered the boat-house he was descried by one who, at first, looked only for curiosity, but who soon looked eagerly to ascertain the meaning of this strange proceeding.

This was Reginald Graham, the English boy, who had been brought from the mountains by Pat O'Connor.

He had taken no particular notice of Willie Curtis at first, as he slunk along the garden; but, on seeing him enter the boat-house, where he knew he had no business, he drew himself to the little opening that served for a window, and peeped in.

He could scarcely understand what the man was doing at first.

But when Curtis replaced the boat and rose to his feet, he muttered to himself—

"Now I think the bhoys will get the worst of it. Now for my revenge!"

Looking around, Willie muttered aloud—

"Shure, and when they played that dirthy thrick on me, they nivir expected this. It's a bath that they were afther giving me in the school, but it's a deeper bath they'll be having themselves, I'm thinking; and," he added, with set teeth, "it 'ud be a good job if they got to the bottom and nivir got up again, the thavin' young omadhauns."

Reginald smiled to himself.

"I think you'll be in the wrong box," he thought, as he glided away unperceived; "I'll turn the tables on you, or my name's not Graham."

He hurried away into the school-house.

There he soon found Pat O'Connor and Marshall, and the three boys were quickly in consultation.

From their loud laughter anyone might have seen they had hit upon a comic plot.

"We'll take Figs into our confidence," said Pat, "for it won't do to tell Mr. O'Shaughnessy. I don't want to get the fellow the sack, though he deserves it. We'll show him that we're not going to run the risk of our lives for him without punishing him."

"But he'll be a nuisance here if he is so spiteful," said Harry.

"Oh! no; to-day's punishment will cure him of that," said Pat; "at any rate, let's try."

The morning soon passed.

At two o'clock dinner was over, and the boys hurried out into the grounds.

Pat O'Connor, Harry Marshall, and Reginald Graham at once made their way towards the boat-house, and soon "The Little Mermaid" was half launched.

Willie Curtis had been called up by one of the other boys to get ready a large boat for a party; and that being done, he stood on the bank watching for the *dénouement*.

"Where are you going, Pat?" asked Harry, speaking, by arrangement, loudly, so that Willie could hear.

"I'm going up to Pier's Point for Mr. O'Shaughnessy," said Pat, "to fetch something for him."

"Can you take me with you?" asked Harry, with a wink.

"Oh! yes," said Pat, "and Reginald too."

And he prepared to enter the boat.

At this moment the usher, Figs, made his appearance.

"Stop a moment, young gentlemen," he said, "stop a moment; you will have to go out a little later."

Pat put on a look of deep concern.

"Why?" he said. "I hope, sir, nothing has happened to offend Mr. O'Shaughnessy?"

"Nothing of that kind, Master O'Connor," said Figs, "nothing of that kind; but Mr. Thaddeus desires Willie Curtis to go on to Pier's Point with this additional note, as there are more things to bring back than he cares to bother you with."

He turned then to Willie Curtis.

"Willie," he said, "Mr. O'Shaughnessy wishes you to go on your errand quickly; so take this skiff, which is the lightest, and row off as quickly as possible."

Curtis turned slightly pale.

"Well, surr, I'm not a furust-rate rower," he said.

"Oh! you're not going for a race," exclaimed Figs, "nor are you expected to show off any fine rowing. So, come; do not make excuses, for Mr. O'Shaughnessy will be angry. There can't be any reasonable excuse at all for objecting to this boat, for it is the pleasantest and lightest in the place."

What was to be done?

There was no room whatever for refusing the order of the schoolmaster.

So, with a rueful face, the man took the paper which Figs held in his hand, and stepped into the skiff.

His only hope of saving himself from a ducking was to row out, and then, as soon as the water began to rush in, turn the nose of his boat towards the shore.

So, with a long pull (and a long face too), he made for mid stream.

But his plan was thwarted.

No sooner had he begun to make headway, than Pat and six of his companions, who had been let into the secret, took their places in the largest boat and pushed off.

"I shan't wait for the skiff, Mr. Finnigan," cried Pat, as they left the shore; "I'll go with the rest."

And they made at once in the direction of Willie Curtis's boat.

As they came nearly alongside, the water began to force itself into the skiff.

"Well, Willie, how are ye getting on?" exclaimed Pat, as they pulled between him and the shore, so as to prevent his reaching it; "if ye go on at this rate, ye'll never reach Pier's Point to-day."

"To tell the solim truth, surr," said Willie,

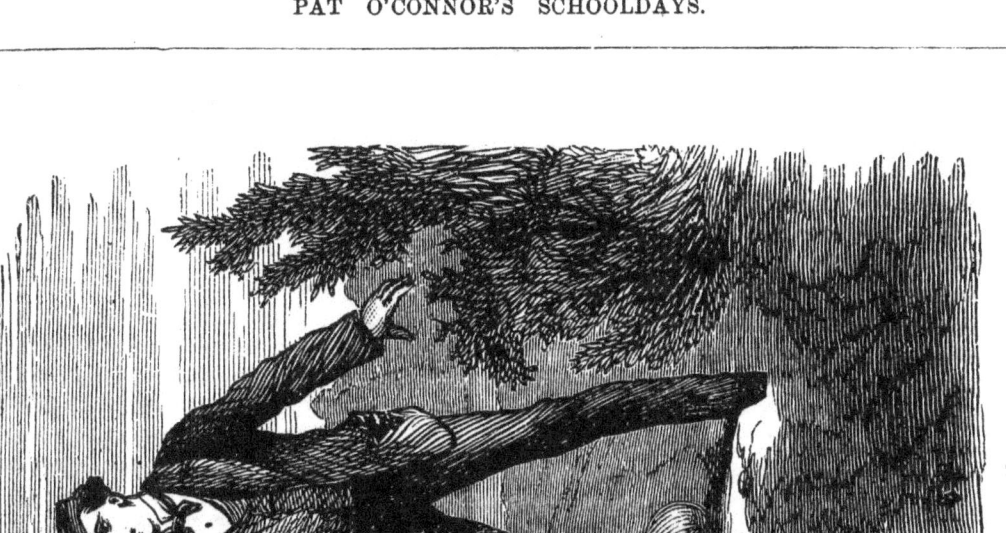

"OCH! MURTHER, BUT I'M KILLED SURE,' CRIED WILLIE CURTIS."

looking very ruefully at the big boat, which still kept in his way, "there'll be no getting to that same place in this boat this blessed day."

"Why not? Have you a boatload of lead on board?" cried Harry.

"No, sir; but I've got a boatload of water," returned Willie. "The boat will be swamped if I don't pull to shore directly."

"How's it getting in?" asked Pat.

"I don't know that same," said Willie.

"Perhaps someone's been cutting a hole in its bottom," said Pat, with a knowing look.

The eyes of the man caught those of our hero.

And in an instant he guessed the truth.

He was being paid out for his spiteful revenge.

He saw, too, that the boys were leagued together against him.

What could he do?

It was best, perhaps, to temporise.

"Will ye be letting me pass yer boat, young jintlemen?" he said. "I must pull ashore."

A laugh was the answer.

"The boat's filling," said Harry, in a whisper.

"Yes; I wonder if the fool can swim," said Pat.

Then he added, turning to Willie—

"Can you swim, Curtis?"

"I can, sir."

"Then you'll have to swim to shore, I'm thinking," said Pat.

"Can't ye take me on board?" asked the serving-man.

"No; we've no room," answered our hero. "Besides, you're too wet; you'd give us all cold."

There was no longer any doubt in the mind of Willie Curtis.

He had undoubtedly been found out, and this was his punishment.

He had nothing to hope from the boys, therefore.

So, with one desperate effort, he dragged the nose of the boat round, and endeavoured to pass by the stern of the other.

In vain.

The very effort he made seemed to suddenly increase the influx of water; and, as he pulled hard, the boat began to settle, and then, with a sudden rush, it went down from beneath him.

A roar of laughter greeted his discomfiture.

But Willie was prepared for the emergency.

He had long foreseen what the result of the adventure would be, and so, when the boat disappeared beneath him, he struck out manfully, and so as to prevent his sinking.

To a certain extent he succeeded, but the kind of miniature whirlpool caused by the sinking of the skiff, drew him down, and effected just the thing that he had desired to prevent—the immersion of his head.

Up he rose, looking half drowned, and pale with anger.

"Hilp!" he cried; "git me aboard your wherry, or I shall be dhrownded before your viry eyes."

"Not more than ye desarve, you murderin' villain," cried one of the Irish lads; "ye know ye've been afther tryin' to drown Pat O'Connor and Harry Marshall."

"And now ye're like a drowned rat, yourself," exclaimed Pat; "but never fear, ye'll be dried well when ye get ashore."

Without condescending to answer the jeers of the lads, or trying to understand what they meant by his "being dried," he struck out as well as he could for shore.

The six lads pulled out manfully, and reached the bank just in time to receive him, after taking from their boat some mysterious articles.

When they had done this, they stood in a semi-circle, holding each an inflated bladder attached to a strong string.

Willie glanced at them in amazement.

What could they be going to do with such things?

He was soon relieved from any anxiety on this point.

"Now then, Willie," cried Pat O'Connor, as the serving man emerged dripping from the waters of the Shannon, "you're looking very wretched; so, as you might catch cold, we'll give you a run across the meadow towards home."

"Shure, and I——" began Willie.

But it was in vain.

Crack went a bladder over his mouth.

"Arrah! now that's not fair," cried Willie.

But whack came a second bladder.

The blows did not fall very lightly.

He looked vengefully at his young tormentors, and then he made a dash at the first lad near him.

Crack came a bladder on the back of his head, and he nearly fell forward.

Then, at a sign from Pat O'Connor, all the boys began an attack upon him at once.

It was useless to attempt to resist them.

The lard bladders went whack, whack in his eyes, against his nose, against his mouth, so incessantly that he was fairly dazzled.

Retreat, therefore, was the best thing.

So, glancing frantically round him, he made a dash for the house, along the edge of the meadow.

The laughing boys pursued him with great gusto.

"This is better than 'hunt the stag,'" cried Pat, as he cracked Willie on the back.

At this point there happened to be the jagged root of a tree, which spread some distance across the path.

The crack of the bladder made him stumble over this, and down he went, splash into a greenish puddle which had been formed by the dripping from the mossy boughs.

Just as he fell, Harry Marshall, who had been keeping his bladder in reserve, gave the prostrate Irish lad a whack with it on the top of his head.

The effect was comic and instantaneous.

The bladder had been filled with pig's blood, and when Willie Curtis rose to his feet, he looked as if every drop of his life-stream had flowed to his head and poured down on him.

"Och, murther, but I'm killed sure," cried Willie.

At this instant, Thaddeus O'Shaughnessy appeared on the scene.

He stared aghast at the serving-man, as he staggered and wiped the blood out of his eyes.

"Why, what on earth is the matter?" asked the schoolmaster. "Has someone been committing a murder?"

Willie Curtis, at first, could make no reply.

Seeing the blood as it streamed off his face, and down his coat in front, he naturally thought that he had cut his head open.

"Shure, and I don't know, sir," he said, "whether I'm murdered or not; but there's a great deal of blood about."

Thaddeus could hardly help smiling, as the man kept putting his hand to the back of his head to find his wounds; and then, as he turned towards the boys, and saw their convulsed faces, he guessed at once that some practical joke had been on foot.

"Pat O'Connor," he said, "will ye explain what this means?"

Pat hesitated only a moment.

Then he told all bravely, not omitting the episode of the bath.

Thaddeus listened as gravely as he could.

"Really, Master O'Connor, and you, Master Marshall," he said, "I cannot permit you to indulge in such practical jokes, and I hope I shall hear no more of them.

"As for you," he added, to Willie, "I cannot help saying that you deserve what you have got. The boys' fun was too much of a good thing, but the scuttling of the boat might have ended in death to the lads. I hope I shall have no more of it."

The man said nothing, but vowing vengeance upon the boys, he passed away towards the house.

Pat and his friends departed to have a bit of fun among themselves, but they all knew that the Irishman would not forgive them.

CHAPTER XXI.

GHOSTS!

SOON after the arrival of Willie Curtis at the school-house, there was another addition to the establishment in the person of Tom McClosky.

He was an oddity.

His hair was of a dull, brick-dust hue, his nose very pug, his eyes were declared by his companions not only to be of different sizes, but of different colours, while his mouth was large and slightly inclined to twist up at one side.

Apparently he had plenty of money and came of a decent family.

But he was frightfully dull.

There was scarcely a lad of ten in the school who didn't know more than he.

However, Thaddeus O'Shaughnessy was just the man to treat with such a boy as Tom McClosky.

He coached him up himself, led him on with kindness, and by degrees—in fact, in the space of a few weeks, he had so improved him that he was able to go into the second class above the young ones.

He was in no wise a pleasant character, however.

He was spiteful to the boys about him, because they knew more than himself, and upon one or two occasions he practised one or two tricks, which he supposed to be funny, but were only spiteful and revengeful.

Salt in the beds, blackbeetles and so forth, were nothing.

Ropes were fastened from bedstead to bedstead to cause the lads to trip up, and on one or two occasions some of them were injured.

At last a watch was set, and the culprit discovered.

At once a council of war was held, and vengeance was the order of the day.

On the second night after the discovery the whole of those in the dormitory were wrapped in sleep, or, at any rate, seemed to be.

It was nearly midnight.

Suddenly a voice said—

"Are you awake, Harry Marshall?"

A snore was the answer.

"Harry," said the voice again, the voice of Pat O'Connor.

"What do you want?" asked Harry Marshall.

"Do you know what night this is?" asked Pat, in a solemn voice.

"No."

"Not the night of the murder?"

"What murder?"

"Why, I thought everyone knew about the murder of the old usher in this room."

"No; that I don't," said Harry. "What is it?"

"Are the other boys asleep, Pat?"

"Yes; I think so."

"That's right, because I don't want to frighten them," said Pat, "especially MacClosky; he'd die with fright if he saw the ghost."

"What ghost?" asked Harry.

"Why, the ghost of the old usher. This is the night he walks."

Tom McClosky was awake, and he shuddered in his bed.

"I hope he won't to-night," said Harry Marshall, "for I'm not partial to ghosts."

"Well, if the story's true, he will," said Pat. "Shall I tell you?"

"Yes, go on. As I said, I don't like ghosts, but you've raised my curiosity, so out with it."

At this moment there was heard a deep groan.

It seemed to come from the wall of the room.

McClosky huddled himself under the bed clothes.

Pat O'Connor exclaimed, in a voice of apparent alarm—

"Did you hear anything, Harry?"

"Yes; I did."

"What was it?"

"It sounded like a groan," said Harry. "I hope the ghost isn't going to walk, after all; it makes me feel shivery."

"Shall I go on with the story?" asked Pat.

"Oh, yes. I can't sleep now, thinking of the ghost," said Harry; "so fire away."

Just at this moment, as luck would have it, the wind howled with a melancholy sound round the towers of the academy, and shrieked like the wailings of a lost spirit.

McClosky fairly trembled.

"I wish the night was over," he murmured.

"Well," continued Pat O'Connor, deepening his voice, "it was on just such a night as this, just such a boisterous and unpleasant night, that one of the big boys in this room murdered the usher.

"The old man was a kindly old fellow enough, and, with some of the boys, was a favourite, but he had given offence to this fellow, whose name was Allenby, and, having been compelled to cause him a thrashing for some grievous offence, the old fellow—O'Connell his name was—was fixed upon as the object of Allenby's deadly vengeance.

"So in the middle of the night, when all the boys were supposed to be asleep, the murderer slunk from his bed and approached that of the usher.

"There was no hesitation in his mind, as it seemed, for he must have killed him with one blow.

"There was only a groaning cry, and then all was still, but that cry had aroused one of the boys, and as he struck a light he saw the murdered man lying weltering in his blood, and the assassin creeping back to his bed.

"The boy was seized and placed in prison, and then committed suicide.

"But the spirit of the old man still walks abroad, and generally as the clock strikes twelve."

As Pat O'Connor spoke there was another long and hollow groan, and the clock began to strike the hour of midnight.

As the last stroke of the clock sounded there was a strange rustling of clothes, and then there seemed to come from out the wall a white-clad figure.

It had a ghostly look upon its face, and its features and its hair were luminous.

It advanced with noiseless steps towards the bed where Tom McClosky lay.

The latter had long since drawn the bedclothes over his face, but when he found that his bedclothes were being pulled from off him, he could not help glancing up.

The sight of the noiseless ghost stalking along the floor of the bedroom at first transfixed him with horror, but then he found his voice, and, with a yell of terror, he leaped from the bed and made his way towards the door.

Here, in his alarm, he was at first unable to find the key, and, as if taking advantage of this, the ghost of O'Connell the usher quickened his pace and hurried as if to clutch him.

At length, however, the boy succeeded in turning the lock, and fled out into the passage. All was in darkness, apparently.

He stood for a moment irresolute; then, seeing that there was a slight light at the end of the passage, just a glimmering through a door that was ajar, he dashed away.

A terrific groan, and then a clattering of something against the windows of the dormitory gave wings to his heels, and on he dashed into the room.

It never occurred to him to ask where he was going.

It might have been the sleeping apartment of Thaddeus O'Shaughnessy for all he knew.

As it was he tumbled headlong over a chair, and, with a howl, lay on the floor.

The occupant of the bed started up in terror, and glanced round him.

The moonlight streamed upon his face, and when Tom McClosky glanced up and saw its ghastly appearance, he gave vent to another howl and hid his face.

It was Willie Curtis who was occupier of the bed, and, being of a superstitious nature, he had the utmost horror of anything spiritual.

So when he saw at the door of the room the same face which had so alarmed McClosky, he uttered a terrific yell and leaped out of the bed.

He had not seen McClosky, and so, in his half-asleep state, he confounded the noise which he had heard with the apparition.

In leaping out, therefore, he came in contact with the limbs of the boy, which were stone cold, and then, with another cry, he fell prostrate on the floor.

The yells, of course, had now aroused the house, and, in a few minutes, Thaddeus O'Shaughnessy and Figs appeared on the scene.

As the master came to the door, and the light of the somewhat dim lamp was shed upon the scene, he could behold nothing at first but a strange struggling mass and a mixture of legs and arms.

"Why, what on earth does this mean?" cried Thaddeus. "Who is this that is struggling on the floor with Willie Curtis?"

"I cannot see yet," said Figs.

Then, as he bent down closer, he said—

"It's McClosky. Tom McClosky, as I live."

Thaddeus seized the boy by the arm and dragged him to his feet.

Willie scrambled to his.

"What is the meaning of this disgraceful scene?" asked Thaddeus.

"Shure, sir, it's meself that doesn't know a wurod about it. All I can till you is that I saw a ghost at the door, and I was so mortally frightened that I leaped out of me bed."

"And pray what is Master Tom McClosky doing here?"

"You'd better ax him, yer honour," replied Willie Curtis, "for I haven't the remotest idea what he wants in my room."

Thaddeus felt "fogged."

What could it all mean?

There was certainly no indication whatever of a practical joke, for both Willie and Tom were evidently in agonies of fear, when master and teacher entered the room.

"What is this about a ghost?" asked Thaddeus. "That is the secret of it all, I expect."

Tom McClosky was the first to speak.

A dim glimmering of the truth entered his heavy mind.

He began to see that he had been made a fool of.

Thaddeus O'Shaughnessy listened severely to the narrative.

Then he said—

"Willie Curtis, go to bed again, and be assured that you are in no danger of ghosts. You have been made the victim of a joke, and I am very sorry for it. But, rest assured, the culprits shall be punished.

"Now, McClosky," he said, turning to Tom, "come with me."

In a few minutes they had reached the dormitory. Thaddeus closed the door.

"Now, then, boys," said he, "this is very serious. I am determined to put a stop to this practical joking. I told you so on a former occasion, and now I shall visit the culprits with condign punishment."

This was a bad stroke of policy on the part of the schoolmaster.

It sealed the lips of everyone in the room.

O'Shaughnessy continued—

"A shameful trick has been played upon Tom McClosky and my serving man also. Nothing can be more dangerous than these jokes about ghosts. It might cause anyone to go into fits. Now, tell me at once, who did this?"

There was a dead silence.

"I repeat, who did this?"

Still no answer.

"Very well, since no one will answer, I will serve all alike. To-morrow, everyone of you shall be punished. I shall put the whole school on bread and water for a week, if the truth is not told, and after that, I shall take severer measures."

This was too much for Pat O'Connor.

It was not in his heart to see the whole school punished for him.

"If you please, sir," he said, "it was I who did this."

The countenance of Thaddeus O'Shaughnessy fell.

Here was his favourite scholar in trouble again.

"Well, Pat," he said, in a voice which showed the intensity of his emotion, "I really am deeply sorry that this has happened. You, of all others too, the one I warned before."

"I am very sorry, sir," said Pat. "But the truth is, that I did this in the interest of the whole school."

"What do you mean by that?" asked Thaddeus.

"It was done to Tom McClosky, sir," returned Pat, "because he has proved himself a sneak and a spiteful fellow altogether to all of us. Several times we have nearly broken our necks through him."

And he gave the history of Tom McClosky's spiteful pranks.

As a man, Thaddeus O'Shaughnessy could not but say in his own heart, that the boys were right.

But as the schoolmaster, he was compelled to take another view of the matter.

"You have no right," he said, "to take into your own hands the punishment of such offences. If you had told me this, I would have punished him. As it is, I must punish *you*. Are you alone in this disgraceful matter?"

"It was my idea," said Pat.

But the boys were not going to stand this. They would not desert their champion.

"No, sir he was not alone," said a chorus of voices. "We were all in it."

"Very well," said the schoolmaster, as he turned away. "Very well, I will see by the morning how I can punish you all. It is shameful that I am to be dragged out of my bed to stop such disturbances."

"We're in for it hot," said Harry Marshall, as Thaddeus passed out of the room. "I wonder what he'll do?"

"Lather us all," said Pat. "You were all duffers not to let me take it. But I'm going to sleep; it'll give me strength for my drubbing. Good night, all."

CHAPTER XXII.

UP IN THE TOWER.

THE dawn of the next day found Figs in the dormitory.

"Shure then, Mr. Figs," said one of the broad Irish lads, "shure then it's fined ye will be, for coming into our dormitory when we're washin'."

Such liberties as these were allowed in the school on such occasions as this.

Figs smiled.

"No—I'll not be fined this time," he said, "for the master sent me. Mr. Pat O'Connor, and you, Mr. Harry Marshall, must remain in the room until either I or Mr. O'Shaughnessy comes to ye."

Pat looked downcast.

This was exactly the worst punishment he could have had inflicted upon him.

To have been thrashed outright would have been more to his mind.

"It would be over and done with," as he said to Harry Marshall as soon as they were alone; "but this'll last goodness knows how long."

At ten in the morning, after four hours of fasting, the door opened, and the servant-man appeared.

There was a smile on his face, but it was one of malice, more than anything else.

"Shure an' it's an illigant breakfast I've brought ye, my young jintlemen," he said; "jest some bread and wather."

"Good enough!" said Pat. "I dare say it's about the same that you've been having as a rule before ye came here."

"Here ye are, and the divil choke ye, ye young blaggard, if ye get meat if I can help it while I'm here," he said.

And he was about to go.

"Stop," said Pat O'Connor; "are you blind of the left eye, Willie?"

"No, surr."

"Are ye blind of the right eye?"

"No, surr."

"Then do ye see this half-sovereign?"

"Well, I should be afther being blind of both eyes, if I didn't see it, surr," said the man.

"Well, then," said Pat, "that's for you, if ye'll be afther doing what I ask ye."

Willie cast a quick glance at the door, and then springing to Pat's side, clutched him by the arm.

"What'll ye be wanting me to do?" asked Willie, eyeing the coin lovingly.

"Why, this, Willie. You'll be the one that'll bring us up our 'bite and sup,' as ye'll call it."

"I shall be that same."

"Then if ye'll bring us up some wine and some meat and so on, during the time we're here, this half-sovereign, good Saxon money, shall be yours."

"And it's meself, Mr. O'Connor, that'll be afther bringing you anything ye like, surr," said the man.

"Then I'll tell ye what we'll have, Willie," said Pat; "it'll just be a nice piece of beef out of the pantry for dinner—pickles, too, if it's possible, and plenty of nice home-made bread. Then for tea we'll have what we cau catch, with the addition of the same as dinner."

Willie laughed.

"Shure, and I'll manage all that, and a good supper for ye too," said he; "and will ye rally gi' me the goulden piece of money?"

"Here ye are, Willie," said Pat; "and remember, afther this, don't bear any more animosity."

The Irish lad's eyes glistened with delight, as he took the half-sovereign.

And a change too went over him.

"Shure and it's meself, surr, that'll do ini-thin' for ye. It's the illigant young jintlemin ye are for forgivin' a bhoy that tried to drown ye. Och, now——"

"Willie Coortis! aire ye comin'?" shouted a voice—the voice of the cook. "Here's the mas-ther's been a-bawlin' and——"

But Willie did not wait to hear more.

He darted a look of intelligence and cunning at the two boys, and took his departure from the room with a celerity which resulted in his rolling half way down the stairs.

Pat and Harry burst into a loud laugh.

"Well, Harry, we're sure of plenty to eat and drink, that's one good job," he said.

"Yes, that is, if we are to stop here," said Marshall.

As if to give his words double effect, the door was pushed open, and Figs entered.

A good-humoured smile was upon the face of the usher.

"Shure, bhoys," he said, "now that you've recrooted yerselves by yer humble repast, I've got bad news for ye."

"What now? I think it's bad news enough to know that we're to be kept on bread and water."

"Well, and it's not pleasant," said Figs, "but still Mr. O'Shaughnessy says your conduct has been outrageous, and ye must be punished. He knows you're brave bhoys—he knows ye de-sarve a great deal for yer courage and so on; but if he let ye do what pranks ye liked, the school would go to the devil."

Pat laughed.

"I think Tom M'Closky deserved it," he said.

"Yes, and it may be that I'm of the same opinion," said Figs; "but then discipline's discipline, and now——"

"Now for the clincher, Mr. Finnigan," said Pat, with a smile, which was but half real, for he knew something most uncomfortable was coming.

"Well, thin, young gentlemen," said Figs, "I tell ye what. The masther says that in consideration of all things, he won't disgrace ye by flogging ye. So you'll be going up to the top of the tower in the left wing, and remain there a week."

"On bread and water!" said Pat.

"Yes."

"Oh! shan t we peg into the beef when we come down?" said Pat O'Connor. "When are we to go?"

"Now, Pat; but I know it's a hard case, and I'd have done the very same myself; so," said the usher, dropping his voice, and glanc-ing round him, as if he was afraid that the walls would hear, "so I've got a little dhrop of the crature just to give you courage; for I know you'll be mighty uncomfortable up there."

The good-natured usher produced from his pocket a goodly-sized bottle of the best Irish whisky, and the boys, cold and shivering after their wretched repast, were nothing loth to partake of a small portion of the warming fluid.

Then the usher led them up towards the place of imprisonment, as it might well be called.

It was a small chamber at the top of the tower of the school.

On one side was a little barred window—the bars were an absurdity which might easily have been dispensed with, considering that the depth was full eighty feet—and on the other was a little fire-place, rusty and quite guiltless of fire, or preparations for one.

There was a kind of truckle bed, sufficiently large to hold the two boys, a table and two chairs, and that was all.

"Oh! shan't we be jolly here?" cried Pat. "See, we can look out of window and count those three trees over there ever so many times a day, and when we're tired of that, we can sit by the empty grate and fancy there's a fire in it, and think how we can pay out Tom McClosky when we come down again."

Figs heard all this with great gravity.

"Oh, Pat," he said, "ye mustn't be too out-rageous. Be as good as ye can, and I'll try if I can't get ye off with the masther."

Then he turned to go, but before he did so, he stopped at the door.

"Look here, bhoys," he said, "you'll be cowld and uncomfortable up here, so I'll leave the bottle with ye. I'm not the one to give bhoys bad advice and tell them to dhrink, but it's mighty cowld up here, and, at any rate, there's the whisky."

And giving them the bottle, and a little wave of the hand, the honest-hearted usher quitted the room.

CHAPTER XXIII.
AS THE NIGHT FELL.

THE day passed without any special incident.

Willie Curtis kept his word.

Instead of the bread and water to which the schoolmaster had so justly confined them, the boys revelled in all the glories of cold beef and pickles, and bread and ale, and hot potatoes.

"Yes, shure, it's the praties ye'd be afther missing, Masther Pat," said Willie, "so ye see I've been thavin' a few for ye. By the token, if the cook finds it out, it's going widout I'd be for a week."

"Well, Willie, ye've been a good boy," said Pat, "and I don't mind giving ye another shilling, but we want a fire."

"Very well, thin, ye shall have one," said Willie, "niver fear; but ye must be patient, for if I'm found out doin' sich things for ye, they'll be sendin' me away or givin' someone else the job, and that 'l be worse than inythink for both you and me."

Pat and Harry Marshall burst into loud laughter as the serving-man departed.

"Well, and what do you think of him?" said Harry Marshall. "Isn't he a queer character?"

"Yes, but not half so bad as we thought him," returned Pat, in the fulness of his heart —his generous, enthusiastic heart. "He'll make our sojourn here pleasant, that's one thing."

Willie was again true to his word.

A roaring fire was provided for them in the afternoon, and as the evening came on, and the one candle was too precious to light yet, they sat in the glow of the logs, and told stories.

It was about twelve o'clock, and the old house was in utter silence, except in the little room where Pat sat with his companion.

They had not been speaking for some moments, when Pat said suddenly—

"I say, Harry; I think I've been here a year longer than you."

"Yes, quite."

"You weren't here when Long Langton was here, the gentleman usher, as we used to call him?"

"No; who was he? Something special, I should think, by his name," said Harry.

"Well, he was something special," said Pat O'Connor; "he was one of the quietest, pleasantest, best-behaved, kindest ushers on the face of the earth."

"Like Figs?"

"Oh! ten times better than Figs," said Pat O'Connor; "though goodness knows Figs is not half a bad fellow. This chap would sacrifice everything for anyone, and I really believe that if anybody had asked him to be hung for him, he would have only hesitated as to the time."

"Then I'll be hanged if I would," said Harry, "but come; I know you are going to tell a story about Long Langton, so out with it."

Pat smiled.

"Ye won't be afraid?"

"No; of what?"

"Remember; this is the very witching hour of night, when ghosts do walk, etc."

"Oh! ghosts must walk if they want to," said Harry; "let the poor things have a little exercise; but for the story—go it, old man."

"Oh! it's not much of a story," said Pat, "only this. Long Langton, it seems, was the son of an Irish gentleman of good family in Connaught. For some reason or another, he had been compelled to quit his native place— some duel or something of the sort, I can't tell you, Harry. At any rate, he didn't care much to appear among his own set any more, so he came to the academy and became our usher. He was all right for a little time. But after a while people came to visit him, until Thaddeus O'Shaughnessy got angry, and said his place was a school, and not one for the reception of visitors. It was about a month after this that the catastrophe happened. Everyone had retired to rest as usual, when suddenly a wild cry rang through the house. Of course

Thaddeus, brave as usual, ran to rouse the usher up. But only Lawrence McMahon was to be found. Long Langton was missing. They sought everywhere, until a last wailing cry resounded through the academy, and then they knew that it came from this part of the building.

"'Something strange must be the matter, Mr. McMahon,' said O'Shaughnessy; 'but certainly the sound comes from the deserted tower.'

"'Then let's go up, sir,' said Mr. McMahon.

"And they did. And what do you think they found there?" asked Pat.

"I guess; I fancy," said Harry, "the traces of a dastardly murder."

"Not far out," said Pat; "though it was worse than the traces. They found the body of Long Langton lying stiff and stark in the moonlight on the floor of the very room we are in."

Harry laughed.

"Pat," he said, "you are good at stories, I know."

"What do you mean?"

"Is this just a tale for the occasion?"

"No," returned Pat; "I swear it's true. All the boys know it, only Thaddeus O'Shaughnessy forbids them to speak of it."

"And what made you think of it now?" asked Marshall.

"Because, in the first place, this is the room in which the deed was done."

"By whom?"

"No one ever knew. Every effort was made to trace his murderers, but in vain."

"Well, to every firstly there must be a secondly. What's the second reason why you thought of it?"

"Because every boy in the school says the place is haunted."

"Haunted!"

Harry Marshall laughed long and loudly. Hark!

Was that an echo—the echo of his voice?

It could not be; but certainly a voice had spoken, and something had rattled down the chimney.

Pat was no coward, but certainly an awe fell over him for the moment.

"What can that be?" asked Harry Marshall. "No wonder the people say it's haunted."

"I don't know what it can be," said Pat, "but certainly it sounded like someone speaking overhead. We must be on our guard."

"Let's get between the bedclothes and pretend to be asleep," said Harry; "then we can listen. Put out the fire—no; we'll want the light of that. Come on."

The two schoolmates had soon crept into bed—dressed as they were, and then, in eager expectation, they waited.

For a time all was still, then a voice was again heard, and the unmistakable sounds of someone descending the wide chimney.

"We must be careful now," said Pat; "this may be a matter of life and death."

"'WHAT DO YOU WANT, MR. HOOLIGAN? THIS IS MY ROOM,' CRIED MARY O'RORKE."

CHAPTER XXIV.

WITH THE TIDE ON THE SHANNON.

ON the night before, a large vessel with blackened sails and straining masts had rolled in from the sea, and floated, as if resting from the storm, upon the broad bosom of the Shannon.

No sooner had it got well out of the roll of the ocean, than it cast anchor, and a boat being lowered, two persons were borne ashore.

The one was as easily recognisable as Captain De Ruyter, the Dutch skipper, as the ship was recognisable as the lugger "Silverhorn."

The captain upon landing took leave of the crew of the skiff.

"I shall pe shoost von 'our ashore," he said, "and ven I returns I shall purn von laight, den I shall expect de boat."

Having given this explicit direction, he led his companion up a narrow path which led to a village, which was somewhat better lit than villages in that part of Ireland usually were.

At the corner of a straggling street, which seemed as if it didn't know where it began or where it was going to end—there stood a curious-looking little house.

A dim light—the dimmest of the dim—burned in the window, but De Ruyter knocked at the door—knocked twice in a peculiar manner.

It was opened at once by a little man with an enormous head.

"Shure, and is it possible that's you?" said he; "you, De Ruyter?"

"Shoost so," cried the smuggler, "it's nopody else; only me and mein vriend here, Jack O'Grady, broder to de Mat O'Grady up at de school yonder."

De Ruyter of course knew nothing of Mat's death.

"Coom in, thin, and wilcome," said the old man; "and," he added, with a grin, "I hope ye've brought plinty of golden suvrins."

"De Ruyter never comes widout de gold; shoost listen to de tinkle ob de coin."

And as he said this he patted his chest.

"Dat is de merry jingle; make de heart tingle. Ha, ha!" laughed the Dutchman, "I am an English boet, you see. Ha, ha! and now shote de door, and ve vill commence bis'ness."

The commodities sold by the old man were of the most strange and miscellaneous description.

Odd parcels dusty with age, implements of agriculture mingled with implements of war, even clothes were there to be seen, but none of these seemed to be the speciality desired by De Ruyter.

"You know vot I vant?" he said.

"No."

"Fireworks. Not de leetle tings dat de jildren play mit, but grate big tings," and he spread out his hands illustratively, "grate tings dat will explode like de bomb."

"Shure and it's meself can accommodate ye, thin," remarked the old man; "I've got things here. that'd blow down a church—staple and all."

As he spoke he made a sign, which De Ruyter understood and answered—the sign of the Men of the Mountain.

"Shoost so," said the Dutchman; "vonce in de zoziety, always in de zoziety. Are dese brudy leetle blay-tings for de boys?"

"Yes, they are that same."

"Thin it's der teifel's in dem, I expects. Let me have a whole sack full mit dem. Have you got any schiedam?"

"Not a dhrap."

"Then, if you vants any, blease to come mit us mit your bote, and ye can hab as moosh as vill make all de beoble in de village droonk for von month. I can zell it jeepe."

In a short space of time the old man had filled the sack with the terrible explosives, and the three were very soon making their way as quickly as possible down the mountain pass.

It was not long before the shore of the river was reached.

Here the old man unmoored a crazy boat; and was soon following in the wake of the wherry containing De Ruyter and his men.

The combustibles were quickly shipped, and the old man received his boat-load of schiedam.

Then the great lugger got under weigh, and began rolling lumberingly along up stream.

There was a good strong breeze blowing, and under its heavy canvas the ship soon spun along wondrously quickly.

It was of course a long distance from the mouth of the river to the Shannon Academy.

So, although it was dawn when the smuggler took up his position, he could not do anything until night fell once more.

And there it lay quietly at anchor, like a simple trader, and quietly the inmates of the school went on with their labours, and Pat O'Connor and Harry Marshall laughed and joked with Willie Curtis up in the room in the tower.

Little did they think what was preparing for them, what hideous fiend was preparing his revenge against a few, reckless of the ruin he would bring on nearly a hundred others.

Hideous fiend indeed.

Nothing else was De Ruyter, under his sleek and laughing exterior.

A man without a heart.

A man without kindly wishes—save three.

A kindly wish for himself, that ranked first; one for the "vrow" he left at home; this was half selfish—and one for the crew of the "Silverhorn," who had fought for him against adverse winds and enemies.

This last was the only unselfish wish in his mind.

But all—self, "vrow," crew, were now swallowed up in one thought.

That of revenge.

So when the shades of night had settled on the bosom of the river, De Ruyter and Jack O'Grady made their way towards the schoolhouse.

They had learned, during their stay on the shore, the death of Mat O'Grady; and the smuggler now had a more willing coadjutor than ever in the person of Mat's brother Jack.

Regardless of danger the two men—for they were both as brave as lions, in spite of their villany—crept up the river in a boat, and landed on the most secluded part of the shore near the school-house.

All was still.

The boys were all in bed, and Thaddeus O'Shaughnessy was half dozing in his chair.

They could see the grand old man as he sat near the window.

Little did he think of the serpents which were crawling towards him, to ruin him—to take the lives of innocent boys, and murder Tim Finnigan.

Of the latter, the brave heart who had sent a coward spy and assassin out of the world—they determined to make sure.

He was to be dispatched at once.

The first thing was to get into the house.

An ordinary burglar would have forced his way in at the door.

But De Ruyter and his companion were not ordinary men, and so they halted on the side lawn.

De Ruyter could fling a lasso as readily and as surely as a Mexican.

And so, having made his loop, he flung it unerringly, and it caught on one of the lofty stacks of chimneys.

It was a thick rope—a ship's rope, quite capable of bearing a man's weight.

So in an instant the Dutchman said—

"Shoost steady de rope a leetle; I'll make de furst dhry."

And up he went.

Up through the darkness, a dizzy, dangerous height, on his errand of ruin and death.

He had soon reached the summit of the house.

Then he gave a peculiar whistle.

A sound, indeed, which was scarcely a whistle, but more like the hiss of a snake.

Then Jack O'Grady, regardless of the swing of the rope, quickly came up to him hand over hand.

They had divided the combustibles between them.

Each had a small sack on his back, tied securely so that it should not sway about and risk ignition.

And now, standing on the roof where they could see the wooded mountains, and the valleys, and the silver sheen of the river, they chuckled to themselves to think that the first step towards their diabolical scheme was successful.

The spot at which they had arrived was the roof of the room in which Pat O'Connor and Harry Marshall had been placed for punishment.

"Dis is von strange ting," said De Ruyter, "smoke out of de chimberly here! Nevar mind; mein pig boots vill put de vire aout."

And he began to descend the chimney, leaving, of course, his sack of "bombs" on the roof with Jack O'Grady.

CHAPTER XXV.

HOW THE FIRE WAS TRIED.

"WHAT is to be done?" whispered Pat. "I don't believe at all in stopping in bed. Be quick; let's move it and crouch down behind it so as to be ready on the moment."

"All right," said Harry.

Pat took up the whisky bottle.

"Going to have a drain to keep up your courage," said Harry, with a laugh.

"No, this is for the thief's head, whoever it is. Come on. That's it."

Of course the noise which De Ruyter made in descending prevented him from hearing any sound below, so he was perfectly oblivious of the fact that anyone was in the room.

Pat O'Connor and Harry crouched behind the bed, and waited.

Presently they saw one huge booted foot descending the chimney and resting on the hob. Then came the other.

Then the whole body cautiously crept down, avoiding the fire, and De Ruyter stood before them.

"The Dutch skipper, as I live," murmured Pat.

"Yes, the villain," whispered Harry. "He's up to some terrible game. But Providence has sent us here to defeat him."

The Dutch skipper had a ship's lantern with him, and he turned the light round the room in every possible direction.

But he could see nothing.

The boys were crouched down well in a corner, and nothing could be seen of them.

"Vell, dis is sdrange. Nopody here—nopody here. Vell, all de petter. Ve vill take de drooble out de vire, or ve shall be blown sky-high. Ha, ha!"

The skipper put his head a little way up the chimney.

"Jack O'Grady," he said, "it is all right, but dere is von leetle vire here dat I must pood out before you come down. You hab de schnapps to keep you varm. I zall not be long time."

He then set vigorously to work to rake out the fire.

This was not a task of long duration.

In a few moments the room was in utter darkness, save for the light of the lantern.

The Dutch skipper looked round for some water to cool the stove.

But in vain.

There was nothing in the room.

The phlegmatic captain, however, was in no way disconcerted.

"Jack," he cried, bawling again up the chimney.

"All right. Shall I come down?"

"No, not shoost now. I vill call ven I vants you."

"But I am shivering."

"Schnapps, mein poy—schnapps. De pipe and schnapps. I vill call you prezently."

And the Dutchman coolly sat down, and took out his pipe, lit it, leaned back in his chair, and seemed to have taken a sudden voyage to the land of dreams.

Pat and his friend still crouched and waited.

Once or twice the idea had occurred to them that now was the time to rush forward and overpower the Dutchman.

But they soon brought reflection to their aid.

It would be better to wait and catch him in some open act of villany.

So they waited patiently, though their hearts went pit-a-pat.

After the lapse of about a quarter of an hour, the Dutchman, who had smoked and smoked quite complacently, without any apparent concern as regarded his companion on the roof, felt the stove with his hand.

It was still warm.

But all danger was over.

He looked up the chimney again.

"Jack, vould you like a varm?"

"Don't chaff, captin. The fireworks will be frozen, shure, if ye lave me up here much longer."

"Den I tell you vat ve vill do," said the Dutchman "ve vill light de vire again ven you comes daoun, and den ve vill warm some schnapps and go about our business mit bleasure."

"But am I to come down, skipper?" shivered Jack.

"Yah, come down. You are in mighty hurry, I'm tinkin'," cried the Dutchman. "Come down. I tink de schnapps habe got into your head."

In a few minutes, the Dutchman, who clambered half way up the chimney, received one of the sacks, then the other, which he carefully deposited on the table.

After this, Jack descended.

Both were, of course, as black as sweeps, and under other circumstances the boys would have felt inclined to burst out laughing.

As it was, however, they saw that some deadly deed was meditated, and their hearts turned sick with horror.

There was plenty of fuel, and in a few minutes Jack O'Grady had lit a fire.

Then they poured a bottle of Hollands into the kettle and made it boil.

This done, they utilised the cups which the boys had had for their tea, and drank the hot grog.

"And now, Jack, ve vill talk about peesiness," said the Dutch skipper.

"All right, skipper. I'm thawed now," said Jack.

"Dat's notin' to do mit me," said De Ruyter, with a grin. "De schnapps have done dat, not me. Now shoost listen. Ve foorst must go to de room of Figs. Hein, are ye listening?"

The boys listened, and what they heard froze their blood with horror.

CHAPTER XXVI.

THE DUTCHMAN'S REVENGE.

AFTER a pause the Dutchman said—

"Vell, ve must shoost make our way first to the bedroom of the yellow, dat dey calls Feegs. He is de von ve must despatch vurst?"

"Yes, the dirthy murtherin' blackguard," remarked Jack O'Grady. "Although nobody saw him do the dade, there's no doubt he did it."

"Vell den, ve vill shoost settle him, vich you can do yourself vid your leetle knife," said De Ruyter. "Den ve vill leave a fire-ball in each of de rooms, and take four down to the bottom of de haouz. Den ve sets fire to a pile, and gets aout as quick as bossible. Den ve zall zee de foinest convlagrashun as ever lit ub de shores of de Zhannon."

Pat gripped Harry Marshall more tightly by the hand, as he whispered—

"The villains! Little do they think that their horrid plans are being overheard."

The Dutchman, as he spoke, took a long pull at the bottle.

Jaek O'Grady was looking moodily in the fire.

"Vell, mein friend?" said De Ruyter.

"Nothin', only I was jist thinking," said Jack.

"Of vat?" said the Dutchman.

"That it would be betther, afther all, if we were to put the knife in 'em one by one."

"Vat, de whole school?"

"Yes. We could go into the rooms, shure, and if we weren't impatient like, there needn't be one man Jack of 'em alive to-morrow to tell the tale."

The Dutchman shrugged his shoulders, while he took a tremendous pull at his pipe.

"Hem!" he said, in an unctuous, sententious voice, "you have no ideas of anytin'. Do you tink dat dey would be all asleep? Von out of so many would be sure to be avake. No, no, mein vriend, trust to de skipper; he is more brudent dan you. Ve virst kill de murderer of Mat O'Grady, and den ve burn up all de rest."

The two villains then drank another glass of whisky, and being now primed for any hideous deed, they rose and approached the door.

The door, as we know, was fastened on the outside.

The Dutchman stood for an instant transfixed.

"Vell," he said, "dis is von strange ting. Here ve are in von room, vere ve finds von fire, and den de room is locked on de aoutside."

"Shure, surr, and it's the skipper himself ought to have been an Irishman," said O'Grady.

"Why?"

"Because, surr, ye've been after makin' the best bull shure I've ever heard on."

"What's that?"

"Shure, sir, ye say it's a strange thing that there's a fire in the room, and so on and so on, and the owner on the other side."

"Vell?"

"Well, surr, shure it wouldn't be just easy for the owner to lock his door on the outside, and the things inside, if he were inside himsel'."

"Ah! ver' vell, ve vill talk aboot dat von oder taime," said the Dutchman. "Meantime, ve vill open dis door. No more delay; von trop of de schnapps, and den to work."

The drains of schnapps were soon dispatched, and then, while the Dutchman smoked his pipe and looked admiringly on, Jack O'Grady took from his pocket some small instruments, and began manipulating the lock.

It was not long before the way was clear.

But not till it was quite clear did the Dutchman move.

"Vell," as he cast his eyes with a kind of scientific glance at the door, "vell, and haf you done?"

"Yes, captain."

"Hein! den I'm ready," said the Dutchman. "Ve vill shoost go ub to de rhoom of Meinheer Vigs. And den ve vill zee."

The door was soon open.

Out into the darkness of the corridor crept Jack.

De Ruyter followed.

The one was overwhelmed, as it were, by a mad desire for revenge.

Revenge for the death of his brother.

His brother.

That was the idea.

In too many countries the thought is nothing.

The tie is as utterly disregarded as the tie between a divorced wife and her husband, to whom for ever more, in the present and the "to be," she belongs.

But in Ireland, for good or bad, the tie of relationship holds good.

And so, as he advanced along the dark corridor, his heart leaped with joy as he thought of the man lying helplessly in his bed—helpless—at his mercy.

The skipper and his mate little knew who were following them, little guessed the retribution that was pursuing them, in the persons of their youngest foes.

On they went.

Presently Finnigan's room was approached.

It was a rule with the ushers that they left their door ajar, in consequence of the devilment of the scholars.

So, as they neared Finnigan's room, they found the door open about an inch.

"Ah, shoost so," said the Dutch skipper, "shoost so. Everytin' is most ready for our blans. Go in vile I vaite."

Jack O'Grady turned to the captain with a quiet chuckle.

"Skipper," he said, "you ain't artful, some?"

"I don't want any of yar over de osheon talk," said De Ruyter; "but vat do you mean by some?"

"Well, skipper," said Jack, "shure and it's meself won't be afther sayin' anythin' against the captain, but I'd be likin' to know why you don't come in wid me."

It was the first time that any suspicion had ever existed between the mate and his captain.

The Dutch skipper shook his fat sides with laughter, laughter so soft and inaudible that it seemed quite impossible that it could ever have proceeded from so ponderous a body.

"You are mad, mein vriend," he cried.

"Why, shure?"

"I did not vant to go into de room of de fig man only for de reason dat I tought you vould like somevon to vatch for you. Ha, ha! if I 'ad, I sould laugh right aoud. But no, I can have no objection to see you let out a leedle blood from Monsieur Figs. I vould ratker—eh, vat vos dat?"

The Dutchman started.

He was no coward, but knowing what a hideous errand he was on, it would not be a matter of surprise if he felt a cold thrill pass through his form as he saw something glide by him.

Something which seemed in the darkness indistinct, shadowy, impalpable.

What he saw was nothing more nor less than the form of Pat O'Connor.

But he could not know this.

"Shure, and is it the bowld captin s frightened of the dark, thin?" muttered Jack O'Grady, in a tone almost of jeering.

"Shoost so," said the captain, as his immense hand closed on the throat of his mate, "shoost so, and Chack O'Grady ees vonting von leetle choke—ha, ha! he can have von now—a leetle choke dat vill send 'im owd of de vorld vorst. But maind, eef de capden——"

"Hush, masther," whispered Jack, who, in spite of all, respected, and even loved the villanous skipper. "Shure, and it's only jokin' I am. If ye kape on like this, bedad, the whole house'll be round yer ears. Arrah, now, lave off."

His words were fair enough.

So were his tones.

But the skipper, even in the uncertain light, saw the glare of murder in his eye, and he knew whom in the future he was to regard as a foe.

The two men crept into the room together.

Figs was sleeping calmly.

His funny little head was reclining on the white pillow as peacefully as a child, and little did he dream in the honesty of his heart what deadly enemies were approaching to destroy him. The Dutchman bent over him.

"Now, shoost so," he said, in a hoarse whisper; "I vill hold de laight vile you faind de heart ob dis funny leetle man."

Jack O'Grady approached.

Hate and murder gleamed in his eyes.

His knife was raised.

The glow of terrible satisfaction was in the expression of the assassin's face, when his throat was gripped, his knife was dashed from his hand, and, at the same moment the Dutch skipper cried—

"Shoost leave ko, mein poy, you grips too hard. And if you don't leave ko, mein knife must stick in your heart."

"Help, help!" was the shouted reply.

"Help, help!"

The cry resounded from the united voices of Pat O'Connor and Harry Marshall.

They knew well that they were dealing with strong men, with whom it would have been madness to attempt to cope for any length of time.

But they were prepared for emergencies, and they knew that their voices would echo loudly along the old corridors of the school.

"Help, help!"

Again the cry resounded.

"Here, here."

"Here."

"Here."

"All right."

The cries came from different parts of the building, and our hero and his friend knew at once that the inmates of the school had been aroused.

"Tonder and blitzen," cried the Dutch skipper; "tonder and blitzen! dey have raoused de blace. Kill dat leetle phoy of yours, Jack O'Grady, and I vill kill dis von. Eh, what? Oh, tamnation!"

It was brave little Figs that gave rise to this last remark.

Suddenly, when no one was aware that he was even awake, he sprang up.

He took in the scene at a glance.

Having no weapon at hand, he was for a moment at a loss for one.

But only for a moment.

Then he raised his pillow and slapped it in the Dutchman's face.

The skipper was so utterly taken aback that he staggered away, and in so doing he let go his hold of Pat O'Connor.

This was fatal to him.

Neither Pat nor Harry Marshall was deficient in strength, and in an instant he felt himself seized by both in an iron grip.

De Ruyter, on this occasion, used his usual phlegmatic pluck.

For a moment he stood perfectly still, and then, by a gigantic effort, he threw his adversaries from him.

Only for a moment this, too.

For Pat and Harry were both determined, and again they flung themselves upon the reckless smuggler.

"Goot phoys," he cried, as he again flung them from him; "goot phoys. You are too goot for dis vorld; you zall go and see your vriends in de next vorld."

And as he spoke he drew a couple of pistols from his belt and presented one at the head of each of the lads.

There were no half measures in the mind of De Ruyter.

He knew that he was in danger.

He knew that the whole house had been, unfortunately for him, aroused, and that his only chance of safety was a bold stroke.

So, ignoring altogether the presence of Figs, who was the very man they had come to destroy, he fired at the heads of the two boys, and then there was a shriek, a yell of pain, and the Dutchman sprang to the window.

"Come on, Chack," he cried; "be quick. Dro de virepalls down; quick, if you vant to pe saive. I have kilt de two poys, and de oder ve can leave for de present. See, dey lie dere inzensible. Quick, madman. De whole zchool is arouse."

CHAPTER XXVII.

A COWARD'S DEED.

WE must not forget Mary O'Rourke.

Sweet Mary.

Mary with eyes of heaven's blue, with love's own dimples on her chin and her cheeks, with love's own smile upon her rosebud lips.

Sweet Mary.

After the adventures she had gone through, she had been left for a time in comparative quietude.

Again and again Harry Marshall had crept up the mountain path, and sought her father's cabin.

There they had sat hour after hour, Harry teaching her the mysteries of literature and history, while Mary, with her arm round his neck, drank in his words.

It was one evening late, some time after the scene at the fair—on the very night, in fact, of the attack upon the school by the Dutchman and Jack O'Grady, that Mary stood at her door talking to her mother.

The scene was a beautiful one.

The cabin was perched on the side of the mountain, and below the landscape, bordered by the silvery Shannon, was perfectly exquisite.

"How lovely is this place, mother," said Mary.

The mother smiled.

"And yet ye'll be glad whin you lave it, honey."

Mary blushed.

"I'll not be glad, mother," she said, "not be glad to lave it; but you remember, years ago, you were glad to leave Connemara with father."

The love light of years ago sprang into the eyes of Mary's mother.

"Yes, shure, mavourneen," she said, "and I was that same. Oh, I can see now, what a weddin' it was; oh, how happy——"

"Good avening, Misthress O'Rourke," said a gruff voice.

And turning, they saw Dan Hooligan.

It was like a cloud suddenly coming between them and the sun.

"Good avenin' till ye," said Mrs. O'Rourke; "and what brings ye up the mountain this blessed avenin'?"

Mary turned and entered the cabin.

"Shure, and it's meself has come to remind ye of yer promise."

"And what might that be, Mr. Hooligan?"

"About Mary, shure."

"Oh! it's toime enough to talk of that," said Mrs. O'Rourke; "besides, my Dennis is not at hoam, and it's useless it ud be for me to say anythin'."

"Thrue for you thin," said Dan; "but all the same, I'll take a sup of the crather wid ye, and I'll wait until he does come."

Mrs. O'Rourke could scarcely refuse this.

Dennis, her husband, and Dan Hooligan were apparently on the best of terms, and so to refuse a "bite or a sup" would have been highly injudicious.

"Come in, and wilcome, Mr. Hooligan," said Mrs. O'Rourke.

And the man entered.

The interior of the cabin was the same as the interior of all the poor tenements on the mountain side.

A trifle more of comfort was noticeable perhaps, here and there, for Harry Marshall had prevailed on Mary now and then to accept money from him to buy her father and mother little things to add to their scanty store.

Dan scowled as he saw the portrait of his boy-rival hung over the fireplace.

But he said nothing.

He looked around anxiously for Mary.

But she was nowhere to be seen.

He cared little for this, however.

The cabin consisted only of two rooms, and he knew, therefore, that she was in the inner chamber.

He sat down accordingly at the fire.

"Will ye be afther ating anythin', Dan Hooligan?" said the old woman; "we've a foine piece of pork, that Harry Marshall—bless his heart, brought up from Shannonside."

"Which he shtole up at the school," said Dan.

"Shtole! not he. He's the jintleman, he is,

and the good-hearted, ginerous bhoy," said Mrs. O'Rourke, as she raked together her peat-fire and made the water boil.

"Bad cess to 'im," cried Dan; "he's too frindly wi' Mary to suit my time o' day."

"And what has that to do with you, Mr. Hooligan?" said the young girl, as she advanced from the inner room.

Dan muttered a curse.

"To do wid me!" he cried, with flashing eyes, as he sprang to his feet; "to do wid me, when ye are me promised bride? Ain't we goin' to be married in a month?"

"Not that I'm knowin' of, Mr. Hooligan," said Mary.

"Ye'll be my woife or—but there," he added, suddenly suppressing his emotion, and tucking under his arm the shillelagh which he had for an instant grasped fiercely in the intensity of his sudden passion, "there, I will not say any more to you; I'll be talkin' to your mother and father."

He sat down again, and looked gloomily at the fire.

Mary retired once more to her room, while Mrs. O'Rourke began brewing some poteen.

In this process she did not neglect herself; and soon two steaming glasses stood on the rude table.

Dan drank his off at a draught; then, when it was replenished, he said—

"What time do ye expect Dennis home, Mrs. O'Rourke?"

"It'll be late, I'm thinking, this night," replied Mrs. O'Rourke.

"Do you know where he is?"

"I don't know that," said Mrs. O'Rourke, "but I fancy it's at some of those meetin's he is."

As she spoke she bent over the fire.

Dan gave one rapid glance around him.

The door of the inner room was closed.

Instantly Dan took from his pocket a handkerchief saturated with chloroform, and dashed it in her face.

She fell at once insensible.

Dan then sprang up, and softly glided across the room to the inner chamber.

As he passed along, he took from his pocket a rope, which he unwound.

Then he pushed open the door, and walked in.

Mary O'Rourke was expecting Harry Marshall, and her hair was hanging in dishevelled masses over her rounded shoulders, while she was glancing at herself in the glass which Harry had presented to her.

Her back was turned towards the door, but she saw the face of Dan Hooligan, as he glided in.

And she knew, from the expression of his features, and the stealthiness of his movements, that he meant harm.

She sprang round and faced him.

Pale as a ghost now as she was, Dan had never seen her look more beautiful.

"What do you want, Mr. Hooligan," she cried, with flashing eyes and heaving bosom; "what do you want? This is my room."

Dan laughed.

"Shure, and that's the reason I'm here," he said.

"I repeat—what do you want?" said Mary. She looked him steadily in the eyes.

And as he gazed at her strong, active form, rendered robust by the bracing air of the mountains, he felt that there must be a fierce struggle for the mastery.

"Shure, and it's yerself I'm wantin'," said Dan.

"Well, speak and go."

"It's not talking to ye I'd be afther," said Dan; "I want to speak to you when I have ye to myself in my cabin. Come on."

"And where would I be going, Mr. Hooligan?" said Mary, with a look of contempt.

"To my place—come quick," he cried.

And he advanced towards her.

"Keep back, I warn ye, keep back," cried Mary; "help, mother, help!"

Dan grinned and drew back, so that the door was free.

"Don't call on yer mither," he cried; "look in there. She'll be quiet, I'm thinking, for an hour or two, unless the docthor's decaved me."

The girl sprang forward, and took an eager glance into the front chamber.

"Fiend! coward!" she cried. "Ah! villain, release me!"

As she had leaned forward and beheld the scene in there, pausing for a moment, as if paralysed, Dan Hooligan had seized her by the arms behind.

Then, in an instant, her wrists were tied, and she was helpless.

She continued to scream and struggle.

"Help! murder! help!"

But there was no answer, save the echo of her own voice.

"Ha, ha!" laughed Dan; "scream away, alanna. There's no one nigh."

"Father, father!" cried the girl.

"That's just about the only one I'm afeard of just now," cried the ruffian, "but ye see he's not here yet. We'll be goin' quick, though, for fear he might interrupt our courtin'.'"

And with that, he suddenly passed a cloth over her mouth and tied it tightly behind her head, so that her cries were completely stifled.

Struggle and writhe now she could.

But of what avail was it, when her wrists were tied?

Lifting her in his strong arms, Dan quickly bore her to the door of the cabin, and looked out.

It was dark now.

A heavy sky brooded over the mountains.

"All's well," he said. "I'm in for luck to-night."

And away he plunged, up the narrow mountain path.

The shanty to which Dan was bearing his prize stood at the very summit of the great hills.

It was a lonely spot, with scarcely a habitation within a quarter of a mile.

It was not, in fact, used as a dwelling-place, even by Dan, except upon occasions when he wanted to hide away.

It contained only a heap of straw, a table and a chair.

But Dan was a son of the mountains, and was inured to hardship and exposure, and here

"MAY THE FAMINE LAST TILL YER'E STARVED TO THE BONE," CRIED DAN HOOLIGAN."

for many a night he had lain, listening to the great winds roaring and raging.

As soon as they had left the cabin of Dennis O'Rourke some distance behind them, he placed her on her feet and forced her along.

It was useless to attempt any resistance now.

It would, indeed, have even been perilous.

For on either side the path, every now and then, shelved down in sudden slopes, which, in some cases, led to the edge of a precipice.

So on they hurried, until at length the shanty was reached. It was pitch dark.

But as soon as Dan had pushed in the helpless girl, and bolted and barred the door, he lit a murky oil lamp, and raked up a peat fire, that had been long mouldering.

Then he poured himself out a drop of neat whisky from a large black bottle.

After this he removed the gag from the mouth of Mary O'Rourke, untied her hands, and sat down on the edge of the heap of straw.

He pointed to the stool.

"Sit down there, Mistress Mary O'Rourke," he said, sneeringly; "the place isn't quite a proper one to bring a bride to, but I'll be givin' ye a bitther home by-and-bye, mavourneen."

The girl eyed him with haughty contempt.

She was free from her bonds now, and on her guard.

"Home! I'll never have a home where you are," said Mary O'Rourke.

"Don't be sayin' that now, Mary dear," cried Dan. "Shure, and the praste'll be here in a moment."

"Let him come."

"I've bargained wid him, my honey," said Dan, "and he'll bring two witnesses, and ye'll be Mrs. Hooligan, Mary alanna, in an hour from now."

"Never! I'll die first."

"Oh, and it's not death we'll be talkin' about, but happiness and love, Mary. Ah! what's that? Holy Vargin protect us! what now?"

No wonder was it that he started back aghast, and nearly fell off his stool.

For up from among the straw, just at the back of Mary O'Rourke, there rose two figures.

Figures clad in long, frieze coats, and wearing black masks.

CHAPTER XXVIII.
THE DUTCHMAN ONCE MORE.

WHEN De Ruyter sprang towards the window, he found that it was latched.

This, of course, caused a momentary delay, and in that moment sprang forward Tim Finnigan, and fastened on his neck.

At the same moment, as with a terrible oath, he strove to free himself from the grasp of the brave little usher, Thaddeus O'Shaughnessy rushed into the room.

He was followed by Laurence McMahon, and several of the boys.

At the same moment Pat O'Connor and Harry Marshall, who had been only slightly wounded, rose to their feet.

The Dutchman saw that he was in a trap.

But his courage did not desert him.

He knew, of course, that escape for the moment was impossible.

But he knew also that friends were near.

With the butt end of one of his pistols, therefore, he dashed out a pane of glass.

Then, in an instant, he had placed a blue light in it, and fired it in the air.

After this he turned to Thaddeus O'Shaughnessy.

"Pray, Mr. De Ruyter, what are you doing in my house?" said the schoolmaster.

He spoke calmly, though his finger was on the trigger of his pistol.

"I gome to see Mr. Vigs," said the Dutchman.

"What for?"

"Shoost to ask him vot he has don mit Mat O'Grady."

"Yes, shure, my brother whom he murdered," cried Jack O'Grady, savagely.

"This is not the time to ask him questions. How did ye enter my house?" said Thaddeus."

"Dat is mein affair," said De Ruyter.

"Excuse me," said Pat O'Connor; "I can explain all, if I may."

"Proceed," said Thaddeus. "I will protect you."

He said this because he saw that the eyes of both the smuggler and Jack were fixed upon the scholar with a vengeful glance.

Quickly, and without hesitation, Pat O'Connor told his story.

The Dutchman, as he listened, was livid with rage.

And he muttered, too, an oath of vengeance.

For even now, surrounded as he was by enemies, he never dreamed of being made prisoner.

Or, at any rate, he never dreamed of suffering punishment.

When Pat had finished, Thaddeus said—

"This is conclusive. Mr. Finnigan, will you please take my mare and ride over to the constabulary? There must be a stop put to this."

Figs lost no time in hurrying on his things.

Then he hastened away, and Thaddeus and his boys were left in charge of the Dutchman.

The latter took out his pipe and lit it.

"Vell, I vill shoost have a smoag," he said, "undil de gonstables coom. Jack, give me de bottle of schnapps."

Within ten minutes more the garden was suddenly lit up by a brilliant light.

"Ha, ha!" cried De Ruyter; "ha, ha, now for mein revenge. Mein phoys are coming."

CHAPTER XXIX.
ON THE ROAD TO DEATH.

DAN HOOLIGAN stood transfixed with horror as he saw the two men.

"And pray, jintlemen," he said, "may I be afther asking what ye're doin' in my own private cabin?"

"You are summoned to the thribunal, Dan."

"And pray what for?" asked Hooligan.

"That's a matther that ye must be settlin' wid our masthers," returned the man; "it's not our place to say, but to do. So come on."

"Come on, where?"

"Wid us."

"Shure, and I've got betther business at home," said Dan, "seein' I'm goin' to be married within an hour to one of the purtiest girls near Ballynara."

"That's nought to do with it," cried the second man. "Put on yer caubeen and follow us quietly."

"Then I'll not be doin' that same," cried Dan. "I don't know what right ye've got to take me at all, at all, and I'll resist to the utmost."

"Ye'll be finding your mistake purty soon then," said the other man; "here's two people against ye, or I may say three, for, from what I've heard, I'm thinking the colleen here will be grateful to be rid of ye."

"I shall, indeed," cried Mary O'Rourke; "it's myself will be helping in anything that ud be getting me out of the way of the big blaggard."

Dan Hooligan was in a terrible rage at this.

His mouth almost foamed with fury.

His eyes glared, his lips became livid.

"The colleen will sing a different tune whin she's bin the mate of the Hooligan for a time," cried Dan. "Give me the summons, and then be off."

"Come," cried one of the men in masks, "we've stood this long enough. Are you coming, or shall we drag you with us?"

"Whin is the summons for?"

"For to-night."

"At what hour?"

"Eleven."

"Then I can be married first and attend the meeting after," cried Dan, with a forced laugh; "so be off wid ye, for a couple of meddlesome vagabonds. Me a-coortin' too, and the praste ixpected ivery blissed minute."

"Seize him," exclaimed the man; "it is getting late now. Mary O'Rourke, unbolt the door."

The girl at once flew to do their bidding.

Dan Hooligan sprang to prevent her.

But in vain.

The two men were beforehand with him and opposed his passage.

One of them held a pistol in his hand.

The other had a coil of rope.

Dan saw he was in their power.

But he had no idea of giving in at once.

He tried to wheedle them out of their purpose.

"Will now, jintlemen, since ye are determined that I shall go up to the mountains wid ye this blessed night, will ye be afther waiting for me? Will ye have the kindness to wait outside while the praste tucks us up and so forth?"

He gabbled in vain.

"Bind him," said the man with the pistol.

If anything was to be done now, it was high time to think of it.

Dan glanced at the wall over the peat fire.

On it was suspended a hanger.

The man approached nearer, and placed the barrel of the pistol close to Dan's head.

Dan staggered back from the gleaming barrel.

"Move an inch towards that weapon," cried the man, "and I will blow your brains out."

His voice and his manner of speaking were quite different to those of his companion.

There was something superior in the ring of his words, and the style of his bearing, and Dan Hooligan felt alarmed and awed.

He dared not move now, as the other man advanced and began to bind him.

Mary O'Rourke, who stood by the open door, could not help indulging in a laugh.

"Sure, and it's the bhoys will be making merry over Dan Hooligan's wedding," she cried; "no matter, better luck next time."

"I'm fearing there will be no sicond toime for 'm, Mary O'Rourke," said the man, in a solemn voice; "he's been doin' what he knows will bring him to death, and he will pay the penalty."

"Shure, and it's meself knows I am innocent, Barney O'Reilly," cried Dan; "it's yer name, I know will now from yer voice. You were always a croakin' owld ravin. Bad cess to ye, I'll be aven wid ye, ye cowardly omadhaun."

Then, turning to Mary, he added—

"Good night, for the prisint, alanna. I'm sorry for ye that the praste didn't come sooner. But, don't be frightened, mavourneen, I'll be your husband to-morrow. So don't be afther runnin' away and losin' yerself on the mountain's side."

"It's not runnin' away I'll be," said Mary; "I'm comin' up the hills with yer, for I don't know my way home, and I'm sure the bhoys will protect me till the mornin'."

"That's thrue for you," said the man, whom Dan had addressed as Barney O'Reilly, "shure and it's the bhoys that will protect you properly. Come on, Dan, the chaps will be waiting for ye."

The helpless prisoner was now seized by the arm and led up the rocks.

He made no further remark now, but sullenly advanced with them up the rugged acclivity.

It was a long and weary journey up the hills, and down again into the valleys, and again up higher hills still.

But at length they reached a tumble-down shanty, which was ablaze with light.

There was very little ceremony on entering here.

Barney O'Reilly gave one shrill whistle, and the door was at once opened.

The man who opened it to them was Terence O'Rafferty.

He stared as he saw Mary O'Rourke with Dan and the others.

"What have ye brought the girl wid ye for?" he cried.

"Shure and we couldn't be afther lavizg her in Dan's cabin all alone, and she there against her will," cried Barney. "She won't split upon us."

"I know that," said Terence. "So, as ye've brought her, take her to the back room, where ye'll find old Mother Dobeen a-brewing whisky, and then come back to the council-room."

The chamber which Terence dignified by the high-sounding title of "council-room" was a wretched place.

The wind rushed in through frequent rents in the wall, forcing the smoke from the peat fire to curl in fantastic coils over the ceiling, and driving it away from the hole which served for a chimney.

So, what with the smoke from the fire, and that from their pipes, the men looked as if they were sitting in a fog.

The fog was not so dense, however, that it prevented Mary from seeing that her father was one of those who sat round the rough table. He met her glance with a dark scowl, but said nothing.

And so, as soon as she had passed into the inner room, the men drew up to the table, the prisoner was placed at the end in a chair, and the proceedings began.

"Dan Hooligan," said the man who had accompanied Barney O'Reilly, and who had not removed his mask, "you know, of course, what you are here for."

"Shure and it's myself does not know that same," said Dan.

"You are accused of being a spy."

"And that's false."

"But what if it's proved?"

"It can't be."

"But, come now, answer me in a straight-forward manner," said the man, sternly. "You know the rules of our society?"

"Yes."

"Well, then, if a man is proved absolutely to be a spy, what ought to be his fate?"

"Shure and he'd be sintenced to death," was the reply.

"Then you've pronounced your own doom," said the man, solemnly. "Now then, Dan Hooligan, you were, on the night of October the 21st, 1839, initiated, when you were quite a boy, into the Society of the United Irishmen."

"Yes."

"You swore, as you valued your life, never to betray a secret belonging to the society?"

"Yes."

"And you knew that if you broke this oath, the penalty would be death?"

"Yes."

"Very well. Now, then, Tom Cartwright, stand forward."

A tall man stood up, and, casting aside his frieze cloak, disclosed a military uniform— the uniform of the 7th English Dragoons.

Dan turned pale.

He knew now what kind of evidence was going to be brought against him.

"Tom Cartwright, you are a soldier in the service of England?" asked the masked man.

"I am, sir, though I'm an Irishman, and I hate the murtherin' Saxon," returned Cartwright.

"Well, you are also a member of our society, and bound by its oaths."

"Yes, sir."

"You know the penalty of giving false information and trying to get a brother member into trouble by false evidence."

"Dith, sir," replied the soldier, simply.

"Well, then, answer me truly. You were one of a squadron of horse soldiers on duty at Ballynara at the time of the fair."

"Yes, sir."

"And you saw Pat O'Connor and his friend go into the colonel's tent."

"Yes."

"And as they went out, you saw Dan Hooligan enter."

"Yes, sir; by the token it wasn't the first time I'd seen him."

"And you heard the conversation between him and the colonel."

"Yes, sir."

"Then repeat it."

"Well, sir, I'd be tellin' a loie if I said I could do that," returned Cartwright, "but I'll tell ye the shubstance."

"That'll do."

"Well, sir," continued the soldier, "Dan Hooligan was with the colonel a long time. He towld him the whole history of the conspiracy, and towld him, too, the day of the risin'.

"And thin, sir," he added, "and thin, bad cess to 'im, he described the cave in the gap, and the secret hiding-place on the island."

A hum, a hoarse murmur of anger, proceeded from the thirty men assembled.

"And was that all?" asked the man.

"No, sir, that wasn't all. The colonel guv him a twenty-pun noat, and Dan agreed to sind, or bring, him informashun up to the last moment, so that we should be all caught like rats in a trap."

"Is that all, Tom Cartwright?"

"Yes, sir; except that he has a free pass to go wherever he likes, and a five-pun noat for every cowardly bit of information he gives to betray his brothers."

The man said these simple words with an emphasis which made the men howl with execration. Dan, bound as he was, sprang up, pale with rage and terror.

"It's a loi," he cried, "a loi! This blaggard is swearin' away me life."

Tom Cartwright turned and looked him fixedly in the face.

"It's thrue; thrue as the day," he cried, "and so I can prove."

"You murtherin' thafe and blaggard," exclaimed Dan, furious at his danger, "where's your proofs?"

"If the bhoys don't belave me," cried Cartwright, "we can fitch the two lads from the school, and they'll tell the truth, I know. They both saw Dan Hooligan there as plain as they saw the colonel."

"Shure, and if I was there, it was only to put the colonel off the scint," cried Dan.

"Then you acknowledge you were there," said the man in the mask.

"Well, I sartinly was there, but it was to thry and find out what the two bhoys from the Shannon Academy were doing," returned Hooligan.

"Search him," cried the leader.

Willing hands soon emptied the pockets of the suspected spy.

On him was found the safe conduct signed by the colonel, besides a scrawl of Dan's own, which fully bore out the theory of his guilt.

Dan's face was livid as these documents were produced.

But he endeavoured to brave it out.

"I know nothing aboot these papers," he said; "I expect they were put there in my pocket on my road here."

A groan followed these words, a groan which, Dan Hooligan knew well, did not portend any good to him.

He tried to speak again, but his voice was drowned in an angry hum, and the man in the mask having obtained silence, rose and said—

"Brothers, you have heard all."

"Yes," was the chorused answer.

"Have you any doubt of Dan Hooligan's guilt?"

"None."

"Then what shall be his doom?"

"Death!"

The word was uttered plainly and unhesitatingly, and Dan, shivering and shuddering, cowered down upon his chair, knowing well that his doom was sealed.

"Take the prisoner away," said the man in the mask, "and let him await us up at Badloe's Point. In his absence we will deliberate upon what his death is to be. Traitors have been abundant lately, and it is time that one of them met with a death that will prove a warning to others."

Two of the men at once sprang up.

One of them was Dennis O'Rourke, the father of pretty Mary.

The other was Tom Cartwright.

The shivering prisoner, whose teeth chattered so that he was unable to speak coherently, though he babbled wildly for mercy, was at once led away and hurried up the rough mountain path, while his cruel, or, at least, his inexorable judges, sat around the rude table, and over their pipes and whisky decided the fate of their comrade.

Dan Hooligan, meanwhile, went up silently with his captors until they reached the summit of the crags known as Badloe's Point.

His mind was in such a whirl with terror and excitement that he did not know what to say.

And so, as his companions preserved an utter silence, he did not utter a word.

At last they reached their destination.

It was a curious place.

A place where a square piece of verdure was to be seen on the summit of the highest point of the hills.

From this point they were able to see around them for miles.

Dan sat down upon a piece of fallen rock, and leaned his head upon his chest.

O'Rourke and his companion folded their arms and leaned against a tree—a forlorn, blighted-looking thing that grew on the edge of a cliff.

Presently the former spoke.

"It'll be a wild night," he said. "The sea yonder is breaking up into white wavelets, and the clouds are coming up in big black banks."

"How long will the bhoys be, do ye think?" asked the other.

"Shure and it's that same I don't know," said O'Rourke; "but I don't suppose they'll be long."

"I hope they won't be," cried the other, "for it's moighty cold up here."

"Oh; but the job won't take long, Tom," said O'Rourke.

It was these words that made Dan Hooligan find his speech.

"Surely they won't be afther killing me

after all, will they, Mr. O'Rourke?" he said, in a voice of supplication.

"Bedad, then, if they changed their minds and didn't, I'd be afther killing ye myself," returned the man.

"And what for?" whined Hooligan.

"For having my colleen up at your shanty against her will," cried O'Rourke, in a furious tone, "ye decaving thief. But the bhoys reached ye in time, or she wouldn't ha' come in so pleasant-like."

"We should ha' bin married in less than an hour, Misther O'Rourke," said Dan, "if ye'd only not sent the bhoys afther me so soon."

"Good luck to 'em that they were so quick," said O'Rourke. "They saved my girl from the dishonour of being the mate of sich a murtherin' blaggard as you, and they saved me from the thruble of blowing yer brains out."

"Oh, Mr. O'Rourke," returned Dan, "it's meself——"

"Howld your coward's tongue," cried O'Rourke. "Here come the bhoys."

CHAPTER XXX.

THE DOOM OF THE TRAITOR.

THE United Irishmen were coming up the rocky path, headed by two men with torches.

Every one of them carried flambeaux, but at present they were not ignited.

They were reserved in order to cast a bright light over the spot where the spy and informer was to meet his fate.

Dan Hooligan watched their advance with horror-stricken eyes.

He felt the approach of death already.

Slowly the men came onwards.

Then, when they had reached the spot where the wretched informer cowered, they drew round him in a circle.

"Stand up, Dan Hooligan," cried the man in the mask.

And, as he staggered to his feet, lights were passed one to another, and in a moment the place was one glow of light.

The prisoner seemed to have grown suddenly older. His features—always ugly—were now drawn down, and pinched, and haggard.

His eyes seemed starting from his head, his mouth hung, and his head drooped forward.

He was the very picture of abject terror.

"Dan Hooligan," again said the man in the mask, in tones which echoed over the cliffs, "you have been, as ye know, doomed to a traitor's death."

"Yes," cried Dan Hooligan in a shrill voice of mingled fear and fury, "yes, I have, by a set of thunderin' thaves who have no more right to do it than the waves of the say."

"You could have had the same power, and have exercised the same power over another when proved to be a traitor," pursued the leader, "and so do not question a power you yourself helped to make; and," he added, "as the deaths which have been meted out to some have not served to deter others from joining the infamous ranks of spies and informers, it has been resolved to make a terrible example of you."

Dan shuddered, but made no reply.

He knew he was doomed now.

"Yes," continued the judge, "we have shot spies, and flung them over rocks, and hung them, and yet the loathsome tribe still flourishes; so, to give more terror to the doom which inevitably follows treachery, we have resolved to bury you alive."

There was an instant's silence.

Then a piercing shriek rang through the night, and the wretched creature fell on his knees, struggling with his hands, as if trying to clasp them together in supplication.

"Spare me! spare me!" he cried. "Sure, and I'll sarve the society like a slave, I will. Shure, and I'm only a poor bhoy, and I was timpted sore by the money, I was. Mercy! mercy!"

"Small mercy ye had towards us," said Terence O'Rafferty. "If ye'd had yer way, the prison and the scaffold would have been the lot of all of us."

"And it's the same will be yer lot now, villains and cowards!" cried Dan, in a shriek of rage, as he staggered again to his feet; "curse ye all! The curse of a dying man fall upon ye all! May the famine last till ye're starved to the bone—may yer children die of starvation before yer eyes—may yer mithers dhrop did at yer fate, and yer daughters die in shame and dishonour—may all the ills of Heaven be upon ye in this life, and the fires of everlasting torment be yer lot in the next!"

The men who stood round were brave, every one of them.

But still, there was something so terrible in this curse, hurled at them by the lips of a man who stood, as it were, on the brink of the grave—that they could not help experiencing a thrill of horror.

Yet they never dreamed of swerving from their purpose.

They one and all regarded him as the attempted murderer of every one of them, and as such, they considered him only justly condemned.

The only one who seemed in no way affected by the awful curse was the man in the mask.

He suffered the wretched spy to finish his invectives, and then, in a calm, cool voice, he said—

"O'Rourke, and five others of ye, dig the grave."

It was a terrible scene now.

The men who, according to instructions, dug a deep hole, instead of a long grave, worked away with a savage will in the red glow of the torches, while Dan, supporting himself against the withered tree, cursed and entreated, and prayed and cursed, in turns.

Again and again the doomed man glanced with a terrible eagerness at the black gulf beneath the cliffs.

He knew that he was fated to die, and the death that was before him was so terrible that a dash, a leap, and a crashing fall down—down from those rugged cliffs upon the jagged beach below—seemed a heavenly mercy too great to be secured.

But it was not to be.

The crowd of men was so closely surrounding him that he could not make the attempt.

And so, with gasping breath, and clenched hands, and a body that writhed in alternate spasms of agony and rage, Dan Hooligan still leaned against the tree and waited.

The men worked with a will.

Soon a deep hole was dug in the soft earth.

The green spot was in a kind of hollow, where rains gathered and soaked in continually.

The man in the mask made no sign, but only a significant gesture.

Then four of the men advanced, seized the unfortunate wretch, and in a moment he was standing in the hole, with his head about a foot below the level of the earth.

Two men held him while the earth was piled in and stamped down on either side.

This was done until he was buried—all but his head, which was so fixed that he could move it neither one way nor the other.

Then the man in the mask advanced closer, and, at a sign from him, the others did the same.

The torches were raised, and the red glow fell upon a face upon which the lines of death were already thickening fast.

"Dan Hooligan," he said, in a solemn voice, "have you anything to say?"

"Nothing, but to renew my curse," returned the white lips.

"Have you made your peace with Heaven?"

"Hiven! And is it you who talk of Hiven? By your cruelty and vindictiveness, shure, I may be standing at Hiven's gates now," cried Dan, "but yer don't know how far ye're standing off from them yoursilves."

"Then you have nothing to say?" said the leader, in his usual cool, collected, and stern voice.

"Nothing more."

"Then end it at once."

The men at once began to shovel in the earth so as to cover his head.

As they did so, and the men looked on with staring eyeballs and set teeth, a wild shriek rent the air, and a white figure rushed in among them.

Rushed in and flung herself on her knees by the side of Dan Hooligan—or, rather, the white, ghastly, death-like face that showed where Dan Hooligan was.

It was Mary O'Rourke.

Mary, his deadly enemy.

All stared, speechless with astonishment, as they saw her kneeling there, with face upraised in entreaty, her hands clasped eagerly, her face deadly pale, the tears pouring down her cheeks.

The men who were shovelling in the earth paused in their hideous labour.

"Oh, mercy—mercy!" cried the girl, wildly. "Surely your hearts are not made of steel—surely ye won't do this terrible thing! Ye've killed him well-nigh with fright. Let him go now, and shure he'll niver betray you again."

"Take her away," growled a voice.

"No, no; not till ye've promised me to let him go," she almost shrieked. "He's me worst enemy—he's been a bad, a wicked man to me, but oh! I can't see him die thus. Be men—be human beings! Don't send the boy out of the world like this. For my sake—for the sake of all the women of Ireland, don't do this dreadful deed!"

A voice, low and trembling, terrible in its subdued tones, coming to her from the earth, like a voice from the grave, was her first answer.

"Heaven bless you, Mary, and forgive me," were the words, coming from the white, parched lips of Dan Hooligan.

Her second answer was a roar of angry voices, sounding like the wild chorus of beasts deprived of their prey.

"Take her away!"

"Away wid her for a meddling fool!"

"O'Rourke, are ye a thraithor too?"

With a howl of anger her father sprang to her side and dragged her from the ground.

"Traitress, ye have bin decaving me—decaving us all," he shouted. "Come away wid ye! Bad cess to the daughter of mine that'd save a black-hearted spy and traitor like Hooligan. Come quietly, softly now, or, bedad, I'll fling ye over the cliff."

The girl, as she was dragged away, seemed quite to lose her senses.

The mountain air was rent with her cries as she was hurried from the scene, and then the men resumed their ghastly work of filling in the grave.

Ten minutes more, and Dan Hooligan's last smothered cry mingled with the agonised shrieks of the girl, who would have saved him.

CHAPTER XXXI.

THE SMUGGLERS TO THE RESCUE—CAPTURED.

WE must now return to the school on the Shannon's banks.

When the Dutch smuggler had shouted in glee that his men were coming to the rescue, he had told the truth.

Matters had been so arranged that only a certain time was to elapse before his return to the "Silverhorn," and so, finding that their captain did not come up to time, twenty of the crew, heavily armed, had rowed up the river in boats.

And now, on the pistol-shot, which was the signal of De Ruyter, the blue light shot up from the foremost boat, and the whole crew landed in the grounds.

Of course, had any houses been immediately adjoining the academy, the thought of an attack upon it would have been utter madness.

But, as it happened the school was quite a quarter of a mile distant from any other human habitation, they expected to be able to make an entry into the place before any aid could come from elsewhere.

So, acting upon the same reckless principles which had actuated Jack O'Grady and Captain De Ruyter, they at once dashed across the grounds and precipitated themselves against the front door.

The door of Shannon Academy, however, was not to be thus easily forced.

It was a strong, iron-bound one, and it resisted every effort to force it for a long time.

During this time, the boys of the Shannon school had flown to the place where they knew a quantity of arms were stacked.

The rifles they had found in the barn at the "Who'd-ha'-thought-it?" were still at the academy.

In fact, Darby had never thought of reclaiming them.

Thaddeus was one of the "Brotherhood," and it was not considered worth while to take them from him.

They were as safe in his custody as in that of anyone else.

So while Figs, McMahon, and the schoolmaster, with one or two others, kept the Dutchman and Jack O'Grady at bay, Pat O'Connor and several of the boys rushed off.

In five minutes they returned, each armed with a rifle.

Thaddeus had quite forgotten the fact that he was so fully armed.

A glow of pleasure overspread his face at once.

And the greater, because the hope of safety came again from his favourite scholar, Pat.

"We're ready, sir," said our hero, "and at your disposal, sir, if ye'll only tell us what to do."

"Brave boys, brave boys!" cried O'Shaughnessy, rubbing his hands, and then taking a rifle from our hero. "Go, six of ye, to each window on this side of the house, and fire down upon the invaders."

"Then I'll remain here," said Pat O'Connor, with brightening eyes; "for there is an enemy here that I have promised to meet face to face."

The Dutch captain met the eye of the brave boy, and he winced.

Aye! the man who had gone through a hundred fights, who had laughed at the revenue coasters, who was as brave as a lion, quailed before the earnest gaze of Pat O'Connor.

He had not forgotten the vow that had been made by Pat, when first they had met on the bosom of the Shannon.

De Ruyter was now taken entirely at a disadvantage. The boys levelled their rifles.

They only awaited the order to fire.

To resist now would have been worse than folly.

"Captain De Ruyter!" cried Thaddeus O'Shaughnessy; "surrender, or your life."

"Vell," said the Dutchman, with a laugh; "I do not vant to go de long shourney shoost yet, and so I vill surrender mit pleasure. Here is mine sword and mine pistols, and mine leetle knife; and now, Mr. Jonessy, vile I am de guest of de worthy zcoolmaster, I zshall be dreeded like von of de vamily.

"Yes," added he, with a loud guffaw; "dere is von leetle weapon dat I have not given up, and dad is mein pipe. I smokes him mit your bermission."

And the daring man took out his large pipe, and lit it.

And all the time his men were battering away at the door, and the scholars were preparing to fire upon them.

When the windows had been well filled with the lads armed for the encounter, Thaddeus leaned out.

The window of his room was just above the

"AT LENGTH I HOLD THE DOCUMENTS WHICH WILL MAKE ME MASTER OF BARRYMORE,' CRIED THE BARRY."

door which the smugglers were striving to batter in.

"Below there! what do you want?"

"Our cabten!" shouted a Dutch sailor.

"He is a prisoner, and will be soon on his way to gaol."

"Ha, ha! shoost so. De cock does crow!" cried the Dutch skipper, with a loud laugh, as he put his head out also. "Mine prave phoys, do not pelieve——"

But he had no time for further speech.

Thaddeus turned and seized him by the throat, and hurled him back into the room.

And here the boys surrounded him, and Pat O'Connor said in a stern voice—

"Captain De Ruyter, we are boys, but these troublesome times make us men. If you cross again towards that window, I will fire."

De Ruyter recoiled, for there was that in the tones of Pat O'Connor, and the rapid movement of his finger to the trigger, that assured him resistance would be certain death.

Meanwhile the colloquy between Thaddeus and the assailing party continued—

"Ev he is a brisoner, he is in the haouz, so ve vill vorce our way in. Go it, vriends."

"I warn you," shouted Thaddeus, "that you are not attacking a place filled with unarmed men. At every window are young and brave fellows, whose rifles cover ye, and——"

"Dere, shots up!" cried another Dutchman, "shots up, we know what viting is. Ve vant de cabden. Ye shoost gib him do uz, and we go our way mid bleasure."

"Then ye refuse to retire!"

"Yes, be tammed to ye."

"Fire, boys!" thundered O'Shaughnessy, and set the example himself.

A shriek of agony rose from among the men. Then a voice cried—

"Get ready de vire balls; set vire to de haouz."

The crashing sound of the rifles, as they poured their deadly volleys from the windows of the academy, went echoing dully over the bosom of the Shannon, and far up among the rugged crags of the mountains.

Yells of agony arose from the huddled throng at the door.

But they did not flinch from their task.

Moving away their wounded, they once more attacked the door, mingling their blows with horrid imprecations and shouts of vengeance.

Huge hammers were brought to bear on the door, and soon even its iron-bound timbers began to crack and splinter.

Thaddeus O'Shaughnessy, pale and yet firm and undaunted, could not but think with dread of a probable conflict between the desperate crew of the "Silverhorn" and the scholars whom he had under his charge.

The Dutch skipper continued to smoke his pipe contentedly, every now and then giving vent to an exclamation.

"Hein! but de phoys vite vell. Ha! dat is von proper blow. Ha, ha! Mister Zchoolmaster, you vill pay for dis."

Thaddeus made no reply, but continued to give his orders.

"Now, then, my lads," he cried, "steady there. Keep yourselves as little exposed as possible. Now, then, fire!"

If he directed his scholars not to expose themselves, he did not act upon the idea himself.

He leaned far out of the window every now and then, so as to be able to command a view of all the windows, and his broad-built, commanding figure formed a ready butt for the rifles of the enemy.

But he seemed, as it were, to possess a charmed life.

Crack! crack! the rifles went at him,

But in vain.

The noble head, with its grizzled hair streaming in the wind, was still protruded from the window.

Presently, just as he was about to issue further orders, a loud crash proclaimed that the door had been forced in.

The Dutchman did not move from his seat.

But he puffed out a large cloud of smoke, chuckled loudly, and said—

"Ha, ha! de dime approaches. Ve vill durn de dables on you, Mister O'Zhounessy."

Already the tramp of men was heard in the passage below.

Already a scuffle on the broad staircase showed that the battle had commenced, when there was a loud shout without, the great bell of the school rang clangingly, and, amid the flare of torches, a troop of dragoons appeared.

In another moment they had ridden round through the great gates into the backgrounds.

Here they dismounted at once from their horses, and drew their long cavalry swords.

With these, and without any regard to the fact that the smugglers had firearms, they rushed into the house.

"Back, boys, back," cried Thaddeus. "Close the windows. Let the soldiers do the rest."

The casements were at once closed, and the boys hurried down, disposing themselves in such positions over the house that they could see a little of what was going on.

The dragoons made short work of the smugglers now.

De Ruyter himself, though he had up to this time pretended to be possessed of such *sang froid*, turned deadly pale.

He saw plainly that his game was up.

At any rate for the present.

There were several sharp tussles on the stairs, several sharp discharges of musketry, followed by groans and cries of pain.

And then came a triumphant cheer.

De Ruyter sprang to his feet.

He had been roused to excitement at last.

"Curse the infernal red coats," he cried. "Tonder and blitzen, but I vill——"

"Advance one step, and you're a dead man," cried Pat O'Connor, levelling his piece as De Ruyter made a step forward, as if to rush to the door.

The Dutchman gnashed his teeth in rage.

"Ha, you zall all pay de dear price for dis," he cried. "De dime vill gome."

At this instant a tall officer, resplendent in plumed helmet and gold lace, entered the room.

He bowed to Thaddeus.

"The affair is over," he said, with a smile; "we have made ten prisoners. Six more are

wounded and cannot be removed, three are dead, one has made his escape across the grounds."

"I am most indebted to you," said Thaddeus O'Shaughnessy, "but there are two prisoners here of greater consequence than the rest."

"Who are they?" asked the dragoon officer.

"Their leader, Captain De Ruyter, of the 'Silverhorn,' and his friend John O'Grady, brother of the serving-man whom I gave in custody a short time since, and who, after escaping from gaol, was found dead on the rocks."

The officer took one rapid glance at the two men who stood bold and defiant, though pale as death.

Then he went to the door and called two of his men by name.

In a moment a couple of stalwart troopers made their appearance.

"Arrest these men," said the officer.

And the troopers at once advanced with handcuffs.

The Dutchman glanced at Jack O'Grady, and made a peculiar sign.

Jack O'Grady evidently understood him at once. He held out his hands instantly, and the steel clasps clicked upon him.

De Ruyter did the same, and the prisoners waited, with a kind of haughty pride, to be taken away.

"Any orders, Mr. O'Shaughnessy?" said the officer.

"I shall come over in the morning," returned the schoolmaster. "I suppose I need not show up to-night?"

"Oh, no," replied the officer. "I have seen enough to justify me in taking the whole lot into custody. Come, gentlemen; we must be going."

"Mit bleasure," said the Dutchman. "You have only done your duty. I do not plame you, but you, Mr. O'Zhaughnessy, remember that De Ruyter never vorgives. You have got de pest ob me to-nide, but it zall not pe long before I have von grand revenge."

And, with the air of an injured king, he stalked from the room, followed by Jack O'Grady, still pale, but bold and defiant.

"We have triumphed to-night," said Thaddeus O'Shaughnessy, "and through my boys, my brave boys. Pat O'Connor and Harry Marshall, you were the first to defeat these villains, and I cannot feel it in my heart to think of punishment. Go to your room, and pray let us hear no more of practical jokes."

It could scarcely be imagined that order could be soon restored in the academy after such an unprecedented thing as the attack upon it by the smugglers, but it was at last.

Then Thaddeus O'Shaughnessy sent round to all the boys some warm drink to cheer them after their battle, and, having been told to take an hour or two extra rest in the morning, they were left to talk of their strange adventures and to drop off to sleep one by one.

CHAPTER XXXII.
INTO THE JAWS OF DEATH.

MEANWHILE, De Ruyter and his companions were taken off by the troopers.

The soldiers were not disposed to walk after riding, and so the prisoners were fastened by ropes or straps, the ends of which were held in the hands of the horsemen.

In this manner they quitted the grounds of the school, and began the ascent of the mountain.

It was very dark, and a chill wind, rushing down from the hills, caused the soldiers to keep their heads bent to avoid the keenness of the blast.

This gave De Ruyter an idea.

An idea which would never have suggested itself to anyone less desperate than the Dutch skipper.

Nothing less than an idea of escape.

To him the bare notion of confinement in a Saxon prison was as bad, and even worse, than death.

Indeed he would seriously have preferred the latter, if met in fair fight.

To risk his life, therefore, under such circumstances was nothing to De Ruyter.

And so in his heart he had conceived a desperate scheme.

The scheme included not only his own escape, but that of Jack O'Grady.

Jack was walking side by side with him, and there was no difficulty, therefore, in communicating with him.

"Jack," he said, "vot are your leetle veelin's naow?"

"I'm thinkin', shure, how much longer we're goin'——"

"Now I hear your voice," returned the Dutchman, speaking in his own native language, "I know that you can hear me. We must escape."

Jack O'Grady was quite conversant with De Ruyter's language.

He answered, therefore, at once—

"Escape! It is not possible."

"Ha, ha! there you are wrong, my friend," returned the Dutch skipper.

"How so? We are handcuffed, and between rows of soldiers," said Jack.

"No matter. Do as I do."

"What is that?"

"You must give a sudden jerk," said the skipper, "when we reach the top of a certain hill."

"How shall I know?"

"I will tell you when," said De Ruyter. "When you jerk yourself out of the hands of the soldiers, dive under the horses' bellies, and roll yourself down the cliff."

"But that is death."

The Dutchman made a gesture of contempt.

"Very well. If you are afraid to risk that, well and good; I will," he said. "I will give you the chance, though. When we reach the cliff, I'll say 'Now.'"

There was silence after this.

The wind kept blowing fiercely, and sweeping in angry gusts down the mountains.

The soldiers, with bent forms, huddled their short cloaks round them.

The last thing in their thoughts was an escape.

Suddenly they reached the summit of a high cliff, from which the ground on one side sloped down steeply, while on the other it was a sheer precipice, going down hundreds of feet into a rocky plain.

De Ruyter had, during their passage up the mountain, succeeded in getting one of his hands into his pocket.

From this he had drawn a small but long-bladed knife.

Now was the critical moment.

It was either escape or death.

Twisting himself suddenly round, he dug the horse in the belly with the knife, and exclaiming in a loud voice—"Now!" he jerked the rope from the hands of the dragoon.

The horse, of course, reared with pain, and began pawing the air, thus aiding De Ruyter in wresting the rope from the hands of his foe.

In an instant all was confusion.

The horse became maddened; De Ruyter dived under its belly, Jack at the same time flung himself forward on his face, and, resolved not to be behind his leader, he rushed after him.

De Ruyter was as brave as a lion, as we have seen.

He did not hesitate a moment.

In an instant, he flung himself over the edge of the cliff, and was at once followed by Jack O'Grady.

The troopers and their officers were for a moment so thunderstricken, that they could do nothing.

A wild cheer rose from the lips of the smugglers.

And one after another the men uttered their exclamations of delight, in their various languages.

"Hurroo! that's the brave capten," cried one.

"Shoost zee how de cabden rolls over, loike de gannon ball," cried another.

"Ha, ha! Monsieur Le Capitaine! he give dem de—vat you call de sleep, eh?" said a third.

And so on, until the officer shouted for silence.

Then he gave some rapid orders, and the men, holding their prisoners tightly, turned their horses and galloped down the slope, towards the spot where the smuggler and his first mate must have fallen.

But what a vain search it was.

It was hundreds of feet below, and as they rushed down, they had, every now and then, to pull up, to prevent their being dashed to pieces over some sudden margin of a precipice.

At length the bottom was reached.

There was no doubt that they could not have rolled further.

But there was no sign of them, living or dead.

Not a trace to show even what spot they had reached.

The officer was white with rage.

But passion could effect nothing.

He had been duped, and he had to be content to make the best of it.

He gave the order, accordingly, to march once more, and away the dragoons went again with the smugglers, but minus the captain and his mate.

CHAPTER XXXIII.

IN THE RUINED ABBEY—MIDNIGHT.

IT was utterly useless for anyone to search for the Dutchman or his companion.

They had completely vanished, and in spite of police and soldiers, nothing could anywhere be seen of them.

The lugger, too, disappeared from the Shannon, and the smugglers who had been captured were therefore brought up by themselves for punishment.

The trial was, of course, a farce.

It was useless for men who had been found in arms, and forcing their way into a house, to plead not guilty.

They accordingly pleaded guilty, and were sentenced to long terms of imprisonment.

Within three weeks all was over.

The people on the mountain-side had, by this time, forgotten the very circumstances of the case.

They were, in fact, so accustomed to such scenes, that they lost all interest in battles, conspiracies and trials, and everything of the kind.

It was about a month after the affair, and the school had returned to its usual routine, when Figs, who was to be married in a few weeks, met The Barry in the grounds.

It was evening time, and very few of the scholars were about.

"Barry," he said, "can I have a word with ye?"

"Certainly, sir."

"And will ye be keeping my secret?"

"Sir, I never betray anyone."

"Well, I don't believe you would, now," said Figs; "but I'd like to have ye promise, for ye'll be so surprised, and maybe angry with me, that ye'll fly off in a paddy, and then good-bye to your reason and my situation."

"Then you have my promise, sir," returned The Barry.

He was now all eagerness.

He felt, indeed, that what Tim Finnigan was about to tell him would have reference to himself.

"Well," said Figs, "you remember Mat O'Grady?"

"I do," returned The Barry, smiling. "I should think everyone in the academy has reason to remember him."

"Well, you know he had papers in his box relating to your estate?"

"Yes."

"And they disappeared?"

"Yes, most mysteriously."

"Well," said Figs, "the mystery is soon cleared up. Both I and O'Grady belonged to the Society of United Irishmen."

"You, sir?" exclaimed The Barry, in complete surprise.

"Yes, I. And I can tell ye that Mr. McMahon is as well," continued Tim Finnigan. "Though, like Mr. O'Shaughnessy, we are members against our will. One of the laws of our society is that we must do what our fellow members ask us. And so, when Mat O'Grady heard that his box was going to be searched, he made a sign to me. I knew at once what he meant, and hurrying up to his room, I abstracted the papers before anyone came up. What to do with them I did not know, and so I went out that very evening and hid them away. What he desired me to do with them, I do not know, and never could guess at. Perhaps he meant me to give them to the leader of the society—perhaps he meant me to abstract them, merely as a piece of revenge. At any rate, when I heard of his death," said Figs, with a grimace at the white lie he had to tell, "I knew I was my own master. I dare not go for them myself," he continued, "for fear of being watched. My life, as it is, is forfeit, and I might be shot down at any moment that I leave the school. But to you the way is open."

"Where are they secreted then?" asked The Barry, eagerly.

"You know the ruined abbey on the hill of Glencarty?"

"Right well I know it."

"Then as you enter the ruins of the arch, you turn to the left, and find yourself in the cloisters?"

"Yes."

"At the end is a little chamber."

"I know it; it is where we used to play," said The Barry. "Many a time have I played hide and seek there, and gone to sleep before they could find me."

"That is the place," said Figs. "Well, when you enter there, you will see a bluish stone in the pavement to the left. Under that are your papers."

The Barry seized his hand.

"Thank you, sir, thank you a thousand times," he said. "How can I ever be grateful enough to you? I will go this night, but——"

He hesitated a moment.

"Why do you hesitate?" asked Finnigan.

"I was going to say something, and then I remembered my promise," said The Barry.

"Speak, do not be afraid," cried Figs.

"Well, sir, I was going to say," replied The Barry, "that I should like to have had Pat O'Connor in my confidence. He is as trustworthy and honourable as he is brave, and I should like to have had him with me in my search."

"You have my permission to tell him," said Figs. "He was with you in your adventures with Mat O'Grady, and so he has a right to be with you in this—that is, if it suits his humour."

"Sure, and he will do that same," said The Barry, joyously; "and Mr. Finnigan, when I recover Barrymore—when I'm the master of the old hall, you shall be my most honoured guest, and, if you will accept it, there's the place of steward, and companion, and adviser, which will be open to you. Oh, Mr. Finnigan, I feel as if I was already The Barry of Barrymore."

Figs smiled.

He could not help sympathising with the enthusiasm of his young friend.

"Well, well," he said, "I hope you will find your hopes realised. Be careful, however; do not be too hasty, or you will give rope to your enemies."

The Barry lost no time in informing Pat O'Connor of the strange adventures in store for them.

As may be readily imagined, his heart beat high with joy.

He was always delighted at scenes of danger and excitement, and he began at once to make preparations for their strange outing.

Among the arms they had discovered in the barn at the "Who'd-Ha'-Thought-It?" he had found two pistols.

These he now loaded, and gave one of them to The Barry.

Then, with true boyish precaution, they filled their pockets with cakes and other niceties, winding up with the remains of the bottle of whisky, which Figs had given the two boys on the night when they were up in the lonely tower.

"But I say, Barry," cried Pat, suddenly, "you've forgotten one thing."

"What is that?"

"Why, we may come through the adventure all right, get the papers, and return, but what then? We mayn't be able to get in again, and if we do, some sneak may split upon us to Mr. O'Shaughnessy."

The Barry thought a moment.

"You're right," he said, "and to tell you the truth, I don't want to get into any more shines with O'Shaughnessy. He's too good to us."

"Yes, but I've an idea."

"Out with it then before it's afther running away."

"We'll ask Figs."

"Ask him what?"

"To let us in. He'll sit up for us."

"Oh, yes, the little man's good enough for anything," said The Barry. "We'll catch him before night and ask him."

They did catch him, as The Barry said, and the good-natured tutor at once assented to his proposition.

So everything was managed properly and satisfactorily.

"Too good to be true," as Pat said; "there's sure to be some muddle at the end."

When midnight approached, the two boys crept out of their dormitory, and slunk downstairs.

Figs was at the back door, and was ready to let them out.

The little man was in high glee.

He never thought of the fact that he was perilling his situation by what he was doing.

His generous little heart was only glad to think that they were going upon an errand which might have the effect of repairing an injustice he had been compelled to commit.

"I'll sit up in my room," said Figs, "and when you come, you must whistle."

"All right," returned Pat, in an undertone, and then the two boys glided away, and hurrying across the grounds, scaled the wall, and were soon making the best of their way up the mountain.

The abbey of Glencarty, perched as it was on the top of a high hill, was an object which could be seen during the daytime for miles around.

Even at night time, when the moon shone, it was an object of observation, for here and there the stone walls stood farth white and grim as if they had been bleached, while in other places the ivy clung lovingly to it.

This night, however, although the moon was high, there was a haze over the hills, and as they passed up, they could see nothing.

"I wish Harry Marshall was with us," said Pat O'Connor; "I know he'd be just in his glory."

"I shouldn't wonder if Figs would have said 'yes' if we'd asked for Harry," returned The Barry, "and yet it would hardly be right for the little man's secret to be known to so many."

"No, perhaps not," said Pat, "but I say, what a miserable night it is."

"Yes, as we leave the Shannon behind us, the moonlight seems to fade away."

"Aye, and a fine old curtain of mist has fallen over the top of the hill of Glencarty."

"True, but it may be moonlight up there all the same," said The Barry. "You know the clouds here sometimes lie quite low."

Chatting thus, they soon reached the summit of the first mound of the Glencarty hills.

Here the words of The Barry were verified.

Above them the hill and its ruined abbey shone in the bright moonlight.

Below them a cloud, through which they had absolutely passed, hung like a circle of vapour round the mountains.

"Well, this is a lonely spot at night," said Pat O'Connor. "I have never been up here except in daylight."

"It's nearly as bright here now," said The Barry; "we're in luck. I feel as if I'd like to stop here all night, and peg into our poteen and cakes."

They were not very long in reaching the abbey.

It was a grand structure, its ruined arches, tesselated pavements, and moss-grown walls forming a wondrous relic of times gone by.

Pat knew it well, but The Barry, who had so often roamed amid its sacred precincts, acted as guide.

"This way," he said, in a voice which awoke the echoes of the old church, "this way; along the cloisters here, and then we shall find the little room."

Pat followed eagerly.

"I say, Barry," he said, "you've forgotten something."

"What's that?"

"A light."

"Not I," said The Barry. "I have a lantern which opens in halves, and gives a splendid light, so we're all right."

About thirty yards of echoing pavement was crossed, and then they reached a door, which swung dejectedly upon its rusty hinges.

Pushing this open, The Barry unfastened his lantern, and they saw that they had entered a small room, where tablets still hung upon the walls, that were green and cracked with age; where the floor was cracked too, and moss-grown; where everything told of the relics of a by-gone time.

"This is a cheerful spot," said Pat, as he glanced round him. "I should think this must be the original 'banquet hall deserted' that the poet sings about."

"We'll get used to it soon," said The Barry. "Let's get the papers first. Then we'll eat our grub and drink a drop of whisky, and then we'll have a song; there's no one to hear us."

As he uttered these words, there sounded near them a hollow groan.

The two lads started back, and glanced at each other in wonder and dismay.

"What on earth can that be?" cried Pat. "It sounded like a ghost with the stomach-ache."

The Barry laughed.

But yet it was a laugh which had no heartiness in it.

"I believe," cried he, "if ye were dying, Pat, you'd have your joke. But, seriously speaking, this isn't at all comfortable. It seems as if, in very truth, we were not alone in this dismal place."

"It does, indeed," said Pat. "But no matter; we are armed."

"Yes, and so may be this 'ghost with the stomach-ache,' as you call it," replied The Barry. "But it doesn't seem to be going to groan any more."

"No. I expect it's only the wind roaring among the old tombs and the ruined walls," said Pat. "Come on; let's commence with the papers."

They experienced little difficulty in discovering the stone spoken of by Figs.

Both were provided with short crowbars, and in a few moments they had knelt on the cold pavement, inserted the sharp ends of the irons between the stones, and begun to prise it up.

In a few moments the stone was raised, and in a small hollow in the centre of the earth beneath it they saw the papers.

With a cry of joy—a glad cry, that echoed through the cloisters—The Barry seized them in his right hand.

"At length," he cried, "at length I hold the documents which will make me master of Barrymore."

"Fool!" exclaimed a voice.

And before either of them was aware of it, an arm was outstretched, and the papers were suddenly snatched from his grasp.

In a moment the lads had sprung to their feet.

They were just in time to see a dark form making its way through an inner door.

The Barry cast one quick glance at Pat O'Connor.

The brave Irish lad at once understood the look.

"I know what you mean, Barry," he cried. "My answer is—on, and I will follow you!"

The Barry waited to hear no more.

Grasping his pistol, and setting his teeth, he rushed through the doorway, and was followed in an instant by Pat O'Connor.

Their way now led them along a wide passage opening into the church, ascending, as it were, along an incline.

On the walls were tablets, in the same manner as those in the little room, while here and there were recesses, in which stood effigies of dead grandees.

The portion of the abbey into which the corridor led was not so ruined as the rest.

The ceiling above them was almost unbroken, while a few yards off was an immense fracture, through which a serpentine flood of moonlight fell on the tesselated pavement.

All around were pillars with strange sculptures, and tombs with oddly-carved figures, and broken columns—ghastly memories of the past that inspired the lads with awe.

They paused as they entered this sacred home of the dead.

They had, in fact, lost their quarry.

They glanced around everywhere, but could see no one.

There was not a vestige of human life visible anywhere.

"What is to be done?" asked Pat.

His voice, though he spoke in modulated accents, resounded with a dismal echo through the ruined abbey.

From out the old effigies at the extreme end of the church a voice seemed to fling back the words—

"What is to be done?"

The Barry grasped Pat by the hand.

"Pat," he said, "I have no right to lead you into danger; but I intend to follow up this adventure now I have once begun it."

"And I, Barry, am going through with you, whatever betides," said Pat O'Connor; "so no false delicacy. Talk no more of it; but let's go on as if it was our mutual interest to succeed."

"Brave friend!" murmured The Barry, "and now what can we do first?"

The two lads glanced round them eagerly.

But they could see nothing but the dim effigies and the dark walls.

The bright belt of moonlight threw everything into shade, and deepened the gloom of the old ruins.

But as they were looking with a certain hopelessness around them, a cloud glided over the face of the moon, and all was in utter darkness.

Through the gloom now, however, they could distinguish a twinkling light at the far end of the edifice.

"See," said The Barry, in an eager undertone; "see! there is a light. We shall discover the secret now."

They were standing in a dark patch of shadow, where, even when the moonlight was falling through the broad fissure in the ceiling, no one could observe them.

"We had better be cautious," said Pat; "they cannot see us now. So let us glide round the sides of the church, and approach the spot by stealth."

So it was done.

The two boys, creeping along in the shadows, were not long before they neared the point whence the light proceeded.

It was a little door leading to an incline similar to that by which they had ascended from the cloisters.

A lamp, dimly lit, was swinging from a rusty chain in the ceiling, and at the end of the corridor was a second door, through which a dull light came.

There was no sound for some moments after they reached the corridor, and the lads at once entered.

Just as they had passed half way down the vaulted thoroughfare they started.

"What was that?" whispered The Barry, laying his hand on Pat's arm.

"It was a man's voice," said Pat.

"But whose? Did it not seem to you familiar?"

They both listened intently for a moment.

Then they heard a chuckling laugh.

"Ha! ha! this is shoosh von grand ting for me; ha! ha! it vill pe vorth von doussand bound to me! not von farding lezz. Ha! ha! It is Chack O'Grady is de glever phoy."

"Good Heaven," cried Pat O'Connor; "it is the Dutch skipper."

"The villain," said The Barry; "come, let us creep closer, and look in."

They stepped forward as noiselessly as they could, and peeped through.

It was true enough.

There, in a dim vault, where a wood fire was burning in an improvised grate, lay De Ruyter on a truckle bed.

His face was a terrible sight to see.

One eye was covered by a bandage, and what could be seen of his features was swollen, and strapped with plaister.

No one else was in the room.

He was lying on his back, and in his hands were the papers so coveted by The Barry.

"Let us rush in and seize the papers," cried Pat O'Connor; "don't delay."

"In then," shouted The Barry.

And while yet the Dutchman was glancing in wonder in the direction of the sound, they rushed in.

They halted at the side of the bed.

De Ruyter clutched the papers, and drew them under the bedclothes, while the one eye through which he could see, glanced at them in anger, and yet, as it were, inquiringly.

"You phoys! Tonder and blitzen, vot ye vont here?"

"I want my papers, nothing more," replied The Barry.

The Dutchman laughed.

"Your babers is it?—ha! ha!" he cried; "dey are mine now. Here—Chack and Pierre—gome in—de enemy has stole a mardge ubon uz. Ha! ha! I smoke mein bibe."

And as he coolly took a whiff from the huge pipe that lay beside him, Jack O'Grady and another man, armed to the teeth, rushed into the vault.

"DE RUYTER PLACED THE BARREL OF HIS PISTOL TO THE HEAD OF A KEG OF POWDER."

CHAPTER XXXIV.

TREACHERY.

PAT O'CONNOR and The Barry saw at once what a terrible trap they had let themselves into. But their hearts did not fail them.

Retreating, they drew their pistols as the two men rushed in ; and retiring, until they nearly reached the wall, they cried—

"Back, or we fire !"

But the men did not seem disposed to come to close quarters.

In fact, to do so would have been utter madness.

The Dutchman at once saw how matters stood, and changed his tactics.

"Ha ! ha !" he cried, with a hoarse chuckle ; "ha ! ha ! I have fridened the phoys, and now dey zall hear all I means. Put away your pistols, mein lads, and come and zit down by me. I do not vant de babers."

"Then why did you take them ?" asked Pat, lowering his pistol.

"I did not take them," said the Dutchman ; "mein vriend Chack brought dem here. I know dat dey are vorth de money—dat is all dat dey are of use to me for."

The two boys glanced at one another.

"Shall we trust him ?" asked Pat.

"No," said The Barry ; "not unless he sends Jack O'Grady out of the room, and his friend too."

"Very well," said Pat ; "we will trust you, Mr. De Ruyter, if you will send your two men away."

"Dat is good," cried the Dutch skipper ; "I knew you vould understand vat I means. Chack, you and your vriend shoost go out von—von leetle vile ; you shall gome in again shoost terickly."

Whatever sign the Dutchman made was not perceptible to the two lads.

But to Jack and his companion it was quite intelligible.

A smile passed over O'Grady's face.

"Come on," he cried to his companion ; "as the skipper thinks he is safe, we will go."

"Zafe ; of course I am zafe wit mine vriends," said the skipper. "I and Mr. O'Connor and The Barry, of Barrymore, may be able to arrange de money between us."

In another moment the two men had quitted the vault.

Pat and The Barry sat down by the side of the sick man's bed.

"Well, Mr. De Ruyter," said our hero, "what is it you propose then ?"

"Vill you listen to me wit bashience ?" said the Dutchman.

"Yes, certainly," said The Barry ; "but we do not wish to be too late, or we may get into trouble."

"Very fell," returned De Ruyter ; "I zall not be long. In de vurst blaice, you know all about de row at de school ?"

"Of course, as I was one of the principals in it," said Pat, "and The Barry here, too."

"Vell, I might have some feeling of enmity towards you, mine vriends," continued De Ruyter, "but I don't have it. I have lost mine sheep through dat, for the audorities have seized it, zo I vants to make some money."

"Well, what then ?" asked The Barry. "I suppose you mean that you wish to make some out of my papers."

"Dat's it," said the Dutchman. "I knew noting of them till shoost now, but as mine friend, O'Grady, made a cabture of dem, I have read zome of dem, and I thinks I may share de gain."

The Barry smiled.

"Well," he said, "it is certainly a strange thing to tell me that I am compelled to share my property with you because one of your men stole my papers."

"Ha, ha ! not zo," exclaimed the Dutchman, "not zo. I means dat I shall be able to help you to get your rights, if you pays me vell."

"And how do you propose to aid him ?" said Pat.

"Why, dat is told easily," cried the Dutchman. "You must see Mr. Singleton."

"What," said The Barry, "meet and make terms with my worst enemy."

"Make derms with 'im ; nod at all," said De Ruyter. "Ve vill get him down here into dese volts, and den we vill tell him dat if he does not give up de other babers that are spoken about in this backet, ve vill shoost close him up in de room yonder until he dies of starvation."

"But I can get my rights by law," said The Barry, "without acting in this underhand way."

De Ruyter shook his head.

"No, no," he said, "I do not like de law. The law people do ask too many questions. Dey might want to know how I escape from de soldiers afder the attack on de zchool, and dey might put me into lodgings vere I shoold not have shoost mine own vay."

"But you need not appear in the matter at all," said The Barry.

"And I needn't have any of the proceeds," said the Dutchman. "Dat is not shoost mine plan ; I vant de management of the matter meinself."

"And if we refuse to let you ?"

The Dutch skipper made a gesture, as much as to say—

"That is your affair."

"You must blease yourselves," he said, "but I dell you plainly, you would have to stop here den, undil you had changed your mind."

"Then you wish us to consider that we are prisoners," said The Barry, flushing with indignation.

"Shoost so," said De Ruyter.

"And the papers, where are they to remain ?"

"In my hands," said the Dutchman.

Pat and The Barry rose from their positions, and retired into a corner of the vaults.

"What is to be done ?" asked The Barry. "We are in a pretty position."

"Yes, we are caged," said Pat. "But we are armed and might force our way out, if we are plucky."

"I don't see how," returned The Barry. "I think we should only make a muddle of it. We had better act with stratagem."

"But in what way ?"

"Let him think that we agree with him, and then we must devise some plan of action."

" You mean that we must do anything to escape from this place," said Pat.

" That's it," returned The Barry, " but we must not let him know what we are consulting about."

" True," said Pat O'Connor, " so let's return to his bedside at once."

" Well, phoys," said the Dutch skipper, " well, what have you decided upon ?"

" Decided to hear your idea about when Mr. Singleton is to come here," said Pat.

" To-morrow night."

" And supposing he refuses to come ?" answered Pat.

The smuggler smiled.

" Ve vill not ask him in the usual way ; ve vill bring him."

" At what time ?"

" At any time you like. Shoost ven you likes. After it has come dark, if dat vill suit you."

" And you keep the papers ?"

" Yes ; and you, too," said De Ruyter.

The two lads had an expression of dismay on their faces as they heard this.

This was worse than ever.

" Why do you want us to remain here ?" said Pat.

" Because I do not vant Thaddeus O'Zhaughnessy and de constables down upon me here."

" But you have us both in your power ; at any rate, you have The Barry," said Pat, " and his being in your hands is the same as my being so."

" I cannot zee at all," returned the Dutchman, " how he is in mine power."

" Certainly, you have the papers which will make The Barry master of Barrymore," returned our hero ; " and if you saw any show of his betraying you or my doing so, you could burn the papers, and with that would disappear all his hopes for the future."

The Dutchman thought a moment.

" Vell, it vould not be vorth your vile to betray me," said he. " I vill strike the pargain mit you, if you vould only do von ting."

" And what is that ?" asked Pat.

" If you vill only svear upon your vords of honour dat you vill not betray me," said the skipper.

" Well, then, we will agree to that," said The Barry ; " only we should like to know what you expect to receive from us, when we have succeeded."

" What is the Barry property worth ?" asked the Dutchman.

" Ten thousand a year."

" Den you will sign a baber, giving me five tousand pounds, if all goes vell," said De Ruyter.

" I agree to that," said The Barry, almost joyfully. " We shall go now, and to-morrow night at nine we will be here again."

" Could it not be earlier than that ?" said Pat.

" No, we must do another slope from school," said The Barry, " for if we came earlier, we might have to stop late and be in trouble all the same."

" Very well, as we have begun with it, we'll go on with it," said Pat. " I'll come what time you like."

A few preliminaries were then arranged, and the two boys, taking leave of the Dutchman, were soon once more in the open air.

" We made a regular mull of the whole affair," said Pat O'Connor, as they hurried down the hills.

" Yes, that we have," returned The Barry. " I shall always be ashamed to think of this night's adventure."

" Well, we must hope that to-morrow night will make up for all," said Pat. " Never say die."

When they reached the school, they found that, true to his word, Figs had sat up for them.

No one knew a word about what they had done.

" Well, have you succeeded ?" said he, as he let them into the passage.

" No."

" You didn't find the papers ?"

" Yes, but we had them taken from us again."

" Then that's your own fault. I've done all I can for you," said the usher. " It's out of my hands now. But ye can tell me all in the morning."

When Tim Finnigan did hear all on the following morning, he shook his head in grave doubt.

" I'm afraid you have got to deal with the wrong man," said he.

The Barry looked sadly concerned.

" Do you mean that he will betray us ?" said he.

" I do not know what you mean by betraying you," said Figs ; " but this much I know, that I do not believe you will see him or the papers this evening."

" Then why did he suffer us to escape ?" said Barry.

" He has some deep design it in, depend on it," said the usher ; " however, time will show. I will do my best to help you to go to-night, but I feel certain that the game will be a useless one."

Figs' prophecy proved too true.

Just in the dusk of the evening, as they were waiting in anxiety for the time to come to start, a boy brought a letter addressed to Pat O'Connor.

It was from De Ruyter, and ran as follows—

" MASTER PAT O'CONNOR,—You and your vriend, The Barry, thought you were going to pe very clever last night. Dat is vere you made a great mistake. I do not make mein pargens mit de phoys. I makes dem mit de men ; so I have sold de babers to Mister Zingleton, and peg to remain, mit mein gomblements, your vriend,

" DE RUYTER.

" Bostcribt.—If yer feel inclined to gome and see the old abbey to-night, gome mit all de bleasure, mit a tousand zoldiers, if you like. But de pirds have flown."

The Barry turned deadly pale, and staggered to a seat in the playground as he read this letter.

" All my hopes are gone ; my life is crushed," he said. " I wish we had not trusted him, but had fought it out."

"My dear Barry," cried Pat, as he took his friend's hand and pressed it, "if we had done as you say, our lives would have been forfeited. As it is, we have still our health and strength left to follow up our enemies and discomfit them."

CHAPTER XXXV.

THE TRAP-DOOR—UNDER THE RUSHING WATERS.

BOYS' natures have an elasticity which is not possessed by men.

Although, therefore, The Barry felt at first crushed and ruined by the loss of the papers, he soon roused himself.

Pat O'Connor, of course, was the one who did the most towards cheering him up.

It was about a month after the scene in the vaults of the old abbey that Pat O'Connor met The Barry in the playground, with a face that was brimfull of fun.

"Barry, old fellow," he cried, "I've got somthing in my head that'll cheer you up properly."

"What's that?" said The Barry. "I suppose it's some devilment again."

"Well, it's a joke," returned Pat, with a look of deprecation, "but scarcely comes under the head of devilment."

"Well, what is it?"

"Come aside here," said Pat, "and I'll tell ye; only, if we take anybody but Harry Marshall into our confidence, we shall spoil everything."

"Where is Harry?"

"Oh, he's sure not to be far off," said Pat, "Ah, there he is. Here, Harry."

Harry Marshall at once came hurrying up.

"Why, what's up, Pat?" he cried. "You look as pleased as if you'd picked up fifty pounds."

"Well," he said, "I haven't picked up that, but I've picked up a lark. You just listen."

Further deponent must not say at present.

All we need remark is that the lads were both delighted at the proposal made by Pat, and the plan was agreed to be put in practice on the following night.

It would take, in fact, until then to make proper preparations for the fun, to which they were all looking forward with such eagerness.

At length the wished-for time came.

It was at the hour when lessons were going to be learned that the plan was to be carried out.

The lamp had purposely been half emptied of its oil (there was no gas in the Shannon school), and the schoolroom was in semi-darkness.

The desk of Tom McClosky was situated near the centre of the room, and upon it was a little lamp of his own.

It was now eight o'clock, and the whole surroundings of the school were quiet.

It was a rather boisterous night, though, and through the trees the wind howled dismally at intervals, bringing, as it were, to the old academy the voices of the far-off hills.

The scholars were all of them busily engaged in their studies, when suddenly a strange phenomenon was seen.

The lamp went out.

The little lamp also on the desk of Tom McClosky grew dim, and burned with a tiny, phosphorescent-looking light.

At the same time, Tom found himself running rapidly backwards, chair and all, while his desk as rapidly ran the other way; not before, however, it had half tilted over, and flung the ink in his face.

"Oh, murder! help! murder!" he shouted, in a loud voice.

But he did not move, neither did anyone move to help him.

Tom himself, when he came to a standstill, was frightened to move one way or the other.

He knew not, in fact, what there was to fear.

But he was, of course, aware that something extraordinary had happened.

A chill air seemed to rise from the floor and blow, like the atmosphere of a sepulchre, on his face.

He trembled at the idea of falling into some unknown depths.

"Help, help!" he cried again.

No one in the room moved.

But soon there was heard the sound of approaching footsteps, and someone dashed into the room.

In an instant there was the sound of a heavy fall.

A man's voice, muffled, and coming, as it were, from the earth, was heard bawling—

"Here, a light! Help! I'm smothering!"

"Just my luck," said Pat O'Connor. "Here's the wrong party tumbled down the hole. Let's get a light."

"Better leave it alone," whispered Harry Marshall. "Here's someone coming down the passage with a lamp."

He had scarcely spoken the words when the door opened, and Thaddeus O'Shaughnessy himself appeared, bearing a bright light.

In an instant the most ludicrous scene presented itself.

On his seat, clinging to it like grim death, was Tom McClosky.

At his feet yawned a black hole, caused by the sliding away of a panel, while down in the hole below was a human head.

It was perfectly impossible to tell whose head it was.

The owner of it had fallen into a mass of dirt and cobwebs, and his features and his hair were perfectly black with powdery filth.

"What on earth is the meaning of all this?" cried Thaddeus, as his eyes fell on the form of Tom McClosky, and then on the head of the "man below," and then on the tilted desk, which had half disappeared down the dark abyss. "Is my schoolroom to be turned into a stage for a pantomime?"

Tom was about to answer, when the voice of the miserable man among the cobwebs cried—

"Pray, someone help me up."

"Why, is that you, Mr. Finnigan?" exclaimed O'Shaughnessy. "Bless me! What can it all mean?"

He stooped down as he spoke, and extended his hand to the wretched usher, who at once assisted himself up by clinging with one hand to the side of the open panel.

In a few moments he was standing on the floor of the schoolroom, looking such a deplorable object, that Thaddeus himself could not forbear laughing.

"What have you been doing, Mr. Finnigan," he said ; "this is most extraordinary conduct before the pupils."

Figs was now vigorously wiping the dirt off his face, and by degrees a little of his original countenance was visible.

"You see, Mr. O'Shaughnessy," he said, "I know nothing about it, only that I'm nearly smothered."

"How did you come down that hole?" said the schoolmaster.

"That's what I can't tell, sir," said Figs ; "except that I rushed into the room, and suddenly fell headlong through this opening, into the hole yonder, where I found myself in utter darkness, among all the cobwebs and dirt that have been collecting since the creation of the world."

"Well, I should like to understand all about it," said Thaddeus, first examining the hole very carefully, and then glancing round the room in search of someone who was likely to be the culprit ; "I really believe that this is the result of some practical joke."

"I can't see how that can be," said Figs ; "I don't think that anyone in the school knew of this place."

"I did not, for one," said Thaddeus ; "and so perhaps you are right."

He turned towards the boys again, however.

"Do any of you know anything of this matter?" he asked.

Of course there arose a perfect chorus of—

"No, sir! no, sir!"

In this answer Pat, Harry, and The Barry did not join, thus avoiding the telling of a lie.

Their silence was not observed, and for once the three boys succeeded in their piece of fun, without harming anyone, and without getting themselves into trouble.'

"I say, Harry Marshall," said Pat, as they went up to bed that night. "I say, I've another adventure in store for us."

"What's that?—another spree?" cried Harry.

"I don't know how it will turn out," said Pat ; "but it's about that hole again."

"It'll never do to open it afresh," said The Barry ; "it'll be suspected."

"Not in the way you mean," said Pat, "but in another."

"What then?"

"Why, the place must lead somewhere, and I vote," said Pat, "that one night we explore it."

"Capital," cried both his friends at once, "and the sooner the better."

It may be as well, before we enter upon this fresh adventure, to explain how the lads managed their fun.

Pat had been left alone in the schoolroom for a while, and a small bolt had caught his attention near Tom McClosky's desk.

He found, on examination, that when this bolt was pulled, it tilted the desk clean over, and slid a panel rapidly along the floor.

This panel consisted of two planks, and was wide enough for a chair to stand on.

He had no time to do more than turn the desk over into its place, and run the panel back, before others came in.

The idea of the lark at once suggested itself, and we have seen how it was carried out.

On the night following the lark, Pat Harry and The Barry crept out of the dormitory, and made their way into the schoolroom.

The whole house was wrapped in slumber, and there was not much fear of their being disturbed.

They carefully closed the door, however, and one of them held the desk, while another drew the bolt.

The panel flew back, and the dark opening was disclosed.

As before, the friends provided themselves with lanterns, pistols, and some provisions, as if they had been going on a long journey.

And then, in a few moments, they had let themselves down into the dark hole, and started on their perilous adventure.

The lads took the wise precaution of not fastening the falling trap-door for fear someone might close it down.

They had resolved to make a regular voyage of discovery, and so they glanced round them on all sides eagerly.

It was a strange place, indeed, that they found themselves in.

It was not a deep place, but a kind of narrow cellar, which had evidently been used as a place of concealment for goods or men.

It was built solidly, and for some time it was impossible to see any place through which persons could escape.

Presently, however, Pat O'Connor, as he leaned down, saw a round hole, just large enough for a man to crawl through.

"Here we are" he cried, as he threw the light of a lantern full upon the aperture ; "I'm first."

And in a few moments he was making his way through.

The place where he now found himself was a narrow passage, along which there came to his ears a dull, murmuring sound.

But there was evidently an outlet, as he could tell by the sweeping air, which ever and anon rushed along the subterranean way.

"Come on, boys," he said ; "it's all right. I'll be pilot."

And so on he went cautiously.

For a short distance he had to go on his hands and knees, which was a matter of considerable difficulty, as he had to hold his lantern as well.

But presently the way became higher, and he was able to rise and walk.

This he did very cautiously.

Of course this subterranean passage, made more than a hundred years ago, might be full of pitfalls, and so he went on close to the wall, keeping his eyes fixed on the ground.

The walls were green and slimy with damp, and unclean things moved upon the ground.

As they advanced, the sound of great waters became louder, and they soon became aware that they were making straight for the Shannon river.

"I wonder what this was made for," said The Barry; "I hope we're not running straight into the water."

"We can't be doing that," said Pat O'Connor, "for the waters would have made their way hither long before this. It's more likely that it will lead to some underground cavern. However, here we are! There are steps."

They had arrived, in fact, at a series of rugged steps, cut out in the clay and stone.

There were about twenty of these, and at the bottom of them they found themselves in a second subterranean way, of a far different character from the first.

It was built artificially, with walls like those of a tunnel, not dug out of the solid earth.

Here, as they advanced, they could hear the rush of the great waters over their heads.

"We're underneath the Shannon," exclaimed The Barry; "I hope we've not started on a long journey as before, which will lead us to nothing."

"I hope it will not be like that," said Pat, "for we should be too late to get in, maybe."

Away along the passage they hurried, keeping a good look-out for pitfalls, until at length about half the width of the great river was reached.

Here the passage took a sudden turn.

Pat O'Connor raised his lantern to see if there was any visible outlet. But no. All was utter darkness. A long black way, without a single ray of light.

"Well, boys, do as ye like," said Pat, "this place seems interminable."

"Oh! I'm for going on," cried The Barry.

"So am I," said Harry.

"Then on it is," said Pat.

And with uplifted lantern he once more advanced.

They had gone about five hundred yards or more, when they fancied they saw a faint glimmer of light.

The boys stopped an instant to consult.

"There's a light, sure enough," said Pat O'Connor, "but it doesn't look like the light of day."

"What can it mean then?" asked The Barry.

"I don't know. I suppose we're in for another adventure. But come; we must go on more cautiously."

They advanced now as slowly as possible, and presently they heard, above the roar of the waters, the voice of a man singing a song.

As they approached nearer, they heard the voice plainly. A voice which made The Barry and Pat O'Connor start in wonder.

It was the voice again of their enemy De Ruyter, the captain of the "Silverhorn."

> "I have left mein vrow in Sharmany,
> Mein vrow and yunkers too,
> And now mein leetle sheep is gone,
> Hein! Blitzen, vot for do?
>
> De river vlows above mein head,
> Hein! tonder, all too vide
> For me to svim to Sharmany
> To zee mein leetle bride.
>
> So I must shtop a leetle vile,
> Until mein vounds are vell,
> And den mein voes shall rue de day
> Ven de hand of Ruyter fell."

"By Jove!" cried Pat, "if it isn't the Dutchman, and by his singing like that, he must be all alone. We'd better hurry in and try and capture him."

The eyes of The Barry lit up with pleasure.

"Yes," he said, "let's hasten on; for if I can't get my papers restored, I can have vengeance."

"I'm with you," cried Harry Marshall.

And the three boys advanced.

In a few moments they arrived at a door through which they could see a sight which edified them excessively.

The Dutchman, still with a bandage round his head and his arm in a sling, was sitting before a roaring fire in the midst of the island cave.

Round him were the kegs of powder and the firearms just as they had been when Thaddeus O'Shaughnessy had been taken prisoner by the United Irishmen, and sent over to the island in charge of Terence O'Rafferty.

On the table before him was a steaming glass of grog, and in his mouth was the mouthpiece of his huge pipe.

From the latter there arose at rapid intervals a huge cloud of smoke, which with his one eye he watched as it curled up to the ceiling.

The door was just ajar, and with a sudden rush they burst into the subterranean room.

De Ruyter, whose nerves were never shaken by any dangers which might present themselves, however suddenly, looked up calmly with his pipe still in his mouth.

He recognised the boys in a moment, with the exception of Harry Marshall.

"Ah! mein little vriends," he said, "vy did you not knock at de door?"

"Because we're cold," said Pat, "and we've fallen in love with your fire."

"And noting else?"

"A little other matter," said The Barry. "I've come for my papers."

"I've zold dem, I told you zo before," said De Ruyter; "so if you are cold, you have made yourzelves cold for no burbose."

"Captain De Ruyter," said The Barry, "I don't believe you. I believe you have never parted with them, and that you have kept them back with some dark design."

The face of The Barry was stern, and his lips were white, as he spoke, and the Dutchman saw that whatever Pat O'Connor might have said in pretended joke, the boys had come there with a firm resolution not to be trifled with.

"Ye must peleeve shoost vot ye like, mein young vriend," said De Ruyter, "but I know von ting. You escaped from me vonce ven you poked your noses into mein blace up at the abbey ruins, but dis time you shall not escape me. I will kill you all and vling you into the Shannon."

"If we chose to escape now, we could," said Pat O'Connor, "and you could do nothing towards preventing us. But that is not our idea. We are well armed, and we give you a choice between two things."

The three boys drew their pistols as Pat spoke.

De Ruyter smiled grimly.

"Very goot," he said, "very goot. And vot are dose tings?"

"Either to go quietly with us or be shot."

"Ha, ha! very goot," laughed De Ruyter,

"very goot inteed. Now, my fine vellows, I give *you* de choice between two tings. Either to go or to be blown to atoms. Either go back to de zchool or go a long shoorney mit me."

And as he spoke, De Ruyter, by a rapid movement, placed the barrel of his pistol to the head of a keg of powder close at hand.

CHAPTER XXXVI.
THE CAPTURE OF THE DUTCHMAN.

FOR an instant the boys were so dismayed that they drew back in alarm.

"Of what avail would it be, if you were to do such a thing?" said The Barry, with as much calmness as he could muster. "If you were to blow us up, you would not receive any comfort from it?"

The Dutchman smiled a grim smile, still holding the pistol to the barrel.

"Ha, ha!" he cried, "dat is shoost vere you mistakes all de whole ting. If I do not dreaten to blow up de powder, ye takes me a brisoner and I go to gaol. I am not vond of de gaol. Mein mind is for de free, free air and de bountain saides, and I vish either to be free or be dead. Hein, it is not much matter vich. Den I have got de zatisfaction of knowing dat I hab not gone away into de land of spirits alone; and I leave no von who can do de laugh and jeer against me."

"You do not give a very satisfactory reason for murdering us," said Pat O'Connor, "but I do not see any cause why you should go to gaol, or why you should kill us."

"Then vy do you not go avay, and let me be at beace?" said the Dutchman.

"Give us the papers, or tell us where they are, and there will be no fear of either your being hurt or ourselves," returned The Barry.

"Tonder and blitzen!" exclaimed De Ruyter, in an apparent rage, "vot for you dhry to drive me mad? I tell you I have sold de babers to Mr. Singleton."

"I do not believe a word of it," returned The Barry.

But at this instant, Harry Marshall whispered gently in his ear.

The Barry at once made a sign to Pat, which was unseen by the Dutchman.

"Well, it is useless parleying here," cried he; "we have an objection to being blown up, and besides that, we had better apply to Mr. Singleton in the first place before going any further. So good evening, Mr. De Ruyter, and pleasant dreams."

The Dutchman laughed.

"Vell, vell, de phoys vill be phoys. Ha, ha! ven I vas a yonker, I used to tink mineself a great man too. But dere, I made my mistake like de oder beoble. Good night mein phoys. Ha! tonder. Vot is dat?"

Well might he ask.

While yet the pistol was directed at the top of the powder keg, a sudden deluge of water caught him in the face.

This caused him at once to start back in his chair, and the pistol fell from his grasp.

In an instant the captain was helpless.

The three boys seized him, and before he had time to attempt even to rise to his feet, he was bound and in their power.

"Shoost so, Mr. De Ruyter," said Pat O'Connor, with a laugh. "I think the cold water cure is a capital cure for the blowing-up you promised."

The Dutchman made no reply.

He rolled his eyes fiercely, but not a sound escaped his lips.

But, just as Harry Marshall opened the door, he burst forth into a fit of terrible cursing.

"Ah, be —— ! mein fine yonkers," he said, "ve vill have de score on our side yet. Ya have caught de Totchman, but, mind, he is as slippery as von feesh. And ven he escape, he bite like de shark. I vant no more talk mit you. Lead on and I vollow!"

"You are mistaken if you think we mean you any harm," said Pat O'Connor. "If you will only confess that you have not sold the papers, and that you know where they are, we will leave you free."

The Dutchman here lost some of his usual equanimity.

His eyes suddenly flashed.

"Ya, I vill tell you," he cried, "vere de babers are. But ye must bromise to release me, if I does so."

The Barry clutched Pat O'Connor by the arm.

"Don't trust him, Pat. Don't believe a word he says," he whispered; "he is deceiving us. I can see it in his eye. We have obtained a victory now. Let us carry it out."

"Good," said Pat; "come on, De Ruyter. You have betrayed us once, and we will never trust you again."

The Dutch skipper said no more.

He saw he was in the hands of those who, young as they were, were determined not to give in one iota, and so he resolved not to humiliate himself by saying a word in deprecation of anything they might do.

He walked quietly with them.

Just as they entered the subterranean, or rather the sub-aqueous passage, the unmistakable sound of a boat was heard grating on the pebbly shore of the island.

The fire of hope once more leaped to the eyes of the Dutchman.

"Ha! ha! I vill be save yet," he cried, "here, help, help! Chack! Chack!"

In an instant The Barry rushed towards the Dutchman, and tied a handkerchief round his capacious mouth.

Then, with a boy holding each arm, he was hurried along the passage

There was no escape.

They knew their way well now; they were certain that there were no pitfalls.

So they hurried the old Dutchman on, until the perspiration ran down his cheeks, and his fat sides fairly quivered with the exertion ne was forced to make.

At length, after a long run, they reached the cellar beneath the schoolroom, and assisted the unwilling Dutchman up.

Then they rearranged the flooring, and having set everything as it was before, they prepared to rouse up the schoolmaster.

In th first place, they removed the gag from De Ruyter's mouth.

"You can shout as much you like here," said

"'BACK! ADVANCE A STEP, AND YOU ARE A DEAD MAN!' CRIED O'SHAUGHNESSY."

Pat O'Connor, "and the louder the better, for you will save us the trouble of rousing the schoolmaster."

"All right, mein yong vriends," he said, "'ave your little games; I vill have mein game prezently."

"And now," said Pat, disregarding entirely the words of the Dutchman, "who is to go up to Mr. O'Shaughnessy? It won't be a pleasant job, I can tell you, whoever goes."

"Draw lots then," said Harry Marshall.

Accordingly, three pieces of paper were torn in the usual way, and held in the hand of young Marshall while the others drew.

The lot fell to Pat O'Connor!

Our hero made a wry face.

"Well," he cried, "it's fair, and I must abide by it."

As he said the words, he advanced boldly to the door, and began to ascend the stairs.

He knew that in the first place Thaddeus would be very angry.

The brunt of this he must of course bear.

But then, the capture of the Dutchman, who was the ringleader in the attack on the house, would be in his favour.

So he made his way to the door of the schoolmaster's room, and tapped gently.

Gentle as the tap was, it moved the door, and he saw at once that it was open.

As no answer was returned, he pushed it slightly.

The schoolmaster was not in bed.

He was sitting at the table, with his head leaning on one hand, while in the other he held something, at which he was intently gazing.

"Mr. O'Shaughnessy," said Pat O'Connor, in a low voice.

There was no answer.

A terrible thought passed through the mind of our hero.

He advanced on tiptoe, and took a rapid glance at the schoolmaster.

His eyes were closed.

Could he be dead?

Or was he sleeping, with that miniature in his hand?—that portrait of a young girl, with fair hair and heavenly eyes.

Pat touched him lightly on the shoulder.

"Mr. O'Shaughnessy," he said.

The schoolmaster started from his sleep, and glanced in dismay around him.

Then, before he spoke, he hurriedly concealed the portrait in his breast.

"What are you doing here, Pat O'Connor?" he cried, indignantly.

"I am on no errand of curiosity," he answered, "believe me, sir. I would not have disturbed you, but I have something of great importance to tell you."

Thaddeus still looked very grave.

"It must, indeed, be something of extreme importance to warrant you in coming to me in the middle of the night. But as I am not disposed to think that you would wilfully deceive me, speak on. Poke the fire, as it is cold."

Pat O'Connor did as he was directed, and sat down.

Then, without any hesitation—first begging Mr. O'Shaughnessy to hear all before he judged —he told all the boyish piece of adventure on which he had been engaged.

Thaddeus listened attentively.

Then he said—

"I think you are the most incorrigible lot of boys that ever a master had to deal with; but your vagabondism generally leads to some good. Where is this ruffianly Dutchman?"

"In the schoolroom, sir."

"And you say this passage led from the island to that room?"

"Yes, sir."

"No one knew of it then," said O'Shaughnessy. "I know I didn't, and those ruffians could not either, or they would have swarmed into the house in secret without getting down by way of the chimney. But come, let us descend!"

The schoolmaster and his favourite pupil made their way at once to the schoolroom, where the Dutchman still sat in his chair, bound and helpless, and the other two boys were on a form, conversing in low murmurs unintelligible to the skipper.

As for him, he had not uttered a word since the departure of Pat O'Connor.

He had contented himself with revolving plans of vengeance, and already in his mind compassing the death and destruction of all his enemies. Pat O'Connor at the head of them.

Harry Marshall and The Barry looked up with a sheepish look, as Thaddeus O'Shaughnessy entered.

They saw at once all was right, by the expression of his face.

"Well, Mr. De Ruyter," he said, "so we meet again."

"Mit pleasure," said the skipper. "I vas brought here against my vill, and I am zorry I am here; but I always like to see a gentleman."

"You will see another gentleman directly," said O'Shaughnessy, "and that is the governor of the gaol."

"Oh! then you are de one dat has poot dese phoys ub to deir branks, eh!" exclaimed the Dutchman; "den bad luck to you. I vill be even mit you yet!"

"Of that we will speak another time," said Thaddeus, "because I care as much for your threats as I do for the whistling of the wind. About these papers—have you got them?"

"No, shoost as I said before," replied De Ruyter, "I have zold de bapers to Mr. Singleton."

"It is, I am certain, a lie," said Thaddeus O'Shaughnessy, "but, however, I am not your judge. As you say you sold the papers to Mr. Singleton, I can strike no bargain with you. If, however, you had had the papers still in your possession, I would have set you free, but now—Pat, fetch Willie Curtis."

The Dutchman bit his lip.

Pat rose at once from the form, and approached the door.

De Ruyter knew well what was about to follow.

"Shoost von moment," he said, "Mister O'Zonessy, shoost von moment."

"Well, what do you want?"

"Vot ye send for Willie Curtis for?" asked the captain.

"In order that he may go for the constables," returned Thaddeus ; " I have no wish or right to keep you here."

"Vell now, one moment, as I said. If I could get de babers from Mr. Singleton, what den ?"

Thaddeus O'Shaughnessy frowned darkly.

"Come," he said, "it is the middle of the night, and I cannot have my school disturbed. I want no prevarication. If you have these papers yourself, or know where you can put your hand upon them, well and good. I will undertake to set you free after you have placed them in my possession. If not, then I shall instantly send for the constables."

The Dutchman did not long hesitate now.

He saw that he was fairly trapped, and so, after muttering a hideous curse, he said—

"Vell, I vant to go home to mein vrow and mein yonkers, and I have no money. So, though I do not like to go pack on my vord, as you beoble say, I can give you the papers dis very night."

"Where have we to go for them ?"

"You must follow me to the island," returned the Dutchman, "and row in de pote to shore, onless you can go up de hills from your gates."

"Up where ?" asked Thaddeus.

The Dutchman saw that the schoolmaster suspected him, and he laughed loudly.

"Ha, ha !" he cried, "you zuspect me. Vell, be it so. I am a man among a lot of phoys dat are as pig devils as all the Shannon phoys put together in a pot and poiled mit de same number of Irish. Surely you vill trust yourself alone by meself."

"I will," said Thaddeus, "with these lads with me, and all well armed. How do we know into what ambush you may lead us ?"

The Dutchman shrugged his shoulders.

"Do as you please. Tonder and blitzen, I can do no more than you asked me. If you do not vont to gome, don't gome."

"Very well, we will come."

"And you will give me mein hands free, eh ?"

"When we are a little way up the hills, yes," said Thaddeus.

Then he turned to the boys, saying—

"Boys, as I have said nothing of this adventure on which you proceeded on your own account, are you prepared to carry it out ?"

"Yes, yes, sir," was the chorussed response ; "we want to come with you."

"Well, then, put on your great coats, wrap yourselves up warm, and come," said the schoolmaster.

CHAPTER XXXVII.

UP IN THE MOUNTAINS ONCE MORE.

WITHIN half an hour the schoolmaster and his pupils, with the Dutch captain, were making their way up the mountain path.

The Dutchman was still bound.

Thaddeus had filled his pipe, and placed it in his mouth.

But further indulgence than this, he had declared he would not grant until they neared their destination.

This, according to De Ruyter, was a cave in the mountains, situated in the very face of a precipice.

A place known by the gloomy name of Callaghan's Fall.

After they had neared this spot, the bonds were quickly removed from the hands of the skipper.

He stretched himself like a goose on a common.

"Ah, shoost so ! dat is goot !" he cried. "Now I smoke mein bibe broberly, not hanging from mein mouth like a vorm. Ve have not far to go now."

"I know the place well," said Thaddeus O'Shaughnessy. "I know it to be a gloomy and dreary spot. If there is any treachery, remember we're armed, and the first bullet that is fired shall seek your heart."

"Shoost so," said the Dutchman ; "but you zee ve shall not meet anypody there."

"So much the better," said O'Shaughnessy.

And then silence fell over all.

The hills were wrapped in utter quiet.

The moon was shining brightly, and the shadows of one great hill fell heavily upon another.

At length, when they had reached a point high up on the mountains, the Dutchman paused.

"Dis way," he cried ; "you zee de mouth of de cliff cavern."

Sure enough it was so.

The gloomy mouth of the cave, from which, years and years before, the rebel O'Callaghan had fallen in escaping from his pursuers, and been dashed to pieces, could now plainly be seen.

"Yes," said Thaddeus.

"Well, then," returned the Dutchman, "in dere are the babers."

"Proceed, then."

"Ha, ha, mein vriends, are you not afraid to go dere mit me, eh ?"

"I am afraid of no man," said Thaddeus ; "lead on. If you attempt to betray us, you are a dead man."

The Dutchman shrugged his shoulders contemptuously.

But he made no remark.

Turning to the left, he passed along a rugged mountain path between two walls of rock, and presently the whole party emerged upon a little basin, as it were, surrounded by high boulders.

It was an awful-looking place, resembling the crater of an extinct volcano.

Here, without pausing a moment, he made his way in the direction of a dark passage, which soon led them to the cave called Callaghan's Fall.

This, if the other was awesome, was absolutely terrible.

It was a cave, certainly, but a cave from which a dozen fissures led away in different directions, evidently, from the wild winds they let in, leading to the upper rocks.

"Well, this is a nice spot to invite anyone to," said Thaddeus. "Do you swear the papers are here ?"

"Hein ; you are suspicious," said De Ruyter. "What for do I bring you up to de mountain cave in the middle of the night if I do not vant to earn mein way to de vrow and to my yonkers, and to Sherm'any, hein ?"

" I believe in nothing you say," returned Thaddeus O'Shaughnessy, "nothing whatever. As regards what you do, I can believe that because I can see it. Where are the papers ? I wish for no delay."

The skipper did not in any way resent the imperious tone in which the schoolmaster spoke.

" This way," he said, "only it is full of danger. Has anyone got a light ?"

Thaddeus was alarmed for a moment.

This was, in fact, a thing of which he had not thought.

" I have a lantern," said Pat O'Connor, and as he drew it from his pocket and opened it, the cavern showed a hundred fantastic shapes and shadows.

"Dis vay !" cried De Ruyter. "Hold the light, Mr. O'Shaughnessy. Dis vay, dis vay."

Thaddeus was taken quite off his guard.

Taking the lantern from the hands of Pat O'Connor, he followed the skipper as he led the way to the very edge of the cave's mouth.

The boys looked on uneasily.

Indeed, they followed closely.

"Take care," said Pat, "take care, Mr. O'Shaughnessy. You know what a dangerous place this is."

These words recalled Thaddeus to himself.

He thanked Pat by a look.

" I know its danger, Pat," he said, "and shall take good care."

At this moment the Dutchman started.

" Hein !" he cried, "what is that ?"

The four listened.

The sound of voices was heard at the mouth of the cavern.

"Villain ! you have betrayed us !" cried Thaddeus O'Shaughnessy, springing forward.

The Dutchman waved him back.

"Madman !" he cried, "you are shoost— quite—quite mad ! How could I give informashuns to mein friends ven de phoys took me from de island, and so brought me up here, all by meinselve ? I have no one here, I swear. I will go mit you to de mouth of de cave."

And he strode on in advance.

They followed him.

His manner was so confident that their suspicion of treachery was, unfortunately, for the moment allayed.

Whoever it was about the cave, they were evidently not there at the Dutch skipper's bidding. No one, however, could be seen.

The moonlight delved down, as it were, into the basin.

"Vell, it must have been de echo of mein own voice," said the Dutchman; "ve vill return. But no—what's dat ?"

As he spoke, voices were again heard, just above their heads.

"Tonder and blitzen !" he exclaimed, " dere dey are again. Ha, ha ! but dey little know dat de smuggler De Ruyter is here."

They all listened again.

The unmistakable sound of voices was once more heard overhead.

" What is to be done ?" asked Thaddeus, in a stern undertone.

" I don't know."

"But you must be aware who these people are," said Thaddeus.

"Not know at all—how can I know ?" said the skipper, in irritation ; "perhaps they are shoost some passing strangers. "But," he added, as if a sudden light had entered his mind, "you poys can vatch at de entrance to the cave, and den we can find de papers."

"Very well," said Thaddeus, quite unsuspectingly. "Pat O'Connor, you and your companions can watch the entrance to the cave. We shall not be long."

In his inmost heart Pat O'Connor felt a fear that Thaddeus O'Shaughnessy was being led into an ambush.

But he could not gainsay his orders, and so he and his companions remained to guard the entrance, while the smuggler led the way once more to the perilous mouth of the cavern, where the fall was a hundred and fifty feet sheer upon rough and jagged rocks.

They all listened.

Each was as anxious as the other.

At length Pat said—

"What do you think of this affair, Barry ?"

" I don't like it."

" I fancy it is some ambush," said Marshall.

"No one is near."

" True, but there is Callaghan's Fall, the terrible spot where the rebel died."

"Surely De Ruyter would not attempt that," said The Barry.

"Attempt it ? You do not know what a desperate man he is," said Pat.

"But we should kill him if he hurt the master," said The Barry.

The three boys remained silent for a moment.

Then Pat said—

"No one seems coming this way. Indeed, I believe the voices were only the result of his knowledge of ventriloquism. Let's creep in and take a peep."

The words had scarcely left his mouth, when a loud shout resounded through the cavern.

It was the voice of Thaddeus O'Shaughnessy.

"Help, help !" he cried.

" I knew it, I knew it," exclaimed Pat, excitedly ; "follow me."

And he dashed into the cave.

The sight they saw froze their very blood.

The lantern, which Pat O'Connor had lent his master, was stuck in a niche in the rock, and by the dim light it shed over the cavern, they could see Thaddeus O'Shaughnessy struggling with the Dutchman.

The moonlight struggled with the feeble light of the lantern, and they could see that the face of De Ruyter was absolutely convulsed with rage.

Thaddeus was pale.

Not with fear, of course, but fear through knowledge of the danger of his position, and his resolute determination not to be worsted by his enemy.

But what was to be done ?

As the two men closed, they were locked in a deadly embrace.

The Dutch skipper, as we know, was destitute of all arms.

The pistol, which had been wrested from his hand by Harry Marshall when he dashed the water in his face in the island cavern, was the only weapon he had possessed, and the boys, having deprived him of this, he of course had to depend upon his own hands.

Thaddeus had a pistol.

But the onslaught of the Dutchman had been so sudden, that he had had no time to do anything but resist hand to hand, and foot to foot.

And now on the perilous edge of the cavern they closed, scarcely a foot separating them from the terrible depth, where either or both might be dashed in pieces a hundred and fifty feet below.

The boys stood for a moment in horror.

What was to be done?

The men were so closely embraced in their death struggle, that it was quite impossible to fire without the chance of wounding the wrong one.

They neared the combatants.

But what could they do?

It was useless to stand there and gaze on such a fearful scene.

But as it was, there seemed nothing for it but to stand and gaze on the death of the Dutch skipper, or Thaddeus, or both, unless they wished to send their friend prematurely to the next world.

Before they had made their appearance in the cavern, the Dutchman had slowly and methodically endeavoured to drag the schoolmaster to the edge of the cavern.

But on their appearance, knowing that if he remained still, he would become an excellent mark for the scholars to fire at, he began whirling round and round, dragging Thaddeus with him.

Ever narrowing the space between them and the mouth of the cavern.

He seemed quite reckless as to whether death overtook him with the schoolmaster.

All he knew was that he had been worsted in a transaction.

This was quite enough to enrage him.

Quite enough to make him perfectly oblivious of his own danger.

"De Ruyter," cried Pat O'Connor, in a loud voice, "beware!"

"Ha, ha!" shouted the Dutch skipper, in a voice full of rage, as he dragged the schoolmaster nearer the edge of the rock. "You see, mein phoys, I tink more of mein revenge dan I do of mein life. We go to the dark kingdom together!"

"Not so, De Ruyter," said Pat, in a voice which astounded him, so firm, cool, and collected was it. "You are mistaken in us, and in the man with whom you are now dealing. He would rather die than give in, and he would rather die by our hands than by yours. So release him at once, or I shall chance the death of my master, and fire."

The Dutchman took no notice.

His blood was up, and he was utterly reckless.

Thaddeus, powerful as he was, seemed no match for his stout antagonist, who dragged 'im, with an apparently irresistible force, towards the cliff's edge.

He struggled violently, and with any other man he would no doubt have had an excellent chance.

But the Dutchman seemed endowed with a supernatural—a demoniacal strength, and the schoolmaster plainly saw that unless aid came, he would fall a certain victim to his determined foe.

The words of Pat O'Connor exactly echoed his own sentiments.

"Brave boy!" he cried, "brave boy! You have said exactly the words which would have come from my own heart. Do not think of me. Fire!"

It was a perilous risk.

They were whirling round and round; dragging here, dragging there.

Now almost stumbling on the floor of the cave, now almost staggering to the edge of the precipice.

Pat turned to The Barry with a pale face.

"Shall I risk it?" he said.

"Yes, yes, anything," he cried. "If you feel any confidence in your aim, fire."

Pat only thought a moment.

Then he said, in a loud voice—

"Mr. O'Shaughnessy, shall I fire?"

The men were now struggling on the very brink of the cave.

It could be but a matter of an instant.

"Yes, yes!" exclaimed Thaddeus, "fire away. Don't think of me. I will not give this ruffian the satisfaction of knowing that he has wreaked his revenge upon me."

Pat whispered to his companions.

Then he advanced and took steady aim at the Dutchman.

"Heaven preserve you, dear master!" he cried.

"Bless you, my boy! Dear boys—all of you," cried the schoolmaster, "remember, if I die, I do not hold you responsible for anything."

Pat waited until the Dutchman, in his struggles, was near to him.

Then, with a deep-drawn breath, he fired.

Every one of the boys felt his heart stand still as the smoke rolled forth and the report echoed through the cave.

But The Barry had heard Pat's whisper, and acted on it.

As Pat fired he sprang forward and made a grab at the master's legs.

Dead or alive, they were determined that they would recover the body of Thaddeus O'Shaughnessy, and save him from the terrible doom of dashing down those awful depths, to be crushed into a shapeless mass.

The Barry, as he seized Thaddeus, threw himself back on the floor of the cavern, and Harry Marshall clutched him so that he should not be dragged back in the recoil.

In an instant the smoke cleared away.

As it did so, a cry of joy arose from the lips of the three boys.

There, standing with The Barry clutching his ankle, was Thaddeus O'Shaughnessy, perfectly unhurt.

At the edge of the precipice, just at the corner of the cave, was the Dutch skipper

He was staggeringly clutching at the rugged rock, and his face was pale and his eyes dull.

From a wound in his forehead was welling some blood, which was slowly trickling down his cheek.

After all, the shot had taken effect, without injuring Thaddeus, who stood firm as a rock.

Suddenly, however, a new phase of the subject was seen.

During the struggle—the last of it—the smuggler had contrived to drag from the pocket of Thaddeus his pistol.

This now, with unsteady hand but determined aim, he raised, and pointed at the schoolmaster.

But death had claimed him for his own.

The pistol exploded.

Its contents were lodged somewhere in the cliff, but Thaddeus still remained untouched.

De Ruyter, completely upset by his last effort, rolled towards the brink, clutching frantically at the rugged rocks, and fell, with a wild, gurgling cry, down—down into the awful depths below.

The depth was so great that they could hear nothing.

But still, for a few moments they stood breathless, until the time arrived when it was likely all was over.

Then slowly Thaddeus turned to his scholars.

"Boys," he said, "this is a sad and terrible affair; but the wretched man has his deserts. He was a wicked and reckless villain, and has been rightly punished.

"But now," he added, "I have some idea that what this wretched man said was the truth; so we will search everywhere in this cavern for these papers. I feel convinced they are here."

"Then, why did he bring us here to kill you, in the very place where he knew we could find the papers?" said Pat O'Connor.

"I think his attempt to kill me was a sudden fit of anger," said Thaddeus, "a sudden feeling that I had overreached him, and that he would not let me triumph. Come, let us seek in these fissures, towards which he pointed. They may be there."

"At any rate, it is worth the trial," said Pat O'Connor.

The Barry smiled.

"You are too good to me, sir," said he. "Why should you trouble like this for one who can never, perhaps, requite you for your kindness to him?"

Thaddeus O'Shaughnessy patted him gently on the head.

"My boy," he said, "unless I am very mistaken, you will have the chance, before long, of amply repaying everyone you love. But, for myself, I neither claim nor expect, nor would receive any reward. But I feel sure that you will recover your own in spite of all."

The search began now in earnest.

The three boys and their master spread themselves in different directions, and every fissure in the cavern was explored.

At length, with a triumphant cry, The Barry jumped from the crevice he was searching, where the grey light of morning was struggling in from above.

"Here, here!" he cried. "I have them—at last I have them."

Thaddeus O'Shaughnessy and the two boys at once rushed to his side.

It was quite true.

The Barrymore papers were at length within his grasp.

For an instant The Barry felt so overwhelmed by his good fortune that he could scarcely speak.

But after awhile, he was about to address a few words to his master and his two friends, when a rush of feet was heard.

Then, just as they were preparing their weapons, four armed men rushed into the cave.

At their head was Jack O'Grady, drunk, and furious with anger.

"Where is the captain?" he cried, in a loud voice. "Tell us, or yer lives are not wurruth a moment's purchase—quick! Bhoys, livel your rifles."

And at the words, the four men whom Jack commanded levelled their loaded weapons at the heads of Thaddeus and the boys.

CHAPTER XXXVIII.
OUT OF THE FIRE!

As Thaddeus O'Shaughnessy and his three scholars glanced at the four ruffians, with their rifles levelled at their heads, they were for a moment dismayed.

Indeed, they could see no reasonable hope of escape.

Thaddeus O'Shaughnessy had no firearms; Pat O'Connor had fired his, and The Barry and Harry Marshall were of no use against four ferocious men.

"Where is the capten of the 'Silverhorn'?" cried Jack O'Grady.

As he spoke, there was heard the unmistakable roll of a drum.

The four men started, but they did not swerve from their purpose.

They kept their rifles still pointed towards the schoolmaster and his scholars.

"I know not where he is now," said Thaddeus O'Shaughnessy, calmly, "but this I do know, that he and I had a fight on the edge of the cliff here, and he is now a hundred and fifty feet below."

Jack O'Grady uttered a howl of rage.

He waited to give no orders to his men, but leaped madly forward.

"Curses on ye," he cried; "I'll take yer life meself!"

As he sprang in the direction of the schoolmaster, however, The Barry raised his pistol, and in an instant Jack O'Grady, with a loud cry, fell prostrate.

In a moment Thaddeus had possessed himself of his musket, and raised it.

"My men!" he cried, addressing the astonished companions of the O'Grady, "do you hear yonder drum?"

He pointed as he spoke towards the roof of the cavern.

Through the entrance of the cave there rolled the sound of a drum and fife band, approaching every moment nearer.

"Yes, shure," said one of the men, known as Mat Barrigan; "but what o' that?"

And he made as if to spring towards the body of his fallen leader.

"Back!" cried Thaddeus, as he kept his rifle levelled against the head of Barrigan; "advance a step and you are a dead man!

"That band is the band of an English regiment; if they hear this constant firing, they will enter the cave, and then your fate is certain. Your leader is dead; let us go, and we will take no further steps. If not, do as you please; we will fight to the death, and abide our chance."

The three boys had taken advantage of the parley to reload their pistols.

The men conferred for a moment in an undertone, and in Irish, keeping their weapons still levelled, and their faces to their foe.

Then, on a sudden, Mat Barrigan fired.

It was a treacherous shot, aimed badly, in the excess of his rage.

The ball whizzed uncomfortably near to the head of Thaddeus, and flattened against the rock at his back.

In an instant the shot was returned, and Mat Barrigan, pierced through the brain, fell by the side of Jack O'Grady.

"At them, boys! we must escape from this den of murderers."

Before the other men could recover their presence of mind, the three boys had fired, and one of the men fell dead, while the other two were badly wounded.

The fight even then, however, was a severe one.

The men of course had their muskets, which they fired, wounding Thaddeus and Harry Marshall severely.

And—after they had discharged them, they could still club them and use them murderously.

But Thaddeus O'Shaughnessy was a tower of strength in himself.

His musket was whirled with terrific force round his head, and as Harry and The Barry rushed at the man who was thus left disengaged, Pat O'Connor quietly loaded his pistol.

Again he took aim.

Again one of the reckless men fell dead.

The other staggered towards the entrance of the cave, just as some English soldiers, who had been attracted by the sound of constant firing, rushed in at the cave's mouth.

Seeing the "redcoats," he halted on the margin of the precipice.

"Stand back there!" he cried; "shure and if it's a poor bhoy's life ye want, ye can have it, but it'll be meself will be makin' ye a present of it."

The sergeant who had entered at the head of the English soldiers, halted, but made no reply to him.

"What does this all mean, sir?" he cried, addressing Thaddeus O'Shaughnessy, whom, as he stood by the side of his three scholars, he recognised as the famous schoolmaster of the Shannon academy.

In a few words, Thaddeus had explained to him the whole state of affairs.

"Well," said the sergeant, "here are four senseless; there's only that mad-looking chap over yonder to take."

"And shure, then, it's that mad-looking fellow ye won't take," cried the Irishman; "it's meself belongs to a brotherhood that has sworn never to be taken alive by any of the myrmidons of the murtherin' Saxon; so away wid ye, or it's Dennis Maloney'll dash himself down the rocks in spite of his three children and the missus."

"Oh! he's one of the preaching lot," cried the sergeant, with a grin; "come, Mr. Bologny, or whatever you call yourself, surrender quietly, or you'll be taken by force."

The man, as he spoke, approached close to the Irishman.

The latter backed to the very edge of the fearful cliff.

"Stand back, I say!" he cried; "shure and haven't I told ye before, if ye want me life, I'll make ye a present of it? But the dhivil a bit of a Saxon gaol am I a-going into."

The sergeant laughed.

"None of yer boasting, Mr. Bologny," he said; "here, Andrews, let's have those handcuffs."

The man addressed as Andrews at once produced a pair of handcuffs.

With these the sergeant and he approached the cave's mouth.

Dennis Maloney was now standing as it were with one foot hanging over the verge of the precipice.

"Back—back, I say!" he cried.

But no more.

His face was pale and determined.

He had flung his musket already into the deep abyss; and now Thaddeus saw plainly that he meant what he said.

"Excuse me," he said, in an undertone, to the soldier, "that man must be arrested by stratagem. He will kill himself rather than yield."

"One more out of the way," cried the sergeant, brutally; "it will save the English government the trouble of hanging him; come on, Andrews."

The two men at once advanced to the margin of the cliff.

But they soon paused as they reached it, and uttered a startled cry.

Neither had expected what happened, in spite of the warning of Thaddeus O'Shaughnessy.

With a wild "Hurroo!" which was the cry of a half-maddened enthusiast, Dennis Maloney gave a leap into the deep abyss, after first hurling his shillelagh full in the face of the sergeant.

"Great Heaven! he has killed himself," cried Pat O'Connor, with pale lips.

"I knew it," said Thaddeus, "I warned them of it. But perhaps it is for the best. Maybe the poor fellow is best out of his misery; for he would have swung at the county gaol of a surety."

"Well, I'm sure I never believed it," said the sergeant, who, brute as he was, was dismayed at the result of his impetuosity, and in fact looked absolutely crestfallen. "I thought it was only boasting; I've seen a good deal of it in my time."

"Ye see, you are an Englishman, and I am an Irishman," said Thaddeus, "and I know

"'SEE, THERE SHAN'T BE A HOUSE CONTAINING A SAXON STANDING,' SAID O'REILLY."

better than you the nature of my countrymen ; but it is of no use talking. The mischief is done—and this terrible slaughter cannot be prevented. I will go with you and give you the necessary information, and then I suppose I can leave the rest in your hands."

"Just so, sir," said the sergeant, somewhat lugubriously ; "my men, turn those bodies on their backs and follow me."

In a few moments the soldiers had done as he bade them, and placed the bodies in a corner.

Then the whole of the occupants of the cave made their way up the mountain's side, and in the light of the early morning they found themselves at the door of the constabulary.

Here the statements of Thaddeus and his scholars were taken down, and once more they took their way towards the academy.

Very little more was heard of this affair.

The bodies of De Ruyter and Dennis Maloney were found crushed and mangled at the bottom of the abyss, and a formal verdict was given of "suicide."

And so, apparently, the affair died out and was done with.

But in the minds of those who knew the state of Irish thought at that moment, it was one more preparation for the tempest that was to come.

CHAPTER XXXIX.

THE CLUE TO A MYSTERY.

DURING the time that Reginald Graham had been at the Shannon academy, Thaddeus O'Shaughnessy had received regularly instalments of money on behalf of the young English lad.

No explanation, however, had been given in reference to the peculiar circumstances under which he had been sent to the school.

He had received letters, it is true, but they had only given vague addresses to which notes could be addressed in regard to Reginald's health.

They contained no information, and in fact the disjointed and sometimes incoherent expressions which were in them served rather to create than to dispel mystery.

At length, one evening, about a fortnight after the scene at Callaghan's Fall, as Thaddeus O'Shaughnessy, tired after more than an ordinary day of fatigue, was in his study sitting at his table, with his head leaning on his hand, Willie Curtis announced a visitor.

"Who is it ?" asked the schoolmaster, somewhat testily ; "it is a strange hour at which to pay visits."

"Shure, surr, and shall I tell him you're not in, and don't want to see 'im ?" began Willie Curtis.

The master interrupted him.

"I asked you a question, please answer me," he said ; "who is it that has called ?"

"A jintleman, surr, a raal jintleman, bred and born, I'm thinking."

"Did he give any name ?"

"Shure, surr, and maybe it's written down on this piece of paper," returned the serving man, and with the words he drew from his pocket a card, which he had been thumbing

and twisting about until it was as black and greasy as if it had been kicking about the place for a week.

However, it was just possible to decipher the name—

"Mr. Herbert Graham."

The schoolmaster rose with an exclamation of pleasure.

"Tell the gentleman I shall be most happy to see him," he said.

And then he murmured, as Willie disappeared with his usual scrape—

"Now, at last there will be a chance of getting at the bottom of this mystery."

It was with great impatience that he waited the arrival of the stranger.

There arrived presently in the room, a tall, military-looking man of about five-and-forty years of age, who wore his left arm in a sling, and had a scar on his forehead as if from a sabre cut.

His face was deadly pale, not with any sudden emotion, but with a pallor which was the result of some great grief gone by.

He bowed in an elegant and graceful manner as he entered the room.

"I have the infinite pleasure, I believe," he said, "of standing in the presence of Mr. Thaddeus O'Shaughnessy."

"Yes, sir, that is my name," said the schoolmaster ; "and I presume I stand in the presence of Mr. Herbert Graham."

"Certainly ; and of a grateful man," he said.

And in a warm manner, discarding all formalities, he held out his hand.

The schoolmaster grasped it, and shook it heartily.

"Sit down, sir," he cried, "and make yourself at home. There is no doubt that if you have crossed the hills, you have had enough of the dew ; so now I'll give you some mountain dew of a different sort."

So saying, he passed to the door and called for Willie Curtis.

Having given his directions, he returned to the fireplace, and sat down opposite his guest in his easy chair.

"I have taken the liberty," he said, "of getting a bed ready for you ; I know this would not be a nice night for you to leave this place, or to find a lodging, no matter in which direction you went. I hope you will remain."

The stranger's eyes flashed with pleasure.

"You are indeed a good friend," returned the guest ; "if all had been to me in other days as you are, I should have been a different man !"

"And are you indeed the father of Reginald Graham ?" asked Thaddeus, eagerly.

"I am !"

"Heaven !" exclaimed the schoolmaster ; "how did you escape from those enemies that night ?"

"They fired at me, and grazed my temple," said Graham, "but at the moment the shot stunned me. They thought they had killed me, for I staggered away down the mountain path, and was lost amid the mists. Since then they have lost sight of me, although they have sought for me—Heaven knows—long, and far enough !"

Thaddeus O'Shaughnessy saw that his guest was lost in the thoughts of the past.

So he left him for a moment to recover himself ere be said—

"May I ask, without rudeness, what is the cause of your great trouble?"

"Certainly, Mr. O'Shaughnessy, you may," said Herbert Graham. "That is one of my objects in coming here."

"I am glad to hear it," said Thaddeus; "for I confess that I am very curious. But would you not like first to see your son Reginald?"

As the schoolmaster moved towards the door, his visitor caught him by the arm.

Mr. O'Shaughnessy turned and looked his visitor in the face.

"No—not before you know all," said the stranger. "I know well Reginald has been in good and kind hands, and I would rather explain to you who and what I am before I meet him."

"Very well," said Mr. O'Shaughnessy, as he brewed a large glass of whisky each, and produced some of his finest cigars. "I will listen attentively."

I will not tell the story of Reginald Graham's life as it was told by him to the schoolmaster; for it would take too long.

In brief, I will narrate it in my own words.

In the county of Devonshire there is a place called Talmar Hall.

This, at the time the episode occurred of which I am about to write, was in the possession of a gentleman named Graham—Horace Graham, who had bought it from one Count De Talmar, who had for a long while been domesticated in this country.

Horace Graham, when he came to the Hall, brought to it a wife and two sons.

The husband and wife were by no means good friends; and indeed it was reported throughout the whole countryside that the Hall was the scene of frequent domestic quarrels.

At length the wife died.

For a year Horace Graham kept single, but at the end of that time he brought to the old house a young and beautiful bride.

Things went on better now; for the new wife, strange to say, though having no children of her own, took a great fancy to the two boys.

But the one she loved was Herbert.

She saw at once the dark and stern nature of Mortimer, and the soft and yielding nature of Herbert, the younger brother.

At length Horace died.

The wife was left in uncontrolled possession of the property, but at the age of twenty-one, Mortimer Graham was to inherit everything.

Herbert was, according to the will, made merely subservient to his brother.

As the time approached for the coming of age of Mortimer, his character so openly developed itself, that he became an object of dislike to everyone in the place.

Often quarrels broke out between him and his brother and his stepmother, and at length, the latter, stung by some insult which was more than she could bear, called Herbert into her private room, and told him a terrible secret.

There had been a flaw in the marriage of his father and mother, at the birth of Mortimer; a flaw which was rectified before the birth of Herbert.

Here, then, was something that would at once crush the hopes of the eldest son, for in the event of Mortimer not taking the property, Herbert would be of necessity the next heir.

But the insulted wife did not find in Herbert the pliant character she had expected.

To her he was kind and gentle.

But when the question was raised of dispossessing his brother of his property, he firmly though gently declined.

"No, mother," he said; "to make myself master of Talmar Hall, I should have to take away my brother's character; and that I will never do."

All persuasion was useless.

He resisted everything.

For a time, consequently, Mrs. Graham desisted from her endeavours.

She hoped, in fact, that Mortimer would behave himself better, and so not give rise to further quarrels.

But she hoped in vain.

Mortimer became worse and worse.

He took to drink, sought bad company, and brought disgrace in every way on the ancient name.

At length, therefore, she took a sudden determination.

Without consulting Herbert, she disclosed to her lawyer the whole circumstances.

Mortimer was at once informed of all.

Of course, a terrible scene ensued between the two brothers.

In vain Herbert declared that he knew nothing of the actions of his stepmother.

In vain he offered to sign the property away to his brother.

Mortimer would listen to nothing.

Nothing, except a duel between them to the death, would satisfy his fierce resentment.

To avoid this, Herbert, taking with him as much money as he could scrape together, fled from Talmar Hall.

His stepmother was terrified by the result of her diplomacy,

She had hoped that by what she had done she would have brought Mortimer to his senses.

She had never dreamed of the maddened fury that she had evoked.

It was in vain she endeavoured to pacify the elder brother.

He would listen to no manner of reason.

Knowing well that he had lost his birthright, as it were; knowing that he had lost even his name, Mrs. Graham did all she could to calm his rage.

But in vain; and accordingly, she disposed of a large portion of the property before Mortimer came of age, and gave Herbert the proceeds.

With this, as I have said, he left the Hall, and soon after the stepmother left also.

Mortimer was left in undisputed possession of the place.

At first he swore that he would have nothing to do with it. But he soon altered his tune.

He had command of a fine estate, and was complete master of all.

So he had changed his mind; gave directions, as soon as his majority arrived, as to how the property was to be improved, and then——?

Did he marry a wife, and strive to settle down in happiness?

No.

It was not in his heart to do this.

He set out on a voyage of vengeance.

Everywhere where Herbert went after this, he was hunted down.

He married a woman he loved.

She died by strange means, just as she gave birth to Reginald.

He went thence a broken-hearted man; and then—when he had settled down with his little child, in another place, he was driven thence by the foul calumnies spread about by his brother.

Finding that this did not destroy the brother, who had, as he thought, taken from him his name, Mortimer Graham began a more terrible scheme of vengeance.

He plainly and openly made attacks on the lives of Herbert and his boy Reginald.

No matter whither he fled, he was pursued.

At length, wearied out by constant chasings, he made his way to Ireland.

But here everything was worse.

Among the starving peasantry Mortimer found ready tools for his vengeance.

The wilder and more distant the regions to which he fled, the more peril Herbert had to encounter.

At length, on that misty night, on the dim hills, his dangers culminated.

Wounded, hunted, scarcely knowing what to do or which way to turn, he had given to Pat O'Connor the charge of his only child, and fled away down the mountain pass.

It was then that he received the wound from the pistol that had grazed his forehead like a cut from a sword.

"And now," asked Thaddeus, when Herbert Graham had reached this point in his story, "is the hunting and pursuit over?"

"Yes, all."

"Is your brother forgiving at last?"

"He is dead," said Herbert; "but as for forgiveness, he had nothing to forgive."

"I beg pardon; I mean, did he repent?"

"Yes; and he left a will giving to me everything," said Herbert. "'Of course,' he added in the private letter which accompanied his testament—

"'Of course it is all yours by right, but let it be thought that I leave all to you of my own free accord, that my head may not go in utter shame and dishonour to the grave.'"

"And did he ask your forgiveness?" asked Thaddeus.

"Yes, he confessed all, and asked me to forgive him. I shall not repeat now what he said in his letter," said Herbert Graham, "but it was a letter which I could not but answer in a friendly spirit. He begged me to come and see him, and I went. I was too late, however, for he died about an hour before I reached the Hall. It was better so, perhaps, for such a meeting between us must have been a terrible one."

There was a pause now.

Neither, in fact, felt inclined to speak.

But at length, as Thaddeus brewed another glass of grog, he said—

"I suppose you would like to retire to bed after this?"

"Yes, and I have changed my mind in one thing," said Mr. Graham. "I should like to see my boy before I retire, though I do not wish to wake him."

So as they passed up the stairs, they paused a moment at the door of the dormitory.

Thaddeus O'Shaughnessy opened it gently, and the two passed in.

"There is Reginald," said the schoolmaster.

The father took a glance at the ruddy, healthy face of his son, and grasping the master's hand, pressed it warmly.

Then he knelt by the side of the bed, and pressed a kiss upon the forehead of his sleeping child.

———

CHAPTER XL.

A DEPARTURE AND A FROLIC.

THE next day was a whole holiday at the Shannon Academy.

The first thing in the morning, of course, was an interview between Reginald and his father, and an affecting one it was, as may be imagined.

Then came an interview with Pat O'Connor, whom he thanked for his brave championship of his son, and to whom he gave a diamond ring and an invitation, at any time, to come to Talmar Hall.

And then, of course, there must be a holiday, and Mr. Graham must send for cakes and fruit, and all manner of good things.

It was a glorious day.

But it ended in sorrow for Pat and some others.

For Reginald Graham quitted the academy with his father.

He gave a handsome recompense to Thaddeus for all his kindness, and an invitation to Devonshire, and as the father and son quitted the school, the boys assembled in the courtyard, and cheered them so lustily that the echoes of the shouts rang up the misty hills.

There was a void left in the school when Reginald went.

Everyone in the school had liked him.

Even those who had at first felt an inclination to annoy him, because of his age and size, had learned to love him.

Indeed, since the night on which Dan Hooligan, as the agent of Herbert Graham's enemies, had made his attack upon the boy in the grounds, he had gathered to himself many friends, and his place was felt to be vacant for many days.

But as the old-fashioned and now worn-out saying has it—"Boys will be boys."

They regretted him; but the studies which they pursued with ardent zeal, and the fun which they had in the playground, and the genial companionship of all, soon banished sorrow, and they only looked forward to the time when school would be a thing of the past, and they would meet their friends again on the busy platform of life.

A short time after the departure of Reginald Graham, one of the scholars, named Robert

Erwell, approached Pat O'Connor one evening in the playground, and beckoned him apart from his fellows.

"Pat," he said, "there's a jolly chance now of paying out Tom McClosky."

Pat laughed.

"Poor fellow," he said, "it's almost time we left him alone, unless, indeed, he's been up to some more pranks."

"And that he has," said Erwell.

"What now, then?" asked Pat.

"Oh, nothing new," replied the boy; "they've been all the old things again, salt in the boys' beds, beetles, nettles, ropes across the rooms, and so on. But he's getting outrageous, and something must be done in the way of retaliation."

"Well, and what is it you propose?" said Pat. "I've used up all my pranks, I think."

"I'll tell you, then," said the other boy; "only let us keep everything dark. Harry Marshall can help us, and so can The Barry; but don't let us have anyone else in the swim."

"We'll leave The Barry out," returned Pat O'Connor. "To-morrow is the day on which he has to meet Mr. Singleton in regard to his property, so it won't do to get him into any scrape beforehand. Surely I and Harry and you are enough to have a lark with one boy."

"Very well then; listen."

Pat did so.

And heartily he laughed as he did.

Excusing himself to his companions, after a moment, he made his way into the school-house, and presently they had dived into the precincts of a large ante-room, which was just outside the pantry.

What they did there, we shall see presently.

They emerged after awhile, and returned again to the playground.

Here they saw Tom McClosky

The latter at once approached Pat O'Connor.

"O'Connor," he said, "it's my birthday."

"Ah! many happy returns of the day," cried our hero; "I hope you're going to stand a treat."

"Well, I was going to," said McClosky, "but to tell the truth, my people haven't sent me a blessed stiver."

"How's that?"

"I don't know. I expect the post has miscarried," said Tom; "for my people never let me in like that. But at any rate, we can have a spree, if you're game."

"Tell us how?"

"Why, you know that everything is preparing for Figs' wedding."

"Yes."

"Well, down in the pantry there are fruit and every kind of dainty 'in galore,' as the people say," returned McClosky; "a little won't be missed."

"I don't quite see," said Pat.

"It's easy enough," returned McClosky; "when all the school is asleep, we'll creep down here, and fill a box full of good things."

"Yes."

"Then we'll cart it up into the dormitory, and we'll have a fine tuck-out," said Tom McClosky.

"All right," said Pat, with feigned delight; "you can have my box. It's down in the room, empty."

"Thanks, that'll do stunning," said McClosky; "we'll come down at ten."

"Yes, I'm game," said Pat; "but don't let's conspire too much, or we shall be observed and suspected."

Never dreaming of the plan which was being hatched against him, Tom McClosky retired delighted, in anticipation of the tuck-out which had been arranged for the night.

At length the hour approached.

As usual, all was quiet, for everyone in the Shannon Academy went at the same hour to bed every night.

McClosky, Pat O'Connor, and Harry Marshall had retired to their beds half dressed.

All the boys in the dormitory were in the fun, and they eagerly looked forward to the dénouement of the adventure.

Down the four conspirators crept.

At every creak of the great stairs they started.

But everyone appeared to be at rest, and although, had anyone been awake, it would have been easy to detect their progress down the stairs, they reached the ground floor in safety, and descended into the room next the pantry.

"Hold this light," said Pat, taking a lantern from his pocket, and placing it in McClosky's hand; "I'll see to the boxes."

The unsuspecting McClosky took the light, while Pat and Harry Marshall lifted a narrow, thin deal box on top of another.

After some mysterious actions, which were lost on Tom, Pat opened the cupboard.

"Now then, McClosky," he cried, "give the light to Marshall, and help me in with the things."

Tom did at once what he was directed.

Then Pat, seizing a pot of marmalade, cried—

"Here you are, old man; quick."

Tom seized it, and placed it in the box.

"Here's some jam."

And this was placed in the box.

Some oranges and apples, and figs and cakes, and an abundance of good things followed.

With a broad grin, Tom McClosky placed the things one after another in the box.

All the time, Erwell was on his hands and knees arranging something behind him.

It was nothing more nor less than a huge tub full of soapy, greasy water, large enough to hold a man at full length.

Of what use it would be to them in their adventure, it would have been impossible to say.

At any rate, Erwell's face was on the broad grin all the time that he was performing his mysterious movements.

Presently, the box of dainties was nearly full.

Pat now made a sudden start.

"Ah!" he cried, "what's that?"

Tom turned pale, and in staggering aside, put his hand through the top of a jar of jam.

"It sounded like someone coming downstairs," said Harry Marshall; "let's go and see."

Harry and Pat crept to the door and listened.

There was not a sound for a few moments.

Then Pat said—

" I think all's right now. There doesn't seem to be anybody about. Take up the box, Tom, and I'll hold the light."

There was a loud clattering at this moment, and Tom, who was now in darkness, cried in a loud voice—

" What's that? Oh, dear, what's the matter ?"

" Nothing," said Erwell; " only I stumbled over something. Be quick; take up the box."

Unfortunate Tom.

He seized the box with all his force, thinking, naturally, that it would be heavy.

Alas ! for human expectations.

There was a false bottom, one that could be slid onwards, and the noise which Tom had heard, was the falling of the jam pots and cakes, and so on, into an empty box beneath.

The consequence was, Tom fell back with a crash, and tumbled with a flop and a splash into the tub of unclean and greasy water.

It was an awful sell for poor Tom.

Instead of the dainties which he had expected, his mouth was filled with a horribly nauseous fluid which nearly choked him.

And to make matters worse, he heard some one descending the stairs with a heavy step.

It sounded like the step of Thaddeus O'Shaughnessy.

Scrambling up out of the tub, dripping like a drowned rat, he made for the door, hoping to hide in the corner away from the dreaded eyes of the master.

In vain.

As he rushed to the door, it opened, a sudden light broke in, and Lawrence McMah n, cane in hand, appeared on the scene.

Tom looked round in dismay for his companions.

But they had disappeared.

Alone he had to face his fate.

CHAPTER XLI.

THE BARRY ON HIS NATIVE HEARTH.

TOM McCLOSKY, terrified in the presence of his teacher, could say nothing in exoneration of his conduct.

Why was he there?

If he told the truth, he would, of course, be splitting on his companions to no purpose.

He would be proved by his own words to be the ringleader in an attempt at theft, whereas the others could show that they had only joined in it to make a fool of him.

So he stammered out some incoherent story about coming down to get his box, and finding it empty, and so falling into the filthy water.

Of course Lawrence McMahon didn't believe a word he said.

His answer was an order to remove a certain portion of his garments, and the cane was flourished about that room in a most extraordinary manner for several minutes, while Tom's head went down, and his heels went up.

When he was released from the master's cane, his face and another part of his body were one as red as the other, and he made no reply to the command of " go to bed," uttered in a loud and authoritative voice.

He howled most lugubriously as he went upstairs, and when he entered the dormitory and removed his things, he rubbed the parts affected and then struck an attitude of theatrical defiance, which made all the boys burst with laughter.

" You cowardly, sneaking hounds !" he cried. " You wretched, paltry humbugs ! To let me into a trap like that, and then to leave me."

" Who was the thief ?" cried one voice.

" Who wanted to give a treat with stolen property ?" cried another.

" Who was going to run away with an empty box ?" exclaimed another.

" Who had a bath in the suds ?" said a fourth.

Tom McClosky fairly tore his hair and danced with rage.

" You may laugh and jeer if you like," he cried, " but you'll find my revenge shall be a real one."

The yell of laughter which followed this threat so enraged McClosky, that he fairly darted into bed, muttering curses beneath his teeth.

" You'll see," he growled, " how I'll pay you out before the week's over. Pat O'Connor, and you, Harry Marshall, will be the first ; the rest shall follow."

" All right," cried Pat with a laugh, " all right. And now we'll go to sleep and dream of it."

The next day was a half-holiday, and while the other boys were amusing themselves like rational beings in the playground, or the gardens, or on the river, Tom McClosky wandered about alone.

Alone to nourish his deadly vengeance.

For a long time he could think of nothing to suit his purpose.

But it occurred to him at last, that not having a fertile brain of his own, he should be better off if he consulted another.

There was a difficulty in his mind as to whom he should apply to aid him.

At any rate, whoever it might be, it would be better than none at all, on the principle that two heads are better than one.

So as he espied Willie Curtis coming across the lawn, it struck him at once that he might do for his plan. Accordingly he accosted him.

" Where are you off to, Willie ?" he said.

" Shure, and it's meself's going on an errand for the masther," said Willie.

" And how far ?"

" Shure, and I haven't measured the disthance," said the man, " but I'm thinking that as I'll have to go there and back, it'll be two miles."

" You're going to Piers Point."

" I am that same," said Willie.

" Will you bring me something on the sly, if I pay you well for it ?"

" Is it asking me ye are, surr, when you know a poor bhoy'll always be after earning an honest penny," said the man, deferentially.

" Well, then, you know Twistem's the chemist up there ?"

"Is it the man you mean that sells the nasty stuff that's supposed to make ye well?" said Willie.

"Yes, that's the chap. Well, I want ye to buy me some chloroform."

"Chloroform! And shure, what's that?" cried Willie, in a voice expressive of intense surprise.

"Never mind what it is," said McClosky; "I know what it is for, and that's a lark."

"And what will ye give me if I help you?" said Willie, in his cautious, cunning way.

"I'll give you five shillings," answered Tom, "if you'll only say nothing about it."

"You're shure it's nothing that'll be afther getting a poor bhoy into throuble now?" said Willie Curtis, suspiciously.

"Trouble! No; it's only a bit of fun, and as it's a game I'm going to have with Pat O'Connor and Harry Marshall, two of the favourites, I don't want anyone to know anything about it. Here's the money—a shilling for the chloroform, and five shillings for yourself."

Willie Curtis took the money with a grin.

"All right, sir," he cried. "I'll bring it back shure, safe enough."

And off he went.

Tom McClosky went on his way rejoicing.

"Now," said Tom, "I'll have a revenge they little dream of. I don't care," he added, between his clenched teeth, "if it ends in their death."

And having given vent to this virtuous exclamation, he was able to join the others in the playground with a cheerful heart.

Meanwhile, we must follow the fortunes of Willie Curtis.

His first visit was to Tony Foster's cabin, for it was little else, where strong spirits could be had cheap.

Tony Foster was an Englishman, and a fine trade he drove by cheating the Irish.

He had the necessary licence, but, as Terence O'Rafferty used to say, paraphrasing the words of the famous song, which has travelled all over the world—

"Shure, there's a sly cupboard behind the back stairs,
And Tony is often seen fiddling there."

And this same cupboard, communicating by a trap-door, and an underground way, with a back part of the premises—could have told strange stories of secret gallons of whisky, brought from unlicensed stills

As Willie Curtis hurried up to the door of the little "inn," as it was called—"The Toad in the Hole" was the name of it—he saw several men lounging at the doors.

He was greeted by several.

In his journeys to and fro he had made many acccquaintances.

Among them was Terence O'Rafferty, his pipe in his mouth, and a gloomy, depressed, far-off look in his eyes, as if he was looking forward to some terrible event.

Willie, proud of his five shillings, at once ordered some grog for himself and two or three of the others, and having thoroughly warmed himself, as he termed it, he hurried again on his road to Piers Point, although his head was by no means as clear as it had been when he started.

Looking round, he saw Barney O'Reilly hurrying forward, and he accordingly waited.

"Well, Mr. O'Reilly," said Willie, "and what would you please to want?"

"I'm coming along nearly all the way to Piers Point," said Barney, "and as I'm not wanting to see you destroyed, I'm come to tell you to beware of the tinth of next month."

Willie turned pale.

"Shure, and what'd that be for?" he said.

"It's not myself that can explain to you that same," said O'Reilly, "but I tell ye that on the night of the tinth of next month, from sivin till the morning's light, it'll be safer for ye to be up on the dark mountains, than in the old school by the Shannon. Oh, there'll be sich a bonnie fire hereabouts, we shall be able to warrum our hands instead of wasting our peat."

"But the masther—shure he——"

Barney O'Reilly's brow grew dark.

"Don't talk of him," he cried, in a hoarse voice, "he's a traithor and a thafe. Bad luck to ye if I thought you'd be afther betraying us, I'd——"

Willie waived him away.

"There, don't be afther frightening a bhoy," he cried. "Shure, and I'm not such a fool as to risk my own life for other people. I'll keep dark, and I'll be at Tony Foster's all night if there's enough to drink."

"All right then; I only warned you because you've often stood a dhrink to me," said Barney O'Reilly; "but shure, it's not at Tony Foster's ye ought to be that same night, but in the ranks of the Boys of the Mountains. See," added the man, maddened by enthusiasm and drink, "see, there shan't be a house containing a Saxon standing on the morning of the eleventh. No, we'll pull the houses down about their ears, and them we don't burn we'll drive into the Shannon."

The man who had sworn to keep the plot a secret, had disclosed it to a lad of eighteen, without even demanding an oath that he would not tell.

"But the bhoys of Shannon Academy are nearly all Irish," said Willie.

"They are, but they stick to that infernal traither, Thaddeus O'Shaughnessy," cried Barney, fiercely, "and the whole herd must go with him. But adieu, Willie, and mind ye kape your tongue between your teeth."

Willie then shook hands with Barney O'Reilly, and they parted.

All along the road to Piers Point the serving man was worried by conflicting thoughts.

When he had just entered the Shannon school as a serving man, he had been made a butt of, and had cursed the day when he had ever caught sight of its towers.

But since then all was changed.

The boys who had made game of him, and upon whom he had endeavoured to wreak a deadly revenge, were now kind and considerate to him.

Thaddeus O'Shaughnessy himself had always been a kind master.

And now?

He was asked to save himself, and stand by while this master and these pupils were doomed to a terrible death.

"THE MAN FAIRLY STAGGERED BACK."

His feelings were wrought up to such a pitch, that like a great many other weak-minded people, he made his way into another poteen shop directly he reached the village.

This made him still more muddly than ever, and by the time that he reached the chemist's, he was fairly tipsy.

But he pulled himself together, and the cunning look in his eyes was attributed by the chemist, Mr. Twistem, to the usual slyness of his nature.

Twistem, however, soon discovered the truth.

For Willie Curtis took off his hat, and began to twirl it round and round, and scratch his head, and looked most wofully silly.

"Well," said Patrick Twistem, smiling, and leaning both his hands upon the counter, "and what can I do for you, Mister Curtis?"

"And it's meself doesn't know that same," said Willie.

"What do you come here for then?" said Twistem, still grinning.

"Shure, sir, one of the young jintlemen up at the 'kademy gave me a shillin', and tould me to bring him some—some—and I don't know what that 'some,' may be, surr."

"Maybe it's a sum ye can't reckon up," said Twistem. "What was it for?"

"I don't know, sir," said Willie, "only I know he said it was for a lark."

"A lark, eh? Is it jalap?"

"No, surr, it wasn't jollup," said Willie; "it was more like a cauliflower."

The chemist began to smell a rat.

"Was it chloroform?" he asked, still laughing.

Willie gave a leap of delight.

"Ah shure, it's Mister Twistem's the clever man," he cried; "that's it—chloroform, and I said cauliflower; but it's all the same."

"To you, perhaps it may be," remarked the man of drugs; "but did ye say it was for a lark?"

"Yes, surr."

"Ah, I understand," said Twistem. "I'll get it ready for you in a moment."

Whether it was chloroform or not that he placed in the bottle we cannot say.

At any rate, whatever compound it contained, it smelt like chloroform, and to Willie that was enough.

He paid his money and departed, staggered his way towards the shop where he had to make his purchases for Thaddeus O'Shaughnessy, and then having visited Mrs. O'Frannagan's whisky bar, he hastened back towards the school.

He was completely fuddled now, and having only a dim idea that he had purchased a cauliflower for Tom McClosky, he rang the bell, and was admitted by Kathleen the cook, who saw at once what a state he was in.

"Oh, you blaggard!" she cried. "Is this the way that you go for the masther's errands?"

Willie began a kind of war dance, peculiar to himself.

"And glad I am that you're not the masther," he said. "What are ye afther, minding other people's business for?"

Then with a hop, skip and a jump, he dashed into the kitchen, shouting at the top of his voice—

"Oh, my, oh ! Charmin' Julia Callaghan !"

He wound up inside with a ferocious jig, that nearly shook every bit of crockery off the shelves.

After this he flung himself down into the great wooden armchair by the fire, and burst into a roar of laughter.

"And I'm shure," said the cook, bridling up. "You're a disgrace to the 'kademy."

Willie put on a look which was meant to be intensely interesting.

"Wait till I've shown you what I've got for ye," he said.

And he brought from his pocket a bottle, containing what he would have called the "crather."

The face of the cook at once showed that she was mollified.

"Well, now, you know, Mr. Coortis," she said, "you shouldn't be afther coming into a rispictible house like this when you're in a state that's a disgrace to a pig."

"Whist now," exclaimed Willie.

But Kathleen was one that would have her way, and not to be interrupted.

"Ye'll be listening to me, if you plase, Mr. Coortis," she remarked. "I was going to remark that I forgive ye because you've behaved as a jintleman in bringing me home something; but I'm hoping ye won't be afther doing it again."

Willie Curtis, having received a couple of glasses at the hands of the buxom cook, poured out two jorums of whisky, and they drank it off at a gulp.

"And pray, Master Coortis," said Kathleen, smiling as she wiped her lips, "pray, Mister Coortis, where ha' ye been?"

"Well, I can soon tell ye that same," said Willie, with many a hiccup. "I've been to post a litter for the masther, and I brought him some coffin drops (cough drops, perhaps, he meant) and a variety of other articles, and then I brought a cauliflower for Master Tom McClosky."

"Shure, and if you've brought a cauliflower for Master Tom McClosky," said Kathleen, "I'd be liking to know where it is, for ye haven't it wid ye."

Willie, by this time, was so thoroughly stupefied, that he didn't remember whether it was really a cauliflower or chloroform which he had brought for the scholar.

So he glanced in a most idiotic manner round him—on chairs, and table, and sideboard.

But seeing nothing in the vegetable line anywhere about him, he fairly collapsed, and having muttered something about "Lord 'elp us !" he sank back in his chair, and was soon snoring.

At this moment the bell rang, and Kathleen had to depart to the upper regions.

As she did so, leaving the door ajar, a figure crept in quietly.

The figure of Tom McClosky.

He had heard all the conversation, and had understood, of course, the mistake which the man had made about the "cauliflower."

Hoping still that Willie had brought what

he wanted, he glided up to the man, and shook him.

"Willie!" he cried.

There was no answer.

"Willie!" he said, in a louder key.

Still no reply.

"It's all right," he muttered.

And then with the ease of a practised thief, he felt the pockets of the sleeping serving man.

In a few moments he succeeded in extracting from one of them the little bottle containing the chloroform.

This he had just succeeded in placing in the pocket of his own coat, when Kathleen reappeared.

"Shure, and what is it you're wanting, Master McClosky?" she said.

Like all servants, she was indignant at her room being invaded.

"I've come for my cauliflower," said Tom, "which I sent Willie Curtis for."

"And what would ye be wanting wid a cauliflower, Master Tom?" said Kathleen.

"That's nothing to do with anybody so long as I pay for it," returned McClosky, "only I know as I gave him a shilling to get it with, I shall certainly expect him to account for the money."

And with these words he passed from the kitchen and upstairs.

He had now in his hand what he hoped would be the instrument of his revenge.

CHAPTER XLII.

THE REVENGE OF TOM MACCLOSKY.

It was very early when the boys retired to bed—about half-past eight or nine.

But it was quite dark, and just before the usual hour, Tom crept up with a large bundle.

In this was contained two large and strong ropes.

These he placed underneath his bed, and then hurried away in search of a boy named Tim Cornish, a poor little lad, whose father must have sent his son to school with the last money he possessed, so wretched—so poverty-stricken was he in appearance when he entered the academy.

Thaddeus O'Shaughnessy had soon, somehow or another, made a difference in his "outer man."

Otherwise he was no different.

His mind had always been as weak and as narrow as his face; as sneaking as his general manners.

He had never yet had an opportunity of showing off his evil propensities, but Tom McClosky soon recognised one of his own kidney.

To this fellow then he applied in this scheme of his for revenge.

"I say, Tim Cornish," he said, "do you want to earn half-a-crown?"

The boy grinned.

"Shure, and I would that," he said.

"Well, then, if you'll help me to-night to have a lark with Pat O'Connor and Harry Marshall, I'll give you half-a-crown," returned Tom McClosky; "now listen, and I'll explain."

He bent low over the boy, and whispered an explanation in his ear.

Little did he know what ears heard it besides his own.

At length the time for rest came, and the boys retired to their beds.

The place was soon quiet, and all the lads were apparently asleep.

About eleven o'clock Tom McClosky rose from his bed, and approached the couch where lay Tim Cornish.

"Now then, Tim, come on," whispered Tom.

Tim, in the prospect of his half-crown, at once roused himself up.

"All right," he said, and as Tom McClosky approached the bed of Pat O'Connor, he went to the window, and began slowly to raise it.

He was enabled to raise it noiselessly, and soon the cool breezes of night were blowing into the room.

While this was being done, Tom quickly passed over the faces of Pat O'Connor and Harry Marshall a handkerchief saturated with the liquid which Willie Curtis had purchased of Mr. Twistem.

The boys lay still, utterly motionless in the bed.

Quickly Tom McClosky slipped upon them, under the arm-pits, the ropes which he had brought up from below.

Then he quietly lifted Pat O'Connor out of his bed, and carried him to the open window.

"Now then, Tim," he cried, "help us."

With great precaution the two boys lowered Pat O'Connor out into the dark night.

Then, as soon as they had assured themselves that Pat was on the ground, they did the same by Harry Marshall.

"They're square now," said Tom McClosky, in a whisper; "now I think I'll manage the rest myself."

And urged on by his revenge, he slid down the rope with the agility of a monkey.

Tom seemed indeed to be endowed suddenly with supernatural powers.

He raised Pat O'Connor in his arms, and hurried down to the margin of the river.

Here he placed the lad in the boat, and leaving him there, he hastened back for Harry Marshall.

Harry was soon placed by the side of his companion, and Tom McClosky prepared to push the skiff off into the stream.

But as he did so a strange phenomenon presented itself.

The two supposed insensible bodies rose from the seats of the boat; a rope was flung over the head of McClosky, and the skiff was shoved off from the shore.

Then, before Tom could recover himself, two powerful arms had seized the oars, and away the boat sped.

At the same time a roar of laughter echoed over the bosom of the river, and Tom, as he was plunged into the water, saw in the moonlight the faces of the two boys, whom he had designed to float senseless and helpless on the bosom of the dangerous stream.

Pat O'Connor and Harry Marshall pulled with a mighty will.

They had in fact overheard all the plot between Tom and Tim.

Unknown to the young conspirators, they had been lurking near the spot where the conversation had been going on, and they were accordingly primed for the adventure.

Tom McClosky, therefore, found that he was in the wrong box.

Dragged through the water by the rope, which cut him under the armpits, he was at first nearly choked by the water, so sudden was his immersion.

But after a moment he managed to grasp the rope with his hand, and so to ease himself along.

As he did so, his head being thus raised above the water, he shouted at the top of his voice—

"I say, Pat, have a little mercy! help! help then! Oh! Ugh! I'm choking."

Of course as the night was chill, it was not a very pleasant journey for the two boys, rowing as they were in their sleeping shirts.

But they had no need to go very far to effect the purpose they had in view, which was to place an effectual damper on the practical joking of Master Tom McClosky.

The ducking was enough to do this, and by the time they had rowed about fifty yards, he was completely blown, and lay like a log on the water.

"It's time we drew him, Pat," said Harry Marshall; "we don't want to kill him quite."

So they stopped the boat, and began pulling him in.

He was exhausted, but was still able to speak.

"This is a shame, Pat," he said.

"And pray, what do you call what you were doing?" asked our hero.

"Only a lark!"

"A lark do ye call it? Well, I don't see much of a lark in it," said Marshall. "I only know you might have killed us."

"I'm sure I didn't mean anything of the kind," said Tom McClosky, shuddering with the cold. "But hadn't we better get back to the school?"

"Oh, I'm all jolly," said Pat, giving Harry a nudge.

"But I'm wet to the skin," shivered the unlucky McClosky.

"That's your own fault, my boy," said Pat O'Connor; "it's the old game of setting the trap, and catching your own finger first. Let's go for a row, Harry."

Without another word the two young lads began to pull out into the centre of the river.

"Pull wild, Harry," whispered Pat O'Connor.

The boat's nose began to move about, but at length turned in the direction of the opposite side of the river.

"I say, this won't do at all," cried Pat O'Connor, in a voice of pretended seriousness. "McClosky, you must really steer; the tide's too strong."

"Oh! ugh! this is too bad," cried Tom McClosky, who was now so cold that he could hardly articulate his words; "I'll steer to shore, and chance it."

The two boys did not gainsay him, for they saw he was rapidly getting frozen.

So with a loud laugh, they let him guide the boat towards shore, and pulled away as vigorously as they could.

On reaching the shore, they all three ran along the lawn in the direction of the school.

The rope was then still dangling, and Tim Cornish was at the window above.

Pat at once whispered to Tom—

"Now look here, Tom, call out 'All right, Tim,' or we'll put you in the water-butt."

"All right, Tim," cried McClosky; "slacken the rope. I'm coming."

"Now then," said Pat; "I'm going up first."

So up he went.

As soon as he reached the top of the rope, he caught Tim Cornish by the neck, kicked him and flung him on a bed.

"You shall have it, my sneak," said he; "wait till a trial comes, then you'll get it hot."

Then he leaned out of the casement, saying—

"All right; come on, friends."

In a few moments Tom McClosky and Harry Marshall were standing in the room.

McClosky was at once hurled on the bed in the same undignified manner as Tim had been.

"This day week there shall be a trial by jury," said Pat O'Connor; "and then you'll see what the school will say to a chap who runs the risk of murdering his schoolmates to have a paltry revenge."

Tom McClosky said nothing.

He knew he was "in for it," and to make any fuss would only make it worse for him.

So he crawled to bed, and, snuggling himself up in the bedclothes, tried to go to sleep.

For a long time he could not.

Visions of a tribunal formed of his schoolmates were before his eyes, and punishment, consisting of knotted handkerchiefs and so on, floated before him.

But at length he dozed off, and dreamed of rushing waters, rheumatism, and ague.

CHAPTER XLIII.
HEAVEN DEFEND THE RIGHT!

THE papers, which The Barry had obtained after so much trouble and danger, were overhauled at last, and there was no doubt left on the minds of any of those who read them that the young scholar was the rightful owner of Barrymore.

He obtained leave of Thaddeus O'Shaughnessy, therefore, to go up to the "big house," as the peasantry called it, to demand from Mr. Singleton a restitution of his rights.

Thaddeus would have gone with him.

But The Barry begged to be permitted to go alone.

With the pride that was innate within him, he wished to go up to the house of his ancestors alone, and, face to face with his enemy, claim his right.

So he passed up the mountain path boldly by himself.

Every boy in Shannon School knew the errand he was on: and a ringing cheer it was that resounded over the schoolgrounds as he trotted off on the back of O'Shaughnessy's pet pony, "Nora."

Nora had often been mounted before by The Barry, and she knew her rider well.

So off she went at her best speed, and it was not long before she had carried her rider out of sight.

The adventure upon which the lad had started was a daring one.

But his heart never failed him.

The day was clear, the breezes blew freshly from the river, and nature altogether looked so bright and fair that he felt inspirited for his journey, and seemed already to behold success crowning his efforts.

So on he went without pausing—his heart beating more quickly as the gates of Barrymore were approached.

At length he neared the home of his fathers.

It was a fine place, a splendid specimen of the rugged old castles of Ireland.

It was disfigured only by the modern wing which Mr. Singleton had added to it.

A wing which was quite out of keeping with the rest of the building.

The rugged walls of the old part of the Hall were covered with moss and lichens, and every here and there were fractures to show where, in former days, the balls from the enemy's cannon had been hurled against them.

It overlooked, in its ancient grandeur, miles and miles of the fair countryside, with its hills, streams and valleys; and The Barry's heart swelled within him as he thought how soon he might be the possessor of so fair a place.

He tied his pony to the ring in one of the old marble gate-posts, and then rang the bell loudly.

A liveried man-servant came pompously down to the entrance.

"And what is it you'd be afther wantin'?" asked he, with a strong Dublin accent.

"I wish to see Mr. Singleton."

The servant saw that the speaker was a gentleman, and so he was as civil as his coarse nature would allow.

"And what might be the name I'd be afther givin' him?" he asked.

"The Barry of Barrymore!" returned the lad, boldly.

The man fairly staggered back.

"Shure, and am I to give sich a message as that to the masther?" he cried; "I'm thinking he'll be afther throwin' me out o' window if I do!"

"You must chance that, then," said The Barry, "for see him I will."

Ordinary Irish hospitality would not permit him to leave the young gentleman standing outside the gates.

So he flung back the great iron portals, and then led the way to the hall, decorated with stags' heads and bulls' horns, pieces of armour, ancient carvings, and pictures dull with age.

Here he left him, and proceeded to the room where Mr. Singleton was sitting with his daughter, Lizzie.

The young girl was reading to him out of his favourite author, and the gleam which shot from his ferret eyes showed that he was greatly enjoying himself.

When he heard the name of The Barry announced, his brow contracted and his cheek paled.

"What does the insolent young rascal want?" he cried.

Lizzie was pale too.

But she put her hand gently on her father's arm.

"Hush, father!" she said, "you know he looks upon this place as his own; do not be too hard upon him."

The father made no reply to her, but turned to the servant.

"Admit The Barry," he said to the serving man.

In a few moments the lad and the man who had usurped his rights were standing face to face.

The Barry cast one furtive glance at the fair young girl, and bent his head.

Then he turned haughtily to her father.

"Pray be seated, sir," said Mr. Singleton, "and do me the honour of explaining why you are here."

"I am here, sir," said The Barry, firmly, declining the proffered seat, "I am here to inform you, in the first place, that the papers which prove my right to this hall and the estates belonging to it, have at length come into my possession."

Singleton was livid with rage.

"What means this intrusion?" he said. "You know that you have no right here."

"Sir," said The Barry, "I have come here in all politeness and honesty of purpose, but if you dare me, I will do the worst."

"I do dare you!" shouted Singleton, losing all command over his temper, and starting up; "away from my hearth, away! and do your worst!"

The Barry turned very pale.

"Well," he said, "since you have dared me, I will tell you that if you carry this tone, not a roof shall shelter you in a month."

Mr. Singleton stood almost aghast as he heard the daring words of The Barry.

"How dare you," he cried, "insult me thus in my own house?"

The Barry smiled.

"Sir," he said, "I am afraid that any mention of insult will come but badly from *you*. You speak of your own house. This house is *not* yours."

Mr. Singleton clenched his fists, and advanced nearer to the young Irish lad.

"It is only the remembrance that once your ancestor had a right——" he began.

But The Barry interrupted him.

"There, you may spare your breath, Mr. Singleton," he said. "I shall believe nothing that you say. All I have to tell you is this: my papers prove that Fergus McCarthy, who sold you this estate, had no right to sell it at all. You were told, or you chose to believe, that my father had mortgaged his property to this McCarthy; but the truth was, that there was nothing of the kind. My father was ill, and under the influence of others, and was forced into signing documents."

"This is all madness," exclaimed Mr. Singleton, in a tone of fury. "Who will believe such a story?"

"Everyone," said The Barry, "because I have witnesses to all."

"Witnesses? Then let them tell their false stories," said Mr. Singleton. "I will listen to no more. Pray leave my place, and let your further proceedings be in a court of law."

"Very well, be it so," returned The Barry.

And, with a slight bow to Lizzie, he walked haughtily from the room.

Mr. Singleton turned very pale as The Barry passed out.

With a step that almost tottered, he went across the room, and sat down on his great armchair by the fire.

Here he buried his head in his hands, muttering to himself—

"That boy will try and ruin me; but, by Heaven, he shall not."

As he spoke, his daughter had crept to his side.

Here she knelt, and placed her arms around him.

"Father," she said, "you have done wrong in dismissing him when he is in one of these haughty moods. Why did you not try and compromise the matter?"

"Compromise! No," he cried, suddenly, starting up again. "I will do better than compromise."

And, without further explanation, he rushed from the room.

"Heaven help us," said his daughter; "I fear he meditates some desperate deed. And yet, how can I do anything to prevent it?"

Meanwhile Mr. Singleton hurried down to a room near the servants' hall.

Here he rang the bell, and there appeared the serving-man who had opened the front gates to The Barry.

"Phil Measom," he said, "is Jack Donegan at home?"

"Yes, surr."

"Tell him I want him then, and return yourself with him."

The man bobbed, and, hurrying away, soon returned with a broad, thickset fellow, whose face was as round as an apple, and whose nose looked as if it had been stuck on "permiscous," as the servant girls say.

His eyes, however, small though they were, were cunning and cruel-looking, and there was in them an expectant glance as if he was hoping to be given some deed of violence to perform.

"Close the door, Phil," said his master, "I have something important to tell you; and I have only a few moments to say it in."

"Very well, surr," said Phil Measom, "we'll listen with all our ears, surr."

"And keep what I say a secret," added Mr. Singleton.

"As secrit as the oath of the Mountain Boys," said Jack Donegan.

"Good. You see a storm is coming on?"

"Yes, surr. I can see that the black clouds are rolling up, and will soon break over the Pass of Barryfoil."

"Before The Barry can reach the Pass, the tempest will break," said Mr. Singleton, "and he will be compelled to seek refuge in one or other of the mountain caves."

Jack Donegan listened eagerly now.

He saw some chance of cruel and bloodthirsty work, and a greedy look came into his eyes.

Mr. Singleton saw plainly that he would have little difficulty in removing from his path The Barry of Barrymore, so, leaning forward, he looked from one to the other of the two men, and said—

"If you will follow The Barry, and contrive that he shall be taken on board a vessel going abroad, I will give you fifty pounds apiece, and pay your passages to America."

The men's faces beamed with satisfaction.

"Oh, sure, surr," said Phil Measom, "and you are the illigant and ginerous gintleman. But if we take 'im down to the Shannon, we'll have to pay the captain to take him away."

"I know that well," said Mr Singleton; "so now be off. Here are ten pounds to give the captain of the ship, and a sovereign apiece to keep the devil out of your pocket. When you return, and say all is right, I'll give you what I promised."

The money was delivered over, and the men, grinning at the anticipation of the "blood money," as it might be called, hurried off in the direction of the Pass of Barryfoil.

"Shure and we've got our wish at last," said Phil Measom, as they passed rapidly down the mountain pass; "we'll be able to leave this land where there are no praties or anythin' to ate, and we'll be off to Ameriky."

"Yes, with a hundred and ten pound betwixt us besides our passage money," said Jack Donegan.

"A hundred and tin? Shure and it's only a hundred you're maning."

"No, I mane a hundred and tin," said Jack Donegan.

"And how do you mean that?—how do you prove it?" asked Phil.

"Shure and it's aisy enough," said Jack Donegan, with a diabolical smile. "The masther's going to pay our fares to America, isn't he?"

"He is that same."

"Well, and there's fifty pounds each for us for the job."

"Yes, shure."

"And then there's tin pounds for the captain of the vessel that's to take him away."

"Yes; but that won't come into our hands."

Jack grasped his companion's arm.

"Shure and ye've got no sinse, at all—at all," cried he. "Don't ye see that if the Barry goes abroad, he can return at any time to worry Mr. Singleton again? The masther doesn't mean that at all—at all. He means to get rid of 'im altogether, shure. We'll take 'im down to the side of the river, and give him his last duckin', and we'll tell the masther he's floatin' away to sea, which'll be the truth, after all."

"Good for ye, Jack," said Phil Measom; "we'll do as ye say, and as the masther won't want us near him after such a deed as this, we'll be out and on our road to the West before anyone's the wiser."

And so the two assassins made their way down the mountain pass.

The storm had now burst in all its fury.

The wind swept in terrific gusts over the mountains. The rain came down in bucketfuls, the lightning flashed, and the thunder boomed like terrific artillery.

The Barry's progress had been reckoned rightly by Mr. Singleton. He had just reached the Pass of Barryfoil when the storm broke.

The pass was a narrow way between two precipices, and in such weather as this it was impossible for either man or beast to cross it.

Sure-footed, therefore, as was the little pony which Thaddeus O'Shaughnessy had lent him, he was compelled to go into one of the caves with his trusty steed, and await the passing away of the storm.

There were a number of these caves in the vicinity of the pass, and strange and weird-looking they were.

They were like the caverns on the seashore, wide and apparently washed by large waves, while here and there great fissures were visible, fashioned, as it would seem, by some convulsion of nature, and leading to inner caves, which in their turn conducted far away beneath the mountain.

The Barry had in former times often visited these caves, and even if he had not, he was not at present in a mood to think of curiosity.

His whole thoughts were naturally in a bewildering state of excitement.

That he could make himself master of Barrymore, he, of course, had not the least doubt.

But there had been a lingering hope in his mind that he should not be compelled to use the worst measures for the recovery of his property for the sake of Lizzie, whom, in spite of her Saxon blood, he loved dearly.

But love now yielded to duty.

He had sworn on his father's grave to wrest the property from the hands of those who had obtained it by fraud, and this vow was far more sacred than even the feelings of his heart.

He was thinking of this—of her—of the future, which would have in it so much more of brightness, when there was a sudden rush of feet behind him, and a blow from the stick of Phil Measom felled him to the earth.

Then the gag was thrust in his mouth, his wrists and ankles were bound as best they could be, and the two assassins waited for the storm to abate.

It was full an hour before it did so, and at the expiration of this time, they took him up in their arms, and hurried with him towards the shores of the Shannon.

*　　*　　*　　*　　*

It was nearly midnight when Phil Measom and Jack Donegan returned to Barrymore.

They were both so full of drink that their steps, as they came up the mountain path, were unsteady and even staggering.

But their minds were in no way affected by the mountain dew they had imbibed.

When Mr. Singleton saw them, he recognised at once the fact that they were somewhat intoxicated.

But he had seen them in the same state on many occasions, and took no notice of it.

"Well," he said, " and how have you succeeded?"

"Shure, surr," cried Phil Measom, "shure, surr, we've succeeded properly."

"Is he gone?"

"He is that same, surr," said Jack, quickly; "he's floating away down the Shannon by this time."

"And where is he bound to?"

"It's one of the German shmugglers where he's got on board," said Phil; "and the captain didn't exactly say where he was bound to. But he understands this—that you don't want to see the lad again."

Mr. Singleton looked into the men's eyes, and guessed somewhat of the truth.

"Surely," he cried, "surely, you haven't ——"

"The Shannon river's very treacherous," said Phil Measom; "and I don't think he'll come back, surr."

A ghastly look overspread the face of Mr. Singleton.

"Say no more," he said; "you had better leave this place at once. Ireland is no safe home for you."

"We should be glad to go as soon as we can," said Phil.

"To-night?"

"Yes, to-night, surr."

"But you've been drinking?"

"Oh, that doesn't matter, surr," said Jack Donegan; "we won't lose our money. There's none of the Irish bhoys would rob us, and there's none of the English bhoys would ever think that two poor lads would have so much money."

The Master of Barrymore hesitated a moment.

"You are sure you will leave the country?" said he.

"Yes, surr."

"Well, then, I will trust you," said Mr. Singleton; "I will write you out a cheque at once, and you must proceed to Dublin. Here are five pounds to start with. In Middle Abbey Street, Dublin, you will find the private banking firm of Messrs. Dawson and Pigott. They will cash this cheque for you for fifty pounds apiece. I have not deducted the five pounds from either."

The men bowed their acknowledgments, and in a few moments Mr. Singleton had gone up into his own room, and written out the cheque.

The men received it with faces beaming with delight.

Their thoughts were only of the " fortune " they had just made, and of their future prospects in America.

They soon took leave of their master, and were once more making their way down the mountain path towards the road by the Shannon school.

They paused at Tony Foster's, had a dram, and then hurried on towards the spot where the coach started for Callingasloe Station, on the railway to Dublin.

Singleton breathed more freely when the next dawn broke.

It mattered not to him through what hideous path he trod, so long as that path led to peace, wealth, and contentment.

"'YOU KNOW NOTHING OF WHAT BECAME OF HIM?' SAID THADDEUS O'SHAUGHNESSY."

No. 9.

PRICE ONE HALFPENNY.
[PUBLISHED EVERY FRIDAY].

CHAPTER XLIV.

WILLIE MAKES A DISCOVERY AND REVEALS A PLOT.

OF course the utmost consternation existed in the Shannon academy, when it was found that The Barry had disappeared.

Thaddeus O'Shaughnessy at once made his way up to Barrymore.

Mr. Singleton received him with the most complete and even pretentious politeness.

"He was delighted," he said, "to see the distinguished schoolmaster, who had made his name famous on all that part of the Shannon."

Thaddeus bowed in answer to the compliment, but there was a sternness evident on his lips and on his brow.

"Mr. Singleton," he said, "I should have great pleasure in coming here, were it under other circumstances; as it is, I come on a most unpleasant errand."

"And pray, sir, what is that?" said Singleton, with a look of pretended astonishment.

"I came to demand of you the person of The Barry, a pupil in my school, and the reputed owner of this property."

"Demand of me his person?" asked Mr. Singleton in surprise. "I really am at a loss to understand your meaning."

"Mr. Singleton," cried Thaddeus, "you cannot pretend to be blind to the fact that The Barry claims, on good authority, all these estates."

"I am quite sure he claims them, but as to the authority on which he does do so, it may be a disputed matter," returned Mr. Singleton.

"And he came here last night to make a claim against you?"

"He did."

"Where is he then?"

"How can I tell?" answered Singleton. "He came here, remained not a quarter of an hour, and departed from the Hall just before the storm broke."

"And you swear that you know nothing of what has become of him?" said Thaddeus O'Shaughnessy, in the same stern voice as before.

"Sir," cried Singleton, in a tone of pretended indignation, "sir, if the word of an English gentleman is not good enough, his oath is worth nothing."

"That is a mere prevarication," said Thaddeus, "nothing but prevarication, and I refuse to accept it in answer to my question."

Singleton bridled up at this.

"Refuse?" he cried. "Then suppose I refuse to give any answer?"

"Then I shall give information to the police, and have the matter investigated."

"Do as you please, then," returned Singleton. "As you have come in this spirit, I decline to have anything more to do with it."

Thaddeus retired at once to the door, and resumed his hat.

"Very well," he said, "within a week you shall hear from me again."

He little knew what would happen within that week.

Singleton cared little for his threat.

The Barry had gone, the two men had gone, and there seemed to him to be no trace by which he could in any way be connected with the disappearance of the young heir to the Hall.

Without any further conversation between them, Thaddeus O'Shaughnessy quitted the place and made his way in the direction of the academy.

Within twenty-four hours the necessary information was in the hands of the constabulary, and the proper preparations made to bring to light the extraordinary disappearance of The Barry.

It was on the evening before the day when Barney O'Reilly had warned Willie Curtis to be out on the mountains rather than in the academy, that a man entered the yard of the school after ringing at the great bell.

Attached to a rope which he held in his hand was the little pony which had borne The Barry so bravely up the mountains.

He was a little man, with red, curly hair, and ferret eyes, and a mouth on which there lurked an incessant grin.

"That's the masther's pony, shure," cried Willie Curtis.

"It is that same," said the man, "and my name is Timothy Beamish, and I'm wantin' to see the masther, Mister O'Shaughnessy, Heaven presarve him."

"And what'll ye'll be afther wantin' wid 'im," said Willie.

"Hurroo! and ye'd be afther asking me what I've got to say to the master. Bad manners till ye, I'll tell him meself," said the little man.

And Tim Beamish snapped his finger in a manner which indicated supreme contempt.

Willie Curtis muttered some words which Beamish did not hear, and then hurried away to inform his master.

He came out in a few moments and beckoned to Beamish, who was standing in the centre of the yard.

Tim, still drawing the little pony after him, at once made his way to the porch.

"I'm to take the pony to the stables, and you're to stop in the hall," said Willie, with an air of grandeur.

"Shure, and it's not meself as ud be wantin' to rob Mr. Shaughnessy of his little horse," said Tim, with a laugh; "but I'll be askin' ye to remember that it was Tim Beamish that brought it home."

Will deigned no reply.

He simply waved his hand with a ridiculous kind of majesty towards the porch of the house, and hurried away with the favourite pony of Thaddeus O'Shaughnessy, which looked most deplorable, with his hair wet and bedraggled as if he had been rolled in the mud.

No sooner had Willie disappeared round the corner than Tim peered out, and after seeing that the coast was clear, he went on tiptoe into the passage itself and listened attentively to hear if anyone was about.

Of course, my readers have not forgotten that the dwelling house was parted off from the school house by two doors.

Not even a murmur, therefore, came to Tim Beamish as he listened.

A diabolical grin overspread his features as he found that all was silent.

Then he quickly took from his pocket some little parcels, which he placed in various corners of the hall and passages.

He was kneeling, connecting one of these packets with a wire that was to pass under the door and out into the yard, when Willie Curtis returned.

He was too ignorant and too inexperienced to repress a slight exclamation of surprise and even fear.

But Tim Beamish was too much engaged in his task, whatever it might be, to hear him, and as Willie had approached almost noiselessly, Tim heard nothing.

Naturally, Willie's first thought was, that the proper thing that was to be done would be to make a dash at the intruder and tell Mr. O'Shaughnessy.

But his cunning in a moment came to his aid, and he was checked from doing anything precipitate.

So he went back on tiptoe, and then approached noisily, whistling the refrain of Rory O'More.

In an instant Tim Beamish, who had succeeded in passing out the wire, took a seat in the hall, and began twiddling his caubeen in his hands.

"Well, and ye've housed the pony, then?" said he.

"Shure, and I have that; and have ye seen Mr. O'Shaughnessy?"

"No, I've seen no one," returned Tim, "and I'm getting tired of waiting."

"Then, I'm shure you needn't wait, for I'm thinkin' Mr. O'Shaughnessy is busy, or he'd come."

At this instant, the schoolmaster made his appearance.

He stared, on seeing Willie raise his hand cautiously to his lips.

But he had been used to so many strange events lately, that he made no remark.

Turning at once to Tim—

"Well, Mr. Beamish, and what do you want with me?"

"Shure, hasn't Willie Curtis tould ye that I've brought 'ome yer little pony, surr?" said Tim.

"He did, and pray where did you find it?" asked the schoolmaster.

"Up in the mountain cave, nearly starved," said Tim Beamish.

"And have you seen anything of The Barry?"

"Who, surr?" asked Beamish, with an attempted ingenuousness of look.

"Come, no nonsense; I asked you a civil question. Answer it," said Thaddeus.

"Shure, and I can't answer what I don't understand," said Tim Beamish; "I've brought you home a pony, but I don't know anybody of the name of Barry, except the Tom Barry who lives up at the corner of——"

"Come, I don't want to hear that," said Thaddeus; "I want to know whether in the cave where you found the pony, ye saw any signs of a human being."

Tim assumed his knowing look again.

"Well, surr," he said, "I don't know 'xactly what ye mane by signs of a human bein'; but you could see there'd been a shtruggle, for the ground was all kicked up like."

Thaddeus turned slightly pale.

"Can you take me to the spot?" said he, excitedly.

Willie Curtis, who was standing behind Beamish, made a most significant sign, which Thaddeus at once understood.

"I can, surr," said Tim, "at any time you like."

"Then, if ye'll call in the morning, I'll give you a job," said Thaddeus, "meanwhile, what award do you expect?"

"I'll leave that to you," said Tim Beamish. "I suppose a suvrin wouldn't hurt your honour?"

"No, certainly not," cried Thaddeus, putting his hand in his pocket and ferreting out the required coin; "here you are, and to morrow at ten o'clock I shall expect you."

The man took the coin, pocketed it, and after touching his hat, sidled away.

"Cunning rascal!" muttered Thaddeus, as Willie let him out of the gates; "I wonder what Curtis can mean by his signs. I'll wait here until he comes back."

Willie was not long before he returned.

He was very excited, as could be told from his wild eyes and red face.

"Shure, surr," he said, "and I'm hoping you'll not be afther bein' cross wid me for making grimaces at ye, but that Tim Beamish is a dirthy blaggard."

"And what makes you think so?" said Thaddeus.

In a moment Willie had told his story in regard to the mysterious packages, and the wire.

It was not long before the schoolmaster had searched one of them, and found, as he had expected, that it was filled with the most explosive compound that could be invented.

"This is the work of those fiends the Mountain Boys," said Thaddeus O'Shaughnessy, "but we'll be even with them yet; give me the packages and we'll fling them into the river, then we'll make up packages of the same kind as they are, and leave the wire, so that even if they have spies in the house, they will fancy their plans have not been disturbed."

Willie hesitated only a moment now.

He had not taken any oath that he would not divulge the secrets which Barney O'Reilly had so incautiously confessed to him on the occasion of his journey in search of the "cauliflower."

So he said, taking his master's hand meanwhile, and gazing up wistfully into his face—

"Surr, I know you're not the one to betray a poor bhoy."

"Betray you?" cried Thaddeus O'Shaughnessy; "why should I?"

All he had seen and heard lately was enough to make him suspicious of everyone.

But there was something in the man's manner which seemed to tell him that he was not trying to deceive his master.

"Speak on," added O'Shaughnessy, "speak on; whatever it is, you will not find me tell a word to a living soul."

Willie hesitated no longer.

He had on his mind ever since the day he had been sent for the chloroform, the necessity of doing something to save the master and the scholars from the fate which he felt sure, from Barney O'Reilly's words, hung over them.

So, without any beating about the bush, he asked his master to step out into the yard, where no one could overhear them.

And then he told all he had heard from the wretched enthusiast.

"It will be a difficult matter," said Thaddeus, "to counteract the designs of these ruffians, and it is so late, too. But still, if ye take the pony, you could reach the constabulary in an hour."

"Thrue for you, surr," said Willie Curtis, "thrue for you. But if any of the dhevils see me, there'll be little of Willie Curtis left."

"You can take my pistols," said Thaddeus, "and go along the lower mountain path. You will not be observed there; I would go with you myself, but I must remain here to look after my scholars, and my presence would make things all the worse for you."

"Very well, surr," said Willie, with a sudden burst of courage, "very well, surr, I'll go. And Heaven help me, surr, as I make all haste to be back with ye."

"Would ye like one of the other men with you?" said Thaddeus.

"No—I thank ye, surr," cried Willie. "I'd rather trust no one but myself, and then I can't be blamed if anything goes wrong."

"Very well, get the white mare out; she'll go quicker than the pony, besides, the pony is tired and worn out, and might break down. By the time you're ready, I'll bring down the pistols."

And so saying, the schoolmaster hurried into the house, and made his way to the school premises.

CHAPTER XLV.

THE RISING OF THE BOYS OF THE MOUNTAIN.

On reaching the little room where Thaddeus often received visitors, the master sent for Lawrence McMahon and Tim Finnigan.

"Now, gentlemen," he said, "it is time for us to throw off the mask. We are all three members, as I know, of the United Irishmen's Society. But how were we made so? Against our will. I have thought again and again over the matter, and I feel convinced that when a man takes an oath against his will, he is not morally bound to keep it.'

"That is true in my opinion," said Lawrence McMahon, "but just think of the danger to you and to all if we were to say a word in regard to the conspiracy."

"Certainly the danger is great," said Thaddeus, "and I should not dream of perilling my life and the lives of my friends by betraying anything in regard to the Society. But if we can defeat them, that will be a different matter."

"And how is that to be done?" cried Mac-Mahon.

"Listen, and I will tell you," remarked Thaddeus.

Then quickly he recounted to his surprised and alarmed hearers the news he had heard from Willie Curtis, and the scene he had witnessed in the hall.

"This almost absolves us from all connection with the Society," said Finnigan; "it is one of the rules that we are to be informed of every action that is coming forward. Every proposed plan is at once to be told to every one of the members. So they have broken faith with us, and must expect us to do the same by them."

"That is all very well as regards our own feelings," said Thaddeus, "but we should get little good from them by such pleading. The thing is this—we must save the scholars to-night, if we cannot save the school."

"We cannot do the latter without the help of the military," said McMahon.

"Well, I will run down—dispatch Curtis, and return," said Thaddeus, as he took out his pistols and examined them; "he will not be long, I hope, going to the constabulary office and back, not at any rate more than two hours. During that time we may be able to do something to prepare for these ruffians."

Thaddeus hastened down the stairs, and found Willie Curtis at the hall door, with the tall white mare ready saddled, and looking fresh and ready for work.

Willie himself had a kind of dogged look of determination on his face.

Thaddeus saw at once that he could be depended upon.

"Here ye are, my man," said he, in a cheery voice, "here are your pistols, here is the letter to the chief of the constabulary; and here is a small bottle of whisky to keep life in you."

"Shure, and it's yerself's the kind gentleman," cried Willie Curtis, as he took a preliminary gulp at the whisky; "the mare's in furst-rate condishun, surr, and'll rattle me over there in the twinkling of a bidpost."

And he leaped on the back of the white mare, and was ready for a start.

"Hivin bliss ye, surr," he added, "Hivin bless you. May the bhoys be late, and when they come, may they get more than they bargain for. If I never return, surr, remember, I've done me best for ye all!"

And trotting his mare to the gate, he passed out, the schoolmaster himself opening it for him, and closing it after him, pulling up the heavy bolts and passing across it also a massive chain.

Then he hastened up to the room where Lawrence McMahon and Tim Finnigan were waiting for him.

They rapidly now made their plans.

It was decided to barricade the doors, put up the strong wooden shutters at the windows, and leave one door open at the rear of the premises for escape in case of need.

The great gates were barricaded, and the boys were stationed at the casements, where they could see through loopholes all that passed below.

It was a time of intense excitement.

Eagerly those in the academy watched for every sign and listened for every sound.

At length, as they looked upwards towards the mountains, they beheld a number of lights moving and flickering.

"Here they come!" cried Thaddeus; "see, there are the torches on the mountain side."

A thrill passed through every heart at these words.

They knew now the struggle was approaching.

CHAPTER XLVI.

THE COMING OF THE MOUNTAIN BOYS.

THE hearts of all in the academy beat high in expectation.

They knew that a terrible struggle was coming—a struggle brought on by vengeance for the death of the O'Gradys and the Dutch skipper.

Willie Curtis could not return for some time, and before then the danger would be nearly over.

But still all stood bravely to their posts, and watched eagerly for the coming of the foe.

On they came, their torches flashing brightly over the mountains, and their forces coming down the paths in waving irregular lines.

Presently, as they came nearer, there was heard the roar of voices, and then Thaddeus O'Shaughnessy felt his heart swell as he knew that the struggle was about to commence.

He felt, of course, the folly of the whole affair.

He knew how utterly powerless a few ignorant peasants were to defeat the trained bands of English soldiers.

He knew, too, that a rising could only result in banishment for some, and death to others.

But still he was aware what mischief could be effected; what homes desolated; what ruin brought upon innocent women and children.

And now there burst upon the view of the scholars the whole maddened crowd of insurgents, eager for the struggle and panting for revenge.

The United Irishmen, full five hundred in number, were armed with guns and pikes.

In their midst was an old cannon with a rattle-trap kind of carriage, which had to be assisted every now and then over the inequalities of the ground.

But still the array was formidable enough to make the heart of Thaddeus O'Shaughnessy leap with excitement.

Presently the storm of wrath broke.

With a loud and savage "Hurroo!" the United Irishmen dashed forward, and the attack on the gates commenced.

They of course expected but a feeble resistance.

They had no conception that Willie Curtis could betray to his master the secret of the coming onslaught, and so when they discovered how the academy had been placed in a state of defence, there burst from them a perfect roar of fury.

But they made no delay.

Bringing up the cannon, they placed it in front of the gates, and took aim.

No one had bargained for this.

"This is getting serious," said Thaddeus to Lawrence McMahon; "I wish the boys were well out of it."

"It cannot be helped, sir," said McMahon; "they will fight bravely, you will see, and depend upon it, their friends will never complain, because they have been asked to assist in defending the place which has been a home to them."

At this moment, the cannon had been placed in position, and one of the men advanced to fire it.

The fuse was already in his hand, when there was a flash from one of the windows in the room, and the gunner fell pierced through the brain.

"Who fired that shot?" exclaimed Thaddeus O'Shaughnessy.

"It was Pat O'Connor," said Tim Finnigan; "he has saved the gate."

A cheer rang out from the boys.

Then Harry Marshall advanced to the loophole.

"I will watch for the next man," said he, and levelled his rifle.

Again one of the United Irishmen advanced to the side of the gun and tried to apply the fuse.

But he shared the same fate as his predecessor.

There was another report, and the gunner, flinging up his arms, fell with a thud to the earth.

"This won't last," said Thaddeus; "they will never stand such slaughter as that. Ah! here it comes."

The attacking party raised their muskets, and fired a deadly volley at the windows from which the shots had been fired.

The shots clattered through the shutters.

But no one was wounded.

The diversion thus caused, however, had its intended effect, and a rush of men surrounded the gun.

Then there came a thundering roar, and a crash, and a cannon ball went dashing through the gates, splintering them to pieces.

In an instant, there was a volley from all the windows as there came a rush of men, with bludgeons and crowbars, who attacked vigorously the broken gate.

But their first success had inspired them with fresh courage, and they kept on their dangerous task in spite of the fact that numbers dropped round them.

"Now comes the press," said McMahon; "boys, pull yourselves together, and we will defeat them yet."

Crash! crash!

There was a rattling volley of musketry, and several of the men, who dashed in through the splintered gates, fell like bullocks before the hands of the slaughterman.

But this could not last long.

The men were in far too great numbers to be defeated by persons firing from windows.

They rushed in a body to the front door of the academy, and under the protection of the great portico, they began an attack on it.

It was difficult now, as it had been in the case of the Dutchman's followers, to fire down upon them as they made their assaults, and so, for some time, the men within the courtyard were able to work away without let or hindrance.

But, presently, as the men on the outer side of the great wall began to bring the cannon into the courtyard, a most tremendous fire was opened from the loopholes, and the United Irishmen began to fall like birds before the shot of the sportsman.

Then there came another sound.

The unmistakable galloping of horses, and the rumbling of cannon-wheels.

And in another moment, the flash of helmets and swords showed that the dragoons had come down from the mountains.

"Now there will be little more of it," said Thaddeus; "I hope for the best."

But, as he spoke, there was a strange smell. A blue smoke came curling up into the room, and an unnatural heat pervaded the place.

Tim Finnigan rushed hurriedly to the door.

The usher, in fact, guessed in a moment that something terrible had happened.

He was confirmed in his idea when he reached the landing.

The place was on fire, and every now and then a strange hissing sound told that more than the natural agency of fire was at work.

He hurried back at once to the side of O'Shaughnessy.

"Sir," he said, "the place is on fire. The villains have succeeded after all."

"Well, then," cried Thaddeus, "we had better descend at once. The back staircase may yet be open."

Then turning to the boys, he cried—

"Boys, the place is on fire; follow me quickly."

Laurence McMahon had at the same time rushed up to the upper floor where the rest of the scholars were, and brought them quickly down.

So, in less than five minutes, the whole of the boys of the Shannon were hastening down to the basement story.

By the time they had reached the bottom of the back staircase, the fire had taken good hold of the premises; but the dragoons too had now succeeded in becoming masters of the situation.

The United Irishmen, however, had made their dispositions well.

On seeing that they were being worsted in the encounter, they began retreating towards the river.

They saw with intense satisfaction, that the fire had taken well hold of the premises, and in the glow of the flames which lapped up against the windows, they retreated towards the banks of the river, where, in the uncertain gloaming, could be distinguished plainly the form of a large vessel.

A dark-looking hull, very much resembling the "Silverhorn," which had so often come down the river under the command of De Ruyter, the Dutch skipper.

Towards this then it was that they made their way.

Their arrangements had been taken admirably.

While the men had been descending the mountain paths, a number of boats, each containing but a single rower, had made their way over the surface of the river in the direction of the Shannon School, while the great lumbering vessel came slowly on in their wake. Pursued by the dragoons, they made a gallant stand on the margin of the water, and a number of them, facing about, protected the others while they embarked on board the wherries.

Then some sprang into the water, and swam or dived after the boats.

The dragoons could do no more now.

They fired, certainly, and dashing into the water, cut down as many as they could.

But these were very few.

Most of them got off to the ship, which then, firing two shots at the schoolhouse, turned and proceeded lazily down the river.

And so, while the schoolhouse blazes upwards towards the sky, and sends a red glow to the heavens for miles around, we will follow the mad enthusiasts on their next voyage of ruin.

CHAPTER XLVII.

THE ATTACK ON BARRYMORE—THE COMPACT.

ON nearing the point opposite which lay the island where the boys had made their celebrated capture of the Dutchman, the ship lay to once more, and the boats, which had been towed along, again received a freight, and were rowed towards shore.

Landing at the same spot where Thaddeus O'Shaughnessy had been sent out on the river with Terence O'Rafferty, the men, whose numbers were now reduced to three hundred and fifty, counting the dead, wounded and prisoners, took their way with unimpaired energy up the mountain path.

Their destination now was Barrymore Hall.

It was far up on the hills, and it took them some time to reach it.

But at length they came up on the broad plateau which faced it, and with a wild " Hurroo !" as before, presented themselves before the astonished inmates.

Mr. Singleton, of course, had had no warning of the approach of the United Irishmen.

Indeed, little could have been said as a reason for the attack at all, except that he was an Englishman, and as such connected in their minds with famine and the absence of potatoes, and so on.

Looking out of his window as he heard the great bell ring, he saw a mass of human beings dancing like infuriated demons, waving their torches, and seemingly under the influence of drink or madness.

His daughter Lizzie was at his side as he glanced out.

"What can this mean ?" he asked. "Great Heaven ! they scarcely seem human in their anger."

"I should be afraid to say what I think it means," said Lizzie, "or I might rouse your anger as well."

"No, speak, my child, speak. It may give me a chance of appeasing them," said Singleton, who, villain and impostor as he was, was yet as brave as a lion, and was reckoning up mentally the number of men he could bring for the defence of the place.

"It is, father, I think," said Lizzie Singleton, in a low voice, "it is because they have taken up the cause of The Barry. Oh, father, if I could only have persuaded you to have made some compromise with him."

Her father's face grew dark with passion.

But still he restrained himself.

He had asked her to give him the reason, and in face of the great danger which threatened them both, he could not give way to any feelings of animosity.

"Compromise," he said. "I do not understand you. Compromise with one who has endeavoured to turn me and you out of our home? No, no, I could not compromise with him."

"You may yet have to do so, father," said his daughter, in a low voice, "for if The Barry were here, he could save us all."

As they were speaking, they had been still gazing out upon the mob that were dancing about like demons outside the gates.

Of course their conversation did not last long, but in the few minutes that it did last, Mr. Singleton saw at once that a deadly attack was intended.

The men were swarming round the gates, and battering away at them without the slightest warning.

"Stay here, Lizzie," he said; "do not expose yourself to danger at this window. I must ask these people what they require of me."

And he passed out.

On reaching the door, knowing well that he would be the first object of the people's resentment, he sent forward one of his men to ask what they wanted.

"You know well what we want," said one of the first, who was none other than Barney O'Reilly, "we want the masther."

"And what for?" asked the serving-man who had gone out.

"To hang him up to the nearest tree," returned Barney, "the murtherin' Saxon. But we don't want to be botherin' wid you. We want him, and if we don't have him, we'll burn the place down about your ears, and it'll be worse for ye all."

Singleton saw at once that it was of no use to attempt to compromise matters with such a wild mass of ragamuffins as those who were assembled round his gates.

So when the man returned with the threatening message which had been thundered at him by Barney O'Reilly, the Englishman said—

"How many persons can we reckon in the house?"

"Well, surr," said the man, "there's me and Tom Bates, and——"

"Come, come, there's no time to reckon," cried Mr. Singleton; "bring them all up into the hall, and see that the arms are brought up also."

Meanwhile, the mob at the gates began to thunder at them.

They had, of course, lost their cannon during the *mélée* with the soldiers, and they had nothing to dash the gates in but their bludgeons and the ends of their muskets.

These they plied vigorously for some time.

But then a new idea presented itself.

If one of them could scale the gates before the fire from the house began, he could open them without danger to himself.

Barney O'Reilly was the one who suggested this.

And in an instant he had begun clambering up the iron work, and was soon at the summit.

But he had reckoned without his host.

As he began to descend, Mr. Singleton came out from his room with his rifle.

In an instant he had taken aim, and Barney O'Reilly fell into the yard—dead.

Dead!

Pierced through the brain.

Such a sudden and deadly aim caused the crowd to pause for a moment.

But only for that moment.

Then there was a howl of execration, and instead of one man, half-a-dozen began clambering over the gates.

Singleton loaded his rifle quickly.

But of what avail was it?

Barney was one of the greatest enthusiasts, and one of the most popular men among them, and if all six who were climbing over the gate had fallen victims, there would have been a hundred volunteers to take their place.

So though Singleton again took deadly aim, and another of the besiegers came tumbling down into the courtyard mortally wounded, the other five descended in safety.

And then in an instant the bars were broken, and the bolts shot, and the mob was at liberty to enter.

By this time the ten servants who belonged to the hall had assembled in the passage, and fired a volley at the besiegers.

But this was all they could do.

There was nothing for it now but to close the great inner door, and make as good a resistance as possible.

Accordingly the iron-bound door was closed, the chains and bolts arranged, and a barricade of chairs, tables, and other furniture hastily constructed.

Of course this occupied some time, and the infuriated mob were already hammering at the door before the barricade was half completed.

But it was of immense strength, and seemed scarcely to yield at all to the fierce blows of the enemy.

As the attack went on, a little figure came gently out of one of the rooms near, and Lizzie stole to her father's side.

"Father," she said, "I think I can save you all, at any rate for a time."

"You," said the father, with a smile; "and may I ask how?"

"We are in the new house now, are we not?"

"Yes."

"Well, you know there is a private communication between this and the old castle, known only to you and me?"

"True, my child," said Mr. Singleton, "I know now what you mean. You intend that we shall make our way into the old castle, and remain there while they are battering down this door?"

"Yes, and while one of the men rides off for assistance."

"That is a good plan, my girl," said Singleton. "Come, my friends," he added, in a loud voice, "follow me."

Used to tacit obedience, the retinue, if so they could be termed, made no demur, but at once followed him as he made his way towards the secret door, which led to a subterranean way between the two houses.

It was not more than five minutes before they had entered the old castle, leaving no trace whatever of their means of transit.

Just as they passed in they heard a loud crash, which showed that the door was beginning to give way.

Leaving the men and the trembling female domestics below in the grand old hall of Barrymore, Singleton and his daughter ascended to one of the chambers, from which they could see all that was going on.

See it also without any chance of being observed themselves.

It was a maddening sight for Lizzie, for the Irishmen, now infuriated by the sight of blood, and by the frequent applications they made to the bottles which they had brought with them, shouted wild songs, and reeled about in grotesque dances, and came and went quickly and frequently through the great gates.

In their hands they brought in great logs of wood, and young saplings, and hedge stakes, which they piled in an immense heap beneath the portico of the new hall.

Singleton turned pale, and Lizzie, seeing him do so, pressed his arm.

"I know your feelings, father," she said. "They are going to burn the place down, and we are powerless to prevent it."

"Unless, indeed, we fire upon them, and disclose our presence here, which is the very thing which we do not wish," said her father.

"Let us hope for the best," said Lizzie; "maybe Phelim M'Carthy may bring us help before we think of it. He has been gone now more than a quarter of an hour."

As she spoke, there was a loud roar from below, and then a simultaneous movement among all the crowd.

At the risk of being observed, Lizzie leaned over, and peered more boldly through the loophole window.

She drew back in surprise, and with a deep blush upon her cheeks.

"What is it?" asked Mr. Singleton.

"The crowd have stopped heaping up the pile," she said, "and someone is speaking to them?"

"Who can it be?"

"I should know him anywhere," returned Lizzie; "it is The Barry."

Singleton staggered back in dismay.

"The Barry!" he cried, "it is impossible. He has gone far hence."

"Be not deluded," said his daughter; "whoever has told you that, has told you falsely."

Mr. Singleton now, without another word, made his way to another part of the suite of apartments, where a large bay window bulging out enabled him to take a better view of the great courtyard.

He saw in an instant that what his daughter said was true.

There, standing between the maddened mob and the door, was The Barry, whom he had hoped was either safe at the bottom of the sea or far away abroad.

At the risk of discovery, he, like Lizzie, leaned out of the window and listened.

The Barry was speaking in a loud voice.

"Irishmen," he cried, "will ye destroy a place that has such memories as this has? Will you destroy the home that can be mine within a week? The punishment which I can inflict upon him will be more than you can. I can prove him the impostor and rogue that he is, and without danger to myself or to you, while you can only destroy this place at deadly peril to yourselves."

Of course this speech was not made consecutively.

It was interrupted frequently by shouts and groans.

But The Barry went persistently on.

"Back, madmen!" he cried, as some of them who were most influenced by whisky advanced towards the door once again, "back! If you wish to revive the glories of old Ireland, do not destroy one of its old strongholds, which is about to return into the hands of one who will revive its ancient hospitality and renown. The Barrys of old were always friends of the peasantry, and so will I be."

Much more in this way he said.

The men began to listen more attentively.

At length Terence O'Rafferty advanced.

He had taken no part in the attack on the Shannon School.

He dared not, of course, do or say anything to prevent it, although he would like to have saved Thaddeus O'Shaughnessy and all connected with him.

But in the attack on Barrymore Hall it was a different affair.

Not knowing that The Barry was in possession of papers to enable him to assert his rights, he looked upon this as a splendid opportunity of punishing one who had oppressed the peasantry, and who was in a position to which he had no right.

"We'd no idea shure that ye were afther havin' a chance of recoverin' yer propherty, surr," said he, "and it's none of us are wishin' to spoil it for ye."

"Then retire," said The Barry.

"But it isn't your place, surr, to shtick up for the one who has robbed you and yours," said Terence; "if we shtop from the attack, will ye give up the Saxon to us?"

The Barry looked at him in indignation.

"Give him up to you that he might die without the chance of a trial," cried he, "die by the hands of murderers? No, no. You must be mad to think that I would agree to it. Rather than do that, I would stand here and defend him!"

A sneer went over the face of Terence O'Rafferty.

"Then, what we have to do is to go on, shure. If ye're defending the one that has been the manes of disthroying——"

"Defending him I am not," exclaimed The Barry, "but I object to murder; leave him to me, and before many hours are over his head, he will be in the gaol of Clare."

This statement calmed the people a little.

"If that's the case," said Terence O'Rafferty,

"of course, it's different. I'll spake to the bhoys, and see what they say."

He moved to the spot where the thickest of the throng was, and spoke for some time in earnest tones.

Then, as The Barry stood calmly though inwardly eager, watching their faces and their movements, he returned towards the door where the heap of faggots lay ready for the torch.

"Shure, Mr. Barry," he said, "shure, and if you promise that the murtherin' Saxon shall be given up to the soldiers when they come, we'll go away. But ye must let some of us remain here to see how matters stand."

"I agree to that at once," said The Barry, in the fulness of his heart.

He little thought of the treachery of those with whom he had to deal.

Terence, however, saved him from himself.

"Shure, Mr. Barry," he cried, in a low tone, as he leaned over him, "shure, Mr. Barry, ye're not half a politishun, though ye're brave enough for a jineral. If we lave ye here, without someone to pertect ye, ye'll be shot down like a rabbit."

"What is to be done, then?" asked The Barry. "I must take my chance."

"It naden't be, shure, Mr. Barry," he said; "if ye'll only guarantee that tin of us shall be safe from the rid coats, when they come up the hills."

"How can I guarantee your safety?" said The Barry. "I will do this, however, I will retire with you into a corner of the great courtyard where we cannot be attacked until the 'red coats,' as you call them, come. Then I will say that you are my friends."

"That's enough for me," returned Terence O'Rafferty. "I will see that everything is right."

As calmly as a schoolmaster addressing the children under his care, Terence went among the throng, and in a few moments the men began to move away through the great gates of the courtyard.

Terence O'Rafferty had kept with himself ten of the most sober of the men, and with The Barry he made his way into the corner of the courtyard, where they were completely out of the way of those who could have shot at them from the windows of the castle.

It was not long before there was heard in the distance the sound of the approaching soldiery.

They came up the mountain path at double quick time, for their officer, after the affair at the Shannon School, was in no good humour.

The gates being open, the soldiers rode straight into the courtyard, and having driven their horses in among the pile of faggots and logs that were heaped before the door, they knocked loudly.

They had come, of course, to protect Mr. Singleton and his household, and now, having seen the departure of The Barry and his friends, he naturally was anxious to receive them.

So in a moment the servants of Mr. Singleton were hurrying across the courtyard in the direction of the great door.

Before, however, they could reach it, Terence O'Rafferty and The Barry had dashed across the yard, and the latter had spoken to the officer in command.

Just before the door was opened, The Barry had placed in the colonel's hand a paper.

The Barry and Terence stood on one side, while the interview between the colonel and Singleton took place.

"Well," said the officer, "you sent one of your men to me. Why did you do so?"

"For my protection I sent," said Mr. Singleton. "I was assailed here by nearly four hundred persons, armed, and I had only ten persons beside myself to protect the Hall."

"Good; and pray what was the cause of the disturbance?"

"That," said Singleton, "is a matter which I must answer for before another tribunal, not before you. You have come here to protect me and my household from violence, and I demand a guard for the night."

"You can have a guard for the night without doubt," said the officer, with a grim smile, "for I have here an order for your arrest, on a charge of attempted kidnapping and also of holding this place under a false tenure."

Mr. Singleton turned pale.

"Under whose information do you hold this order for my arrest?"

"The information of The Barry, the rightful owner of this place, Mr. Singleton," said the officer. "I hope you will not attempt any resistance; it would only be folly."

Mr. Singleton turned to one of his men.

"Tom," he said, "give me my great coat and my whip; and bring round my grey mare."

Within ten minutes, he was in the centre of the soldiers, and on his way from the house, where he had so long lorded it as master.

"I shall be with you before dawn has fairly broken," said The Barry. "I have one word to say to Miss Singleton."

He said this in a low voice, not overheard by her father.

The officer bowed, and then The Barry hurriedly entered the Hall.

Lizzie retreated as she saw him.

But The Barry was too quick for her, and had reached the door of the room, to which she was hurrying, before she could enter.

"Miss Singleton, Lizzie!" he cried, "one word with you, and then I will go."

"Do not address me," said she, "you have caused the arrest of my father."

The Barry closed the door, in spite of the angry looks of the servants that filled the Hall.

"Lizzie," he said, "I am the only one who can save your father from a shameful imprisonment. I have saved his life this day, at the peril of my own, in spite of the fact that he has all this time, robbed me of my birthright, and my fortune. Say but one word, and the houses of the Barrys and the Singletons shall be joined, and all animosity shall cease."

He advanced towards her, and caught her by the wrist.

"Lizzie!" he cried, drawing her towards him, "you know that I love you, and I would do no injury to your father, but I have sworn that I will see to the rights of my family: I have sworn that The Barrys of Barrymore shall be reinstated in their ancient home. I cannot break my vow, but by keeping it, I need not do you an injury."

"How so, sir?" cried the young girl.

Lizzie spoke in apparent indignation; but her flushed cheeks and downcast eyes showed plainly that she was not really so angry as she seemed.

"I will tell you," said The Barry, bending over her, earnestly. "Because I will forgive your father; because I will make you my wife, and the houses of the Singletons and the Barrys can be joined, as I said before. Speak, Lizzie, speak but one word, and all will be well."

What could the young girl say?

She had long loved The Barry, and she knew well that her father had done him a great injustice.

"Rescue my father," she said, "and I will be yours."

He glanced for one moment into her bright eyes.

Then she was clasped in his embrace; one fervent kiss passed between them, and then he hurried towards the door.

"Good bye, Lizzie!" he said. "I will not meet you face to face again, until I bring your father with me."

"Noble heart!" exclaimed Lizzie, as she watched him pass across the court yard, "surely, in the whole country, there cannot be such a brave and generous mind as his."

Meanwhile, giving the word to Terence and his men to follow him, The Barry hurried on towards the constabulary.

Here, till the morning, Mr. Singleton would be confined, and here, therefore, would be his only chance of seeing him.

There was no difficulty in obtaining an interview.

It was only a matter of a few minutes before he stood in the presence of the man who had robbed him of his property.

Mr. Singleton eyed him in indignation.

"Boy," he cried, "have you come here to triumph over me?"

"No, sir," said The Barry, "I have come to save not only your life, but your honour."

"So you are come here to insult me?" were the words of Mr. Singleton.

"Certainly not," repeated The Barry; "I am here to save you."

"To save me. I think the very words show that you desire to insult me, since you know it to be impossible," returned Mr. Singleton.

"It is not impossible; and not only that, if you accede to my terms," said The Barry, "you need not leave the Hall at all, and more than that, the property will still remain in the family."

Mr. Singleton glanced at him earnestly.

"What do you mean?" he asked; "pray explain yourself, and not keep me in suspense."

"I mean this, then," The Barry said, "that I love your daughter."

Singleton fairly staggered back in surprise.

"Love my daughter?" he cried, "she——"

"She loves me also."

Singleton was silent for a few moments, pacing to and fro, like a caged lion.

Then stopping before The Barry, he said—

"And if I consent to this union, you will forgive me?"

"Yes."

"And rescue me?"

"I will."

"And never throw up in my child's face, the fact that her father—well, as you say—usurped your property?"

"Never—as I wish for happiness," said The Barry; "my hand upon it."

And the enemies grasped hands.

Mr. Singleton's face expressed a variety of emotions, and for a time his lips quivered, so that he could not make any reply.

At length he said—

"You are a brave and a generous lad, and I willingly give my consent. But how you can save me, I know not."

"Leave that to me," said The Barry; "consider, in fact, that you are a free man. Of course I am young yet to talk of marriage. I will arrange in regard to your return to Barrymore, and in two years from this time, when I have returned from the travels I wish to take, I will be your daughter's husband."

Some further conversation took place on the same subject, and then they parted.

Both were well pleased.

The Barry, to win so easily the girl of his choice.

Mr. Singleton, to think that he had a prospect of release from imprisonment and shame.

*　　*　　*　　*　　*

Meanwhile, for a time, we must return to the school on the Shannon.

The flames had got such a hold on the building that nothing could be done.

True, the broadly-flowing river was at the end of the grounds, and the little fire-engine that was always kept on the premises was plied vigorously.

But of what use was this thin stream of water, when applied to such a tremendous volume of flame?

There was a huge column of steam, and a fizz—fizz as the water fell upon the burning mass.

But no appreciable difference was made in the conflagration; and away the flames went up towards the sky; merrily, fiercely illuminating the country for miles around.

There being no chance of extinguishing the fire, the scholars were all turned out in order, and then came the question where were they to go?

There was no place in the neighbourhood capable of holding such a number, except Barrymore Hall, and in spite of their ignorance of what was going on, they were by no means disposed to seek aid of the Saxon.

The officer in command of the company of dragoons settled the question.

"We have plenty of tents up at the quarters, Mr. O'Shaughnessy," he said, "and the boys are welcome to them. It'll not be a very comfortable night for them—but it'll be better than nothing."

"I am sure I am much obliged to you, sir," said Thaddeus; "and as the lads can camp in the barrack-yard, it will be warmer than out on the hills."

It was useless to keep all the boys to watch

the conflagration, which it was impossible to put out, and so under the charge of Laurence McMahon the sixty lads were marshalled in military array, and marched up the mountain paths towards the Ballynara Barracks.

Thaddeus and Tim "Figs" remained behind with Willie Curtis and some of the military—using their best endeavours to extinguish the flames and save even a portion of the building.

But all in vain.

The flames grew and grew—higher and higher—fiercer and fiercer, until they began at length to lower and the skeleton walls held a mass of red beams—falling about in fiery tangles and ever and anon sending up thousands of sparks into the sky.

When dawn came there was nothing left of the old academy but a mass of red-hot ruins, and Thaddeus O'Shaughnessy. turned with a sigh from the scene of so many trials and so many pleasures.

He was not absolutely a ruined man, but in the bank where he had hoarded up his savings there was a mere pittance; and his property was uninsured.

He heaved a bitter sigh as he went up the mountain path.

It was a sigh that included his regret at losing his pupils, and the place which had afforded him so much pleasure, where, in fact, many of the happiest years of his life had been spent.

A sigh, too, to think that the portrait of the one he had loved and lost had been consumed in the flames which had been lit by the madly enthusiastic Men of the Mountains.

But he said not a word to anyone of his intentions or his feelings.

He rode on the horse which was provided for him by one of the officers, and in silence made his way to the barracks, where his boys were under tents asleep.

Here he was placed in the officers' quarters, and, tired out, he was soon wrapped in slumber.

CHAPTER XLVIII.
TIME'S CHANGES.

Of course, it was impossible for a few days after the disgraceful outrage which had so changed the whole life of Thaddeus O'Shaughnessy, to collect his thoughts, or even to frame any plan for the future.

At the end of a week, however, he had resolved what to do.

He would communicate to the parents of the boys the position in which he and they found themselves, and then retire altogether from business.

But it was not to be.

It was at the moment that he came to this determination that a letter was brought to him.

The handwriting startled him, but the black edge startled him more.

It was signed "Aline," and was written in a fine though trembling hand.

It contained a long account of what had occurred years ago.

And then it said—

"Thaddeus, I am dying. Before this reaches you I shall be cold in the grave; but I send to you my living image in the daughter whom I love. Forget, Thaddeus, that she is the child of your rival. I was forced to marry him; and I loved you always. But, in begging you to accept the responsibility of being her guardian, I beg also that you will accept something more substantial. I have heard of your misfortune in the burning of the academy. I know well how much your heart is set upon the school, and the scholars whom you have brought up. And so, since I wish you to regard my child as your own, and to take the charge of her, which I know is a great responsibility to demand at your hands, I have left my whole fortune to you, with the proviso that you rebuild the academy; not that I wish to confine you against your will to duties that may have become distasteful to you, but because I desire to erect a monument, which shall be understood by you and me, to the love of long ago, which might have brought to both of us such happy fruits. Accept the dearest love and kind wishes for the future of the one whose heart was always yours.

"ALINE."

There was a postscript stating that Aline, the daughter, would reach Ballynara at 6 p.m. on the third day.

A cheque for a thousand pounds was enclosed, with a memorandum stating that the total amount placed to the account of Thaddeus O'Shaughnessy in the Dublin Bank was twenty-five thousand pounds.

At first, the schoolmaster was so utterly taken aback by this announcement that he could scarcely believe his senses.

And then came the question, should he accept the fortune?

And why not?

He could undertake the responsibility offered him—the charge and guardianship of Aline's child. He could rebuild his school, he could complete the teachings of his pupils, and in the society of the young girl think of the past, which had once been to him such a happy one.

There was a certain sacrifice of pride in this, it might be thought by some; but not in this case.

Thaddeus knew well the character of the woman who had left him the money, and placed her own conditions on its use.

And so, without hesitation, he made the proper communication to the lawyers, accepting the fortune, telling them to place the money to his account in the Bank of Dublin, and begging that Miss Aline Beresford would come as she said to her appointment.

Punctually to the moment the train arrved at Ballynara station, and there stepped from one of the first-class carriages a young girl about seventeen, dressed in deep mourning.

She wore on her bosom a white camellia, and Thaddeus O'Shaughnessy, who had taken Pat O'Connor with him as a companion, at once passed to her side.

"Have I the pleasure of seeing Miss Aline Beresford?" he said, bowing.

"Yes, sir; are you Mr. O'Shaughnessy?" she answered, in a low, sweet voice.

"Yes, I am Thaddeus O'Shaughnessy," he said, taking her hand, " and a very old friend of your mother."

The young girl blushed deeply.

"Yes, I know it," she said ; " I have heard a great deal of you from my mother. You were the one of all the world she loved the best—except, perhaps, me."

The arch and winning smile with which these words were accompanied, had their due effect upon Pat O'Connor.

He felt a strange and unusual sensation in his heart ; and he involuntarily drew nearer to the young girl.

She caught the expression of his eye, and a deep blush overspread her features.

Then she turned towards O'Shaughnessy, and took his arm, bowing to Pat O'Connor, but taking no more notice of our hero.

On the road to Ballynara town proper they indulged in a variety of reminiscences until they reached the hotel where Thaddeus O'Shaughnessy had engaged apartments for Aline.

Having seen that she was well taken care of, and having left her in charge of Kathleen, the old cook of the academy, he returned to the barracks and his boys.

A month passed.

During this time a great change had taken place in and about Ballynara.

Mr. Singleton had been released from prison on the assurance of The Barry that he had been led into the matter by a designing knave, and he had returned to Barrymore Hall.

A large building had been taken by Thaddeus, in the town, and with the concurrence of the parents of all the scholars, they had been placed here under the tuition of their old tutors.

The old academy had been already demolished, and the foundations of the new one had been commenced.

Often and often, when he could spare an hour or two from his duties, the master of the boys of the Shannon passed down from the mountains and gazed contentedly and with folded arms on the reconstruction of the house which had become to him almost a hobby.

As for the Boys of the Mountains—the misguided followers of interested enthusiasts, they had received a series of desperate reverses.

The "rebellion," as they termed it, and the "movement" which they chose to regard as so formidable, were confined in reality to a few hundreds, and what they imagined would result in the overthrow of the English rule, ended only in a few skirmishes, always finishing by the utter rout of the insurgents.

Terence O'Rafferty and about two hundred of the most desperate of the men, had flown up into the mountains.

Here in caves and fissures they maintained a wretched existence ; some of them even having their wives and children with them.

So raging at the failure of the great enterprise, they began to brood over desperate enterprises, and on the very day that Tim Figs led to the altar his Kathleen—Kathleen Moriarty—a meeting was held in one of the great caves to consult over the punishment of the "traithers."

And the principal "traither" of all was Thaddeus O'Shaughnessy.

CHAPTER XLIX.
NEWS FROM FRANCE.

THE great cave presented a most extraordinary appearance on the night when the men met together to consult upon the punishment of the traitors.

There was no solemn conclave.

There were no set speeches ; no regular resolutions proposed and carried ; no appeals to rhetoric ; no gushes of flowery eloquence.

But there was a stern determination—a sad, weary desperation on the brows of the assembled men, and although women and children formed a portion of the assemblage, and the fathers and husbands talked to their wives and offspring, it could be seen they were in eager expectation of something or someone.

It was a picturesque scene.

The peasantry were gathered in groups round fires, which cast their red glow upon grimed and woebegone faces and tattered garments.

Here and there a woman was busy preparing some supper, while another, seated on the rocky floor, leaned her head on her husband's knee, and bewailed in tears the "day whin ye wint afther the blaggart praching min."

Presently there was a shout without.

"He's comin'."

Sentries had been posted at intervals outside along the mountainous path, and a shrill whistle went from one to the other, until the man posted at the door of the cave cried—

"All right. Rory's comin'."

And in a few moments a man, wrapped in a heavy cloak and wearing a peaked cap and high riding boots, entered the cavern.

He affected quite the style which had vogue in the days when the "great rebellion" was talked of, and in fact, on his first entrance into the cave, he had the appearance of Laurence Raturier.

But as he came forward into the light, he displayed the well-known features of Rory O'Neil.

Rory, the robber of the hills.

There was a terrible scowl upon his face ; and an awful gash fresh bleeding in his forehead, showed that he had been in the wars.

He flung his cloak off as he entered, and approaching the fire, threw himself into a large chair, and wiped the blood from his brow with his handkerchief.

"Well, Rory," said Terence O'Rafferty, impatiently, as he neared the side of the bold outlaw, "what news ?"

Rory took out his sword, and showing that it was broken in halves, flung it into the fire.

"What's that ?" cried Terence O'Rafferty.

"Shure, and that's me broken sword," cried Rory, " and the cause is as broken as that is."

"Why, what is the matther now ?" cried O'Rafferty ; " have the Frinch desaved us ?"

Rory O'Neil made a gesture of contempt.

"The Frinch !" he said, with a shrug of the shoulders ; " shure that's the drhame that's been desaving ould Ireland for so many years. What do ye think the Frinch 'ud be makin' war with England for just to free a country that's no use to them, and that couldn't kape itself free, if it repaled the Union ?"

The Irishmen around him groaned and gazed at him aghast.

"Och, and ye're never goin' to turn against us, Rory, and be a traither to your word afther all ?"

The man flashed his eyes savagely round him.

"Traither ? Shure, and there's not a man in the company dare say that Rory O'Neil 'ud be a traither," he cried. "It's not that, it's not that."

And he shook his head sorrowfully.

Terence O'Rafferty gazed upon him very sternly.

"Look here, Misther O'Neil," he said, "you know what ye're talkin' about, and that's just what we don't. Ye're sittin' there a-waggin' of yer head, and a-talkin' like an old riddle-monger, while we want to hear what the Frinch capten said, and what luck ye've had on the return journey."

Rory turned upon Terence a glance of lofty contempt.

"Shure, and it's not myself that's account-able to you, Mr. O'Rafferty," he said, "or to anyone here for that matter, except as a mem-ber of the United Irishmen. But I'll tell ye, and then, perhaps, ye'll be afther returning paceably to yer homes, and becoming what the Saxons call 'paceable members of society.'"

And he laughed a jeering laugh.

"Well, we don't want to quarrel, especially at such a time as this," said O'Rafferty; "so go on, O'Neil, and tell us all that has happened to ye."

"Give us a glass of potheen, and let it be shtrong," said Rory O'Neil, "and I'll tell ye all."

There were a dozen glasses ready for him when he said this, but Rory was apparently in no humour to drink more than he absolutely required.

He took the first glass offered to him, drank it off at a draught, and said—

"Ye know you chose me to go down to the bay and see if Laurence Raturier had arranged all with the Frinch capten, either to give us help or to transport us—wives and children and all—over to Ameriky.

"Shure, and I wint to the 'Bay of Dublin,' as they call the place where we were to meet, and there was Raturier. He smiled when he met me, and he held out his hand.

"'I'm glad to see you.' he said, 'and I hope now you are here, ye will not return to those madmen, but come across the seas with me. You'd make a fine soldier.'

"I looked at 'im in surprise, as ye may think.

"'What do you mane by madmen ?' cried I; 'are ye after deluding the poor bhoys up in the mountain caves, that have given up their homes and iverything for the good of ould Ireland ?'

"When I said that, I thought he'd have had a fit with laughin'.

"'Shure, and it's killin' me ye'll be,' he cried; 'the good of ould Ireland ! Why, do ye think a poor handful of ragamuffins, half-armed, and without any discipline, could con-tend against the soldiers of England ?'

"'That's thrue for you,' says I; 'but we thought the Frinch——'

"I could not go on any furder, for this man, who jinerally looked so grave and stern, burst out in laughter again.

"'What 'ud the French be doing over here ?' cried he.

"'Shure, an' wasn't it yerself that towld us they were comin' ?'

"'Oh, that's nothin',' said he; 'it was my business to say so. But shure, and how could ye think that the French people would go to war with England jist because the praties had got the blight in 'em ?' and he laughed again.

"I felt as if I'd like to have hit him clean in the eye, when he told me how he'd been desavin' us.

"But I kept myself from strikin' 'im, because I knew he'd have lots of his people round, and I wanted to get back to ye.

"'It's a cruel thing, Mr. Raturier,' said I, 'to desave the poor bhoys.'

"'Oh, it's time they were punished for their folly,' cried he; 'it's been "the French are comin'" for fifty years, and now they know that no one cares for 'em half so much as England, perhaps they'll be inclined to be a little more paceful.'

"Then I knew that the blaggart was an agent, a spy of the Saxons, and I was de-tarmined to put a mark on 'im."

The men now leaned forward, pulling their seats nearer, and peering eagerly into his face.

"So," said Rory, after filling up another bumper, "so I got up afther telling him that I thought he was a thafe and a liar, which he took with a broad grin, telling me to go back to my native bogs and grow praties.

"'Thinks I to myself,' continued Rory, "thinks I, ye'll never go back to your native bogs, if Rory's got a thrue aim, and a ha'porth of powther and ball.'"

And Rory glanced slowly round at his com-panions.

Taking another drink of whisky, Rory said—

"So I goes back to Dave Murphy's cabin, where I'd lift my rifle, and I waits till dark. It was nearly about an hour but shure, and it seemed a wake, before the big blaggart came out.

"And thin as he went along the river bank, up towards the cliff that overhangs the bay, I followed 'im. He was all alone, and divil a bit of a shanty or a cabin in sight. So when I got to the tap of the hill, where his figure stood out black against the moonlit sky, I raised my rifle.

"Not a bit of pity had I for the murtherin' thafe. I only saw in him an inimy to the ould counthry, and who'd bin paid by the Saxons to lead us into a thrap. So I never waited an instant, but fired. My love for Ire-land steadied my aim, and I hit 'im fair in the head.

"I never even heard a cry, but he toppled over the edge of the cliff, and I saw him no more. He went over as dead as a shot rabbit, and bad luck to 'im."

A ringing cheer came from the lips of all present as Rory stopped.

"Oh, it's Rory's the clever boy," exclaimed all ; " and here's success and long life to him."

And their glasses were raised and chinked, and the cavern re-echoed with the sounds of welcome and rejoicing over the death of the "inimy of ould Ireland."

"And now," said Rory O'Neil, "there's one more traither I've got to dispose of, and that's Thaddeus O'Shaughnessy."

A hush fell over the company.

Everyone knew well the schoolmaster of the Shannon Academy.

Everyone knew what a grand old man he was.

Everyone knew what a perilous task it would be to attack him.

Yet if he was a traitor, he must die.

That was the oath of the society, and they were determined to keep it to the letter.

"Is he a traither, too ?" asked one of the men.

"A traither ! a double-dyed one," cried Rory ; "it's he that caused the slaughter of our boys, and led the rid-coats up to our caves. I'm going to kill 'im to-morrow."

And Rory whiffed his pipe as if he had spoken about the sticking of a pig.

As he spoke, a dark figure detached itself from among the others, and made his way to the mouth of the cave.

It was Terence O'Rafferty.

The men were too eager to notice him.

Just glancing round to see if he was watched, he was about to plunge out into the dark night, when he remembered one thing.

He had been too precipitate.

His errand, of course, was to save Thaddeus O'Shaughnessy.

But to do this, he must hear more.

So he sauntered back as if he had been only glancing out upon the night, and lit his pipe at the blazing peat fire.

"Ye'll have a difficult job, I'm thinking," he said, "if ye're afther the schoolmaster, for he's surrounded by an army of bhoys."

Rory laughed.

"Shure, and ye must think me a senseless omadhaun," said he, "if ye fancy I'm going to attack 'im in the middle of the school. Shure, and don't I know that he goes every ither night to visit Darby McFergus, the landlord of the 'Pig and Murphy,' and it's comin' across the bridge at Clany, over the blessed river that took the body of the spy to the ocean, I'll tumble him in, jist to look after his friend."

"Shure, and ye talk as if Thaddeus O'Shaughnessy was a gossoon," said O'Rafferty. "Where will he be while ye're puttin' him in the river ? Do ye think that the schoolmasther has had all his senses burnt out at the fire ?"

Rory turned towards him with a scowl.

"It's meself that knows that ye're a frind to the spy, the one that murthered Mat O'Grady and his brother," said he, "but beware !"

He shook his fist threateningly at Terence.

Terence dug his hands deep into his pockets, while his pipe was elevated towards his nose.

"Is it yerself I'm to beware of ?" he asked, with a scoffing smile, "because if ye mane that —I laugh at ye. Ye can go following min in the dark, and firing at 'em behind their backs —but dhivil a bit of a fair fight ye'd 'ave."

Rory sprang up blusteringly.

"Shure, and what do ye mane ?" he cried ; "is it a fight ye're manin' ? Ye shall have it as soon as I have settled Thaddeus O'Shaughnessy."

"Very well, and perhaps before," said Terence O'Rafferty ; "at iny rate, when ye want yer head crushed, I'm at yer sarvis, for when we do fight, it'll be no Ballynara whacking, but a battle to the death."

And he turned away.

He had heard enough for his purpose now.

He did not know the hour or even the day when the attack on Thaddeus was to be made.

But he knew where to watch, and he resolved to save him, if he waited weeks.

He sauntered to the cavern mouth again, and spoke to one of the sentries.

Then he passed on unchallenged, for all knew him, and quickly went down the mountain path.

Once down in the lowlands he felt himself safe.

Safe, at least, from Rory and his friends.

A price was set upon his head by the English.

But of this he took no notice.

All he wanted was to save Thaddeus O'Shaughnessy ; and this he resolved to do at all risks to himself.

Meanwhile, down in the town of Ballynara everything was progressing favourably.

The academy on the shores of the Shannon was progressing capitally.

The school went on as usual.

Except as regards Pat O'Connor, whom the sweet eyes of Aline Beresford had conquered and subdued.

He felt now that there was something more to live for than there had been, and even more sedulously than ever he had been pursuing his studies.

He had lost the companionship of The Barry, who had started on his travels with a private tutor, but still he had Harry Marshall, who, happy in the frequent society of Mary O'Rourke, was always a cheerful friend.

No one guessed the vile plans which were being prepared for the overthrow of all.

It was on the fourth evening after the scene in the cave that the schoolmaster left the new school which had replaced for a time the Shannon Academy, in order to visit his friend, Darby McFergus, at the sign of the "Pig and Murphy."

It was a very lonely road to travel.

The tavern stood on the verge of the mountain road, and before it could be seen nothing but the delving valley and the darkly-flowing river that passed through it.

Just about a hundred yards from this was the bridge of which Rory O'Neil had spoken, and here the assassin was now waiting, hoping that by a treacherous stab he could dispatch him, or at any rate so wound him that he could seize him and fling him into the stream.

But as he stood there in the shadow of the trees, a tall form suddenly confronted him.

The form of Terence O'Rafferty.

"Rory O'Neil," he said, "a word with you."

Rory started.

"A word wid me?" he said; "and what for?"

"You're here to murder Thaddeus O'Shaughnessy."

"And if I am, it's only to fulfil my oath," said Rory.

"Then in this case ye'll not do it," said Terence.

"And pray who is to prevent me?" inquired Rory.

"Myself," cried O'Rafferty, in an angry voice; "be off, or it'll be the worse for ye."

Rory's answer was a treacherous spring.

But Terence was ready for him.

He knew the character of the man with whom he had to deal.

A heavy bludgeon was in his hand, and as Rory aimed a desperate blow at him with the knife, it was knocked from his hand, and fell glistening into the waters of the river.

The rest of the struggle was a wrestle, in which strength was the predominating principle.

Rory O'Neil was of course the younger and stronger man.

Nearer and nearer he dragged his adversary to the river's brink.

But just as Terence stood half stunned and wounded on the edge of the swift-rushing waters, a man's form came dashing down the incline.

A blow sent Rory, unconscious and helpless, into the boiling flood—and Terence stood—saved. Saved by Thaddeus O'Shaughnessy.

There was little more heard of the insurgents after this.

Fate had declared against them, and they gradually dispersed unmolested to their homes.

Thaddeus, in due course of time, returned to his academy, newly built in splendid style, and Pat, having finished his course of studies, went to Dublin University for a time.

In three years after there was a triple wedding at Ballynara church—the wedding of The Barry with Lizzie Singleton, of Harry Marshall and Mary O'Rourke, and of Pat O'Connor with Aline Beresford, the ward of Thaddeus O'Shaughnessy; and none danced so merrily on that day or sang louder than Tim Figs and his wife Kathleen, and Terence O'Rafferty and his Kathleen, and none so welcome at the wedding feast as Thaddeus O'Shaughnessy and Reginald Graham, the lad who had been saved on the misty mountain tops by Pat O'Connor, the merriest of the Boys of the Shannon.

THE END.

Important Announcement.

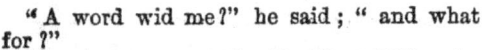

Another New and Exciting Story will shortly be issued. It is now in preparation. Look out for the date and particulars in either

THE BOYS OF ENGLAND,

THE HALFPENNY SURPRISE,

OR

THE BOYS' COMIC JOURNAL.

www.ingramcontent.com/pod-product-compliance
Lightning Source LLC
Chambersburg PA
CBHW082011170626
46817CB00009B/3065